UTOPIA

A NEW TRANSLATION

BACKGROUNDS

Norton Critical Editions in the History of Ideas

AYLORD

⫸ A NORTON CRITICAL EDITION ⫷

SIR THOMAS MORE

UTOPIA

A NEW TRANSLATION
BACKGROUNDS
CRITICISM

⫸⫷

Translated aud Edited by

ROBERT M. ADAMS

UNIVERSITY OF CALIFORNIA AT LOS ANGELES

W · W · NORTON & COMPANY

New York · London

Copyright © 1975 by W. W. Norton & Company, Inc.

W. W. Norton & Company, Inc., 500 Fifth Avenue, New York, N.Y. 10110
W. W. Norton & Company Ltd., 37 Great Russell Street, London WC1B 3NU

All Rights Reserved

Published simultaneously in Canada by
Penguin Books Canada Ltd,
2801 John Street, Markham, Ontario L3R 1B4.

Library of Congress Cataloging in Publication Data
More, Thomas, Sir, Saint, 1478–1535.
    Utopia: a new translation, backgrounds, criticism.
    (A Norton critical edition)
    Bibliography: p.
    1. Utopias. I. Adams, Robert Martin, 1915–
II. Title.
HX8111516.E975   321'.07   75–17737
ISBN 0-393-04397-5
ISBN 0-393-09256-9 pbk.

Printed in the United States of America

9

Contents

v

vi · *Contents*

Preface

Utopia is one of those mercurial, jocoserious writings which turn a new profile to every advancing generation, and respond in a different way to every set of questions which is addressed to them. Though small in size and flippant in tone, it is in fact two very heavy books. The first part propounds a set of riddles which every sincere man who enters public life is bound to ask himself, whether he is living in early-capitalist England, late-capitalist America, or any other society dominated by the money-mad and the authority-intoxicated. He must think, What good can I do as an honorable man in a society of power-hungry individuals? What evil will I have to condone as the price of the good I accomplish? And how can I tell when the harm I am doing, by acting as window-dressing for evil, outweighs my potential for good? The second part of *Utopia* offers a set of no less disturbing questions. For example, Can a community be organized for the benefit of all, and not to satisfy the greed, lust, and appetite for domination of a few? How much repression is a good society justified in exercising in order to retain its goodness? And finally, When we give some persons power in our society (as we must), and appoint others to watch them (as we'd better), who is going to watch the watchers? Can we really stand a society in which everybody watches everybody?

Almost everyone has seen that these are some of the major questions the *Utopia* raises; they include many of the classical questions of political economy and social organization. As for what answers the author of *Utopia* provided, we are still in dispute; he was a complex man who understood very well that it is not always safe or politic to speak one's entire mind—even supposing it is ever possible. Most of the authorities whose essays are assembled at the back of the book try to calculate the answers More gave to his questions by studying the way in which they are framed or the context in which they occurred to him. Some see him as a man modern far beyond his era, proposing prophetic remedies for the problems of an outworn social system; others see him as a conservative, medieval-minded man whose ideal community was patterned on that of the monastery. Still others deny that he meant anything at all, preferring to describe his book as a joke. Some feel that the book can be understood in terms of its literary form or genre, in terms of its predecessors among the imaginary commonwealths, or in terms of the ideals prevalent among More's literary friends on the Continent. Some find the key to its equivocal patterns of meaning in an equivocal pattern of syntax; some argue that Utopia was a real place located in Peru, and Hythloday a real man who had visited it and talked with More. A gamut of speculation is thus offered to the reader, spreading, if not from the sublime to the ridiculous, at least from the plausible to the improbable.

But, whatever the book "really" meant when it was written, one aspect of it which our materials do not properly emphasize (simply because of lack of space) is the enormous influence it had on men's minds. It had this influence not only on socialist Utopians of the nineteenth century like William Morris and Edward Bellamy, but on men of its own time, the sixteenth century. America had been discovered for fewer than twenty-five years when the *Utopia* appeared in print. Europeans knew very little about the new land beyond the ocean, and what information they got from the first explorers was sparse, ill-written, and, worst of all, not very interesting, especially when it was accurate. Just at this moment, More appeared with a finished and elegant literary production, describing some enchanting people who, in addition to all the "natural" virtues like innocence, simplicity, and native honor, had some very sophisticated institutions perfectly suited to comment on the most notorious abuses of contemporary Europe. No wonder the book took European readers by storm. Naive folk of the early sixteenth century swallowed More's account of Utopia as a fair description of the New World; tougher and more practical men still tended, when they came to America, to see the natives as potential Utopians or ex-Utopians. In Mexico and South America the best and most generous of the explorers tried to form the tribes and pueblos they discovered into little Amaurots. These, of course, disintegrated; but throughout the centuries and across most of the American latitudes, there have rarely failed to be found little groups of true believers whose social ideals owed something to the inspiration of More's *Utopia*. The book is thus of special interest to Americans, North and South; it helped to make us what we are today by determining, not our immediate institutions, but the level of our expectations. And in the long run that may be the most important, though the least formal, of our institutions.

If, then, it was a mere joke, More's book was one of the most appealing and influential jokes ever made—consequently, one of the cruelest. And that, I think, takes it outside the limits of More's character. The power of the book's idealism is a real ingredient of its structure; that fact has been demonstrated, not in a learned article, but by the testimony of history. We may interpret it as we will, but the way a book like *Utopia* has been read and lived across the centuries is an authentic part of its nature. However we choose to read it, we cannot deprive it of qualities it has proved on the pulses of mankind. On these terms it cannot be other than a compassionate and generous book, as well as a witty one—a book which is interested in living people and the way they live, not just in verbal phantoms and personae. To read it is a test of one's own temper. We in the United States should be particularly aware of this book as we come up on the two hundredth anniversary of our own generous, perilous experiment.

ROBERT M. ADAMS

Translator's Note

Translations, according to a cynical, sexist wheeze, are like mistresses; the faithful ones are apt to be ugly, and the beautiful ones false. This glib cliché can be supplemented by another one, declaring that the translator's game always involves an effort to have his cake and eat it too. He wants to catch, to savor, to crystallize in his mind the special qualities of his original, and at the same time to transfuse them into an entirely different medium, readable modern English. Thomas More's *Utopia* is not cast in artificial or ornate literary language, as his age understood it. The Latin More uses is simple, conversational, everyday prose such as a lawyer, a diplomat, or a humanist might employ about the normal occasions and business of daily existence. But it is quite unlike modern English in several important respects. The sentences are longer and less tightly knit in patterns of subordination. The main idea of a sentence may be hidden in an ablative absolute, or hung out at a considerable distance in space and syntax. Because it is an inflected language, Latin can scatter the ingredients of a sentence about more loosely than English does, in the assurance that a reader will be able to assemble them within his own mind. An English sentence is expected to do more of the reader's work for him. At the same time, Latin, or at least More's lawyerly Latin, has a whole mass of delicate innuendoes and qualifications at its disposal—double negatives, ironic appositives, pseudo-antitheses, and formal (but only formal) correlatives. To represent the structure of More's Latin syntax in English would create the impression of a whirling chaos; reproducing his stylistic nuances would give rise to a mincing and artificial English, as of a rhetorical sophist. And in either case, the real flavor of More's book, which is casual and colloquial, would be lost completely.

A constant temptation of the translator is to go for one quality of his original at the expense of all the others. More's long, loosely articulated sentences can be made swift and clear by rearranging some of their parts and omitting others; his rhetorical structure can be retained, at the cost of sacrificing the colloquial and conversational flavor of his book. In trying to respond to all four demands (for clarity, completeness, colloquial ease, and a sense of contour in the prose), I have consulted from time to time the work of my predecessors. Three in particular proved suggestive and challenging.

Ralph Robynson's 1551 rendering is a superb achievement; it still withstands the severest test of any translation, close comparison with the original. To be sure, Robynson is so anxious to squeeze out every drop of More's meaning, that he sometimes translates one word by two or four or more; and his language, after more than four-hundred years, requires no less glossing and translation than the original text. H. V. S. Ogden (1949) is swift, deft, and modern; but to gain these qualities, he omits not only elements of More's meaning but most of the nuances of More's expression. It is an extraordinarily *flat* translation, as if written for someone in a great hurry; and it occasionally misrepresents to odd effect the actual sense of the Latin. Finally, Father Edward Surtz's (1965) recension of the (1923) translation by G. C. Richards strives as earnestly as Robynson for completeness of expression. But, following a Latinate word order, this version is generally stiff and sometimes wooden; its sentences, with their intricate turnings and grammatical suspensions, often defy articulation by the mouth of anyone who knows and cares for English idiom. Yet all three translations catch intersecting and overlapping sectors of an original which is richer than any of them. In the process of making my own text, I consulted these various versions freely, and even when dissatisfied with the work of one of my predecessors, drew from it the stimulus of disagreement. A. E. Housman dedicated his great edition of Manilius *in usu editorum*—for the use of those future editors who, he supposed, would *really* study the complexities of a text to which he had merely indicated the first approaches. Less formidably, any "new" translation of a much-translated text can best define itself as a temporary trial balance, for the guidance of future translators in their search for a miracle which will reverse the action of the old philosopher's stone. For where the alchemist's dream was of turning lead to precious gold, the translator's dream is that he may somehow be kept from reducing gold to common lead.

This translation is dedicated to the memory of Mr. William Nagel of the Horace Mann School for Boys, who more than forty years ago taught me—reluctant and ungrateful infant that I was—the rudiments of the Latin tongue.

R.M.A.

The Text of
Utopia

CONCERNING THE BEST
STATE OF A COMMONWEALTH
AND THE NEW ISLAND
OF UTOPIA

A Truly Golden Handbook

No Less Beneficial Than Entertaining
by the Most Distinguished and Eloquent Author
THOMAS MORE
Citizen and Sheriff of the Famous City
of London

[The word "Utopia" is compounded from Greek *ou* and *topos*, meaning "no place"; there may also be a pun on *eutopos*, meaning "good place." More sometimes spoke of his book by a Latin equivalent, Nusquama, from *nusquam*, nowhere. This whole ornate title is translated from the title page of the March 1518 edition—the third—published by Froben at Basle.]

BOOK ONE

The most invincible King of England, Henry the Eighth of that name, a prince adorned with the royal virtues beyond any other, had recently some differences of no slight import with Charles, the most serene Prince of Castille,[1] and sent me into Flanders as his spokesman to discuss and settle them. I was companion and associate to that incomparable man Cuthbert Tunstall,[2] whom the King has recently created Master of the Rolls, to everyone's great satisfaction. I will say nothing in praise of this man, not because I fear the judgment of a friend might be questioned, but because his learning and integrity are greater than I can describe and too well-known everywhere to need my commendation—unless I would, according to the proverb, "Show the sun with a lantern."[3]

Those appointed by the prince to deal with us, all excellent men, met us at Bruges by prearrangement. Their head man and leader was the Margrave, so called, of Bruges,[4] a most distinguished person. But their main speaker and guiding spirit was Georges de Themsecke, the Provost of Cassel,[5] a man eloquent by nature as well as by training, very learned in the law, and most skillful in diplomatic affairs through his ability and long practice. After we had met several times, certain points remained on which we could not come to agreement; so they adjourned the meetings and went to Brussels for some days to consult their prince in person.

Meanwhile, since my business permitted it, I went to Antwerp.[6] Of those who visited me while I was there, Peter Giles[7] was more welcome to me than any of the others. He was a native of Antwerp,

1. The Prince of Castille is the future Charles V (Carlos Quinto), as yet only fifteen years old and under the guardianship of his grandfather, but about to become King of Castille, then King of Spain, and, before he was twenty-one, Holy Roman Emperor. As part of his royal possessions, he inherited the Low Countries. The matters in dispute between him and Henry were certain Dutch import duties, against which the English government protested by declaring an embargo on all exports of wool to Holland. In retaliation for this act Charles was hinting at an expropriation of the English fleet, or such parts of it as he could get his hands on.
2. An admired scholar and influential cleric, though not yet a bishop, Cuthbert Tunstall (1474–1559) was appointed Ambassador to Brussels in May 1515, and a year later became Master of the Rolls.
3. Analogues of this saying are scattered through the *Adagia* of Erasmus, an immense collection of proverbs and pop-ular sayings: see especially No. 1407 in the *Opera* (Leyden, 1703–6) II, 556.
4. J. (for Jean or Jacques) de Halewyn, Seigneur de Maldeghem, was Margrave of Bruges. Bruges itself, after a rich commercial flowering in the fourteenth century (when it was the central distributing point and an important manufacturing center for English wool), was losing some of its commercial clout in the early sixteenth century, partly because its harbor was silting up.
5. Georges de Themsecke, Provost of Cassel, was a native of Bruges, author of a regional history, and chief magistrate of Cassel, a small town between Dunkirk and Lille.
6. Antwerp and Brussels are about equidistant (sixty miles) from Bruges.
7. Peter Giles (1486?–1533) had been a star pupil of Erasmus, and was now (1515) town clerk of his native Antwerp, as well as a poet and editor of Latin texts.

a man of high reputation, already appointed to a good position
and worthy of the very best: a young man distinguished equally by
learning and character. Apart from being cultured, virtuous, and
courteous to all, with his intimates he is so open, trustworthy, loyal,
and affectionate that it would be hard to find another friend like
him anywhere. No man is more modest or more frank; none better
combines simplicity with wisdom. His conversation is so merry,
and so witty without malice, that the ardent desire I felt to see
my native country, my wife and my children (from whom I had
been separated more than four months) was much eased by his
agreeable company and pleasant talk.

One day after I had heard mass at Nôtre Dame, the most beautiful
and most popular church in Antwerp, I was about to return to
my quarters when I happened to see him talking with a stranger, a
man of quite advanced years. The stranger had a sunburned face, a
long beard, and a cloak hanging loosely from his shoulders; from his
appearance and dress, I took him to be a ship's captain. When
Peter saw me, he approached and greeted me. As I was about to
return his greeting, he drew me aside, and, indicating the stranger,
said, "Do you see that man? I was just on the point of bringing
him to you."

"He would have been very welcome on your behalf," I
answered.

"And on his own too, if you knew him," said Peter, "for there is
no man alive today can tell you so much about unknown peoples and
lands; and I know that you're always greedy for such information."

"In that case," said I, "my guess wasn't a bad one, for at first
glance I supposed he was a skipper."

"Then you're not quite right," he replied, "for his sailing has not
been like that of Palinurus,[8] but more that of Ulysses, or rather of
Plato. This man, who is named Raphael—his family name is
Hythloday[9]—knows a good deal of Latin, and is particularly
learned in Greek. He studied Greek more than Latin because his
main interest is philosophy, and in that field he found that the
Romans have left us nothing very valuable except certain works of
Seneca and Cicero. Being eager to see the world, he left his patri-

8. The pilot of Aeneas slept over his
steering oar, fell overboard, and perished: *Aeneid* V.832 ff. Palinurus is a
type of the careless traveler, Ulysses is a
type of the man who learns from traveling, and Plato (who made trips to Sicily
and Egypt) is a type of the man who
travels to learn.
9. Raphael will not be known specifically
as the "affable archangel" till Milton
writes *Paradise Lost* a century and a
half hence; still, he is already known as

a comfortable, sociable archangel, as
contrasted with Michael the warrior:
witness his befriending of Tobias in the
apocryphal Book of Tobit. The first root
of "Hythloday" is surely Greek *huthlos*,
meaning "nonsense"; the second part of
the name may suggest *daien*, to distribute, *i.e.*, a nonsense-peddler. A fantastic
trilingual pun could make the whole
name mean "God heals [Heb., *Raphael*] through the nonsense [Gr., *huthlos*]
of God [Lat., *dei*]."

mony to his brothers (he is Portuguese by birth) and took service with Amerigo Vespucci.[1] He accompanied Vespucci on the last three of his four voyages, accounts of which are now common reading everywhere; but on the last voyage, he did not return home with the commander. After much persuasion and expostulation he got Amerigo's permission to be one of the twenty-four men who were left in a fort at the farthest point of the last voyage.[2] Being marooned in this way was altogether agreeable to him, as he was more anxious to pursue his travels than afraid of death. He would often say, "The man who has no grave is covered by the sky,' and 'The road to heaven is equally short from all places.'[3] Yet this frame of mind would have cost him dear, if God had not been gracious to him. After Vespucci's departure, he traveled through many countries with five companions from the fort. At last, by strange good fortune, he got, via Ceylon, to Calcutta,[4] where by good luck he found some Portuguese ships; and so, beyond anyone's expectation, he returned to his own country."

When Peter had told me this, I thanked him for his kindness in wishing to introduce me to a man whose conversation he hoped I would enjoy, and then I turned toward Raphael. After greeting one another and exchanging the usual civilities of strangers upon their first meeting, we all went to my house. There in the garden we sat down on a bench covered with turf to talk together.

He told us that when Vespucci sailed away, he and his companions who had stayed behind in the fort often met with the people of the countryside, and by ingratiating speeches gradually won their friendship. Before long they came to dwell with them safely and even affectionately. The prince also gave them his favor (I have forgotten his name and that of his country), furnishing Raphael and his five companions not only with ample provisions, but with means for traveling—rafts when they went by water, wagons when they went by land. In addition, he sent with them a most trusty guide who was to introduce and recommend them to such other princes as they desired to visit. After many days' journey, he said, they came to towns and cities, and to commonwealths that were both populous and not badly governed.

1. Amerigo Vespucci's last two voyages were made for the King of Portugal, so a Portuguese nationality was natural for Hythloday. By making him a foreigner, More also disposed of him conveniently out of range of the curious. Vespucci, born in Florence, but employed by the monarchies of Spain and Portugal, claimed to have made four trips to America between 1497 and 1504. His account of these voyages (excerpted below, pp. 233–238) circulated widely through Europe after its publication in 1507, and did more to make him famous than the earlier and more substantial explorations of Columbus and Cabot.

2. Cape Frio, near Rio de Janeiro in Brazil.

3. Both these dicta are from classical sources: Lucan, *Pharsalia* VII.819; and Cicero, *Tusculan Disputations* I.104.

4. More covers in a prepositional phrase the distance from Eastern Brazil to Ceylon, a distance of about fifteen thousand miles. Somewhere in there is Utopia.

To be sure, under the equator and as far on both sides of the line as the sun moves, there lie vast empty deserts, scorched with the perpetual heat. The whole region is desolate and squalid, grim and uncultivated, inhabited by wild beasts, serpents, and also by men no less wild and dangerous than the beasts themselves. But as they went on, conditions gradually grew milder. The heat was less fierce, the earth greener, men and even beasts less savage. At last they reached people, cities, and towns which not only traded among themselves and with their neighbors, but even carried on commerce by sea and land with remote countries. After that, he said, they were able to visit different lands in every direction, for he and his companions were welcome as passengers aboard any ship about to make a journey.

The first vessels that they saw were flat-bottomed, with sails made of papyrus-reeds and wicker, or occasionally of leather. Farther on, they found ships with pointed keels and canvas sails, very much like our own. The seamen were skilled in managing wind and water; but they were most grateful to him, Raphael said, for showing them the use of the compass, of which they had been ignorant. For that reason, they had formerly sailed with great timidity, and only in summer. Now they have such trust in the compass that they no longer fear winter at all, and tend to be overconfident rather than secure. There is some danger that through their imprudence, this discovery, which they thought would be so advantageous to them, may become the cause of much mischief.

It would take too long to repeat all that Raphael told us he had observed, nor would it make altogether for our present purpose. Perhaps in another place we shall tell more about the things that are most profitable, especially the wise and sensible institutions that he observed among the civilized nations. We asked him many questions about such things, and he answered us willingly enough. We made no inquiries, however, about monsters, which are the routine of travelers' tales. Scyllas, ravenous Celaenos, man-eating Lestrygonians[5] and that sort of monstrosity you can hardly avoid, but it is not so easy to find good citizens and wise governments. While he told us of many ill-considered usages in these new-found nations, he also described quite a few other customs from which our own cities, nations, races, and kingdoms might take example in order to correct their errors. These I shall discuss in another place, as

5. Scyllas and Lestrygonians are Homeric bogeys, from *Odyssey* XII and X, a monster and a nation that eat men alive. Celaeno was the leader of the Harpies that so tormented Phineus (*Aeneid* III.211 ff.). This is Professor Hexter's "curious paragraph," that marks the transition to the interpolated "dialogue of counsel," which was written and inserted after Book Two was completed. See *More's Utopia: the Biography of an Idea* (Princeton, 1952), Part I, Sec. 3.

I said. Now I intend to relate only what he told us about the manners and laws of Utopians, first explaining the occasion that led him to speak of that commonwealth. Raphael had been talking very wisely about the many errors and also the wise institutions found both in that hemisphere and this (as many of both sorts in one place as in the other), speaking as shrewdly about the manners and governments of each place he had visited briefly as though he had lived there all his life. Peter was amazed.

"My dear Raphael," he said, "I'm surprised that you don't enter some king's service; for I don't know of a single prince who wouldn't be eager to have you. Your learning, and your knowledge of various countries and men would entertain him while your advice and your supply of examples would be very helpful. Thus you might advance your own interest and be useful at the same time to all your relatives and friends."

"I am not much concerned about my relatives and friends," he replied, "because I consider that I have already done my duty by them. While still young and healthy, I distributed among my relatives and friends the possessions that most men do not part with till they are old and sick (and then only reluctantly, because they can no longer keep them). I think they should be content with this gift of mine, and not expect that for their sake I should enslave myself to any king whatever."

"Well said," Peter replied; "but I do not mean that you should be in servitude to any king, only in his service."

"The difference is only a matter of one syllable," Raphael replied.[6]

"All right," said Peter, "but whatever you call it, I do not see any other way in which you can be so useful to your friends or to the general public, apart from making yourself happier."

"Happier indeed!" exclaimed Raphael. "Would a way of life so absolutely repellent to my spirit make my life happier? As it is now, I live as I please, and I fancy very few courtiers, however splendid, can say that. As a matter of fact, there are so many men soliciting favors from the great that it will be no great loss if they have to do without me and a couple of others like me."

Then I said, "It is clear, my dear Raphael, that you want neither wealth nor power, and indeed I value and revere a man of such a disposition as much as I do the greatest men in the world. Yet I think if you would devote your time and energy to public affairs, you would do a thing worthy of a generous and philosophical nature, even if you did not much like it. You could best perform

6. The play on words here rendered by "service" and "servitude" takes the form in Latin of *servias* and *inservias*.

such a service by joining the council of some great prince, whom you would incite to noble and just actions. I am sure you would do this if you held such an office, and your influence would be felt, because a people's welfare or misery flows in a stream from their prince, as from a never-failing spring. Your learning is so full, even if it weren't combined with experience, and your experience is so great, even if you didn't have any learning, that you would be an extraordinary counsellor to any king in the world."

"You are twice mistaken, my dear More," he replied, "first in me and then in the situation itself. I don't have the capacity you ascribe to me, and if I had it in the highest degree, the public would not be any better off through the destruction of my peace. In the first place, most princes apply themselves to the arts of war, in which I have neither ability nor interest, instead of to the good arts of peace. They are generally more set on acquiring new kingdoms by hook or by crook than on governing well those that they already have. Moreover, the counsellors of kings are all so wise that they need no other knowledge (or at least that's the way they see it). At the same time, they accept and even flatter the most absurd statements of favorites through whose influence they seek to stand well with the prince. It is only natural, of course, that each man should think his own opinions best: the old crow loves his fledglings, and the ape his cubs.[7] Now in a court composed of people who envy everyone else and admire only themselves, if a man should suggest something he had read of in other ages or seen in other places, the other counsellors would think their reputation for wisdom was endangered, and they would look like simpletons, unless they could find fault with his proposal. If all else failed, they would take refuge in some remark like this: 'The way we're doing it is the way we've always done it, this custom was good enough for our fathers, and I only hope we're as wise as they were.' And with this deep thought they would take their seats, as though they had said the last word on the subject—implying, forsooth, that it would be a very dangerous matter if a man were found to be wiser in any point than his forefathers were. As a matter of fact, we quietly neglect the best examples they have left us; but if something better is proposed, we seize the excuse of reverence for times past and cling to it desperately. Such proud, obstinate, ridiculous judgments I have encountered many times, and once even in England."

"What!" I asked, "Were you ever in England?"

"Yes," he answered, "I spent several months there. It was not long after the revolt of the Cornishmen against the king had been put down, with great slaughter of the poor folk involved in

7. Another of Erasmus's *Adagia*, perhaps No. 115 or 3964.

it.[8] At that time I was very deeply beholden to the reverend prelate John Cardinal Morton, Archbishop of Canterbury, and in addition at that time Lord Chancellor of England.[9] He was a man, my dear Peter (for More knows about him, and can tell what I'm going to say), as much respected for his wisdom and virtue as for his authority. He was of medium height, not bent with age; his looks inspired respect rather than fear. In conversation, he was not forbidding though serious and grave. When suitors came to him on business, he liked to test their spirit and presence of mind by speaking to them sharply, though not rudely. He liked to uncover these qualities, which were those of his own nature, as long as they were not carried to the point of effrontery; and he thought such men were best qualified to carry on business. His speech was polished and pointed; his knowledge of the law was great, he had a vast understanding and a prodigious memory—for he had improved extraordinary natural abilities by constant study and practice. At the time when I was in England, the king depended greatly on his advice, and he seemed the chief support of the nation as a whole. He had left school for court when scarcely more than a boy, had devoted all his life to important business, and had acquired from his many changes of fortune and at great cost a supply of wisdom, which is not soon lost when so purchased.

"One day when I was dining with him, there was present a layman,[1] learned in the laws of your country, who for some reason took occasion to praise the rigid execution of justice then being practiced upon thieves. They were being executed everywhere, he said, with as many as twenty at a time being hanged on a single gallows. And then he declared that he could not understand how so many thieves sprang up everywhere, when so few of them escaped hanging. I ventured to speak freely before the Cardinal, and said, 'There is no need to wonder: this way of punishing thieves goes beyond the call of justice, and is not, in any case, for the public good. The penalty is too harsh in itself, yet it isn't an effective deterrent. Simple theft[2] is not so great a crime that it ought to cost a man his head, yet no punishment however severe can withhold a man from robbery when he has no other way to eat. In this matter

8. Angered by the greedy taxation of Henry VII, the men of Cornwall revolted in 1497 and marched on London but were defeated at Blackheath and savagely slaughtered.
9. Morton (1420–1500) was a distinguished prelate, statesman, and administrator. More's father, following the custom of the age, sent his son to serve as a page for two years (1490–92) in the cardinal's household; the seventy-year-old cardinal was so impressed with the twelve-year-old More that he arranged for his education at Oxford.
1. It was unusual at that time for a layman to have legal training; but More, who is going to attribute cruel and stupid opinions to this man, wants to dissociate him from the Church and the Cardinal. Hollinshead, the Chronicler, declares that in the reign of Henry VIII alone, 7200 thieves were hanged.
2. Theft is simple when not accompanied by violence or intimidation; when so accompanied, it is robbery.

not only you in England but a good part of the world seem to imitate bad schoolmasters, who would rather whip their pupils than
teach them. Severe and terrible punishments are enacted against
theft, when it would be much better to enable every man to earn
his own living, instead of being driven to the awful necessity of stealing and then dying for it.'

" 'Oh, we've taken care of all that,' said the fellow. 'There are the
trades and there is farming, by which men may make a living unless
they choose deliberately to be rogues.'

" 'Oh no, you don't,' I said, 'you won't get out of it that way.
We may overlook the cripples who come home from foreign and
civil wars, as lately from the Cornish battle and before that from
your wars with France.[3] These men, wounded in the service of
king and country, are too weak to follow their old trades, and too
old to learn new ones. But since wars occur only from time to time,
let us, I say, overlook these men, and consider what happens
every day. There are a great many noblemen who live idly like
drones, off the labors of others, their tenants whom they bleed
white by constantly raising their rents.[4] (This is the only instance of
their tight-fistedness, because they are prodigal in everything else,
ready to spend their way to the poorhouse.) These noblemen drag
around with them a great train of idle servants,[5] who have never
learned any trade by which they could earn a living. As soon as
their master dies, or they themselves fall ill, they are promptly
turned out of doors, for lords would rather support idlers than inva-
lids, and the son is often unable to maintain as big a household as
his father had, at least at first. Those who are turned off soon set
about starving, unless they set about stealing. What else can they
do? Then when a wandering life has taken the edge off their health
and their clothes, when their faces look pinched and their garments
tattered, men of rank will not want to engage them. And country people dare not do so, for they don't have to be told that one
who has been raised softly to idle pleasures, who has been used
to swaggering about with sword and buckler, is likely to look down
on the whole neighborhood, and despise everybody as beneath him.
Such a man can't be put to work with spade and mattock; he will
not serve a poor man laboriously for scant wages and sparse diet.'

3. Though savage early in the fifteenth
century, recent French wars had not
amounted to much. In 1492, Henry VII
briefly supported, or feigned to support,
the independence of Brittany against
Charles VIII, but the matter was quickly
compromised (see below, p. 25, fn. 2).
4. In the endless argument between landlords and tenants, both are likely to
overlook conditions which are the fault
of neither, such as inflation. Still, the
consequences for tenants are generally
worse than for landlords; the abuses at
which More is pointing, through Hythloday, were real and getting worse.
5. The retainers against whom More in-
veighs were the last vestiges of the private armies by which, under feudalism,
every lord had to be followed.

" 'We ought to encourage these men in particular,' said the lawyer. 'In case of war the strength of our army depends on them, because they have a bolder and nobler spirit than workmen and farmers have.'

" 'You may as well say that thieves should be encouraged on account of wars,' I answered, 'since you will never lack for thieves as long as you have men like these. Just as some thieves are not bad soldiers, some soldiers turn out to be pretty good robbers, so nearly are these two ways of life related. But the custom of keeping too many retainers is not peculiar to this nation, it is common to almost all of them. France suffers from an even more grievous plague.[6] Even in peacetime—if you can call it peace—the whole country is crowded with foreign mercenaries, hired on the same principle that you've given for your noblemen keeping idle servants. Wise fools have a saying that the public safety depends on having ready a strong army, preferably of veteran soldiers. They think inexperienced men are not reliable, and they sometimes hunt out pretexts for war, just so they may have trained soldiers and experienced cutthroats—or, as Sallust neatly puts it, that "hand and spirit may not grow dull through lack of practice."[7] But France has learned to her cost how pernicious it is to feed such beasts. The examples of the Romans, the Carthaginians, the Syrians,[8] and many other peoples show the same thing; for not only their governments, but their fields and even their cities were ruined more than once by their own standing armies. Besides, this preparedness is unnecessary: not even the French soldiers, practiced in arms from their youth, can boast of having often got the best of your fresh levies.[9] I shall say no more on this point, lest I seem to flatter present company. At any rate, neither your town workmen nor your rough farm laborers seem to be much afraid of fighting the idle pensioners of gentlemen, as long as they're not weakened by some accident or cowed by extreme poverty. So you need not fear that retainers, once strong and vigorous (for that's the only sort gentlemen deign to corrupt), but now soft and flabby because of their idle, effeminate life, would be weakened

6. Charles VII of France (Joan of Arc's "Dauphin") had tried during the early century to establish a national army; but his successor, Louis XI, reverted to mercenaries, mostly Swiss infantrymen.
7. The quotation is from *Catiline's War*, Chap. XVI.
8. The Romans and Carthaginians both had to fight servile wars against gladiators and mercenaries; the "Syrians" may perhaps be the Turks and Egyptians, who employed alien soldiers under the titles of janizaries and mamelukes; or else the word may refer to much earlier Syrian empires, as described by Polybius v. 31–87.
9. Past English victories over the French included Crécy (1346), Poitiers (1356), and Henry V's triumph at Agincourt (1415); Machiavelli treats it as a commonplace that raw English recruits will always beat French veterans, *Discorsi* I.21. English chauvinism has always maintained that the stout English yeoman, nourished on beef and beer, can overcome ten meager Frenchmen, nourished on sour wine and black bread. (Since the French took up rugby football, less has been heard of this theory.)

if they were taught practical crafts to earn their living, and trained
to manly labor. Anyway, I cannot think it's in the public interest to
maintain for the emergency of war such a vast multitude of people
who trouble and disturb the peace. You never have war unless you
choose it, and peace is always to be more considered than war. Yet
this is not the only circumstance that makes thieving necessary.
There is another one, peculiar (as I see it) to the English people
alone.'

" What is that?' asked the Cardinal.

" 'Your sheep,'[1] I replied, 'that used to be so meek and eat so
little. Now they are becoming so greedy and wild that they devour
men themselves, as I hear. They devastate and pillage fields, houses,
and towns. For in whatever parts of the land the sheep yield the
softest and most expensive wool, there the nobility and gentry,
yes, and even some abbots though otherwise holy men, are not content with the old rents which the land yielded to their predecessors.
Living in idleness and luxury, without doing any good to society, no
longer satisfies them; they have to do positive evil. For they leave no
land free for the plow: they enclose every acre for pasture; they
destroy houses and abolish towns, keeping only the churches, and
those for sheep-barns. And as if enough of your land were not
already wasted on woods and game-preserves, these worthy men
turn all human habitations and cultivated fields back to wilderness.
Thus one greedy, insatiable glutton, a frightful plague to his
native country, may enclose many thousand acres of land within a
single hedge. The tenants are dismissed and compelled, by trickery
or brute force or constant harassment, to sell their belongings. By
hook or by crook these miserable people—men, women, husbands,
wives, orphans, widows, parents with little children, whole families
(poor but numerous, since farming requires many hands)—are
forced to move out. They leave the only homes familiar to them,
and they can find no place to go. Since they cannot afford to wait
for a buyer, they sell for a pittance all their household goods, which
would not bring much in any case. When that little money is gone
(and it's soon spent in wandering from place to place), what
remains for them but to steal, and so be hanged—justly, you'd say!
—or to wander and beg? And yet if they go tramping, they are
jailed as sturdy beggars. They would be glad to work, but they can
find no one who will hire them. There is no need for farm labor, in

1. The wet climate of England provided
ideal conditions for sheep-grazing, and
her insular position kept her from being
overrun by mass armies, whose first activity was always, everywhere, to slaughter stock for food. Thus the English
wool trade was favored from the first. In
a steadily inflating economy, wool, which
could be sold on an international market
for cash, had a special advantage over
other crops, which had to be sold or
even bartered locally. Finally, sheep required less manpower than tillage: a single shepherd with his dog replaced a
hundred plowmen. Petitions, statutes,
and pamphlets of the day provide co-
pious evidence that More was not exag-
gerating.

which they have been trained, when there is no land left to be plowed. One herdsman or shepherd can look after a flock of beasts large enough to stock an area that would require many hands if it were plowed and reaped.

" 'This enclosing has had the effect of raising the price of grain in many places. In addition, the price of raw wool has risen so much that poor people who used to make cloth are no longer able to buy it, and so great numbers are forced from work to idleness. One reason is that after the enlarging of the pasture-land, rot killed a great number of the sheep—as though God were punishing greed by sending upon the animals a murrain, which in justice should have fallen on the owners! But even if the number of sheep should increase greatly, their price will not fall a penny. The reason is that the wool trade, though it can't be called a monopoly because it isn't in the hands of one single person, is concentrated in few hands (an oligopoly, you might say) and these so rich, that the owners are never pressed to sell until they have a mind to, and that is only when they can get their price.

" 'For the same reason other kinds of livestock also are priced exorbitantly, and this is all the easier because, with so many villages being pulled down, and farming in a state of decay, there are not enough people to look after the breeding of cattle. These rich men will not breed calves as they do lambs, but buy them lean and cheap, fatten them in their own pastures, and then sell them at a high price. I don't think the full impact of this bad system has yet been felt. We know these dealers raise prices where the fattened cattle are sold. But when, over a period of time, they keep buying beasts from other localities faster than they can be bred, then as the supply gradually diminishes where they are purchased, a widespread shortage is bound to ensue. So your island, which seemed especially fortunate in this matter, will be ruined by the crass avarice of a few. For the high price of grain causes rich men to dismiss as many retainers as they can from their households; and what, I ask, can these men do, but rob or beg? And a man of courage is more likely to rob than to beg.

" 'To make this hideous poverty worse, it exists side by side with wanton luxury.[2] Not only the servants of noblemen, but tradespeople, farmers, and people of every social rank are given to ostentatious extravagance of dress and too much wasteful indulgence in eating. Look at the eating houses, the bawdy houses, and those other places just as bad, the taverns, wine-shops, and alehouses. Look at all the crooked games of chance like dice, cards,

2. In fact, the court of Henry VII and the style of life in the period 1497–1500, when Hythloday is supposed to be addressing Cardinal Morton, were notably modest and restrained. More is projecting onto the earlier period, perhaps unconsciously, a kind of extravagant display that began in 1509 with the accession of Henry VIII, and was current when he wrote.

backgammon, tennis, bowling, and quoits, in which money slips away so fast. Don't all these lead their habitués straight to robbery? Banish these blights, make those who have ruined farms and villages restore them, or rent them to someone who will rebuild. Restrict the right of the rich to buy up anything and everything, and then to exercise a kind of monopoly. Let fewer people be brought up in idleness. Let agriculture be restored and the wool-manufacture revived, so there will be useful work for the whole crowd of those now idle—whether those whom poverty has already made into thieves, or those whom vagabondage and habits of lazy service are converting, just as surely, into the robbers of the future.

" 'If you do not find a cure for these evils, it is futile to boast of your severity in punishing theft. Your policy may look superficially like justice, but in reality it is neither just nor practical. If you allow young folk to be abominably brought up and their characters corrupted, little by little, from childhood; and if then you punish them as grownups for committing crime to which their early training has inclined them, what else is this, I ask, but first making them thieves and then punishing them for it?'

"As I was speaking thus, the lawyer had made ready his answer, choosing the solemn, formal style of disputants who are better at summing up than at replying, and who like to show off their memory. So he said to me, 'You have talked very well for a stranger, but you have heard about more things than you have been able to understand correctly. I will make the matter clear to you in a few words. First, I will repeat in order what you have said; then I will show how you have been misled by ignorance of our customs; finally, I will demolish all your arguments and reduce them to rubble. And so to begin where I promised, on four points you seemed to me————'

" 'Hold your tongue,' said the Cardinal, 'for you won't be finished in a few words, if this is the way you start. We will spare you the trouble of answering now, and reserve the pleasure of your reply till our next meeting, which will be tomorrow, if your affairs and Raphael's permit it. Meanwhile, my dear Raphael, I am eager to hear why you think theft should not be punished with death, or what other punishment you think would be more in the public interest. For I'm sure even you don't think it should go unpunished entirely. Even as it is, the fear of death does not restrain these men; once they were sure of their lives, as you propose, what force or fear could restrain them? They would look on a lighter penalty as an open invitation to commit more crimes—it would be like offering them a reward.'

" 'It seems to me, most kind and reverend father,' I said, 'that it's altogether unjust to take away a man's life for the loss of someone's money. Nothing in the world that fortune can bestow is equal in value to a man's life. If they say the thief suffers not for the money, but for violation of justice and transgression of laws, then this extreme justice should be called extreme injury. We ought not to approve of these fierce Manlian laws[3] that invoke the sword for the smallest violations. Neither should we accept the Stoic view that considers all crimes equal,[4] as if there were no difference between killing a man and taking a coin from him. If equity means anything, there is no proportion or relation at all between these two crimes. God has said, "Thou shalt not kill"; shall we kill so readily for the theft of a bit of small change? Perhaps it will be argued that God's law against killing does not apply where human laws allow it. But then what prevents men from making other laws in the same way—perhaps even laws legalizing rape, adultery, and perjury? God has taken from each person the right not only to kill another, but even to kill himself. If mutual consent to human laws on manslaughter entitles men freely to exempt their agents from divine law, what is this but preferring the law of man to the law of God? The result will be that in every situation men will decide for themselves how far it suits them to observe the laws of God. The law of Moses is harsh and severe, as for an enslaved and stubborn people, but it punishes theft with a fine, not death.[5] Let us not think that in his new law of mercy, where he treats us with the tenderness of a father, God has given us a greater license to be cruel to one another.

" 'These are the reasons why I think it is unlawful to put thieves to death. But everybody knows how absurd and even harmful to the public welfare it is to punish theft and murder alike. If theft carries the same penalty as murder, the thief will be encouraged to kill the victim whom otherwise he would only have robbed. When the punishment is the same, murder is safer, since one conceals both crimes by killing the witness. Thus while we try to terrify thieves with extreme cruelty, we really invite them to kill innocent men.

" 'Now since you ask what better punishment can be found, in my judgment, it would be much easier to find a better one than a worse. Why should we question the value of the punishments long used by the Romans, who were most expert in the arts of government? They condemned those convicted of heinous crimes to work, shackled, for life, in stone quarries and mines. But of all

[margin handwritten note: GD. POINT]

3. Manlian laws (like those imposed by Titus Manlius in the fourth century B.C.) are very strict, Manlius executed his own son for disobeying one of them: Livy VIII.7.1–22 and Machiavelli, *Discorsi* III.22.
4. That all crimes were equal was maintained by some Stoics and ridiculed by Horace, *Satires* I.3.94 ff.
5. The Mosaic law is that spelled out in the first verses of Exodus xxii. It provides various penalties for theft over and above restitution, but nowhere death. This is contrasted with the "new law" of Christ, under which England is supposed to be operating.

the alternatives, I prefer the method which I observed in my Persian travels among the people commonly called the Polylerites.[6] They are a sizable nation, not badly governed, free and subject only to their own laws, except that they pay annual tribute to the Persian Shah. Living far from the sea, they are nearly surrounded by mountains. Being contented with the products of their own land, which is by no means unfruitful, they have little to do with any other nation, nor are they much visited. According to their ancient customs, they do not try to enlarge their boundaries, and easily protect themselves behind their mountains by paying tribute to their overlord. Thus they have no wars and live in a comfortable rather than a glorious manner, more contented than ambitious or famous. Indeed, I think they are hardly known by name to anyone but their next-door neighbors.

" 'In their land, whoever is found guilty of theft must make restitution to the owner, not (as elsewhere) to the prince; they think the prince has no more right to the stolen goods than the thief. If the stolen property has disappeared, the value of the thief's property is estimated, and restitution is made from it. All the rest is handed over to the thief's wife and children, while the thief himself is sentenced to hard labor.

" 'Unless their crimes were compounded with atrocities, thieves are neither imprisoned nor shackled, but go freely and unguarded about their work on public projects. If they shirk and do their jobs slackly, they are not chained, but they are whipped. If they work hard, they are treated without any insults, except that at night after roll call they are locked up in their dormitories. Apart from constant work, they undergo no discomfort in living. As they work for the state, they are decently fed out of the public stores, though arrangements vary from place to place. In some districts they are supported by alms. Unreliable as this support may seem, the Polylerites are so charitable that no way is found more rewarding. In other places, public revenues are set aside for their support, or a special tax is levied; and sometimes they do not do public work, but anyone in need of workmen can go to the market and hire a convict by the day at a set rate, a little less than that for free men. If they are lazy, it is lawful to whip them. Thus they never lack for work, and each one of them brings a little profit into the public treasury beyond the cost of his keep.

" 'They are all dressed in clothes of the same distinctive color. Their hair is not shaved but trimmed close about the ears, and the tip of one ear is cut off. Their friends are allowed to give them food, drink, or clothing, as long as it is of the proper color; but to give them money is death, both to the giver and to the taker. It

---

6. The name comes from the Greek words *polus* and *leiros*, meaning "much   nonsense." The people are of course imaginary.

is just as serious a crime for any free man to take money from them for any reason whatever; and it is also a capital crime for any of these slaves (as the condemned are called) to carry weapons. In each district of the country they are required to wear a special badge. It is a capital crime to throw away the badge, to go beyond one's own district, or to talk with a slave of another district. Plotting escape is no more secure than escape itself: it is death for any other slave to know of a plot to escape, and slavery for a free man. On the other hand, there are rewards for informers—money for a free man, freedom for a slave, and for both of them pardon and amnesty. Thus it can never be safer for them to persist in a plan of escape than to renounce it.

" 'Thus I've described their policies in this matter. You can see how mild and practical they are, for the aim of the punishment is to destroy vices and save men. The criminals are treated so that they see the necessity of being honest, and for the rest of their lives they atone for the wrong they have done before. There is so little danger of relapse that travelers going from one part of the country to another think slaves the most reliable guides, changing them at the boundary of each district. The slaves have no means of committing robbery since they are unarmed, and any money in their possession is evidence of a crime. If caught, they would be instantly punished, and there is no hope of escape anywhere. Since every bit of a slave's clothing is unlike the usual clothing of the country, how could a slave escape, unless he fled naked? Even then his cropped ear would give him away at once. Might not the slaves form a conspiracy against the government? Perhaps. But the slaves of one district could hardly expect to succeed unless they first involved in their plot the slave-gangs of many other districts. And that is impossible, since they are not allowed to meet or talk together or even to greet one another. No one would risk a plot when they all know joining is so dangerous to the participant and betrayal so profitable to the informer. Besides, no one is quite without hope of gaining his freedom eventually if he accepts his punishment in the spirit of obedience and patience, and gives promise of future good conduct. Indeed, every year some are pardoned as a reward for their submissive behavior.'

"When I had finished this account, I added that I saw no reason why this system could not be adopted, even in England, and with much greater advantage than the 'justice' which my legal antagonist had praised so highly. But the lawyer replied that such a system could never be adopted in England without putting the whole nation in serious peril. And so saying, he shook his head, made a wry face, and fell silent. All the company signified their agreement in his opinion.

"Then the Cardinal remarked, 'It is not easy to guess whether this scheme would work well or not, since nobody has yet tried it out. But perhaps when the death sentence has been passed on a thief, the king might reprieve him for a time without right of sanctuary,[7] and thus see how the plan worked. If it turned out well, then he might establish it by law; if not, he could execute immediate punishment on the man formerly condemned. This would be no more inconvenient or unjust than if the condemned man had been put to death before, yet the experiment would involve no risk. I think vagabonds too might be treated this way, for though we have passed many laws against them, they have had no real effect as yet.'

"When the Cardinal had concluded, they all began praising enthusiastically ideas which they had received with contempt when I suggested them; and they particularly liked the idea about vagabonds because it was the Cardinal's addition.

"I don't know whether it is worthwhile telling what followed, because it was silly, but I'll tell it anyhow, for it's not a bad story and it bears on our subject. There was a hanger-on standing around, who was so good at playing the fool that you could hardly tell him from the real thing. He was constantly making jokes, but so awkwardly that we laughed more at him than at them; yet sometimes a rather clever thing came out, confirming the old proverb that a man who throws the dice often will sooner or later make a lucky cast.[8] One of the company happened to say, 'Well, Raphael has taken care of the thieves, and the Cardinal has taken care of the vagabonds, so now all we have to do is take care of the poor whom sickness or old age has kept from earning a living.'

"'Leave that to me,' said the fool, 'and I'll set it right at once. These are people I'm eager to get out of my sight, having been so often vexed with them and their pitiful complaints. No matter how pitifully they beg for money, they've never whined a single penny out of my pocket. Either I don't want to give them anything, or I haven't anything to give them—it's one of the two. Now they're getting wise; they know me so well, they don't waste their breath, but let me pass without a word or a hope—no more, by heaven, than if I were a priest. But I would make a law sending all these beggars to Benedictine monasteries,[9] where the men could

---

7. In earlier days almost any criminal could take sanctuary in any church and be safe from the law. By More's time, this privilege had been much abridged, but it still applied here and there, and More was hostile to it as adding an element of lottery to the administration of justice.

8. Erasmus, *Adagia*, No. 113, perhaps.

The parallel is not quite exact.

9. The Benedictine order was one of the largest, and also one of the strictest; a lay brother within it would get his full share of work, mostly menial, but would not be admitted even to minor orders. He would be working strictly for the love of God.

become lay brothers, as they're called, and the women could be nuns.'

"The Cardinal smiled and passed it off as a joke; the rest took it seriously. But a certain friar, graduate in divinity, took such pleasure in this jest at the expense of secular priests and monks that he too began to make merry, though generally he was grave to the point of sourness. 'You will not get rid of the beggars,' he began, 'unless you take care of us friars[1] too.'

" 'You have been taken care of already,' retorted the fool. 'The Cardinal provided for you splendidly when he said vagabonds should be arrested and put to work, for you friars are the greatest vagabonds of all.'

"When the company, watching the Cardinal closely, saw that he admitted this jest like the other, they all took it up with vigor—except for the friar. He, as you can easily imagine, was stung by the vinegar,[2] and flew into such a rage that he could not keep from abusing the fool. He called him a knave, a slanderer, a ribald, and a 'son of perdition,' quoting in the meanwhile terrible denunciations from Holy Writ. Now the joker began to jest in earnest, for he was clearly on his own ground.

" 'Don't get angry, good friar,' he said, 'for it is written, "In your patience, possess ye your souls." '[3]

"In reply, the friar said, and I quote his very words: 'I am not angry, you gallows-bird, or at least I do not sin, for the psalmist says, "Be ye angry, and sin not." '[4]

"At this point the Cardinal gently cautioned the friar to calm down, but he answered: 'No, my lord, I speak only from great zeal, as I ought to. For holy men have had great zeal. That is why Scripture says, "The zeal of Thy house has eaten me up,"[5] and we sing in church, "those who mocked Elisha for being bald, as he went up to the house of God, felt the effects of his zeal."[6] Just so this mocker, this rascal, this ribald fellow may very well feel it.'

" 'Perhaps you mean well,' said the Cardinal, 'but you would act in a more holy, and certainly in a wiser way, if you didn't set your wit against a fool's wit and try to spar with a professional jester.'

" 'No, my lord,' he replied, 'I would not act more wisely. For Sol-

1. Specifically, a friar is a member of a mendicant (begging) order, as opposed to a monk who lives, and labors, in a cloister.
2. More's locution reminds the knowing reader of a phrase in Horace's *Satires* I.7.32–33: *italo perfusus aceto*, "soaked in Italian vinegar."
3. Luke xxi.19.
4. Psalms iv.4.
5. Psalms lxix.9.
6. Some children mocked Elisha, son of Elijah the prophet, for his baldness; but he called numerous bears out of the woods, and they ate up the bad children: II Kings ii.23. There is a hymn based on this cautionary tale, by Adam of Saint Victor. In the course of his diatribe the furious friar makes a mistake in his Latin syntax, which a marginal note (by Peter Giles or Erasmus himself) points out; but it is too recondite to be worth translating.

omon himself, the wisest of men, said, "Answer a fool according to his folly,"[7] and that's what I'm doing now. I am showing him the pit into which he will fall if he does not take care. For if the many mockers of Elisha, who was only one bald man, felt the effects of his zeal, how much more effect shall be felt by a single mocker of many friars, who include a great many bald-heads! And besides, we have a papal bull, by which all who mock at us are excommunicated.'

"When the Cardinal saw there was no end to the matter, he nodded to the fool to leave, and turned the conversation to another related subject. Soon after, he rose from table, and, going to hear petitioners, dismissed us.

"Look, my dear More, what a long story I have inflicted on you. I would be quite ashamed, if you had not yourself asked for it, and seemed to listen as if you did not want to miss any of it. Though I might have shortened my account somewhat, I have told it in full, so you might see how those who rejected what I said at first approved of it immediately afterward, when they saw the Cardinal did not disapprove. In fact they went so far in their flattery that they applauded in good earnest ideas that he tolerated only as the jesting of a fool. From this episode you can see how little courtiers would value me or my advice."

To this I answered, "You have given me great pleasure, my dear Raphael, for everything you've said has been both wise and witty. As you spoke, I seemed to be a child and in my own native land once more, through the pleasant recollection of that Cardinal in whose court I was brought up as a lad. Dear as you are to me on other accounts, you cannot imagine how much dearer you are because you honor his memory so highly. Still, I don't give up my former opinion: I think if you could overcome your aversion to court life, your advice to a prince would be of the greatest advantage to mankind. This, after all, is the chief duty of every good man. Your friend Plato thinks that commonwealths will become happy only when philosophers become kings or kings become philosophers.[8] No wonder we are so far from happiness when philosophers do not condescend to assist even kings with their counsels."

"They are not so ill disposed," Raphael replied, "but that they would gladly do it; in fact, they have already done it in a great many published books, if the rulers would only read their good advice. But doubtless Plato was right in foreseeing that unless kings became philosophical themselves, they would never take the advice

---

7. Proverbs xxvi.5. Compare also the previous verse: "Answer not a fool according to his folly, lest thou also be like unto him."

8. Plato, *Republic* V.473.

of real philosophers, drenched as they are and infected with false values from boyhood on. Plato certainly had this experience with Dionysius of Syracuse.[9] If I proposed wise laws to some king, and tried to root out of his soul the seeds of evil and corruption, don't you suppose I would be either banished forthwith, or treated with scorn?

"Imagine, if you will, that I am at the court of the king of France.[1] Suppose I were sitting in his royal council, meeting in secret session, with the king himself presiding, and all the cleverest counsellors were hard at work devising a set of crafty machinations by which the king might keep hold of Milan, recover Naples, which has proved so slippery; then overthrow the Venetians and subdue all Italy; next add Flanders, Brabant, and the whole of Burgundy to his realm, besides some other nations he had in mind to invade.[2] One man urges him to make an alliance with the Venetians for just as long as the king finds it convenient—perhaps to develop a common strategy with them, and even allow them some of the loot, which can be recovered later when things work out according to plan. Another recommends hiring German *Landsknechte* and paying the Swiss to stay neutral.[3] Another suggests soothing the Emperor's wounded pride with a lavish and agreeable lotion of gold.[4] Still another, who is of a different mind, thinks a settlement should be made with the king of Aragon, and that, to cement the peace, he should be allowed to take Navarre from its proper ruler.[5] Another suggests snaring the prince of Castille into a marriage alliance—a first step would be to buy up some nobles of his court with secret pensions.[6]

9. Plato was imported into Syracuse to improve Dionysius the Younger, who had become tyrant by the death of his father in 367 B.C. The anticipated improvement did not come about, and Plato shortly left in disgust.
1. Either Charles VIII, who died in 1498; Louis XII, who died in 1515; or Francis I may have been in More's mind; they were all would-be imperialists who bogged down in the intricacies of Italian political intrigue.
2. The French house of Anjou had various dynastic claims to the rule of Milan and Naples, but after much maneuvering and warfare was driven out of both states by 1513. The enormous program of the French monarchy for unifying its own kingdom (including Brittany and Burgundy, parts of Flanders, but not ultimately Brabant) had preoccupied most French kings of the fifteenth century.
3. Many German mercenaries took service in Italy, either as individuals or in companies, during the incessant warfare that began in 1494; as foot soldiers, they were second in Europe only to the Swiss, whose talents were such that they fre-quently didn't have to fight to get paid: they collected for staying neutral.
4. Maximilian of Austria, Holy Roman Emperor, whom Machiavelli sketches sharply in Chap. XXIII of *The Prince*, had grandiose schemes (he even dreamed of being Pope) but little money. He was always accessible to a bribe.
5. Machiavelli characterizes the tricky Ferdinand of Aragon in Chapter XXI of *The Prince*. Navarre was a small independent enclave astride the Pyrenees, long disputed between Spain and France. In 1512 Ferdinand took one piece of it from Jean III d'Albret; in 1598 Henri IV snapped up the remainder for France.
6. Already in his teens, Charles V was a great matrimonial and diplomatic catch. The question of a French marriage, which would unite the two greatest Continental and Catholic powers, was continually in the air throughout the century. On the use of international bribery as an everyday tactic of European "statecraft," see J. W. Thompson and S. K. Padover, *Secret Diplomacy* (New York, 1965), Chap. 4.

"The hardest problem of all is what to do about England. They all agree that the alliance, which is weak at best, should be strengthened as much as possible; but while the English are being treated as friends, they should also be suspected as enemies. And so the Scots must be kept in constant readiness, poised to attack the English in case they stir ever so little.[7] Also a banished nobleman with some pretensions to the English throne must be secretly encouraged (there are treaties against doing it openly), and in this way pressure can be brought to bear on the English king, and a ruler kept in check who can't really be trusted.

"Now in a meeting like this one, where so much is at stake, where so many brilliant men are competing to think up intricate strategies of war, what if an insignificant fellow like myself were to get up and advise going on another tack entirely? Suppose I said the king should leave Italy alone and stay at home,[8] because the single kingdom of France all by itself is almost too much for one man to govern, and the king should not dream of adding others to it. Then imagine I told about the decrees of the Achorians[9] who live off the island of Utopia toward the southeast. Long ago, these people went to war to gain another realm for their king, who had inherited an ancient claim to it through marriage. When they had conquered it, they soon saw that keeping it was going to be as hard as getting it had been. Their new subjects were continually rebelling or being attacked by foreign invaders, the Achorians had to be constantly at war for them or against them, and they saw no hope of ever being able to disband their army. In the meantime, they were being heavily taxed, money flowed out of their kingdom, their blood was being shed for the advantage of others, and peace was no closer than it ever was. The war corrupted their own citizens by encouraging lust for robbery and murder; and the laws fell into contempt because their king, distracted with the cares of two kingdoms, could give neither one his proper attention.

"When they saw that the list of these evils was endless, the Achorians took counsel together and very courteously offered their king his choice of keeping whichever of the two kingdoms he preferred, because he couldn't rule them both. They were too numerous a people, they said, to be ruled by half a king; and they added that a man would not even hire a muledriver, if he had to divide his

7. The Scots, as traditional enemies of England, were traditional allies of France. Though the pretender Richard de la Pole has been suggested, nobody is really sure of who the "banished nobleman" of the next sentence could be. But the point of the passage is the devious intricacy of the counsellors' thoughts; if there were no banished nobleman, they would find or invent one.

8. One of history's great unanswered problems is why three successive French kings (Charles VIII, Louis XII, and Francis I) felt they had to conquer Italy, when they had more trouble than they could manage simply in governing France properly.

9. The name arises from the Greek *a* ("without") and *chora* ("place"): people from nowhere.

services with somebody else. The worthy king was thus obliged to be content with his own realm and give his new one to a friend, who before long was driven out.

"Finally, suppose I told the French king's council that all this war-mongering, by which so many different nations were kept in social turmoil as a result of royal connivings and schemings, would certainly exhaust his treasury and demoralize his people, and yet very probably in the end come to nothing through some mishap or other. And therefore I would advise the French king to look after his ancestral kingdom, improve it as much as he could, cultivate it in every conceivable way. He should love his people and be loved by them; he should live among them, and govern them kindly, and let other kingdoms alone, since his own is big enough, if not too big for him. How do you think, my dear More, the other counsellors would take this speech of mine?"

"Not very well, I'm sure," said I.

"Well, let's go on," he said. "Suppose the counsellors are discussing various schemes for raising money to fill some other king's treasury. One man recommends increasing the value of money when the king pays his debts and devaluing it when he collects his revenues.[1] Thus he can discharge a huge debt with a small payment, and collect a large sum when only a small one is due him. Another suggests a make-believe war, so that money can be raised under pretext of carrying it on; then, when the money is in, he can make peace with solemn ceremonies—which the simple-minded people will attribute to the piety of their prince and his careful compassion for the lives of his subjects.[2] Another counsellor calls to mind some old moth-eaten laws, antiquated by long disuse, which no one remembers being made and consequently everyone has transgressed. By imposing fines for breaking these laws, the king will get great sums of money, as well as credit for upholding law and order since the whole procedure can be made to look like justice.[3] Another recommendation is that he forbid under particularly heavy fines a lot of practices that are contrary to the public interest; afterward, he can dispense with his own rules for large sums of money. Thus he pleases the people and makes a double profit, one from the heavy fines imposed on law-breakers, and the other from selling licenses. Meanwhile he seems careful of his people's welfare, since it is plain he will not

1. Edward IV, Henry VII, and (after *Utopia* was written) Henry VIII all fiddled with the English currency in ways like those suggested here.
2. Something like this happened in 1492, when King Henry VII not only pretended war with France on behalf of Brittany and levied taxes for the war (which was hardly fought), but collected a bribe from Charles VIII for not fighting it.
3. This had been common practice under Henry VII, whose ministers Empson and Dudley scratched up a great many forgotten laws for strictly mercenary purposes.

allow private citizens to do anything contrary to the public interest except for a huge price.[4]

"Another counsellor proposes that he gain influence with the judges, so that they will decide every case in favor of the king. They should be summoned to court often, and invited to debate his affairs in the royal presence. However unjust his claims, one or another of the judges, whether from love of contradiction, or desire to seem original, or simply to serve his own interest, will be bound to find some way of twisting the law in the king's favor and tripping up his opponent. If the judges can be brought to differ, then the clearest matter in the world will be made disputable, and the truth itself brought into question. The king can then interpret the law as he will, and everyone else will acquiesce from shame or fear. (Afterwards, of course, it will be said that the law has spoken!) There are always plenty of pretexts for giving judgment in favor of the king. Either equity is on his side, or the letter of the law happens to make for him, or the words of the law can be twisted into obscurity —or, if all else fails, he can appeal above the law to the royal prerogative, which is a never-failing argument with judges who know their 'duty.'[5]

"Thus all the counsellors agree with the famous maxim of Crassus: a king who wants to maintain an army can never have too much gold.[6] Further, that a king, even if he wants to, can do no wrong, for all property belongs to the king, and so do his subjects themselves; a man owns nothing but what the king, in his goodness, sees fit to leave him. The king should in fact leave his subjects as little as possible, because his own safety depends on keeping them from growing insolent with wealth and freedom. For riches and liberty make men less patient to endure harsh and unjust commands, whereas meager poverty blunts their spirits, makes them patient, and grinds out of the oppressed the lofty spirit of rebellion.

"Now at this point, suppose I were to get up again and declare that all these counsels are both dishonorable and ruinous to the king? Suppose I said his honor and his safety alike rest on the people's resources, rather than his own? Suppose I said that men choose a king for their own sake, not for his, so that by his efforts and troubles, they may live in comfort and safety?[7] This is why, I

4. For a Christian saint, More has a terrible practical insight into the ways of government hypocrisy, which we sometimes call, indulgently, public relations.
5. "Prerogative" was a catchall phrase, used in those days to justify verbally what couldn't be justified logically, much like "executive privilege" or "the national interest" in our own times.
6. Quoted by Cicero, *De Officiis* I.8.25. Crassus was a rich Roman (his name means "fat") who joined with Pompey and Caesar to form the First Triumvirate. A vindictive Parthian is said to have disproved his maxim by pouring molten gold down his throat (Florus III.11).
7. Though phrased as the hypothetical speech of an imaginary person, this liberal doctrine was a deep element of More's constant thought. One of his little Latin poems contains a couplet which could be translated, "There's no way a ruler should rule longer than his subjects want him to." *Epigrams*, No. 103.

would say, it is the king's duty to take more care of his people's welfare than of his own, just as it is the duty of a shepherd who cares for his calling to feed his sheep rather than himself.[8]

"They are absolutely wrong when they say that the people's poverty safeguards public peace—experience shows the contrary. Where will you find more squabbling than among beggars? Who is more eager for revolution than the man who is most discontented with his present position? Who is more reckless about creating disorders than the man who knows he has nothing to lose and thinks he may have something to gain? If a king is so hated or despised by his subjects that he can rule them only by mistreatment, plundering, confiscation, and pauperization of his people, then he'd do much better to abdicate his throne—for under these circumstances, though he keeps the name of authority, he loses all the majesty of a king. A king has no dignity when he exercises authority over beggars, only when he rules over prosperous and happy subjects. This was certainly what that noble and lofty spirit Fabricius meant when he said he would rather be a ruler of rich men than be rich himself.[9]

"A solitary ruler who enjoys a life of pleasure and self-indulgence while all about him are grieving and groaning is acting like a jailer, not a king. Just as an incompetent doctor can cure his patient of one disease only by throwing him into another, so it's an incompetent king who can rule his people only by depriving them of all life's pleasures. Such a king openly confesses that he does not know how to rule free men.

"A king of this stamp should correct his own sloth or arrogance, because these are the vices that cause the people to hate or despise him. Let him live on his own income without wronging others, and limit his spending to his income. Let him curb crime, and by wise training of his subjects keep them from misbehavior instead of letting it breed and then punishing it. Let him not suddenly revive antiquated laws, especially if they have been long forgotten and never missed. And let him never take money as a fine when a judge would regard an ordinary subject as wicked and fraudulent for claiming it.

"But suppose I should then describe for them the law of the Macarians,[1] a people who also live not far from Utopia? On the day that their king first assumes office, he must take an oath confirmed by solemn ceremonies that he will never have in his treasury at any one time more than a thousand pounds of gold, or its equiva-

---

8. This metaphor is one of the great commonplaces. Ezekiel xxxiv.2 reads: "Woe be to the shepherds of Israel that do feed themselves: should not the shepherds feed the flocks?"
9. Gaius Fabricius Luscinus, who took part in the wars against Pyrrhus, King of Epirus (281–275 B.C.); the saying attributed to him here was actually coined by his colleague M. Curius Dentatus, but it is quite in his spirit.
1. From the Greek *makarios*, "happy," "fortunate."

lent in silver. They say this law was made by an excellent king, who cared more for his country's prosperity than for his own wealth; he established it as a barrier against any king heaping up so much money as to impoverish his people.[2] He thought this sum would enable the king to put down rebellions or repel hostile invasions, but would not tempt him into aggressive adventures. His law was aimed chiefly at keeping the king in check, but he also wanted to ensure an ample supply of money for the daily business transactions of the citizens. Besides, a king who has to distribute all his excess money to the people will not be much disposed to oppress them. Such a king will be both a terror to evil-doers and beloved by the good. —Summing up the whole thing, don't you suppose if I set ideas like these before men strongly inclined to the contrary, they would turn deaf ears to me?"

"Stone deaf, indeed, there's no doubt about it," I said, "and no wonder! To tell you the truth, I don't think you should offer advice or thrust on people ideas of this sort which you know will not be listened to. What good will it do? When your listeners are already prepossessed against you and firmly convinced of opposite opinions, what good can you do with your rhapsody of new-fangled ideas? This academic philosophy is quite agreeable in the private conversation of close friends, but in the councils of kings, where grave matters are being authoritatively decided, there is no place for it."

"That is just what I was saying," Raphael replied. "There is no place for philosophy in the councils of kings."

"Yes, there is," I said, "but not for this scholastic philosophy which supposes that every topic is suitable for every occasion. There is another philosophy that is better suited for political action, that takes its cue, adapts itself to the drama in hand, and acts its part neatly and well. This is the philosophy for you to use. When a comedy of Plautus is being played, and the household slaves are cracking trivial jokes together, you propose to come on stage in the garb of a philosopher, and repeat Seneca's speech to Nero from the *Octavia*.[3] Wouldn't it be better to take a silent role than to say

2. Once again More glances at the previous monarch, Henry VII, who died the richest prince in Christendom and probably the most hated. He combined unscrupulous greed with skinflint stinginess.
3. Most of the plays of Plautus involve low intrigue: needy young men, expensive prostitutes, senile moneybags, and clever slaves, in predictable combinations. *Octavia*, a tragedy like those of Seneca, involving Seneca as a personage, but not by Seneca (though long supposed to be so), is full of high seriousness. In a letter written by Pico to Andrew Corneus and dated 15 October 1492 (More included it with his translation of a tiny *Life of Pico della Mirandola*, published 1510) there occurs this answer to a

suggestion that Pico take service with a prince: "but I see well that as yet you have not known that opinion that philosophers have of themselves, who (as Horace says) repute themselves kings of kings: they love liberty: they cannot bear the proud manners of estate [nobility]: they cannot serve. They dwell with themselves and are content with the tranquillity of their own minds; they suffice themselves and more; they seek nothing outside of themselves" (English much modernized by R. M. A.).

There is a Latin idiom, "scenae servire," which means to go through with the demands of a public performance: Cicero, *Ad Brutum*, 1.9.2. It may have suggested More's metaphor.

(margin notes: "Accusation of being unrealistic", "REAGAN (ACTOR)", "machi.")

something wholly inappropriate, and thus turn the play into a tragi-comedy? You pervert and ruin a play when you add irrelevant speeches, even if they are better than the play itself. So go through with the drama in hand as best you can, and don't spoil it all simply because you happen to think another one would be better.

"That's how things go in the commonwealth, and in the councils of princes. If you cannot pluck up bad ideas by the root, if you cannot cure long-standing evils as completely as you would like, you must not therefore abandon the commonwealth. Don't give up the ship in a storm because you cannot direct the winds. And don't arrogantly force strange ideas on people who you know have set their minds on a different course from yours. You must strive to influence policy indirectly, handle the situation tactfully, and thus what you cannot turn to good, you may at least make less bad. For it is impossible to make all institutions good unless you make all men good, and that I don't expect to see for a long time to come."

"The only result of this," he answered, "will be that while I try to cure others of madness, I'll be raving along with them myself. If I am to speak the truth, I will simply have to talk in the way I have described. For all I know, it may be the business of a philosopher to recite lies, but it isn't mine. Though my advice may be repugnant to the king's counsellors, I don't see why they should consider it eccentric to the point of folly. What if I told them the kind of thing that Plato advocates in his Republic, or which the Utopians actually practice in theirs? However superior those institutions might be (and as a matter of fact they are), yet here they would seem inappropriate because private property is the rule here, and there all things are held in common.

"People who have made up their minds to rush headlong down the opposite road are never pleased with the man who calls them back and tells them they are headed the wrong way. But, apart from that, what did I say that could not and should not be said anywhere and everywhere? If we dismiss as out of the question and absurd everything which the perverse customs of men have made to seem unusual, we shall have to set aside most of the commandments of Christ even in a community of Christians. Yet he forbade us to dissemble them, and even ordered that what he had whispered to his disciples should be preached openly from the housetops.[4] Most of his teachings differ more radically from the common customs of mankind than my discourse does. But preachers, like the crafty fellows they are, have found that men would rather not change their lives to conform to Christ's rule, and so, just as you suggest, they have accommodated his teaching to the way men live,

4. A reminiscence of Luke xii.3: "that which ye have spoken in the ear in closets shall be proclaimed upon the house-tops." Cf. also Matthew x.27, to the same effect.

as if it were a leaden yardstick.[5] At least in that way they can get the two things to correspond on one level or another. The only real thing they accomplish that I can see is to make men feel a little more secure in their consciences about doing evil.

"And this is all that I could accomplish in a prince's court. For either I would have different ideas from the others, and that would come to the same thing as having no ideas at all, or else I would agree with them, and that, as Mitio says in Terence, would merely confirm them in their madness.[6] When you say I should 'influence policy indirectly,' I simply don't know what you mean; remember, you said I should try hard to handle the situation tactfully, and what can't be made good I should try to make as little bad as possible. In a council, there is no way to dissemble, no way to shut your eyes to things. You must openly approve the worst proposals, and consent to the most vicious decisions. A man who went along only halfheartedly even with the worst decisions would immediately get himself a name as a spy and perhaps a traitor. How can one individual do any good when he is surrounded by colleagues who would sooner corrupt the best of men than do any reforming of themselves? Either they will seduce you, or, if you keep yourself honest and innocent, you will be made a screen for the knavery and madness of others. Influencing policy indirectly! You wouldn't have a chance.

"This is why Plato in a very fine comparison declares that wise men are right in keeping clear of government matters.[7] They see the people swarming through the streets and getting soaked with rain, and they cannot persuade them to go indoors and get out of the wet. They know if they go out themselves, they can do no good but only get drenched with the rest. So they stay indoors and are content to keep themselves dry, since they cannot remedy the folly of everyone else.

"But as a matter of fact, my dear More, to tell you what I really think, as long as you have private property, and as long as cash money is the measure of all things, it is really not possible for a nation to be governed justly or happily. For justice cannot exist where all the best things in life are held by the worst citizens; nor

---

5. A flexible yardstick made of lead was particularly useful in the sort of ancient building known as the "Lesbian" style, because of the great number of curved mouldings. Aristotle in *Ethics* V.10.7 uses it as a metaphor for adaptable moral standards.

6. The slave Mitio, speaking of his master, says: "If I provoke or even listen to his madness, I shall be as crazy as he is" (*Adelphi* I.ii.66–67).

7. Plato *Republic* VI.496. This attitude that the wise man should avoid not only politics but public service and even marriage was characteristic of many early humanists. Hans Baron traces in *The Crisis of the Early Italian Renaissance* (Princeton, 1966) the process by which "civic humanism" took its place.

can anyone be happy where property is limited to a few, since those few are always uneasy and the many are utterly wretched.

"So I reflect on the wonderfully wise and sacred institutions of the Utopians who are so well governed with so few laws. Among them virtue has its reward, yet everything is shared equally, and all men live in plenty. I contrast them with the many other nations which are constantly passing new ordinances and yet can never order their affairs satisfactorily. In these other nations, whatever a man can get he calls his own private property; but all the mass of laws old and new don't enable him to secure his own, or defend it, or even distinguish it from someone else's property. Different men lay claim, successively or all at once, to the same property; and thus arise innumerable and interminable lawsuits—fresh ones every day. When I consider all these things, I become more sympathetic to Plato and do not wonder that he declined to make laws for any people who refused to share their goods equally.[8] Wisest of men, he easily perceived that the one and only road to the welfare of all lies through the absolute equality of goods. I doubt whether such equality can ever be achieved where property belongs to individual men. However abundant goods may be, when every man tries to get as much as he can for his own exclusive use, a handful of men end up sharing the whole thing, and the rest are left in poverty. The result generally is two sorts of people whose fortunes ought to be interchanged: the rich are rapacious, wicked, and useless, while the poor are unasuming, modest men who work hard, more for the benefit of the public than of themselves.

"Thus I am wholly convinced that [unless private property is entirely done away with, there can be no fair or just distribution of goods, nor can mankind be happily governed.] As long as private property remains, by far the largest and the best part of mankind will be oppressed by a heavy and inescapable burden of cares and anxieties. This load, I admit, may be lightened a little bit under the present system, but I maintain it cannot be entirely removed. Laws might be made that no one should own more than a certain amount of land or receive more than a certain income.[9] Or laws might be passed to prevent the prince from becoming too powerful and the populace too unruly. It might be made unlawful for public offices to be solicited, or put up for sale, or made burdensome for

8. The Arcadians and Thebans united to build a great city, we are told, and asked Plato to be its legislator. He made communism a condition of his going there, and when the inhabitants would not consent, declined the offer. Diogenes Laertius, *The Lives of the Eminent Philosophers* III.17.

9. From time to time Rome, and many Italian city-states, had passed sumptuary laws regulating finery in dress, number of servants, and quantity of display; agrarian laws limiting land ownership were also often attempted.

the officeholder by great expense. Otherwise, officeholders are tempted to get their money back by fraud or extortion, and only rich men can afford to seek positions which ought to be held by wise men. Laws of this sort, I agree, may have as much effect as good and careful nursing has on men who are chronically or even terminally sick.[1] The social evils I mentioned may be alleviated and their effects mitigated for a while, but so long as private property remains, there is no hope at all of effecting a cure and restoring society to good health. While you try to cure one part, you aggravate the disease in other parts. Suppressing one symptom causes another to break out, since you cannot give something to one man without taking it away from someone else."

"But I don't see it that way," I replied. "It seems to me that men cannot possibly live well where all things are in common.[2] How can there be plenty of commodities where every man stops working? The hope of gain will not spur him on; he will rely on others, and become lazy. If a man is driven by want of something to produce it, and yet cannot legally protect what he has gained, what can follow but continual bloodshed and turmoil, especially when respect for magistrates and their authority has been lost? I for one cannot conceive of authority existing among men who are equal to one another in every respect."

"I'm not surprised," said Raphael, "that you think of it in this way, since you have no idea, or only a false idea, of such a state. But you should have been with me in Utopia, and seen with your own eyes their manners and customs as I did—for I lived there more than five years, and would never have left, if it had not been to make that new world known to others. If you had seen them, you would frankly confess that you had never seen a people so well governed as they are."

"You will have a hard time persuading me," said Peter Giles, "that people in that new land are better governed than in the world we know. Our minds are not inferior to theirs, and our government, I believe, is older. Long experience has helped us develop many conveniences of life, and by good luck we have discovered many other things which human ingenuity could never hit on."

"As for the relative ages of the governments," Raphael replied, "you might judge more accurately if you had read their histories. If we believe these records, they had cities before there were even

---

1. A problem with social reform throughout the ages is that the patient tends to dictate to the doctor what his diagnosis shall be.

2. These preliminary objections are chiefly founded on those of the hardheaded Aristotle, *Politics* II.1–3. Most of them reduce to the prediction (painfully verified in several "egalitarian" societies of our own day) that if you are to make the donkey go without carrots, you will have to hit him often and hard with a stick.

human inhabitants here. What ingenuity has discovered or chance hit upon could have turned up just as well in one place as the other. As a matter of fact, I believe we surpass them in natural intelligence, but they leave us far behind in their diligence and zeal to learn.[3]

"According to their chronicles, they had heard nothing of men-from-beyond-the-equator (that's their name for us) until we arrived, except that once, some twelve hundred years ago, a ship which a storm had blown toward Utopia was wrecked on their island.[4] Some Romans and Egyptians were cast ashore, and never departed. Now note how the Utopians profited, through their diligence, from this one chance event. They learned every single useful art of the Roman civilization either directly from their guests, or indirectly from hints and surmises on which they based their own investigations. What benefits from the mere fact that on a single occasion some Europeans landed there! If a similar accident has hitherto brought any men here from their land, the incident has been completely forgotten, as it will be forgotten in time to come that I was ever in their country. From one such accident they made themselves masters of all our useful inventions, but I suspect it will be a long time before we accept any of their institutions which are better than ours. This willingness to learn, I think, is the really important reason for their being better governed and living more happily than we do, though we are not inferior to them in brains or resources."

"Then let me implore you, my dear Raphael," said I, "to describe that island to us. Do not try to be brief, but explain in order everything relating to their land, their rivers, towns, people, manners, institutions, laws—everything, in short, that you think we would like to know. And you can take it for granted that we want to know everything that we don't know yet."

"There's nothing I'd rather do," he replied, "for these things are fresh in my mind. But it will take quite some time."

"In that case," I said, "let's first go to dinner. Afterward, we shall have all the time we want."

"Agreed," he said. So we went in and had dinner. Then we came back to the same spot, and sat down on the bench. I ordered my

3. Precisely the opposite judgment was reached by early English explorers among the Indians of Virginia. In native ingenuity, they said, the Indians were often superior, but the larger difference lay in European technology. See Thomas Hariot's *Brief and true report of . . . Virginia*, included in Hakluyt's *Principal Navigations*, 1600.
4. In A.D. 315 (about 1200 years before *Utopia* was written), Europeans would have had little to teach the Utopians in the way of technology or social organization; and, as appears later, these early arrivals knew nothing of Christianity. More is trying to indicate that the two cultures started about even, on the path of their development, with the Roman and Egyptian rudiments.

servants to take care that no one should interrupt us. Peter Giles and I urged Raphael to keep his promise. When he saw that we were eager to hear him, he sat silent and thoughtful a moment, and then began as follows:

The End of Book One

* * * * *

BOOK TWO

The Geography of Utopia

The island of the Utopians is two hundred miles across in the middle part where it is widest, and is nowhere much narrower than this except toward the two ends. These ends, drawn toward one another in a five-hundred-mile circle, make the island crescent-shaped like a new moon.[5] Between the horns of the crescent, which are about eleven miles apart, the sea enters and spreads into a broad bay. Being sheltered from the wind by the surrounding land, the bay is never rough, but quiet and smooth instead, like a big lake. Thus, nearly the whole inner coast is one great harbor, across which ships pass in every direction, to the great advantage of the people. What with shallows on one side, and rocks on the other, the entrance into the bay is very dangerous. Near the middle of the channel, there is one rock that rises above the water, and so presents no dangers in itself; on top of it a tower has been built, and there a garrison is kept. Since the other rocks lie under water, they are very dangerous to navigation. The channels are known only to the Utopians, so hardly any strangers enter the bay without one of their pilots; and even they themselves could not enter safely if they did not direct themselves by some landmarks on the coast. If they should shift these landmarks about, they could lure to destruction an enemy fleet coming against them, however big it was.

On the outer side of the island there are likewise occasional harbors; but the coast is rugged by nature, and so well fortified that a few defenders could beat off the attack of a strong force. They say (and the appearance of the place confirms this) that their land was not always an island. But Utopus, who conquered the country and gave it his name (it had previously been called Abraxa),[6] brought

---

5. The island is about the size of England; its likeness to the new moon is perhaps less striking, for a post-Freudian generation, than its resemblance to a womb. See the woodcut "map" or drawing, from the editions of 1516 and 1518, p. 2.

6. The name "Abraxa" connotes mystical antiquity; it was engraved on various stones by the followers of Basilides the Gnostic (second century A.D.), and nobody knows precisely what it means. For what it's worth, the Greek letters making it up have numerical equivalents which add up to 365.

its rude and uncouth inhabitants to such a high level of culture and humanity that they now excel in that regard almost every other people. After subduing them at his first landing, he cut a channel fifteen miles wide where their land joined the continent, and caused the sea to flow around the country.[7] He put not only the natives to work at this task, but all his own soldiers too, so that the vanquished would not think the labor a disgrace. With the work divided among so many hands, the project was finished quickly, and the neighboring peoples, who at first had laughed at his folly, were struck with wonder and terror at his success.

There are fifty-four cities on the island, all spacious and magnificent, identical in language, customs, institutions, and laws. So far as the location permits, all of them are built on the same plan, and have the same appearance. The nearest are at least twenty-four miles apart, and the farthest are not so remote that a man cannot go on foot from one to the other in a day.[8]

Once a year each city sends three of its old and experienced citizens to Amaurot[9] to consider affairs of common interest to the island. Amaurot is the chief city, lies near the omphalos[1] of the land, so to speak, and convenient to every other district, so it acts as a capital. Every city has enough ground assigned to it so that at least ten miles of farm land are available in every direction, though where the cities are farther apart, they have much more land. No city wants to enlarge its boundaries, for the inhabitants consider themselves good tenants rather than landlords. At proper intervals all over the countryside they have built houses and furnished them with farm equipment. These houses are inhabited by citizens who come to the country by turns to occupy them. No rural house has fewer than forty men and women in it, besides two slaves. A master and mistress, serious and mature persons, are in charge of each household. Over every thirty households is placed a single phylarch.[2] Each year twenty persons from each rural household move back to the city, after completing a two-year stint in the country. In their place, twenty others are sent out from town, to learn farm work from those who have already been in the country for a year, and who are better skilled in farming. They, in turn, will teach

---

7. There is a story that Xerxes did something like this at Mt. Athos—not, however, to make an island, but to get his ships across an isthmus; see Herodotus, VII.22–24. The parallel might be insignificant, but More does emphasize later the connections between the Utopians and the Persians, see below, pp. 62, 78.

8. A conscious absurdity, no doubt—since only an exceptional athlete, walking as fast as he can, will cover much more than twenty-four miles from dawn to dusk. Maxima and minima are about the same.

9. From the Greek, implying "dark city." It is probably only a coincidence that a major medieval heretic, whose teachings were responsible for several communist sects of the Free Spirit among the cloth traders of Flanders, was Amaury of Bène (died 1206 or 1207), whose followers were called "Amaurians."

1. Navel, umbilicus; an ancient word for the spiritual as well as the physical center of a nation.

2. From the Greek, meaning head (arché) of a tribe (phylon).

those who come the following year.[3] If all were equally ignorant of farm work, and new to it, they might harm the crops out of ignorance. This custom of alternating farm workers is solemnly established so that no one will have to do such hard work against his will for more than two years; but many of them who take a natural pleasure in farm life ask to stay longer.

The farm workers till the soil, raise cattle, hew wood, and take it to the city by land or water, as is most convenient. They breed an enormous number of chickens by a marvelous method. Men, not hens, hatch the eggs by keeping them in a warm place at an even temperature. As soon as they come out of the shell, the chicks recognize the men, follow them around, and are devoted to them instead of to their real mothers.

They raise very few horses, and these full of mettle, which they keep only to exercise the young men in the art of horsemanship. For the heavy work of plowing and hauling they use oxen, which they agree are inferior to horses over the short haul, but which can hold out longer under heavy burdens, are less subject to disease (as they suppose), and so can be kept with less cost and trouble. Moreover, when oxen are too old for work, they can be used for meat.

Grain they use only to make bread. They drink wine, apple or pear cider, or simple water, which they sometimes mix with honey or licorice, of which they have an abundance.[4] Although they know very well, down to the last detail, how much grain each city and its surrounding district will consume, they produce much more grain and cattle than they need for themselves, and share the surplus with their neighbors. Whatever goods the folk in the country need which cannot be produced there, they request of the town magistrates, and since there is nothing to be paid or exchanged, they get what they want at once, without any haggling. They generally go to town once a month in any case, to observe the holy days. When harvest time approaches, the phylarchs in the country notify the town-magistrates how many hands will be needed. Crews of harvesters come just when they're wanted, and in one day of good weather they can usually get in the whole crop.

Their Cities, Especially Amaurot

If you know one of their cities, you know them all, for they're exactly alike, except where geography itself makes a difference. So

3. We learn later that everyone studies agriculture in school and gets practical experience of it on field trips; in addition, a man who spent half his adult life on the farm would, by the age of forty, have had at least ten and probably fifteen years of experience.
4. Beer and ale are rather strikingly omitted from the list of Utopian drinks. Perhaps More considered them an undue temptation, as being easier to make than wine and more agreeable to the taste of the English workingman. Utopia's drinking habits are more middle class than a plowman accustomed to beer would consider Utopian.

I'll describe one of them, and no matter which. But what one rather than Amaurot the most worthy of all?—since its eminence is acknowledged by the other cities which send representatives to the annual meeting there; besides which, I know it best because I lived there for five full years.

Well, then, Amaurot lies up against a gently sloping hill; the town is almost square in shape. From a little below the crest of the hill, it runs down about two miles to the river Anyder,[5] and then spreads out along the river bank for a somewhat greater distance. The Anyder rises from a small spring about eighty miles above Amaurot, but other streams flow into it, two of them being pretty big, so that, as it runs past Amaurot, the river has grown to a width of half a mile. It continues to grow even larger until at last, sixty miles farther along, it is lost in the ocean. In all this stretch between the sea and the city, and also for some miles above the city, the river is tidal, ebbing and flowing every six hours with a swift current. When the tide comes in, it fills the whole Anyder with salt water for about thirty miles, driving the fresh water back. Even above that for several miles farther, the water is brackish; but a little higher up, as it runs past the city, the water is always fresh, and when the tide ebbs, the water is fresh all the way to the sea.

The two banks of the river at Amaurot are linked by a bridge, built not on wooden piles but on many solid arches of stone. It is placed at the upper end of the city, farthest removed from the sea, so that ships can sail along the entire length of the city quays without obstruction. There is also another stream, not particularly large, but very gentle and pleasant, which rises out of the hill, flows down through the center of town, and into the Anyder. The inhabitants have walled around the source of this river, which takes its rise a little outside the town, and joined it to the town proper so that if they should be attacked, the enemy would not be able to cut off the stream or divert or poison it. Water from the stream is carried by tile piping into various sections of the lower town. Where the terrain makes this impractical, they collect rain water in cisterns, which serve just as well.

The town is surrounded by a thick, high wall, with many towers and forts. On three sides it is also surrounded by a dry ditch, broad and deep and filled with thorn hedges; on its fourth side the river itself serves as a moat. The streets are conveniently laid out for use by vehicles and for protection from the wind. Their buildings are by no means paltry; the unbroken rows of houses facing each other across the streets through the whole town make a fine sight. The

5. From the Greek, meaning "waterless." Many of the details of Amaurot (its situation on a tidal river, its stone bridge, though not the location of that bridge) are reminiscent of London. Even the second little stream, which provides Amaurot's water-supply, suggests the brook known as the Fleet.

streets are twenty feet wide.[6] Behind each row of houses at the center of every block and extending the full length of the street, there are large gardens.

Every house has a door to the street and another to the garden. The doors, which are made with two leaves, open easily and swing shut automatically, letting anyone enter who wants to—and so there is no private property. Every ten years, they change houses by lot.[7] The Utopians are very fond of these gardens of theirs. They raise vines, fruits, herbs, and flowers, so thrifty and flourishing that I have never seen any gardens more productive or elegant than theirs. They keep interested in gardening, partly because they delight in it, and also because of the competition between different streets which challenge one another to produce the best gardens.[8] Certainly you will find nothing else in the whole city more useful or more pleasant to the citizens. And for that reason, the city's founder seems to have made gardens the primary object of his consideration.

They say that in the beginning the whole city was planned by King Utopus himself, but that he left to posterity matters of adornment and improvement, such as could not be perfected in one man's lifetime. Their records begin 1,760 years ago with the conquest of the island, and are carefully preserved in writing. From these records it appears that the first houses were low, like cabins or peasant huts, built out of any sort of timber, with mud-plastered walls and steep roofs, ridged and thatched with straw. But now their houses are all three stories high and handsomely constructed; the fronts are faced with stone, stucco, or brick, over rubble construction. The roofs are flat, and are covered with a kind of plaster that is cheap but fireproof, and more weather-resistant even than lead. Glass is very generally used in windows to keep out the weather;[9] and they also use thin linen cloth treated with oil or gum so that it lets in more light and keeps out more wind.

---

6. For a city on an island with no tradition of civil strife and no record of foreign invasion, Amaurot is heavily fortified—as were almost all the towns of which More had personal knowledge. The twenty feet that he assigns as the width of streets seem to us absurdly inadequate; but for a medieval town they were lavish.

7. Redistributing housing by lottery every decade seems likely to create as many problems as it solves, especially when combined with the shorter cycle of two years in the city and two years in the country. An average stay in any particular house of just five years must make for a nomadic existence at best. The purpose is, of course, to keep people from getting attached to things. For a striking similarity of custom, founded on a wholly different reason, see Vespucci's account of the American aborigines he saw, below, p. 236.

8. How one can have competition between gardeners when anyone is free at any time to pick any fruits or flowers he wants is a practical problem into which More does not enter.

9. During More's day in England window glass was not common; oiled cloth was more frequent.

Their Officials

Once a year, every group of thirty households elects an official, formerly called the syphogrant,[1] but now called the phylarch. Over every group of ten syphogrants with their households there is another official, once called the tranibor but now known as the head phylarch. All the syphogrants, two hundred in number, are brought together to elect the prince. They take an oath to choose the man they think best qualified; and then by secret ballot they elect the prince from among four men nominated by the people of the four sections of the city. The prince holds office for life, unless he is suspected of aiming at a tyranny.[2] Though the tranibors are elected annually, they are not changed for light or casual reasons. All their other officials hold office for a single year only.

The tranibors meet to consult with the prince every other day, and more often if necessary: they discuss affairs of state, and settle the occasional disputes between private parties, if there are any, acting as quickly as possible. The tranibors always invite two syphogrants to the senate chamber, different ones every day. There is a rule that no decision can be made on a matter of public business unless it has been discussed in the senate for three separate days. It is a capital offense to consult together on public business outside of the senate or the popular assembly.[3] The purpose of these rules, they say, is to prevent the prince and the tranibors from conspiring together to alter the government and enslave the people. Therefore all matters which are considered important are first laid before the popular assembly of the syphogrants. They talk the matter over with the households they represent, debate it with one another, then report their recommendation to the senate. Sometimes the question is brought before the general council of the whole island.

The senate has a standing rule never to discuss a matter on the same day when it was first introduced; all new business is deferred to the next meeting. They do this so that a man will not blurt out the first thought that occurs to him, and then devote all his energies to defending those foolish impulses, instead of considering impar-

1. Neither *syphogrant* nor *tranibor* has any distinct meaning or etymological insinuation, nor is there any explanation of why Hythloday consistently uses what he describes as the "older" form of the title.
2. Since the prince normally holds office for life, and his relation to the tranibors is strangely undefined (they meet together regularly, but whether or when he must follow their advice is never stated), it's not clear what "aiming at a tyranny" would involve.

3. This is one of the most savage and least explained laws in Utopia. It seems to apply to the entire population, yet those against whom it is really aimed number only twenty-one—twenty tranibors and the prince. Within two sentences its literal provisions have been violated, for when the syphogrants consult on public matters with their households, they are evidently in contempt of this law.

tially the public good. They know that some men would rather jeopardize the welfare of the state than admit to having been heedless and shortsighted—so perverse and preposterous is their sense of pride. They should have had enough foresight at the beginning to speak with prudence rather than haste.

Their Occupations

Agriculture is the one occupation at which everyone works, men and women alike, with no exceptions. They are trained in it from childhood, partly in the schools where they learn theory, and partly through field trips to nearby farms, which make something like a game of practical instruction. On these trips they not only watch the work being done, but frequently pitch in and get a workout by doing the jobs themselves.

Besides farm work (which, as I said, everybody performs), each person is taught a particular trade of his own, such as wool-working, linen-making, masonry, metal-work, or carpentry. There is no other craft that is practiced by any considerable number of them.[4] Throughout the island people wear, and down through the centuries they have always worn, the same style of clothing, except for the distinction between the sexes, and between married and unmarried persons. Their clothing is attractive, does not hamper bodily movement, and serves for warm as well as cold weather; what is more, each household can make its own.

Every person (and this includes women as well as men) learns a second trade, besides agriculture. As the weaker sex, women practice the lighter crafts, such as working in wool or linen; the heavier crafts are assigned to the men. As a rule, the son is trained to his father's craft, for which most feel a natural inclination. But if anyone is attracted to another occupation, he is transferred by adoption into a family practicing the trade he prefers. When anyone makes such a change, both his father and the authorities make sure that he is assigned to a grave and responsible householder. After a man has learned one trade, if he wants to learn another, he gets the same permission. When he has learned both, he pursues whichever he likes better, unless the city needs one more than the other.

The chief and almost the only business of the syphogrants is to manage matters so that no one sits around in idleness, and assure that everyone works hard at his trade. But no one has to exhaust

4. Among the objects in Utopia which nobody seems to make are glassware, ceramics, books, statuary, horseshoes and harness, wheels, candles, armor, arrows, ships, and musical as well as astronomical instruments. Among the "unex-plained" professions, which people practice but for which they are never trained, are sailors, judges, doctors, nurses, teachers, miners, musicians, plumbers, bakers, and stewards.

himself with endless toil from early morning to late at night, as if he were a beast of burden. Such wretchedness, really worse than slavery, is the common lot of workmen in all countries, except Utopia. Of the day's twenty-four hours, the Utopians devote only six to work. They work three hours before noon, when they go to dinner. After dinner they rest for a couple of hours, then go to work for another three hours. Then they have supper, and at eight o'clock (counting the first hour after noon as one), they go to bed and sleep eight hours.[5]

The other hours of the day, when they are not working, eating, or sleeping, are left to each man's individual discretion, provided he does not waste them in roistering or sloth, but uses them busily in some occupation that pleases him. Generally these periods are devoted to intellectual activity. For they have an established custom of giving public lectures before daybreak;[6] attendance at these lectures is required only of those who have been specially chosen to devote themselves to learning, but a great many other people, both men and women, choose voluntarily to attend. Depending on their interests, some go to one lecture, some to another. But if anyone would rather devote his spare time to his trade, as many do who don't care for the intellectual life, this is not discouraged; in fact, such persons are commended as especially useful to the commonwealth.

After supper, they devote an hour to recreation, in their gardens when the weather is fine, or during winter weather in the common halls where they have their meals. There they either play music or amuse themselves with conversation. They know nothing about gambling with dice, or other such foolish and ruinous games. They do play two games not unlike our own chess. One is a battle of numbers, in which one number captures another. The other is a game in which the vices fight a battle against the virtues. The game is set up to show how the vices oppose one another, yet readily combine against the virtues; then, what vices oppose what virtues, how they try to assault them openly or undermine them in secret; how the virtues can break the strength of the vices or turn their purposes to good; and finally, by what means one side or the other gains the victory.[7]

---

5. Another way of calculating is that if the Utopians work six hours a day and sleep eight, they have ten hours a day free for eating and leisure. But More has done something to mitigate the dangers of this leisure by allocating most of it to the early morning hours. If they go to bed at eight, as he says, and sleep eight hours, the Utopians will rise at four A.M. Work does not start till nine. There may be problems with this timetable, but boredom is only one of them.

6. Renaissance universities got under way at inhumanly early hours; first lecture was between five and seven A.M.
7. Moral games of this general character were popular with Renaissance educators. Jacques Lefèvre d'Etaples invented one of the first sort, and Sir Thomas Elyot (in *The Governor*) mentions one of the second sort. But he may have picked up the idea for it from this passage.

But in all this, you may get a wrong impression, if we don't go back and consider one point more carefully. Because they allot only six hours to work, you might think the necessities of life would be in scant supply. This is far from the case. Their working hours are ample to provide not only enough but more than enough of the necessities and even the conveniences of life. You will easily appreciate this if you consider how large a part of the population in other countries exists without doing any work at all. In the first place, hardly any of the women, who are a full half of the population, work;[8] or, if they do, then as a rule their husbands lie snoring in the bed. Then there is a great lazy gang of priests and so-called religious men. Add to them all the rich, especially the landlords, who are commonly called gentlemen and nobility. Include with them their retainers, that mob of swaggering bullies. Finally, reckon in with these the sturdy and lusty beggars, who go about feigning some disease as an excuse for their idleness. You will certainly find that the things which satisfy our needs are produced by far fewer hands than you had supposed.

And now consider how few of those who do work are doing really essential things. For where money is the standard of everything, many superfluous trades are bound to be carried on simply to satisfy luxury and licentiousness. Suppose the multitude of those who now work were limited to a few trades, and set to producing more and more of those conveniences and commodities that nature really requires. They would be bound to produce so much that the prices would drop, and the workmen would be unable to gain a living. But suppose again that all the workers in useless trades were put to useful ones, and that all the idlers (who now guzzle twice as much as the workingmen who make what they consume) were assigned to productive tasks—well, you can easily see how little time each man would have to spend working, in order to produce all the goods that human needs and conveniences require—yes, and human pleasure too, as long as it's true and natural pleasure.

The experience of Utopia makes this perfectly apparent. In each city and its surrounding countryside barely five hundred of those men and women whose age and strength make them fit for work are exempted from it.[9] Among these are the syphogrants, who by law

---

8. More is rather less than generous to women, who, in addition to selecting, preparing, and cooking the family food, doing the family laundry, making the family clothes, cleaning the house, and doing a thousand other routine tasks of domestic drudgery, were responsible for taking care of the children. This seems to be the contemplated routine, both in More's England and in Utopia (where, in addition, the women are blessed with a full-time trade); if it doesn't constitute "work," that word must have a very special meaning.

9. Figuring six thousand families per city, thirteen adults per family, and three of those too old or feeble for work, we have sixty thousand working adults per city and the same number in the surrounding countryside. So the rate of those exempted from work is under half a percent.

are free not to work; yet they don't take advantage of the privilege, preferring to set a good example to their fellow-citizens. Some others are permanently exempted from work so that they may devote themselves to study, but only on the recommendation of the priests and through a secret vote of the syphogrants. If any of these scholars disappoints their hopes, he becomes a workman again. On the other hand, it happens from time to time that a craftsman devotes his leisure so earnestly to study, and makes such progress as a result, that he is relieved of manual labor, and promoted to the class of learned men. From this class of scholars are chosen ambassadors, priests, tranibors, and the prince himself,[1] who used to be called Barzanes, but in their modern tongue is known as Ademus.[2] Since all the rest of the population is neither idle nor occupied in useless trades, it is easy to see why they produce so much in so short a working day.

Apart from all this, in several of the necessary crafts their way of life requires less total labor than does that of people elsewhere. In other countries, building and repairing houses requires the constant work of many men, because what a father has built, his thriftless heir lets fall into ruin; and then his successor has to repair, at great expense, what could easily have been maintained at a very small charge. Further, even when a man has built a splendid house at large cost, someone else may think he has finer taste, let the first house fall to ruin, and then build another one somewhere else for just as much money. But among the Utopians, where everything has been established, and the commonwealth is carefully regulated, building a brand-new home on a new site is a rare event. They are not only quick to repair damage, but foresighted in preventing it. The result is that their buildings last for a very long time with minimum repairs; and the carpenters and masons sometimes have so little to do, that they are set to hewing timber and cutting stone in case some future need for it should arise.

Consider, too, how little labor their clothing requires. Their work clothes are loose garments made of leather which last as long as seven years. When they go out in public, they cover these rough working-clothes with a cloak. Throughout the entire island, everyone wears the same colored cloak, which is the color of natural wool.[3] As a result, they not only need less wool than people in other

1. The apparent democracy of Utopia is sharply limited by this provision; in fact, what we have here is an incipient managerial class, as in the USSR or, more proximately, in that Brahmin caste which Calvinism tended to breed, for example, in Geneva, Edinburgh, and Boston.
2. Barzanes, "Son of Zeus" in Greek; Ademus, "Without People." In Lucian's dialogue "Menippus," which More trans-

lated, there is a wise and wonderful Chaldean named "Mithrobarzanes," Lucian, *Works*, tr. H. W. Fowler and F. G. Fowler (Oxford, 1965), I, 159.
3. Furs and feathers evidently exist on the island, but are not used for clothing lay people, perhaps because they would raise awkward issues of unequal distribution.

countries, but what they do need is less expensive. They use linen cloth most, because it requires least labor. They like linen cloth to be white and wool cloth to be clean; but they put no price on fineness of texture. Elsewhere a man is not satisfied with four or five woolen cloaks of different colors and as many silk shirts, or if he's a show-off, even ten of each are not enough. But a Utopian is content with a single cloak, and generally wears it for two seasons. There is no reason at all why he should want any others, for if he had them, he would not be better protected against the cold, nor would he appear in any way better dressed.

When there is an abundance of everything, as a result of everyone working at useful trades, and nobody consuming to excess, then great numbers of the people often go out to work on the roads, if any of them need repairing. And when there is no need even for this sort of public work, then the officials very often proclaim a shorter work day, since they never force their citizens to perform useless labor. The chief aim of their constitution and government is that, whenever public needs permit, all citizens should be free, so far as possible, to withdraw their time and energy from the service of the body, and devote themselves to the freedom and culture of the mind. For that, they think, is the real happiness of life.

Social and Business Relations

Now I must explain the social relations of these folk, the way the citizens behave toward one another, and how they distribute their goods within the society.

Each city, then, consists of households, the households consisting generally of blood-relations. When the women grow up and are married, they move into their husbands' households. On the other hand, male children and after them grandchildren remain in the family, and are subject to the oldest parent, unless his mind has started to fail, in which case, the next oldest takes his place. To keep the city from becoming too large or too small, they have decreed that there shall be no more than six thousand households in it (exclusive of the surrounding countryside), each family containing between ten and sixteen adults.[4] They do not, of course, try to regulate the number of minor children in a family. The limit on adults is easily observed by transferring individuals from a household with too many into a household with not enough. Likewise if a city has too many people, the extra persons serve to make up the shortage of population in other cities. And if the population

4. When houses are exchanged by lottery every ten years, the difference between ten and sixteen adults may be very considerable—not to speak of the further difference in the potential number of children. Either all Utopian houses have thirty bedrooms, or there is a lot of squeezing and cramping every ten years.

throughout the entire island exceeds the quota,[5] then they enroll
citizens out of every city and plant a colony under their own laws
on the mainland near them, wherever the natives have plenty of
unoccupied and uncultivated land. Those natives who want to live
with the Utopian settlers are taken in. When such a merger occurs,
the two peoples gradually and easily blend together, sharing the
same way of life and customs, much to the advantage of both. For
by their policies the Utopians make the land yield an abundance
for all, which had previously seemed too barren and paltry even to
support the natives. But if the natives will not join in living under
their laws, the Utopians drive them out of the land they claim for
themselves, and if they resist make war on them. The Utopians say
it's perfectly justifiable to make war on people who leave their land
idle and waste, yet forbid the use of it to others who, by the law of
nature, ought to be supported from it.[6]

If for any reason, one of their cities shrinks so sharply in population that it cannot be made up from other cities without bringing
them too under proper strength, then the population is restored by
bringing people back from the colonies. This has happened only
twice, they say, in their whole history, both times as a result of a
frightful plague. They would rather that their colonies dwindled
away than that any of the cities on their island should get too
small.

But to return to their manner of living. The oldest of every
household, as I said, is the ruler. Wives are subject to their husbands, children to their parents, and generally the younger to their
elders. Every city is divided into four equal districts, and in the
middle of each district is a market for all kinds of commodities.
Whatever each household produces is brought here, and stored in
warehouses, each kind of goods in its own place. Here the head of
each household looks for what he or his family needs, and carries off
what he wants without any sort of payment or compensation. Why
should anything be refused him? There is plenty of everything, and
no reason to fear that anyone will claim more than he needs. Why
would anyone be suspected of asking for more than is needed, when
everyone knows there will never be any shortage? Fear of want, no
doubt, makes every living creature greedy and avaricious—but only

5. The population of Utopia works out,
by crude arithmetic (six thousand families of 13 adults, times fifty-four cities,
with a healthy allowance for country
dwellers and children), to at least ten
million inhabitants, not counting slaves.
6. Every imperialism in the world's history has proceeded on the assumption
that the "natives" don't know what to
do with the land that Providence has un-
fairly bestowed on them, and that superior races are therefore entitled to take
over. Shortly after the First World War,
and probably under its inflammatory influence, a group of German scholars
began polemicizing aginst the *Utopia* as
a blueprint or even an *apologia* for British imperialism. They were so thoroughly
demolished by H. W. Donner, *Introduction to Utopia* (London, 1945) as to
render not only the thesis but its refutation largely obsolete.

man develops these qualities out of pride, pride which glories in putting down others by a superfluous display of possessions. But this kind of vice has no place whatever in the Utopian way of life.

Next to the marketplace of which I just spoke are the food markets, where people bring all sorts of vegetables, fruit, and bread. Fish, meat, and poultry are also brought there from designated places outside the city, where running water can carry away all the blood and offal. Slaves do the slaughtering and cleaning in these places: citizens are not allowed to do such work. The Utopians feel that slaughtering our fellow-creatures gradually destroys the sense of compassion, which is the finest sentiment of which our human nature is capable. Besides, they don't allow anything dirty or filthy to be brought into the city lest the air become tainted by putrefaction and thus infectious.[7]

Every street has its own spacious halls, equally distant from one another, and each known by a special name. In these halls live the syphogrants. Thirty families are assigned to each hall, to take their meals in common—fifteen live on one side of the hall, fifteen on the other. The stewards of each hall meet at a fixed time in the market and get food according to the number of persons for whom each is responsible.

In distributing food, first consideration goes to the sick, who are cared for in public hospitals. Every city has four of these, built at the city limits, slightly outside the walls, and spacious enough to appear like little towns. The hospitals are large for two reasons: so that the sick, however numerous they may be, will not be packed closely and uncomfortably together, and also so that those who have a contagious disease, such as might pass from one to the other, may be isolated. The hospitals are well ordered and supplied with everything needed to cure the patients, who are nursed with tender and watchful care. Highly skilled physicians are in constant attendance. Consequently, though nobody is sent there against his will, there is hardly anyone in the city who would not rather be treated for an illness at the hospital than at home.

When the hospital steward has received the food prescribed for the sick by their doctors, the rest is fairly divided among the halls according to the number in each, except that special regard is paid to the prince, the high priest, and the tranibors, as well as to ambassadors and foreigners, if there are any. In fact, foreigners are very few; but when they do come, they have certain furnished houses assigned to them.

At the hours of dinner and supper, a brazen trumpet summons the entire syphogranty to assemble in their hall, except for those

---

7. In cramped medieval cities, this rule was necessary; even in modern towns, slaughterhouses are still generally located in the outskirts.

who are bedridden in the hospitals or at home. After the halls have been served with their quotas of food, nothing prevents an individual from taking food home from the marketplace. They realize that no one would do this without good reason. For while it is not forbidden to eat at home, no man does it willingly, because it is not thought proper; and besides, a man would be stupid to take the trouble of preparing a worse meal at home when he had a sumptuous one near at hand in the hall.

In the syphogrant's hall, slaves do all the particularly dirty and heavy work. But planning the meal, as well as preparing and cooking the food, is carried out by the women alone, with each family taking its turn.[8] Depending on their number, they sit down at three or more tables. The men sit with their backs to the wall, the women on the outside, so that if a woman has a sudden qualm or pain, such as occasionally happens during pregnancy, she may get up without disturbing the others, and go off to the nurses. A separate dining room is assigned to the nurses and infants, with a plentiful supply of cradles, clean water, and a warm fire. Thus the nurses may lay the infants down, change them, dress them, and let them play before the fire. Each child is nursed by its own mother, unless death or illness prevents. When that happens, the wife of the syphogrant quickly finds a suitable nurse. The problem is not difficult. Any woman who can gladly volunteers for the job, since all the Utopians applaud her kindness, and the child itself regards its new nurse as its natural mother.

Children under the age of five sit together in the nursery. All other minors, both boys and girls up to the age of marriage, either wait on table, or if not old and strong enough for that, stand by in absolute silence. They eat whatever is handed to them by those sitting at the table, and have no other time set for their meals.

The syphogrant with his wife sits in the middle of the first table, at the highest part of the dining hall. This is the place of greatest honor, and from this table, which is placed crosswise of the hall, the whole gathering can be seen. Two of the eldest sit with them, for they always sit in groups of four; if there is a church in the district, the priest and his wife sit with the syphogrant, and preside with him. On both sides of them sit younger people, next to them older people again, and so through the hall, those of about the same age sit together, yet are mingled with others of a different age. The reason for this, as they explained it, is that the dignity of the aged, and the respect due them, may restrain the younger people

8. Every meal is thus cooked for a minimum of 390 persons (30 families averaging thirteen adults). But we must also add the children (males under twenty-two, females under eighteen) and the slaves required to help with these mammoth meals and clean up afterwards, since they have to eat too. The total of those eating in each syphogranty can hardly be short of 700 persons per meal.

from improper freedom of words and gestures, since nothing said or done at table can pass unnoticed by the old, who are present on every side.

Dishes of food are not served down the tables in order from top to bottom, but all the old persons, who are seated in conspicuous places, are served with the best food; and then equal shares are given to the rest. The old people, as they feel inclined, give their neighbors a share of those delicacies which are not plentiful enough to be served to everyone. Thus, due respect is paid to seniority, yet the principle of equality is preserved.

They begin every dinner and supper with some reading on a moral topic,[9] but keep it brief lest it become a bore. Taking that as an occasion, the elders introduce topics of conversation, which they try not to make gloomy or dull. They never monopolize the conversation with long monologues, but are ready to hear what the young men say. In fact, they deliberately draw them out in order to discover the natural temper and quality of each one's mind, as revealed in the freedom of mealtime talk.

Their dinners are light, their suppers rather more elaborate, because dinner is followed by work, supper by rest and a night's sleep, which they think particularly helpful to good digestion. Never a meal passes without music, and the dessert course is never scanted; during the meal, they burn incense and scatter perfume, omitting nothing which will make the occasion festive. For they are much inclined to think that no kind of pleasure is forbidden, provided harm does not come of it.

This is the ordinary pattern of life in the city; but in the country, where they are farther removed from neighbors, they all eat in their own homes. No family lacks for food, since, after all, whatever the city-dwellers eat comes originally from those in the country.

Travel and Trade in Utopia

Anyone who wants to visit friends in another city, or simply to see the country, can easily obtain permission from his syphogrant and tranibor, unless for some special occasion he is needed at home. They travel together in groups, taking a letter from the prince granting leave to travel and fixing a day of return. They are given a wagon and a public slave to drive the oxen and look after them, but unless women are in the company, they usually dispense with the wagon as an unnecessary bother. Wherever they go, though they take nothing with them, they never lack for anything, because they are at home everywhere. If they stay more than a day in one place,

9. Humanists were fond of this social custom, the origins of which were part monastic, part classical.

each man practices his trade there in the shop of the local artisans, by whom he is gladly received.

Anyone who takes upon himself to leave his district without permission, and is caught without the prince's letter, is treated with contempt, brought back as a runaway, and severely punished. If he is bold enough to try it a second time, he is made a slave. Anyone who wants to stroll about and explore the extent of his own district is not prevented, provided he first obtains his father's permission and his wife's consent. But wherever he goes in the countryside, he gets no food until he has completed either a morning's or an afternoon's stint of work. On these terms, he may go where he pleases within his own district, yet be just as useful to the community as if he were at home.

So you see there is no chance to loaf or kill time, no pretext for evading work; no taverns, or alehouses, or brothels; no chances for corruption; no hiding places; no spots for secret meetings. Because they live in the full view of all, they are bound to be either working at their usual trades, or enjoying their leisure in a respectable way. Such a life style must necessarily result in plenty of life's good things, and since they share everything equally, it follows that no one can ever be reduced to poverty or forced to beg.

In the annual gathering at Amaurot (to which, as I said before, three representatives come from each city), they survey the island to find out where there are shortages and surpluses, and promptly satisfy one district's shortage with another's surplus. These are outright gifts; those who give receive nothing in return from those to whom they give. Though they give freely to one city, they get freely from another to which they gave nothing; and thus the whole island is like a single family.

After they have accumulated enough for themselves—and this they consider to be a full two-years' store, because next year's crop is always uncertain—then they export their surpluses to other countries. They sell abroad great quantities of grain, honey, wool, flax, timber, scarlet and purple dye-stuffs, hides, wax, tallow, and leather, as well as livestock. One-seventh of their cargo they give freely to the poor of the importing country, and the rest they sell at moderate prices. In exchange they receive not only such goods as they lack at home (in fact, the one important thing they lack is iron) but immense quantities of silver and gold. They have been carrying on trade for a long time now, and have accumulated a greater supply of the precious metals than you would believe possible. As a result, they now care very little whether they sell for cash or credit, and most payments to them actually take the form of promissory notes. However, in all such transactions, they never trust individuals but insist that the foreign city become officially responsible. When the

day of payment comes, the city collects the money due from private
debtors, puts it into the treasury, and enjoys the use[10] of it till the
Utopians claim payment. Most of it, in fact, is never claimed. The
Utopians think it is hardly right to take what they don't need away
from people who do need it. But if they want to lend the money to
some other nation, then they call it in—as they do also when they
must wage war. This is the only reason that they keep such an
immense treasure at home, as a protection against extreme peril or
sudden emergency. They use it above all to hire, at extravagant
rates of pay, foreign mercenaries, whom they would much rather
risk in battle than their own citizens. They know very well that for
large enough sums of money the enemy's soldiers can themselves be
bought, or set at odds with one another, either secretly or openly.

Their Gold and Silver

For these reasons, therefore, they have accumulated a vast treasure, but they do not keep it like a treasure. I'm really quite ashamed
to tell you how they do keep it, because you probably won't believe
me. I would not have believed it myself if someone had just told
me about it; but I was there, and saw it with my own eyes. It is a
general rule that the more different anything is from what people
are used to, the harder it is to accept. But, considering that all their
other customs are so unlike ours, a sensible man will not be surprised that they use gold and silver quite differently than we do.
After all, they never do use money among themselves, but keep it
only for a contingency which may or may not actually arise. So in
the meanwhile they take care that no one shall overvalue gold and
silver, of which money is made, beyond what the metals themselves
deserve. Anyone can see, for example, that iron is far superior to
either; men could not live without iron, by heaven, any more than
without fire or water. But gold and silver have, by nature, no function that we cannot easily dispense with. Human folly has made
them precious because they are rare. Like a most wise and generous
mother, nature has placed the best things everywhere and in the
open, like air, water, and the earth itself; but she has hidden away
in remote places all vain and unprofitable things.

If in Utopia gold and silver were kept locked up in some tower,
foolish heads among the common people might well concoct a story
that the prince and the senate were out to cheat ordinary folk and
get some advantage for themselves. They might indeed put the gold
and silver into beautiful plate-ware and rich handiwork, but then in
case of necessity the people would not want to give up such articles,

10. The Latin word, here translated
"use," is "usura"—the way to use
money in More's world is to put it out
at interest.

on which they had begun to fix their hearts, only to melt them down for soldiers' pay. To avoid all these inconveniences, they thought of a plan which conforms with their institutions as clearly as it contrasts with our own. Unless we've actually seen it working, their plan may seem ridiculous to us, because we prize gold so highly and are so careful about protecting it. With them it's just the other way. While they eat from pottery dishes and drink from glass cups, well made but inexpensive, their chamber pots and stools —all their humblest vessels, for use in the common halls and private homes—are made of gold and silver. The chains and heavy fetters of slaves are also made of these metals. Finally, criminals who are to bear through life the mark of some disgraceful act are forced to wear golden rings on their ears, golden bands on their fingers, golden chains around their necks, and even golden crowns on their heads. Thus they hold gold and silver up to scorn in every conceivable way. As a result, when they have to part with these metals, which other nations give up with as much agony as if they were being disemboweled, the Utopians feel it no more than the loss of a penny.

They find pearls by the seashore, diamonds and rubies in certain cliffs, but never go out of set purpose to look for them. If they happen to find some, they polish them, and give them to the children who, when they are small, feel proud and pleased with such gaudy decorations. But after, when they grow a bit older, and notice that only babies like such toys, they lay them aside. Their parents don't have to say anything, they simply put these trifles away out of a shamefaced sense that they're no longer suitable, just as our children when they grow up put away their rattles, marbles, and dolls.

Different customs, different feelings: I never saw the adage better illustrated than in the case of the Anemolian[1] ambassadors, who came to Amaurot while I was there. Because they came to discuss important business, the senate had assembled ahead of time, three citizens from each city. But the ambassadors from nearby nations, who had visited Utopia before and knew something of their customs, realized that fine clothing was not much respected in that land, silk was despised, and gold was a badge of contempt; and therefore they came in the very plainest of their clothes. But the Anemolians, who lived farther off and had had fewer dealings with the Utopians, had heard only that they all dressed alike, and very simply; so they took for granted that their hosts had nothing to wear that they didn't put on. Being themselves rather more proud

---

1. "Windy People" in Greek. The story of the absurd Anemolian ambassadors may owe something to a dialogue of Lucian, in which a rich Roman makes a fool of himself by stalking around Athens in a purple robe: "Nigrinus," in Lucian, *Works*, tr. Fowler and Fowler, I, 16.

than wise, they decided to dress as resplendently as the very gods and dazzle the eyes of the poor Utopians by the splendor of their garb.

Consequently the three ambassadors made a grand entry with a suite of a hundred attendants, all in clothing of many colors, and most in silk. Being noblemen at home, the ambassadors were arrayed in cloth of gold, with heavy gold chains on their necks, gold rings on their ears and fingers, and sparkling strings of pearls and gems on their caps. In fact, they were decked out in all the articles which in Utopia are used to punish slaves, shame wrongdoers, or pacify infants. It was a sight to see how they strutted when they compared their finery with the dress of the Utopians who had poured out into the street to see them pass. But it was just as funny to see how wide they fell of the mark, and how far they were from getting the consideration they wanted and expected. Except for a very few Utopians who for some special reason had visited foreign countries, all the onlookers considered this pomp and splendor a mark of disgrace. They therefore bowed to the humblest servants as lords, and took the ambassadors to be slaves because they were wearing golden chains, passing them by without any reverence at all. You might have seen children, who had themselves thrown away their pearls and gems, nudge their mothers when they saw the ambassadors' jeweled caps, and say:

"Look at that big lummox, mother, who's still wearing pearls and jewels as if he were a little kid!"

But the mother, in all seriousness, would answer:

"Hush, my boy, I think he is one of the ambassador's fools."

Others found fault with the golden chains as useless, because they were so flimsy any slave could break them, and so loose that he could easily shake them off and run away whenever he wanted. But after the ambassadors had spent a couple of days among the Utopians, they learned of the immense amounts of gold which were as thoroughly despised there as they were prized at home. They saw too that more gold and silver went into making the chains and fetters of a single runaway slave than into costuming all three of them. Somewhat crestfallen, then, they put away all the finery in which they had strutted so arrogantly; but they saw the wisdom of doing so after they had talked with the Utopians enough to learn their customs and opinions.

Their Moral Philosophy

The Utopians marvel that any mortal can take pleasure in the weak sparkle of a little gem or bright pebble when he has a star, or the sun itself, to look at. They are amazed at the foolishness of any man who considers himself a nobler fellow because he wears clothing of specially fine wool. No matter how delicate the thread, they say, a sheep wore it once, and still was nothing but a sheep. They are surprised that gold, a useless commodity in itself, is everywhere valued so highly that man himself, who for his own purposes conferred this value on it, is far less valuable. They do not understand why a dunderhead with no more brains than a post, and who is about as crooked as he is foolish, should command a great many wise and good people, simply because he happens to have a great pile of gold. Yet if this booby should lose his money to the lowest rascal in his household (as can happen by chance, or through some legal trick—for the law can produce reversals as violent as luck itself), he would promptly become one of the fellow's scullions, as if he were personally attached to the coin, and a mere appendage to it. Even more than this, the Utopians are appalled at those people who practically worship a rich man, though they neither owe him anything, nor are obligated to him in any way. What impresses them is simply that the man is rich. Yet all the while they know he is so mean and grasping that as long as he lives not a single penny out of that great mound of money will ever come their way.

(margin note: neither do I!)

These and the like attitudes the Utopians have picked up partly from their upbringing, since the institutions of their society are completely opposed to such folly, and partly from instruction and the reading of good books. For though not many people in each city are excused from labor and assigned to scholarship full time (these are persons who from childhood have given evidence of unusual intelligence and devotion to learning), every child gets an introduction to good literature, and throughout their lives a good part of the people, men and women alike, spend their leisure time in reading.

They can study all the branches of learning in their native tongue, which is not deficient in terminology or unpleasant in sound, and adapts itself fluently to the expression of thought. Just about the same language is spoken throughout that entire area of the world, though elsewhere it is somewhat more corrupt, depending on the district.

Before we came there, the Utopians had never so much as heard about a single one of those philosophers whose names are so celebrated in our part of the world. Yet in music, dialectic, arithmetic, and geometry they have found out just about the same things as our great men of the past. But while they equal the ancients in almost all other subjects, they are far from matching the inventions of our modern logicians.[2] In fact they have not discovered even one of

2. The scholastic philosophers, traditional enemies of the humanists.

those elaborate rules about restrictions, amplifications, and suppositions which our own schoolboys study in the *Small Logicals*.[3] They
are so far from being able to speculate on "second intentions," that
not one of them was able to conceive of "man-in-general,"[4] though
I pointed straight at him with my finger, and he is, as you well
know, bigger than any giant, maybe even a colossus. On the other
hand, they have learned to plot expertly the courses of the stars and
the movements of the heavenly bodies. They have devised a number
of different instruments by which they compute with the greatest
exactness the course of the sun, the moon, and the other stars
which are visible in their area of the sky. As for the friendly and
hostile influences of the planets, and that whole deceitful business
of divination by the stars, they have never so much as dreamed of
it. From long experience in observation, they are able to forecast
rains, winds, and other changes in the weather. But as to the causes
of the weather, of the flow of the sea and its saltiness, and the origins and nature of the heavens and the universe, they have various
opinions. Generally they treat of these matters as our ancient philosophers did, but they also disagree with one another, as the
ancients did, and are unable to come up with any generally
accepted theories of their own.

In matters of moral philosophy, they carry on much the same
arguments as we do. They inquire into the nature of the good, dis-
tinguishing goods of the body from goods of the soul and external
gifts. They ask whether the name of "good" may be applied to all
three, or applies simply to goods of the mind. They discuss virtue
and pleasure, but their chief concern is human happiness, and
whether it consists of one thing or many. They seem much inclined
to the view of those who think that all or most human happiness
consists of pleasure. And what is more surprising, they seek support
for this hedonistic philosophy from their religion, which is serious
and strict, indeed, almost stern and forbidding. For they never discuss happiness without joining to their philosophic rationalism the
principles of religion. Without these religious principles, they think
that philosophy is bound to prove weak and defective in its effort to
investigate true happiness.

[Their religious principles are of this nature: that the soul of man
is immortal, and by God's goodness it is born for happiness; that
after this life, rewards are appointed for our virtues and good deeds,
punishments for our sins. Though these are indeed religious beliefs,
they think that reason leads men to believe and accept them. And
they add unhesitatingly that if these beliefs were rejected, no man

3. A textbook of logic by Peter of Spain (Petrus Spanheym), later Pope John XXI (died 1277).
4. More is using this entire passage, in the name of that common sense on which the humanists prided themselves, to ridicule logical abstractions.

would be so stupid as not to realize that he should seek pleasure regardless of right and wrong. His only care would be to keep a lesser pleasure from standing in the way of a greater one, and to avoid pleasures which are inevitably followed by pain. Without religious principles, a man would have to be actually crazy to pursue harsh and painful virtue, give up the pleasures of life, and suffer pain from which he can expect no advantage. For if there is no reward after death, a man has no hope of compensation for having passed his entire existence without pleasure, that is, miserably.

In fact, the Utopians believe that happiness is found, not in every kind of pleasure, but only in good and honest pleasure.[5] Virtue itself, they say, draws our nature to this kind of pleasure, as to the supreme good. There is an opposed school which declares that virtue is its own reward.

They define virtue as living according to nature; and God, they say, created us to that end. When a man obeys the dictates of reason in choosing one thing and avoiding another, he is following nature. Now the first rule of reason is to love and venerate the Divine Majesty to whom men owe their own existence and every happiness of which they are capable. The second rule of nature is to lead a life as free of anxiety and as full of joy as possible, and to help all one's fellow men toward that end. The most hard-faced eulogist of virtue and the grimmest enemy of pleasure, while they invite us to toil and sleepless nights and self-laceration, still admonish us to relieve the poverty and misfortune of others, as best we can. It is especially praiseworthy, they tell us, when we provide for our fellow-creature's comfort and welfare. Nothing is more humane (and humanity is the virtue most proper to human beings) than to relieve the misery of others, assuage their griefs, and by removing all sadness from their life, to restore them to enjoyment, that is, pleasure. Well, if this is the case, why doesn't nature equally invite us to do the same thing for ourselves? Either a joyful life (that is, one of pleasure) is a good thing or it isn't. If it isn't, then you should not help anyone to it—indeed, you ought to take it away from everyone you can, as harmful and deadly to them. But if such a life is good, and if we are supposed, indeed obliged, to help others to it, why shouldn't we first of all seek it for ourselves, to whom we owe no less charity than to anyone else? When nature prompts us to be kind to our neighbors, she does not mean that we should be cruel and merciless to ourselves. Thus they say that nature herself prescribes for us a joyous life, in other words, pleasure, as the goal of

More the Speaker vs writer

5. Though they are somewhat idealized Epicureans, the Utopians are not so deeply infused with Christian grace as some of their "defenders" have claimed. For despite his vulgar reputation as a besotted sensualist, Epicurus in his own right really meant by "pleasure" a discriminating intellectual virtue which could easily be exalted into a spiritual and then into a religious principle.

our actions; and living according to her prescriptions is to be
defined as virtue. And as nature bids men to make one another's
lives merrier, to the extent that they can, so she warns us constantly
not to seek our own advantages so avidly that we cause misfortune
to our fellows. And the reason for this is an excellent one; for no
man is placed so highly above the rest, that he is nature's sole concern; she cherishes alike all those living beings to whom she has
granted the same form.

Consequently, the Utopians maintain that men should not only
abide by their private agreements, but also obey all those public
laws which control the distribution of vital goods, such as are the
very substance of pleasure. Any such laws, provided they have been
properly promulgated by a good king, or ratified by a people free of
force and fraud, should. be observed; as long as they are observed,
any man is free to pursue his own interests as prudence prompts
him. If, in addition to his own interests, he concerns himself
with the public interest, that is an act of piety; but if, to secure
his own pleasure, he deprives others of theirs, that is injustice. On
the other hand, deliberately to decrease one's own pleasure in order
to augment that of others is a work of humanity and benevolence
which never fails to benefit the doer more even than he benefits
others. He may be repaid for his kindness; and in any case, he is
conscious of having done a good deed. His mind draws more joy
from recalling the gratitude and good will of those whom he has
benefited than his body would have drawn pleasure from the things
he gave away.[6] Finally they believe (as religion easily persuades a
well-disposed mind to believe) that God will recompense us, for
surrendering a brief and transitory pleasure, with immense and never-
ending joy. And so they conclude, after carefully considering and
weighing the matter, that all our actions and the virtues exercised
within them look toward pleasure and happiness as their ultimate
end.

By pleasure they understand every state or movement of body or
mind in which man naturally finds delight. They are right in considering man's appetites natural. By simply following his senses and
his right reason a man may discover what is pleasant by nature—it
is a delight which does not injure others, which does not preclude a

---

6. Not for its literary merits, but for its
thematic relation to this passage, we
reproduce here a bit of More's verse par-
aphrase of the "XII Rules of John Pico
della Mirandola" involving the virtuous
life:

  Any good work if thou with labor do,
  The labor goeth, the goodness doth re-
    main;
  If thou do evil, with pleasure joined
    thereto,

  The pleasure which thine evil work
    doth contain
  Glideth away, thou mayst him not re-
    strain.
  The evil then in thy breast cleaveth
    behind
  With grudge of heart and heaviness of
    mind.

greater pleasure, and which is not followed by pain. But a pleasure which is against nature, and which men call "delightful" only by the emptiest of fictions (as if one could change the real nature of things just by changing their names), does not really make for happiness; in fact they say, it destroys happiness. And the reason is that men whose minds are filled with false ideas of pleasure have no room left for true and genuine delight. As a matter of fact, there are a great many things which have no sweetness in them, but are mainly or entirely bitter—yet which through the perverse enticements of evil lusts are considered very great pleasures, and even the supreme goals of life.

Among those who pursue this false pleasure the Utopians include those whom I mentioned before, the men who think themselves finer fellows because they wear finer clothes. These people are twice mistaken: first in thinking their clothes better than anyone else's, and then in thinking themselves better because of their clothes. As far as a coat's usefulness goes, what does it matter if it was woven of thin thread or thick? Yet they act as if they were set apart by nature herself, rather than their own fantasies; they strut about, and put on airs. Because they have a fancy suit, they think themselves entitled to honors they would never have expected if they were poorly dressed, and they get very angry if someone passes them by without showing special respect.

It is the same kind of absurdity to be pleased by empty, ceremonial honors. What true and natural pleasure can you get from someone's bent knee or bared head? Will the creaks in your own knees be eased thereby, or the madness in your head? The phantom of false pleasure is illustrated by other men who run mad with delight over their own blue blood,[7] plume themselves on their nobility, and applaud themselves for all their rich ancestors (the only ancestors worth having nowadays), and all their ancient family estates. Even if they don't have the shred of an estate themselves, or if they've squandered every penny of their inheritance, they don't consider themselves a bit less noble.

In the same class the Utopians put those people I described before, who are mad for jewelry and gems, and think themselves divinely happy if they find a good specimen, especially of the sort which happens to be fashionable in their country at the time—for stones vary in value from one market to another. The collector will not make an offer for the stone till it's taken out of its setting, and even then he will not buy unless the dealer guarantees and gives

---

7. In the *Life of Pico della Mirandola*, which More translated, pride of ancestry is much ridiculed. If the ancestor has no honor himself, there's no point in recol-lecting him; and even if he did have honor, he could never leave it to his descendants as an inheritance.

security that it is a true and genuine stone. What he fears is that his eyes will be deceived by a counterfeit. But if you consider the matter, why should a counterfeit give any less pleasure when your eyes cannot distinguish it from a real gem? Both should be of equal value to you, as they would be, in fact, to a blind man.[8]

Speaking of false pleasure, what about those who pile up money, not because they want to do anything with the heap, but so they can sit and look at it? Is that true pleasure they experience, or aren't they simply cheated by a show of pleasure? Or what of those with the opposite vice, the men who hide away money they will never use and perhaps never even see again? In their anxiety to hold onto their money, they actually lose it. For what else happens when you deprive yourself, and perhaps other people too, of a chance to use money, by burying it in the ground? And yet when the miser has hidden his treasure, he exults over it as if his mind were now free to rejoice. Suppose someone stole it, and the miser died ten years later, knowing nothing of the theft. During all those ten years, what did it matter whether the money was stolen or not? In either case, it was equally useless to the owner.

To these false and foolish pleasures they add gambling, which they have heard about, though they've never tried it, as well as hunting and hawking. What pleasure can there be, they wonder, in throwing dice on a table? If there were any pleasure in the action, wouldn't doing it over and over again quickly make one tired of it? What pleasure can there be in listening to the barking and yelping of dogs—isn't that rather a disgusting noise? Is there any more real pleasure when a dog chases a rabbit than there is when a dog chases a dog? If what you like is fast running, there's plenty of that in both cases; they're just about the same. But if what you really want is slaughter, if you want to see a living creature torn apart under your eyes, then the whole thing is wrong. You ought to feel nothing but pity when you see the hare fleeing from the hound, the weak creature tormented by the stronger, the fearful and timid beast brutalized by the savage one, the harmless hare killed by the cruel dog. The Utopians, who regard this whole activity of hunting as unworthy of free men, have assigned it, accordingly, to their butchers, who as I said before, are all slaves. In their eyes, hunting is the lowest thing even butchers can do. In the slaughterhouse, their work is more useful and honest—besides which, they kill animals only from necessity; but in hunting they seek merely their own pleasure from the killing and mutilating of some poor little creature. Taking such relish in the sight of death, even if it's only beasts,

8. Erasmus tells a story about More that he gave his wife a false gem and then teased her (rather meanly) at being disappointed when its falsity was pointed out to her. *Praise of Folly*, tr. and ed. Hoyt Hudson (Princeton, 1970), p. 64.

reveals, in the opinion of the Utopians, a cruel disposition. Or if he isn't cruel to start with, the hunter quickly becomes so through the constant practice of such brutal pleasures.

Most men consider these activities, and countless others like them, to be pleasures; but the Utopians say flatly they have nothing at all to do with real pleasure since there's nothing naturally pleasant about them. They often please the senses, and in this they are like pleasure, but that does not alter their basic nature. The enjoyment doesn't arise from the experience itself, but only from the perverse mind of the individual, as a result of which he mistakes the bitter for the sweet, just as pregnant women, whose taste has been turned awry, sometimes think pitch and tallow taste sweeter than honey. A man's taste may be similarly depraved, by disease or by custom, but that does not change the nature of pleasure, or of anything else.[9]

They distinguish several different classes of true pleasure, some being pleasures of the mind and others pleasures of the body. Those of the mind are knowledge and the delight which rises from contemplating the truth, also the gratification of looking back on a well-spent life and the unquestioning hope of happiness to come.

Pleasures of the body they also divide into two classes. The first is that which fills the senses with immediate delight. Sometimes this happens when organs which have been weakened by natural heat are restored with food and drink; sometimes it happens when we eliminate some excess in the body, as when we move our bowels, generate children, or relieve an itch somewhere by rubbing or scratching it. Now and then pleasure rises, not from restoring a deficiency or discharging an excess, but from something that excites our senses with a hidden but unmistakable force, and attracts them to itself. Such is the power of music.

The second kind of bodily pleasure they describe as nothing but the calm and harmonious state of the body, its state of health when undisturbed by any disorder. Health itself, when undisturbed by pain, gives pleasure, without any external excitement at all. Even though it appeals less directly to the senses than the gross gratifications of eating and drinking, many consider this to be the greatest pleasure of all. Most of the Utopians regard this as the foundation of all the other pleasures, since by itself alone it can make life peaceful and desirable, whereas without it there is no possibility of any other pleasure. Mere absence of pain, without positive health, they regard as insensibility, not pleasure.

They rejected long ago the opinion of those who doubted

9. Seneca provides a relevant analogue: "Natural desires are limited, but those which spring from false opinion can have no stopping point." *Moral Epistles,* XVI.

whether a stable and tranquil state of health was really a pleasure, on the grounds that pleasure made itself felt only when aroused from without. (They have arguments of this sort, just as we do.) But now they mostly agree that health is the greatest of bodily pleasures. Since pain is inherent in disease, they argue, and pain is the bitter enemy of pleasure, while disease is the enemy of health, then pleasure must be inherent in quiet good health. You may say pain is not the disease itself, simply an accompanying effect; but they argue that that makes no difference. For whether health is itself a pleasure or is merely the cause of pleasure (as fire is the cause of heat), the fact remains that those who have permanent health must also have pleasure.

When we eat, they say, what happens is that health, which was starting to fade, takes food as its ally in the fight against hunger. While our health gains strength, the simple process of returning vigor gives us pleasure and refreshment. If our health feels delight in the struggle, will it not rejoice when the victory has been won? When at last it is restored to its original strength, which was its aim all through the conflict, will it at once become insensible, and fail to recognize and embrace its own good? The idea that health cannot be felt they consider completely wrong. Every man who's awake, they say, feels that he's in good health—unless he isn't. Is any man so torpid and dull that he won't admit health is delightfully agreeable to him? And what is delight except pleasure under another name?

Of all the different pleasures, they seek mostly those of the mind, and prize them most highly, because most of them arise from the practice of the virtues and the consciousness of a good life. Among the pleasures of the body, they give the first place to health. As for eating and drinking and other delights of the same sort, they consider these bodily pleasures desirable but only for the sake of health. They are not pleasant in themselves, but only as ways to withstand the insidious attacks of sickness. A wise man would rather escape sickness altogether than have a good cure for it; he would rather prevent pain than find a palliative for it. And so it would be better not to need this kind of pleasure at all than to be comforted by it.

Anyone who thinks happiness consists of this sort of pleasure must confess that his ideal life would be one spent in an endless round of hunger, thirst, and itching, followed by eating, drinking, scratching, and rubbing. Who fails to see that such an existence is not only disgusting but miserable? These pleasures are certainly the lowest of all, as the most adulterate—for they never occur except in connection with the pains that are their contraries. Hunger, for example, is linked to the pleasure of eating, and far from equally, since the pain is sharper and lasts longer; it precedes the pleasure, and ends only when the pleasure ends with it. So the Utopians think pleasures of this sort should not be much valued, except as they are necessary to life. Yet they enjoy these pleasures too, and acknowledge gratefully the kindness of Mother Nature, who coaxes her children with allurements and cajolery to do what from hard necessity they must always do. How wretched life would be, if the daily diseases of hunger and thirst had to be overcome by bitter potions and drugs, like some other diseases that afflict us less often!

Beauty, strength, and agility, these are special and pleasant gifts of nature, and these they joyfully accept. The pleasures of sound, sight, and smell they also accept as the special seasonings of life, recognizing that nature intended these delights to be the particular province of man. No other kind of animal contemplates the shape and loveliness of the universe, or enjoys odors, except in the way of searching for food, or distinguishes harmonious from dissonant sounds. But in all their pleasures, the Utopians observe this rule, that the lesser pleasure must not interfere with a greater, and that no pleasure shall carry pain with it as a consequence. If a pleasure is false, they think it will inevitably lead to pain.

Moreover, they think it is crazy for a man to despise beauty of form, to impair his own strength, to grind his energy down to lethargy, to exhaust his body with fasts, to ruin his health, and to scorn natural delights, unless by so doing he can better serve the welfare of others or the public good. Then indeed he may expect a greater reward from God. But otherwise, such a man does no one any good. He gains, perhaps, the empty and shadowy reputation of virtue; and no doubt he hardens himself against fantastic adversities which may never occur. But such a person the Utopians consider absolutely crazy—cruel to himself, as well as most ungrateful to nature—as if, to avoid being in her debt, he were to reject all of nature's gifts.

This is the way they think about virtue and pleasure. Human reason, they think, can attain to no surer conclusions than these, unless a revelation from heaven should inspire men with holier notions. In all this, I have no time now to consider whether they are right or wrong, and don't feel obliged to do so. I have undertaken only to describe their principles, not to defend them. But of this I am sure, that whatever you think of their ideas, there is not a happier people or a better commonwealth anywhere in the whole world.

In body they are active and lively, and stronger than you would expect from their stature, though they're by no means tiny. Their soil is not very fertile, nor their climate of the best, but they protect themselves against the weather by temperate living, and improve their soil by industry, so that nowhere do grain and cattle flourish more plentifully, nowhere are men more vigorous and liable to fewer diseases. They do all the things that farmers usually do to improve poor soil by hard work and technical knowledge, but in addition they may even transplant a forest from one place to another. They do this not so much for the sake of better growth, but to make transportation easier, in order to have wood closer to the sea, the rivers, or the cities themselves. For grain is easier than wood to transport over a long distance, especially by land.

Their Delight in Learning

The people in general are easygoing, cheerful, clever, and fond of leisure. When they must, they can stand heavy labor, but otherwise they are not very fond of it. In intellectual pursuits, they are tireless. When they heard from us about the literature and learning of the Greeks (for we thought there was nothing in Latin except the historians and poets that they would enjoy), it was wonderful to behold how eagerly they sought to be instructed in Greek. We therefore began to study a little of it with them, at first more to avoid seeming lazy than out of any expectation that they would profit by it. But after a short trial, their diligence convinced us that our efforts would not be wasted. They picked up the forms of the letters so quickly, pronounced the language so aptly, memorized it so quickly, and began to recite so accurately that it seemed like a miracle. Most of our pupils were established scholars, of course, picked for their unusual ability and mature minds; and they studied with us, not just of their own free will, but at the command of the senate. Thus in less than three years they had perfect control of the language, and could read the best Greek authors fluently, unless the text was corrupt. I suspect they picked up Greek more easily because it was somewhat related to their own tongue. Though their language resembles the Persian in most respects, I suspect them of deriving from Greece because their language retains quite a few vestiges of Greek in the names of cities and in official titles.

Before leaving on the fourth voyage, I placed on board, instead of merchandise, a good-sized packet of books; for I had resolved not to return at all, rather than to come home soon. Thus they received from me most of Plato's works and many of Aristotle's, as well as Theophrastus's book *On Plants*, though the latter, I'm sorry to say, was somewhat mutilated.[10] During the voyage I left it lying around, a monkey got hold of it, and out of sheer mischief ripped a few pages here and there. Of the grammarians they have only Lascaris,

---

10. Aristotle is slighted by comparison with Plato; Theophrastus, Aristotle's pupil, was studied in the Renaissance not as a quaint curiosity but as the last word in botanical studies.

for I did not take Theodorus with me, nor any dictionary except that of Hesychius; and they have Dioscorides.[1] They are very fond of Plutarch's writings, and delighted with the witty persiflage of Lucian. Among the poets they have Aristophanes, Homer, and Euripides, together with Sophocles in the small Aldine edition.[2] Of the historians they possess Thucydides and Herodotus, as well as Herodian.

As for medical books, a comrade of mine named Tricius Apinatus[3] brought with him some small treatises by Hippocrates, and that summary of Galen known as *Microtechne*.[4] They were delighted to have these books because they consider medicine one of the finest and most useful parts of knowledge, even though there's hardly a country in the world that needs doctors less. They think when they thus explore the secrets of nature, they are gratifying not only to themselves but the Author and Maker of Nature. They suppose that, like other artists, he created this visible mechanism of the world to be admired—and by whom, if not by man, who is alone in being able to appreciate such an intricate object? Therefore he is bound to prefer a careful observer and sensitive admirer of his work before one who, like a brute beast, looks on the grand spectacle with stupid and blockish mind.

Once stimulated by learning, the minds of the Utopians are wonderfully quick to seek out those various arts which make life more agreeable and convenient. Two inventions, to be sure, they owe to us: the art of printing and the manufacture of paper. At least they owe these arts partly to us, and partly to their own ingenuity. While we were showing them the Aldine editions of various books, we talked about paper-making and typecutting, though without giving a detailed explanation of either process, for none of us had had any practical experience. But with great sharpness of mind, they immediately grasped the basic principles. While previously

1. Constantine Lascaris and Theodore of Gaza wrote Renaissance dictionaries of Greek, much used when that language was first being studied in the West. Hesychius of Alexandria (5th century A.D.) did a valuable book on Greek dialects and idioms; but Dioscorides Pedanius of Anazarba, who lived about the time of Nero, wrote on *materia medica*—a treatise on drugs and herbs, not properly a dictionary at all.
2. The first modern edition of Sophocles was that of Aldus Manutius in 1502. The house of Aldus, established in Venice towards the end of the fifteenth century, was not only the first establishment to print Greek texts in Greek type, but was responsible for some of the best-designed books in the history of the art. Their editions are collectors' items.
3. In effect, "Mr. Silly Nonsense": cf. Martial XIV.1.7: "Sunt apinae tricaeque, & si quid vilius istis" ("They're Apinas and Tricas, and what's lower than that, if anything is.") Trica and Apina were tiny townlets in Apulia, symbolizing ridiculous unimportance.
4. To Hippocrates of Cos (fifth century B.C.) and Galen of Pergamus (second century A.D.) were attributed, in addition to some writings admittedly theirs, dozens of other medical treatises, which were variously translated, expanded, summarized, and combined for use sometimes as medical encyclopedias or sometimes as handbooks of medical practice.

they had written only on vellum, bark, and papyrus, they now undertook to make paper and to print letters. Their first attempts were not altogether successful, but with practice they soon mastered both arts. If they had texts of the Greek authors, they would soon have no lack of volumes; but as they have no more than those I mentioned, they have contented themselves with reprinting each in thousands of copies.[5]

Any sightseer coming to their land who has some special intellectual gift, or who has traveled widely and seen many countries, is sure of a special welcome, for they love to hear what is happening throughout the world. This is why we were received so kindly. Few merchants, however, go there to trade. What could they bring except iron—or else gold and silver, which everyone would rather bring home than send abroad? As for their own export trade, the Utopians prefer to do their own transportation, rather than invite strangers to do it. By carrying their own cargoes they are able to learn more about their neighbors and keep up their skill in navigation.

Slaves[6]

The Utopians enslave prisoners of war only if they are captured in wars fought by the Utopians themselves. The children of slaves are not automatically enslaved, nor are any men who were enslaved in a foreign country. Most of their slaves are either their own former citizens, enslaved for some heinous offense, or else men of other nations who were condemned to death in their own land. Most are of the latter sort. Sometimes the Utopians buy them at a very modest rate, more often they ask for them, get them for nothing, and bring them home in considerable numbers. These kinds of slaves are kept constantly at work, and are always fettered. The Utopians deal with their own people more harshly than with others, feeling that their crimes are worse and deserve stricter punishment because, as it is argued, they had an excellent education and the best of moral training, yet still couldn't be restrained from wrongdoing. A third class of slaves consists of hardworking penniless drudges from other nations who voluntarily choose to become slaves in Utopia. Such people are treated well, almost as well as citizens, except that they are given a little extra work, on the score that they're used to it. If one of them wants to leave, which seldom happens, no obstacles are put in his way, nor is he sent off empty-handed.

5. Apparently, the Utopians have little or no accumulated literature of their own.
6. The Latin word "servus" can imply various degrees of subjection, differences which the Utopians observe. It does not, like the English word "slave," imply simply chattel slavery.

Care of the Sick and Dying

As I said before, the sick are carefully tended, and nothing is neglected in the way of medicine or diet which might cure them. Everything is done to mitigate the pain of those who are suffering from incurable diseases; and visitors do their best to console them by sitting and talking with them. But if the disease is not only incurable, but excruciatingly and continually painful, then the priests and public officials come and urge the invalid not to endure such agony any longer. They remind him that he is now unfit for any of life's duties, a burden to himself and to others; he has really outlived his own death. They tell him he should not let the disease prey on him any longer, but now that life is simply torture and the world a mere prison cell, he should not hesitate to free himself, or to let others free him, from the rack of living. This would be a wise act, they say, since for him death puts an end, not to pleasure, but to agony. In addition, he would be obeying the advice of the priests, who are the interpreters of God's will; which ensures that it will be a holy and a pious act.[7]

Those who have been persuaded by these arguments either starve themselves to death or take a potion which puts them painlessly to sleep, and frees them from life without any sensation of dying. But they never force this step on a man against his will; nor, if he decides against it, do they lessen their care of him. Under these circumstances, when death is advised by the authorities, they consider self-destruction honorable. But the suicide, who takes his own life without the approval of priests and senate, they consider unworthy either of earth or fire, and throw his body, unburied and disgraced, into the nearest bog.

Marriage Customs

Women do not marry till they are eighteen, nor men till they are twenty-two. Premarital intercourse by either men or women, if discovered and proved, is severely punished, and the guilty parties are forbidden to marry during their whole lives, unless the prince, by his pardon, alleviates the sentence. In addition both the father and mother of the household where the offense occurred suffer public disgrace for having been remiss in their duty. The reason they punish this offense so severely is that they suppose few people would join in married love—with confinement to a single partner,

7. The Utopian view of suicide is clearly more Stoic than Christian, but different from both in the very strong emphasis placed on the social element of the deci- sion. No other society (until, perhaps, our own) seems to have contemplated making the life or death of an individual a matter for decision by a committee.

and all the petty annoyances that married life involves—unless they were strictly restrained from a life of promiscuity.[8]

In choosing marriage partners, they solemnly and seriously follow a custom which seemed to us foolish and absurd in the extreme. Whether she is a widow or a virgin, the bride-to-be is shown naked to the groom by a responsible and respectable matron; and, similarly, some respectable man presents the groom naked to his future bride. We laughed at this custom and called it absurd; but they were just as amazed at the folly of all other nations. When men go to buy a colt, where they are risking only a little money, they are so suspicious that though he is almost bare they won't close the deal until the saddle and blanket have been taken off, lest there be a hidden sore underneath. Yet in the choice of a mate, which may cause either delight or disgust for the rest of their lives, people are completely careless. They leave all the rest of her body covered up with clothes and estimate the attractiveness of a woman from a mere handsbreadth of her person, the face, which is all they can see. And so they marry, running great risk of hating one another for the rest of their lives, if something in either's person should offend the other. Not all people are so wise as to concern themselves solely with character; even the wise appreciate physical beauty, as a supplement to a good disposition.[9] There's no question but that deformity may lurk under clothing, serious enough to make a man hate his wife when it's too late to be separated from her. When deformities are discovered after marriage, each person must bear his own fate, so the Utopians think everyone should be protected by law beforehand.

There is extra reason for them to be careful, because in that part of the world, they are the only people who practice monogamy. Their marriages are seldom terminated except by death, though they do allow divorce for adultery or for intolerably difficult behavior. A husband or wife who is an aggrieved party to such a divorce is granted permission by the senate to remarry, but the guilty party is considered disreputable and permanently forbidden to take another mate. They absolutely forbid a husband to put away his wife against her will because of some bodily misfortune; they think it cruel that a person should be abandoned when most in need of comfort; and

8. Cf. Bernard Shaw, "Virtue is the trade unionism of the married" (*Man and Superman*, Act III).

9. More wrote in his own person several epigrams on the topic of choosing a wife: see *Epigrams*, pp. 181–84. His own performance in the matter (choosing the less favored older daughter to avoid hurting her feelings, though the younger one attracted him more) was decorous to the point of seeming a little chilly. When he compares taking a wife to buying a colt (the Latin is "in equuleo comparando"), he can hardly have failed to recall that the maiden name of his first wife, Jane, was Jane Colt. See also Seneca, *Moral Epistle* LXXX: "When you buy a horse, you order its blanket to be removed."

they add that old age, since it not only entails disease but is actually a disease itself, needs more than a precarious fidelity.

It happens occasionally that a married couple cannot get along, and have both found other persons with whom they hope to live more harmoniously. After getting the approval of the senate, they may then separate by mutual consent and contract new marriages. But such divorces are allowed only after the senators and their wives have carefully investigated the case. They allow divorce only very reluctantly because they know that husbands and wives will find it hard to settle down together if each has in mind that another new relation is easily available.

They punish adulterers with the strictest form of slavery. If both parties were married, they are both divorced, and the injured parties may marry one another, if they want, or someone else. But if one of the injured parties continues to love such an undeserving spouse, the marriage may go on, providing the innocent person chooses to share in the labor to which every slave is condemned. And sometimes it happens that the repentance of the guilty, and the devotion of the innocent party, move the prince to pity, so that he restores both to freedom. But a second conviction of adultery is punished by death.

Punishments, Legal Procedures, and Customs

No other crimes carry fixed penalties; the senate sets specific penalties for each particular misdeed, as it is considered atrocious or venial.[1] Husbands chastise their wives and parents their children, unless the offense is so serious that public punishment seems to be in the public interest. Generally, the gravest crimes are punished by slavery, for they think this deters offenders just as much as instant capital punishment, and is more beneficial to the state. Slaves, moreover, are permanent and visible reminders that crime does not pay. If the slaves rebel against their condition, then, like savage beasts which neither bars nor chains can tame, they are put instantly to death. But if they are patient, they are not left altogether without hope. When subdued by long hardships, if they show by their behavior that they regret the crime more than the punishment, their slavery is lightened or remitted altogether, sometimes by the prince's pardon, sometimes by popular vote.

---

1. In Utopia there are thus no legal precedents. The common law of England, in which More had his training, consists of nothing but precedents. Half the predictive value of law (emphasized below) thus vanishes, for no man can ever estimate (in the absence of precedents) the penalty for disobedience. All law is equity law, i.e., up to the individual judge's incalculable intuitions of right and wrong.

A man who tries to seduce a woman is subject to the same penalties as if he had actually done it. They think that a crime attempted is as bad as one committed, and that failure should not confer advantages on a criminal who did all he could to succeed.

They are very fond of fools, and think it contemptible to insult them. There is no prohibition against enjoying their foolishness, and they even regard this as beneficial to the fools. If anyone is so serious and solemn that the foolish behavior and comic patter of a clown do not amuse him, they don't entrust him with the care of such a person, for fear that a man who gets no fun from a fool's only gift will not treat him kindly.

To jeer a person for being deformed or crippled is considered disgraceful, not to the person, but to the mocker, who stupidly reproaches the cripple for something he cannot help.

They think it a sign of a weak and sluggish character to neglect one's natural beauty, but they consider cosmetics a detestable affectation. From experience they have learned that no physical beauty recommends a wife to her husband so effectually as truthfulness and reverence. Though quite a few men are captured by beauty alone, none are held except by virtue and compliance.

As they deter men from crime by penalties, so they incite them to virtue by public honors. They set up in the marketplaces statues of distinguished men who have served their country well, thinking thereby to preserve the memory of their good deeds, and to spur on the citizens to emulate the glory of their ancestors.

In Utopia any man who campaigns too eagerly for a public office is sure to fail of that one, and of all others as well. As a rule, they live together harmoniously, and the public officials are never arrogant or unapproachable. Instead, they are called "fathers," and that is the way they behave. Because the officials never extort respect from the people against their will, the people respect them spontaneously, as they should. Not even the prince is distinguished from his fellow citizens by a robe or crown; he is known only by a sheaf of grain carried before him, just as the high priest is distinguished by a wax candle.[2]

They have very few laws, and their training is such that they need no more. The chief fault they find with other nations is that, even with infinite volumes of laws and interpretations, they cannot manage their affairs properly. They think it completely unjust to bind men by a set of laws that are too many to be read and too obscure for anyone to understand. As for lawyers, a class of men whose trade it is to manipulate cases and multiply quibbles, they have no use for them at all. They think it is better for each man to

2. The grain (prosperity) and the candle (vision) obviously symbolize the special function of each ruler.

plead his own case, and say the same thing to the judge that he would tell his lawyer. This makes for less ambiguity, and readier access to the truth. A man speaks his mind without tricky instructions from a lawyer, and the judge examines each point carefully, taking pains to protect simple folk against the false accusations of the crafty. It is hard to find this kind of plain dealing in other nations, where they have such a multitude of incomprehensibly intricate laws. But in Utopia everyone is a legal expert. For the laws are very few, as I said, and they consider the most obvious interpretation of any law to be the fairest. As they see things, all laws are promulgated for the single purpose of teaching every man his duty. Subtle interpretations teach very few, since hardly anybody is able to understand them, whereas the more simple and apparent sense of the law is open to everyone. If laws are not clear, they are useless; for simpleminded men (and most men are of this sort, and most men of this sort need to be told where their duty lies) there might as well be no laws at all, as laws which can be interpreted only by devious minds after endless disputes. The average, common man cannot understand this legal chicanery, and couldn't even if he devoted his whole mind to studying it, since he has to earn a living in the meanwhile.

Foreign Relations

Some time ago the Utopians helped various of their neighbors to throw off the yoke of tyranny; and since then, these people (who have learned to admire Utopian virtue) have made a practice of asking for Utopians to rule over them. Some of these rulers serve one year, others five. When their service is over, they return with honor and praise to their own home, and others are sent in their place. These countries seem to have settled on an excellent scheme to safeguard their happiness and safety. Since the welfare or ruin of a commonwealth depends wholly on the character of the officials, where could they make a more prudent choice than among Utopians, who cannot be tempted by money? For money is useless to them when they go home, as they soon must, and they can have no partisan or factional feelings, since they are strangers to the affairs of the city over which they rule. Wherever they take root in men's minds, these two evils, greed and faction, are the destruction of all justice—and justice is the strongest bond of any society. The Utopians call these people who have borrowed governors from them their *allies*; others whom they have benefited they call simply *friends*.

While other nations are constantly making treaties, breaking them, and renewing them, the Utopians never make any treaties at all. If nature, they say, doesn't bind man adequately to his fellow man, will an alliance do so? If a man scorns nature herself, is there any reason to think he will care about mere words? They are confirmed in this view by the fact that in that part of the world, treaties and alliances between kings are not generally observed with much good faith.

In Europe, of course, the dignity of treaties is everywhere kept sacred and inviolable, especially in these regions where the Christian religion prevails. This is partly because the kings are all so just and virtuous, partly also because of the reverence and fear that everyone feels toward the ruling Popes.[3] Just as the Popes themselves never promise anything which they do not most conscientiously perform, so they command all other chiefs of state to abide by their promises in every way. If someone quibbles over it, they compel him to obey by means of pastoral censure and sharp reproof. The Popes rightly declare that it would be particularly disgraceful if people who are specifically called "the faithful" did not adhere faithfully to their solemn word.

But in that new world which is scarcely removed from ours by geography so far as it is by customs and life style, nobody trusts treaties. The greater the formalities, the more numerous and solemn the oaths, the sooner the treaty will be broken. The rulers will find some defect in the wording of it, which often enough they deliberately inserted themselves, so that they're never at a loss for a pretext. No treaty can be made so strong and explicit that a government will not be able to worm out of it, breaking in the process both the treaty and its own word. If such craft, deceit, and fraud were practiced in the contracts of businessmen, the righteous politicians would raise a great outcry against both parties, calling them sacrilegious and worthy of the gallows. Yet the very same politicians think themselves clever fellows when they give this sort of advice to kings. As a consequence, plain men are apt to think that justice is a humble, plebeian virtue which is far beneath the majesty of kings. Or else they conclude that there are two kinds of justice, one which is only for the common herd, a lowly justice that creeps along the ground, encumbered with chains; and the other, which is the justice of princes, much more free and majestic, so that it can do anything it wants and nothing that it doesn't want.

This royal practice of keeping treaties badly is, I suppose, the reason the Utopians don't make any; doubtless if they lived here in Europe, they would change their minds. However, they think it a bad idea to make treaties at all, even if they are faithfully observed.

3. The irony here lies thick to the point of sarcasm. Not to speak of English kings, all the crowned heads of Europe —Ferdinand of Spain, Maximilian of Austria, and three successive French kings—were ruthless and casual violators of treaties. But they were far outdone by the successive Popes of the day, Alexander VI and Julius II, who raised duplicity to a fine art.

The treaty implies that men who are separated by some natural obstacle as slight as a hill or a brook are joined by no bond of nature; it assumes that they are born rivals and enemies, and are right in aiming to destroy one another except insofar as the treaty restrains them. Moreover, they see that treaties do not really promote friendship; for both parties still retain the right to prey upon one another, unless extreme care has been used, in drawing up the treaty, to outlaw freebooting.[4] The Utopians think, on the other hand, that no man should be considered an enemy who has done you no harm, that the fellowship of nature is as good as a treaty, and that men are united more firmly by good will than by pacts, by their hearts than by their words.

Warfare

They despise war as an activity fit only for beasts,[5] yet practiced more by man than by any other beast. Unlike almost every other people in the world, they think nothing so inglorious as the glory won in battle. Yet on certain fixed days, both men and women alike carry on vigorous military training, so they will be fit to fight should the need arise.[6] They go to war only for good reasons; among these are the protection of their own land, the protection of their friends from an invading army, and the liberation of an oppressed people from tyranny and servitude. Out of human sympathy, they not only protect their friends from present danger, but avenge previous injuries; they do this, however, only if they themselves have previously been consulted, have approved the cause, and have demanded restitution without effect. Then and only then they think themselves free to declare war. They take this final step not only when their friends have been plundered, but also when their friends' merchants have been subjected to extortion in another country, either through laws unfair in themselves or through the perversion of good laws.

This and no other was the cause of the war which the Utopians waged a little before our time on behalf of the Nephelogetes against the Alaopolitans.[7] Under pretext of right, a wrong, as they saw it, seemed to have been inflicted on some Nephelogete traders residing among the Alaopolitans. Whatever the rights and wrongs of the quarrel, it developed into a fierce war, into which the neighboring nations poured all their resources, thereby inflaming mutual hatreds.

4. More has in mind a kind of trade mixed with blackmail and occasional informal piracy, common enough in his day, but for which we have now no proper denomination.

5. A folk etymology, mistaken like most of them, derived *bellum* (war) from *belua* (beast). Erasmus used it in the *Adages*, "Dulce bellum inexpertis."

6. The citizen-soldier has been idealized since classical days and was the object of Machiavelli's fondest hopes (Chap. XIII, *The Prince*).

7. "People born in the clouds" versus "people without a country."

Some prosperous nations were ruined completely, others badly shaken. One trouble led to another, and in the end the Alaopolitans were crushed and reduced to slavery (since the Utopians weren't involved on their own account) by the Nephelogetes—a people who, before the war, had not been remotely comparable in power to their rivals.

So severely do the Utopians punish wrong done to their friends, even in matters of mere money; but they are not so strict in standing up for their own rights. When they are cheated in any way, so long as no bodily harm is done, their anger goes no further than cutting off trade relations with that nation till restitution is made. The reason is not that they care more for their allies' citizens than for their own, but simply this: when the merchants of allies are cheated, it is their own property that is lost, but when the Utopians lose something, it comes from the common stock, and is bound to be in plentiful supply at home; otherwise they wouldn't have been exporting it. Hence no one individual has to stand the loss. So small a loss, which affects neither the life nor the livelihood of any of their own people, they consider it cruel to avenge by the death of many people. On the other hand, if one of their own is killed or maimed anywhere, whether by a government or a private citizen, they first send envoys to look into the circumstances; then they demand that the guilty persons be surrendered; and if that demand is refused, they are not to be put off, but at once declare war. If the guilty persons are surrendered, their punishment is death or slavery.

The Utopians are not only troubled but ashamed when their forces gain a bloody victory, thinking it folly to pay too high a price even for good goods. But if they overcome the enemy by skill and cunning, they exult mightily, celebrate a public triumph, and raise a monument as for a mighty exploit. They think they have really acted with manly virtue when they have won a victory such as no animal except man could have won—a victory achieved by strength of understanding. Bears, lions, boars, wolves, dogs, and other wild beasts fight with their bodies, they say; and they are all superior to us in strength and ferocity; but we outdo them all in shrewdness and rationality.

The only thing they aim at, in going to war, is to secure what would have prevented the declaration of war, if the enemy had conceded it beforehand. Or if they cannot get that, they try to take such bitter revenge on those who have injured them that they will be afraid ever to do it again. These are their chief concerns, which they go after energetically, yet in such a way as to avoid danger, rather than to win fame and glory.

As soon as war is declared, therefore, they have their secret agents set up overnight many placards, each marked with their official seal, in the most conspicuous places throughout the enemy territory. In these proclamations they promise immense rewards to anyone who will kill the enemy's king. They offer smaller but still very substantial sums for killing any of a list of other individuals whom they name. These are the persons whom they regard as most responsible, after the king, for plotting aggression against them. The reward for an assassin is doubled for anyone who succeeds in bringing in one of the proscribed men alive. The same reward, plus a guarantee of personal safety, is offered to any one of the proscribed men who turns against his comrades. As a result, the enemies of the Utopians quickly come to suspect everyone, particularly one another; and the many perils of their situation lead to panic. They know perfectly well that many of them, including their prince as well, have been betrayed by those in whom they placed complete trust—so effective are bribes as an incitement to crime. Knowing this, the Utopians are lavish in their promises of bounty. Being well aware of the risks their agents must run, they make sure that the payments are in proportion to the peril; thus they not only offer, but actually deliver, enormous sums of gold, as well as large landed estates in very secure locations on the territory of their friends.

Everywhere else in the world, this process of bidding for and buying the life of an enemy is condemned as the cruel villainy of a degenerate mind;[8] but the Utopians consider it good policy, both wise and merciful. In the first place, it enables them to win tremendous wars without fighting any actual battles; and in the second place it enables them, by the sacrifice of a few guilty men, to spare the lives of many innocent persons who would have died in battle, some on their side, some on the enemy's. They pity the mass of the enemy's soldiers almost as much as their own citizens, for they know common people do not go to war of their own accord, but are driven to it by the madness of their rulers.

If assassination does not work, they sow the seeds of dissension in enemy ranks by inciting the king's brother or some member of the nobility to scheme for the crown. If internal discord dies down, they try to rouse up the neighboring peoples against the enemy, by reviving forgotten claims to dominion, of which kings always have an ample supply.[9]

When they promise their resources to help in a war, they send money very freely, but commit their own citizens only sparingly. They hold their own people dear, and value them so highly that they would not exchange one of their citizens for an enemy's king.

8. This is not altogether ironic; regicide was considered ignoble and treacherous until the sixteenth-century wars of religion made it common practice and produced formal, learned justifications of it.
9. More seems to have forgotten that these devices, which he admires in the Utopians, were cited as examples of low craft in unscrupulous courtiers, and indignantly repudiated by Hythloday in Book I; cf. above, pp. 23–24.

Since they keep their gold and silver for the purpose of war alone, they spend it without hesitation; after all, they will continue to live just as well even if they waste the whole sum. Besides the wealth they have at home, they have a vast treasure abroad since, as I described before, many nations owe them money. So they hire mercenary soldiers from all sides, especially the Zapoletes.[1]

These people live five hundred miles to the east of Utopia, and are rude, rough, and fierce. The forests and mountains where they are bred are the kind of country they like—tough and rugged. They are a hard race, capable of standing heat, cold, and drudgery, unacquainted with any luxuries, careless of what houses they live in or what they wear; they don't till the fields, but raise cattle instead. Most of them survive by hunting and stealing. These people are born for battle and are always eager for a fight; they seek it out at every opportunity. Leaving their own country in great numbers, they offer themselves for cheap hire to anyone in need of warriors. The only art they know for earning a living is the art of taking life.

They fight with great courage and incorruptible loyalty for the people who pay them, but they will not bind themselves to serve for any fixed period of time. If someone, even the enemy, offers them more money tomorrow, they will take his side; and day after tomorrow, if a trifle more is offered to bring them back, they'll return to their first employers. There's seldom a war in which a good number of them are not fighting on both sides. It happens every day that men who are united by ties of blood and have served together in intimacy through long campaigns, but who are now separated into opposing armies, meet in battle. Forgetful of kinship and comradeship alike, they furiously run one another through, with no other motive than that they were hired for paltry pay by opposing kings. They care so much about money that they can easily be induced to change sides for an increase of only a penny a day. They have picked up the habit of avarice, and none of the profit; for what they earn at the risk of their lives, they quickly squander on debauchery of the most squalid sort.

Because the Utopians give higher pay than anyone else, these people are ready to serve them against any enemy whatever. And the Utopians, who seek out the best possible men for proper uses, hire these, the worst possible men, for improper uses. When the situation requires, they thrust the Zapoletes into the positions of greatest danger by offering them immense rewards. Most of these volunteers never come back to collect their pay, but the Utopians faithfully pay off those who do survive, to encourage them to try it

---

1. "Busy sellers"; the Swiss were the best known and ablest mercenaries of Europe (a remnant still survives as the Swiss Guard in the Vatican); they correspond in many ways with the Zapoletes.

again. As for how many Zapoletes get killed, the Utopians never worry about that, for they think they would deserve very well of all mankind if they could exterminate from the face of the earth that entire disgusting and vicious race.

Beside the Zapoletes, they employ as auxiliaries the soldiers of the people for whom they have taken up arms, and then squadrons of all their other friends. Last, they add their own citizens, including some man of known bravery to command the entire army. In addition, they appoint two substitutes for him, who hold no rank as long as he is safe. But if the commander is captured or killed, the first of these two substitutes becomes his successor, and in case of a mishap to him, the other. Thus, though the accidents of war cannot be foreseen, they make sure that the whole army will not be disorganized as a result of misfortune to the commander.

Only volunteers are sent to fight abroad; they are picked men from within each city. No one is forced to fight abroad against his will, because they think a man who is naturally a bit fearful will act weakly at best, and may even spread panic among his comrades. But if their own country is invaded, they call everyone to arms, posting the fearful (as long as they are physically fit) on shipboard among braver men, or here and there along fortifications, where there is no place to run away. Thus shame at failing their countrymen, desperation at the immediate presence of the enemy, and the impossibility of flight often combine to overcome their fear, and they turn brave out of sheer necessity.

Just as no man is forced into a foreign war against his will, so women are allowed to accompany their men on military service if they want to—not only not forbidden, but encouraged and praised for doing so. They place each woman alongside her husband in the line of battle; and in addition they place around him all of a man's children, kinsmen, and blood- or marriage-relations, so that those who by nature have most reason to help one another may be closest at hand for mutual aid. It is a matter of great reproach for either partner to come home without the other, or a son to return after losing his father. The result is, that as long as the enemy stands his ground, the hand-to-hand fighting is apt to be long and bitter, ending only when everyone is dead.

As I observed, they take every precaution to avoid fighting in person, so long as they can bring the war to an end with mercenaries. But when they are forced to take part in battle, they are as bold in the struggle as they were formerly prudent in avoiding it as long as they could. In the first charge they are not fierce, but gradually as the fighting goes on they increase in valor, putting up a steady, stubborn resistance. Their spirit is so strong that they will die rather than yield ground. They have no anxieties about making a living at home, nor any worry about the future of their families (and that sort of worry often daunts the boldest spirits); so their spirit is exalted and unconquerable. Knowing the job of warfare and know-ing it well gives them extra confidence; also from childhood they have been trained by example and instruction in the first principles of patriotism; and that too adds to their courage. They don't hold life so cheap that they throw it away recklessly, nor so dear as to grasp it avidly at the price of shame, when duty bids them give it up.

At the height of the battle, a band of the bravest young men who have taken a special oath devote themselves to seeking out the opposing general. They attack him directly, they lay secret traps for him, they hit at him from near and far. A continuous supply of fresh men keep up the assault as the exhausted drop out. In the end, they rarely fail to kill or capture him, unless he takes to flight.

When they win a battle, it never ends in a massacre, for they would much rather take prisoners than kill a lot of people. They never pursue fugitives without keeping one line of their army drawn up under the colors and ready to renew the fight. They are so care-ful of this that if they win the victory with this last reserve force (supposing the rest of their army has been beaten), they would rather let the enemy army escape than be tricked into pursu-ing them with their own ranks in disorder. They remember what has happened more than once to themselves: that when the enemy seemed to have the best of the day, had routed the main Utopian force and scattered to pursue the fugitives, a few Utopians held in reserve and watching their opportunity have suddenly attacked the dispersed enemy at the very moment when he felt safe and had low-ered his guard. Thereby they changed the fortune of the day, snatched a certain victory out of the enemy's hands, and, though conquered themselves, were able to overcome their conquerors.

It is not easy to say whether they are more crafty in laying ambushes and traps or more cautious in avoiding those laid for them. Sometimes they seem to be on the point of breaking and run-ning when that is the very last thing they have in mind; but when they really are ready to retreat, you would never guess it. If they are too few to attack, or if the terrain is unsuitable, they shift their ground silently by night and slip away from the enemy by some stratagem. Or if they have to withdraw by day, they do so gradually, and in such good order that they are as dangerous to attack then as if they were advancing. They fortify their camps very carefully with a deep, broad ditch all around them, the earth being thrown inward to make a wall; the work is done not by workmen but by the sol-diers themselves with their own hands. The whole army pitches in, except for a guard which is posted around the workers to prevent a surprise attack. With so many hands at work, they complete great fortifications, enclosing wide areas with unbelievable speed.

The armor they wear is strong enough to protect them from blows, but does not prevent easy movement of the body; in fact, it doesn't interfere even with their swimming, and part of their military training consists of swimming in armor. For long-range fighting they use arrows, which they fire with great strength and accuracy, and from horseback as well as on the ground. At close quarters they use not swords but battle-axes, which, because of their sharp edge and great weight, are lethal weapons, whether used in slashing or thrusting. They are very skillful in inventing machines of war, but conceal them with the greatest care, since if they were made known before they were needed, the enemy might turn them to ridicule and lessen their effect. Their first consideration in designing them is to make them easy to carry and aim.[2]

When the Utopians make a truce with the enemy, they observe it religiously, and will not break it even if provoked. They do not ravage the enemy's territory or burn his crops; indeed, so far as possible, they avoid any trampling of the crops by men or horses, thinking they may need the grain themselves later on. Unless he is a spy, they injure no unarmed man. When cities are surrendered to them, they keep them intact; even when they have stormed a place, they do not plunder it, but put to death the men who prevented surrender, enslave the other defenders, and do no harm to the civilians. If they find any of the inhabitants who recommended surrender, they give them a share in the property of the condemned, and present their auxiliaries with the rest, for the Utopians themselves never take any booty.

When a war is ended, they collect the cost of it, not from the allies for whose sake they undertook it, but from the conquered. They take as indemnity not only money which they set aside to finance future wars, but also landed estates from which they may enjoy forever a healthy annual income. They now have property of this sort in many different countries, which over the years has increased little by little, and has been augmented in various ways, till it now amounts to over seven hundred thousand ducats a year.[3]

2. The military devices of the Utopians are a patchwork of different notions from the common knowledge of the day. The camps are fortified like Roman camps. English archers had won famous victories over the French at Crécy and Agincourt; and the Parthians, as well as the Scythians, were famous in antiquity for their ability to shoot arrows accurately from horseback. The "machines" are evidently like Roman ballistae, arietes, scorpiones (dart-hurlers, battering-rams, stone-throwers); but the emphasis on their portability probably reflects contemporary experience with cannon, which were terribly hard to drag over muddy medieval routes.

3. These are doubtless Venetian ducats, a common medium of international exchange. The sum would translate into half as many English pounds of the time but would have to be multiplied by as much as fifty to get a rough modern equivalent in dollars. The point is simply that it's a whopping sum of money.

As managers of these estates, they send abroad some of their own citizens, with the title of Financial Factors. Though they live on the properties in great style and conduct themselves like great personages, plenty of income is still left over, to be put in the public treasury, unless they choose to give the conquered nation credit. They often do the latter, until they happen to need the money, and even then it's rare for them to call in the entire debt. And of course some of the estates are given, as I've already described, to those who have risked great dangers in their behalf.

If any foreign prince takes up arms and prepares to invade their land, they immediately attack him in full force outside their own borders. They are most reluctant to wage war on their own soil, and no necessity could ever compel them to admit foreign auxiliaries onto their island.

Religions

There are different forms of religion throughout the island, and in each particular city as well. Some worship as a god the sun, others the moon, and still others one of the planets.[4] There are some who worship a man of past ages who was conspicuous either for virtue or glory; they consider him not only a god but the supreme god. Most of the Utopians, however, and among these all the wisest, believe nothing of the sort: they believe in a single power, unknown, eternal, infinite, inexplicable, far beyond the grasp of the human mind, and diffused throughout the universe, not physically, but in influence. Him they call father, and to him alone they attribute the origin, increase, progress, change, and end of all visible things; they do not offer divine honors to any other.

Though the other sects of the Utopians differ from this main group in various particular doctrines, they all agree in this main head, that there is one supreme power, the maker and ruler of the universe, whom they all call in their native language Mithra. Different people define him differently, and each supposes the object of his worship is the special vessel of that great force which all people agree in worshipping. But gradually they are coming to forsake this mixture of superstitions, and to unite in that one religion which seems more reasonable than any of the others. And there is no doubt that the other religions would have disappeared long ago, except for various unlucky accidents which befell certain Utopians who were thinking about changing their religion. All the others

---

4. The various lights in the heavens are appropriate objects of worship for a people influenced by Persian thought, which represented Mithra or Mazda, the spirit of light, as the supreme force of good in the universe. More could have learned a great deal about the ancient Persians from his reading of Pico della Mirandola.

immediately construed these events as a sign of heavenly anger, not chance, as if the deity who was being abandoned were avenging an insult against himself.[5]

But after they had heard from us the name of Christ, and learned of his teachings, his life, his miracles, and the no less marvelous devotion of the many martyrs who shed their blood to draw nations far and near into the Christian fellowship, you would not believe how they were impressed. Either through the mysterious inspiration of God, or because Christianity is very like the religion already prevailing among them, they were well disposed toward it from the start. But I think they were also much influenced by the fact that Christ had encouraged his disciples to practice community of goods, and that among the truest groups of Christians, the practice still prevails.[6] Whatever the reason, no small number of them chose to join our communion, and received the holy water of baptism. By that time, two of our group had died, and among us four survivors there was, I am sorry to say, no priest; so, though they received instruction in other matters, they still lack those sacraments which in our religion can be administered only by priests.[7] They do, however, understand what they are and earnestly desire them. In fact, they dispute vigorously among themselves whether a man chosen from among themselves could be considered a priest, even if not ordained by a Christian bishop. Though they seemed on the point of selecting such a person, they had not yet done so when I left.

Those who have not accepted Christianity make no effort to restrain others from it, nor do they criticize new converts to it. While I was there, only one of the Christians got into trouble with the law. As soon as he was baptized, he took on himself to preach the Christian religion publicly, with more zeal than discretion. We warned him not to do so, but he soon worked himself up to a pitch where he not only preferred our religion, but condemned all others as profane in themselves, leading their impious and sacrilegious followers to the hell-flames they richly deserved. After he had been going on in this style for a long time, they arrested him. He was tried, not on a charge of despising their religion, but of creating a

5. The ridicule is obviously pointed against superstitious interpretation of mere natural accidents. Yet the Utopians believe in miracles and are apparently commended for doing so: see below, p. 82 and note.
6. The communist practice of the disciples is described in Acts ii.44-45 and iv.32-35; see below, in the "Backgrounds" section, p. 99. Many monastic and ascetic orders made a practice of abolishing private property for their members. The Latin word that More uses for "groups" is *conventus*, which means "gatherings" but has given rise to

the English cognate *convents*.
7. Of the seven sacraments recognized by the Catholic church, a layman can officiate at no more than three. He can perform a marriage, he can act in case of necessity to baptize, and under conditions of extreme urgency he can even grant absolution which has a certain sacramental value. But he cannot possibly ordain a new priest or consecrate the bread and wine for communion; so where there is no duly ordained priest, crucial elements of the Christian religion are missing.

public disorder, convicted and sentenced to exile. For it is one of their oldest institutions that no man's religion, as such, shall be held against him.

Even before he came to the island, King Utopus had heard that the inhabitants were continually quarreling over religious matters. In fact, he found it was easy to conquer the country because the different sects were too busy fighting one another to oppose him. As soon as he had gained the victory, therefore, he decreed that every man might cultivate the religion of his choice, and might proselytize for it, provided he did so quietly, modestly, rationally, and without bitterness toward others. If persuasions failed, no man was allowed to resort to abuse or violence, under penalty of exile or enslavement.

Utopus laid down these rules, not simply for the sake of peace, which he saw was in danger of being destroyed by constant quarrels and implacable hatred; but also for the sake of religion itself. In matters of religion, he was not at all quick to dogmatize, because he suspected that God perhaps likes various forms of worship and has therefore deliberately inspired different people with different views. On the other hand, he was quite sure that it was arrogant folly for anyone to enforce conformity with his own beliefs by means of threats or violence. He supposed that if one religion is really true and the rest false, that true one will prevail by its own natural strength, provided only that men consider the matter reasonably and moderately. But if they try to decide these matters by fighting and rioting, since the worst men are always the most headstrong, the best and holiest religion in the world will be crowded out by blind superstitions, like grain choked out of a field by thorns and briars. So he left the whole matter open, allowing each individual man to choose what he would believe. The only exception he made was a positive and strict law against any person who should sink so far below the dignity of human nature as to think that the soul perishes with the body, or that the universe is ruled by mere chance, rather than divine providence.[8]

Thus the Utopians all believe that after this life vices are to be punished and virtue rewarded; and they consider that anyone who opposes this proposition is hardly a man, since he has degraded the sublimity of his own soul to the base level of a beast's wretched body. They will not even count him as one of their citizens, since he would undoubtedly betray all the laws and customs of society, if not prevented by fear. Who can doubt that a man who has

---

8. Like many Christians of More's day, the Utopians are rather dogmatic about a point (the immortality of the soul) which they themselves consider a point of faith, not of demonstration. Among those holding that the world began as a chance concatenation of atoms, More might have had in mind Lucretius.

nothing to fear but the law, and no hope of life beyond the grave, will do anything he can to evade his country's laws by craft or break them by violence, in order to gratify his own private greed? Therefore a man who holds such views is offered no honors, entrusted with no offices, and given no public responsibility; he is universally regarded as a low and sordid fellow. Yet they do not afflict him with punishments, because they are persuaded that no man can choose to believe by a mere act of the will.[9] They do not compel him by threats to dissemble his views, nor do they tolerate in the matter any deceit or lying, which they detest as next door to deliberate malice. The man may not argue in the presence of the common people in behalf of his opinion; but in the presence of the priests and other important persons, they not only permit but encourage it. For they are confident that in the end his madness will yield to reason.

There are some others, in fact no small number of them, who err in the opposite direction, in supposing that animals too have immortal souls,[1] though not comparable to ours in excellence, nor destined to equal felicity. These men are not thought to be evil, their opinion is not thought to be wholly unreasonable, and so they are not interfered with.

[Almost all the Utopians are absolutely convinced that man's bliss after death will be enormous and eternal;] thus they lament every man's sickness, but mourn over a death only if the man was torn from life anxiously and against his will.[2] Such behavior they take to be a very bad sign, as if the soul, being in despair and conscious of guilt, dreaded death through a secret premonition of punishments to come. Besides, they suppose God can hardly be well pleased with the coming of one who, when he is summoned, does not come gladly, but is dragged off reluctantly and against his will. Such a death fills the onlookers with horror, and they carry away the corpse to the cemetery in melancholy silence. There, after begging God to have mercy on his spirit, and pardon his infirmities, they bury the unhappy man. [But when a man dies blithely and full of good hope, they do not mourn for him, but carry the body cheerfully away, singing and commending the dead man's soul to God.] They cremate him in a spirit more of reverence than of grief, and

9. More, who in later years took part in the burning of obstinate heretics—i.e., Protestants—would have done well to remember these wiser words of his early middle age. His exact phrase here is "nullo afficiunt supplicio."
1. Pythagoreans, who believed in the transmigration of souls from form to form, were particularly likely to concede them to animals.

2. More's emphasis on cheerful dying is humanist in tone. When Pico was dying, we learn from the biography that More translated, "he lay always with a pleasant and merry countenance, and in the very twitches and pangs of death, he spake as though he beheld the heavens open."

erect a tombstone on which the dead man's honors are inscribed. As they go home, they talk of his character and deeds, and no part of his life is mentioned more frequently or more gladly than his joyful death.

They think that recollecting the good qualities of a man helps the living to behave virtuously and is also the most acceptable form of honor to the dead. For they think that dead persons are actually present among us, and hear what we say about them, though through the dullness of human sight they are invisible to our eyes. Given their state of bliss, the dead must be able to travel freely where they please, and they are bound to want to revisit their friends, whom they loved and honored during their lives. Like all other good things, they think that after death freedom of motion is increased rather than decreased in all good men; and thus they believe the dead come frequently among the living, to observe their words and actions. Hence they go about their business the more confidently because of their trust in such protectors; and the belief that their forefathers are physically present keeps men from any secret dishonorable deed.

Fortune-telling and other vain forms of superstitious divination, such as other people take very seriously, they consider ridiculous and contemptible.[3] But they venerate miracles which occur without the help of nature, considering them direct and visible manifestations of the divine power. Indeed, they report that miracles have frequently occurred in their country. Sometimes in great and dangerous crises they pray publicly for a miracle, which they then anticipate with great confidence, and obtain.

They think that the careful investigation of nature, and the sense of reverence arising from it, are acts of worship to God. There are some people, however, and quite a few of them, who for religious motives reject learning, pursue no studies, and refuse all leisure, but devote their full time to good works. Constant dedication to the offices of charity, these people think, will increase their chances of happiness after death; and so they are always busy. Some tend the sick; others repair roads; clean ditches; rebuild bridges, dig turf, gravel, or stones; fell trees and cut them up; and transport wood, grain, and other commodities into the cities by wagon. They work for private citizens, as well as the public, and work even harder than slaves. They undertake with cheery good will any task that is so rough, hard, and dirty that most people refuse to tackle it because of the toil, boredom, and despair involved. While constantly

3. Pico della Mirandola, whom More greatly admired, strongly condemned astrological divination. The opinion expressed below, that miracles can occur even in non-Christian countries, is standard Catholic doctrine.

engaged in heavy labor themselves, they secure leisure for others, and yet they claim no credit for it.[4] They do not criticize the way other people live, nor do they boast of their own doings. The more they put themselves in the position of slaves, the more highly they are honored by everyone.

These people are of two opinions.[5] The first are celibates who abstain not only from sex, but also from eating meat, and some of them from any sort of animal food whatever. They reject all the pleasures of this life as harmful and look forward only to the joys of the life to come, which they hope to deserve by hard labor and all-night vigils. As they hope to attain it quickly, they are cheerful and active in the here and now. The other kind are just as fond of hard work, but prefer to marry. They don't despise the comforts of marriage, and they think as their duty to nature requires work, so their duty to their country draws them to beget children. They avoid no pleasure, unless it interferes with their labor, and gladly eat meat, precisely because they think it makes them stronger for any sort of heavy work. The Utopians regard the second sort as more sensible, but the first sort as the holier men. If anyone claimed to prefer celibacy to marriage, and a hard life to a comfortable one, on the grounds of reason alone, the Utopians would think him absurd. But since these men claim to be motivated by religion, the Utopians respect and revere them. There is no subject on which they are more careful of jumping to conclusions than this matter of religion. These then are the men whom in their own language they call Buthrescas, a term which may be translated as "especially religious men."

Their priests are men of great holiness, and therefore very few. In each city, there are no more than thirteen, one for each church.[6] In case of war, seven of them go out with the army, and seven substitutes are appointed to fill their places for the time being. When the regular priests come back, the substitutes return to their former posts—that is, they serve as assistants to the high priest, until one of the regular thirteen dies, and then one of them suceeds to his position. The high priest is, of course, in authority over all the others. Priests are elected, just like all other officials, by secret popu-

4. I.e., they are direct enemies of sloth, gluttony, avarice, pride, envy, and lust, and implicit enemies of anger, the seventh of the deadly sins. These ascetic Utopians are clearly congenial to More, in whom the strain of penitential, self-mortifying feeling ran very deep; their constant pursuit of disagreeable and painful activity contrasts with the laziness attributed to European monks in Book One.

5. The Latin word for "opinions" is *haereses*—despite the sinister overtones of English "heresy," the Latin means simply "schools of thought."
6. As there are nearly 120,000 adults (plus children and slaves) in each city and its suburbs, the thirteen churches of each city must be able to accommodate, no doubt in several shifts, 10,000 worshippers apiece.

lar vote, in order to avoid partisan feeling.[7] After election they are ordained by the college of priests.

Their chief functions are to preside over divine worship, decree religious rites, and act as censors of public morality.[8] For a man to be summoned before them, and scolded for not living an honorable life, is considered a great disgrace. As the duty of the priests is simply to counsel and advise, so correcting and punishing offenders is the duty of the prince and the other officials, though the priests may and do exclude from divine service persons whom they find to be extraordinarily wicked. Hardly any punishment is more dreaded than this; the man who is excommunicated incurs great disgrace and is tortured by the fear of damnation. Not even his body is safe for long, for unless he quickly convinces the priests of his repentance, he will be seized and punished by the senate for impiety.

The priests are entrusted with teaching the children and young people.[9] Instruction in good manners and pure morals is considered just as important as the accumulation of learning. From the very first they try to instill in the pupils' minds, while they are still young and tender, principles which will be useful to preserve the commonwealth. What is planted in the minds of children lives on in the minds of adults, and is of great value in strengthening the state: the decline of a state can always be traced to vices which arise from wrong attitudes.

Women are not debarred from the priesthood, but only a widow of advanced years is ever chosen, and it doesn't happen often.[10] Except for women who are priests themselves, the wives of priests are the most important women in the whole country.

No official in Utopia is more honored than the priest. Even if one of them commits a crime, he is not brought into a court of law, but left to God and his own conscience. They think it wrong to lay human hands on a man, however guilty, who has been specially consecrated to God as a holy offering, so to speak. This custom is the easier for them to observe, because their priests are very few and very carefully chosen. Besides, it rarely happens that a man selected for his goodness and raised to high dignities wholly because of his moral character will fall into corruption and vice. If such a thing should happen, human nature being as changeable as it is, no great

7. The election is popular and the ballot secret; but the slate is radically limited to the very small class of the professionally learned; see above, p. 43 and note.
8. Priests do not seem to hold secular office in Utopia, as, for example, Cardinal Morton and Cardinal Wolsey did in More's England. They hardly could, there being so few of them.
9. In view of their many other functions and small numbers (13 priests to supervise the morals of 120,000 adults plus—let's say—half as many children), priests cannot be the only teachers. They evidently supervise the teaching program.
10. Among the early Christians, women frequently served in an ambiguous ecclesiastical office known as "deaconess"; whether they were actually priestesses is not wholly clear.

harm is to be feared, because the priests are so few and have no power beyond that which derives from their good reputation. In fact, the reason for having so few priests is to prevent the order, which the Utopians now esteem so highly, from being cheapened by numbers. Besides, they think it would be hard to find many men qualified for a dignity to which merely ordinary virtues could never raise them.

Their priests are esteemed as highly abroad as at home, which can be seen from the following fact: Whenever their armies join in battle, the Utopian priests are to be found, a little removed from the fray but not far, wearing their sacred vestments and down on their knees. With hands raised to heaven, they pray first of all for peace, and then for victory to their own side, but without much bloodshed on either hand. Should their side be victorious, they rush among the combatants and restrain the rage of their own men against the enemy. If any of the enemy see these priests and call to them, it is enough to save their lives; to touch the robe of a priest will save all their property from confiscation. This custom has brought them such veneration among all peoples, and given them such genuine authority, that they have saved the Utopians from the rage of the enemy as often as they have protected the enemy from their own men. Instances of this are well known. Sometimes when the Utopian line has buckled, when the field was lost, and the enemy was rushing in to kill and plunder, the priests have intervened, separated the armies, and concluded an equitable peace. There was never anywhere a tribe so fierce, cruel, and barbarous as not to hold their persons sacrosanct and inviolable.

The Utopians celebrate the first and last days of every month, and likewise of each year, as holy days. They divide the year into months, which they measure by the orbit of the moon, just as they measure the year itself by the course of the sun. In their language the first days are known as the Cynemern and the last days as the Trapemern,[1] which is to say "First-feast" and "Last-feast." Their churches are beautifully constructed, finely adorned, and large enough to hold a great many people. This is a necessity, since churches are so few. Their interiors are all rather dark, not from architectural ignorance, but from deliberate policy; for the priests think that in bright light the congregation's thoughts will go wandering, whereas a dim light tends to concentrate the mind and encourage devotion.

Though there are various religions in Utopia, as I've said, all of them, even the most diverse, agree in the main point, which is worship of the divine nature; they are like travelers going to one desti-

---

1. *Cynemern* really means, in Greek, "dog-day," *Trapemern* "turning-day."

nation by different roads. So nothing is seen or heard in the churches that does not square with all the creeds. If any sect has a special rite of its own, that is celebrated in a private house; the public service is ordered by a ritual which in no way derogates from any of the private services. Therefore in the churches no image of the gods is to be seen, so that each man may be free to form his own image of God after his heart's desire, in any shape he pleases. There is no special name for God, apart from the common word *Mithra*. Whatever the nature of the divine majesty may be, they agree to refer to it by that single word, and their prayers are so phrased as to accommodate the beliefs of all the different sects.

On the evening of the "Last-feast" they meet in their churches, and while still fasting they thank God for their prosperity during that month or year which is just ending. Next day, which is "First-feast," they all flock to the churches in the morning, to pray for prosperity and happiness in the month or year which is just beginning. On the day of "Last-feast," in the home before they go to church, wives kneel before their husbands and children before their parents, to confess their various failures and negligences, and beg forgiveness for their offenses.[2] Thus if any cloud of anger and resentment has arisen in the family, it is dispersed, and they can attend divine services with clear and untroubled minds, for they consider it sacrilege to worship with a rankling conscience. If they are conscious of hatred or anger toward anyone, they do not take part in divine services till they have been reconciled and cleansed their hearts, for fear of some swift and terrible punishment.

As they enter the church, they separate, men going to the right side and women to the left. Then they take their seats so that the males of each household are placed in front of the head of that household, while the womenfolk are directly in front of the mother of the family. In this way they insure that everyone's behavior in public is supervised by the same person whose authority and discipline direct him at home. They take great care that the young are everywhere placed in the company of their elders. For if children were trusted to the care of other children, they might spend in childish foolery the time they should devote to developing a religious fear of the gods, which is the greatest and almost the only incitement to virtue.

They do not slaughter animals in their sacrifices and do not think a merciful God, who gave life to all creatures, will be gratified with the shedding of blood. They light incense, scatter perfumes, and burn a great number of candles—not that they think these practices profit the divine nature in any way, any more than human prayers

---

2. It is not specific that the husbands have anything to confess or anywhere to confess it.

do; but they like this harmless kind of worship. They feel that sweet smells, lights, and rituals elevate the mind, and lift it with a livelier devotion toward the adoration of God.

When they go to church, the people all wear white. The priest wears a robe of many colors, wonderful for its workmanship and decoration, though not of materials as costly as one would suppose. It has no gold embroidery nor any precious stones, but is decorated with the feathers of different birds so skillfully woven together that the value of the handiwork far exceeds the cost of the most precious materials. They add that certain symbolic mysteries are hidden in the patterning of the feathers on the priest's robes, the meaning of which is carefully handed down among the priests. These messages serve to remind them of God's benefits toward them, and consequently of the gratitude they owe to God as well as of their duty to one another.

As the priest in his robes appears from the vestry, the people all fall to the ground in reverence. The stillness is so complete, that the scene strikes one with awe, as if a divinity were actually present. After remaining in this posture for some time, they rise at a word from the priest. Then they sing hymns to the accompaniment of musical instruments, quite different in shape from those in our part of the world. Many of them produce sweeter tones than ours, but others are not even comparable. In one respect, however, they are beyond doubt far ahead of us, because all their music, both vocal and instrumental, renders and expresses natural feelings, and perfectly matches the sound to the subject. Whether the words of the hymn are cheerful, supplicatory, troubled, mournful, or angry, the music represents the meaning through the melody so admirably that it penetrates and inspires the minds of the ardent hearers. Finally, the priest and the people together recite certain fixed forms of prayer, so composed that what they all repeat in unison each individual can apply to himself.

In these prayers, the worshippers acknowledge God to be the creator and ruler of the universe and the author of all good things. They thank God for benefits received, and particularly for the divine favor which placed them in the happiest of commonwealths and inspired them with religious ideas which they hope are the truest. If they are wrong in this, and if there is some sort of society or religion more acceptable to God than the present one, they pray that he will, in his goodness, reveal it to them, for they are ready to follow wherever he leads them. But if their form of society is the best and their religion the truest, then they pray that God will keep them steadfast, and bring other mortals to the same way of life and the same religious faith—unless, indeed, there is something in this variety of religions which delights his inscrutable will.

Then they pray that after an easy death God will receive each of them to himself, how soon or how late it is not for them to say. But, if God's divine majesty so please, they ask to be brought to him soon, even by the hardest possible death, rather than be kept away from him longer, even by the most prosperous of earthly careers! When this prayer has been said, they prostrate themselves on the ground again; then after a little while they rise and go home to dinner. The rest of the day they pass in games and military training.

Now I have described to you as accurately as I could the structure of that commonwealth which I consider not only the best but the only one that can rightfully claim that name. In other places men talk very liberally of the common wealth, but what they mean is simply their own wealth; in Utopia, where there is no private business, every man zealously pursues the public business. And in both places, men are right to act as they do. For among us, even though the state may flourish, each man knows that unless he makes separate provision for himself, he may perfectly well die of hunger. Bitter necessity, then, forces men to look out for themselves rather than for others, that is, for the people. But in Utopia, where everything belongs to everybody, no man need fear that, so long as the public warehouses are filled, he will ever lack for anything he needs. Distribution is simply not one of their problems; in Utopia no men are poor, no men are beggars. Though no man owns anything, everyone is rich.

For what can be greater riches than for a man to live joyfully and peacefully, free from all anxieties, and without worries about making a living? No man is bothered by his wife's querulous complaints about money, no man fears poverty for his son, or struggles to scrape up a dowry for his daughter. Each man can feel secure of his own livelihood and happiness and of his whole family's as well: wife, sons, grandsons, great-grandsons, great-great-grandsons, and that whole long line of descendants that gentlefolk are so fond of contemplating. Indeed, even those who once worked but can do so no longer are cared for just as well as if they were still productive.

Let me now make bold to compare this justice of the Utopians with the so-called justice that prevails among other nations—among whom let me perish if I can discover the slightest scrap of justice or fairness. What kind of justice is it when a nobleman or a goldsmith or a moneylender, or someone else who makes his living by doing either nothing at all or something completely useless to the public, gets to live a life of luxury and grandeur? In the meantime, a laborer, a carter, a carpenter, or a farmer works so hard and so constantly that even a beast of burden would perish under the load;

and this work of theirs is so necessary that no commonwealth could survive a year without it. Yet they earn so meager a living and lead such miserable lives that a beast of burden would really be better off. Beasts do not have to work every minute, and their food is not much worse; in fact they like it better. And, besides, they do not have to worry about their future. But workingmen not only have to sweat and suffer without present reward, but agonize over the prospect of a penniless old age. Their daily wage is inadequate even for their present needs, so there is no possible chance of their saving toward the future.

Now isn't this an unjust and ungrateful commonwealth? It lavishes rich rewards on so-called gentry, bankers and goldsmiths and the rest of that crew, who don't work at all, are mere parasites, or purveyors of empty pleasures. And yet it makes no provision whatever for the welfare of farmers and colliers, laborers, carters, and carpenters, without whom the commonwealth would simply cease to exist. After the state has taken the labor of their best years, when they are worn out by age and sickness and utter destitution, then the thankless state, forgetting all their pains and services, throws them out to die a miserable death. What is worse, the rich constantly try to grind out of the poor part of their meager wages, not only by private swindling, but by public tax-laws. It is basically unjust that people who deserve most from the commonwealth should receive least. But now they have distorted and debased the right even further by giving their extortion the color of law; and thus they have palmed injustice off as "legal." When I run over in my mind the various commonwealths flourishing today, so help me God, I can see nothing in them but a conspiracy of the rich, who are fattening up their own interests under the name and title of the commonwealth.[3] They invent ways and means to hang onto whatever they have acquired by sharp practice, and then they scheme to oppress the poor by buying up their toil and labor as cheaply as possible. These devices become law as soon as the rich, speaking through the commonwealth—which, of course, includes the poor as well—say they must be observed.

And yet, when these insatiably greedy and evil men have divided among themselves goods which would have sufficed for the entire people, how far they remain from the happiness of the Utopians, who have abolished not only money but with it greed! What a mass of trouble was uprooted by that one step! What a multitude of crimes was pulled up by the roots! Everyone knows that if money

3. In this famous, vehement assertion of his most radical position, More is in fact echoing the words of Saint Augustine, in *The City of God*, IV, 4: "Remota justitia quid sunt regna nisi magna latrocinia?" ("Take away justice, and what are states but giant rip-offs?")

were abolished, fraud, theft, robbery, quarrels, brawls, seditions, murders, treasons, poisonings, and a whole set of crimes which are avenged but not prevented by the hangman would at once die out. If money disappeared, so would fear, anxiety, worry, toil, and sleepless nights. Even poverty, which seems to need money more than anything else for its relief, would vanish if money were entirely done away with.

Consider if you will this example. Take a barren year of failed harvests, when many thousands of men have been carried off by hunger. If at the end of the famine the barns of the rich were searched, I dare say positively enough grain would be found in them to save the lives of all those who died from starvation and disease, if it had been divided equally among them. Nobody really need have suffered from a bad harvest at all. So easily might men get the necessities of life if that cursed money, which is supposed to provide access to them, were not in fact the chief barrier to our getting what we need to live. Even the rich, I'm sure, understand this. They must know that it's better to have enough of what we really need than an abundance of superfluities, much better to escape from our many present troubles than to be burdened with great masses of wealth. And in fact I have no doubt that every man's perception of where his true interest lies, along with the authority of Christ our Saviour (whose wisdom could not fail to recognize the best, and whose goodness would not fail to counsel it), would long ago have brought the whole world to adopt Utopian laws, if it were not for one single monster, the prime plague and begetter of all others—I mean Pride.

Pride measures her advantages not by what she has but by what other people lack. Pride would not condescend even to be made a goddess, if there were no wretches for her to sneer at and domineer over. Her good fortune is dazzling only by contrast with the miseries of others, her riches are valuable only as they torment and tantalize the poverty of others. Pride is a serpent from hell which twines itself around the hearts of men; and it acts like the suckfish[4] in holding them back from choosing a better way of life.

Pride is too deeply fixed in the hearts of men to be easily plucked out. So I am glad that the Utopians at least have been lucky enough to achieve this commonwealth, which I wish all mankind would imitate. The institutions they have adopted have made their community most happy, and as far as anyone can tell, capable of lasting forever. Now that they have rooted up the seeds of ambition and faction at home, along with most other vices, they are in no

4. The relatively small remora (*Écheneis naucrates*) has a suction plate atop its head, by which it attaches itself to the underbelly of larger fishes or the hulls of ships. Impressed by the tenacity of its grip, the ancients fabled that it could stop ships in their course. More is not above a pun here; the remora *remoratur*, i.e., "holds back."

danger from internal strife, which among us has been the ruin of many other states that seemed secure. As long as they preserve harmony at home, and keep their institutions healthy, the Utopians can never be overcome or even shaken by their envious neighbors, who have often attempted their ruin, but always in vain.

When Raphael had finished his story, it seemed to me that not a few of the customs and laws he had described as existing among the Utopians were quite absurd. Their methods of waging war, their religious ceremonies, and their social customs were some of these, but my chief objection was to the basis of their whole system, that is, their communal living and their moneyless economy. This one thing alone takes away all the nobility, magnificence, splendor, and majesty which (in the popular view) are considered the true ornaments of any nation. But I saw Raphael was tired with talking, and I was not sure he could take contradiction in these matters, particularly when I remembered what he had said about certain counsellors who were afraid they might not appear wise unless they found out something to criticize in other men's ideas.

So with praise for the Utopian way of life and his account of it, I took him by the hand and led him in to supper. But first I said that we would find some other time for thinking of these matters more deeply, and for talking them over in more detail. And I still hope such an opportunity will present itself some day.

Meanwhile, though he is a man of unquestioned learning, and highly experienced in the ways of the world, I cannot agree with everything he said. Yet I confess there are many things in the Commonwealth of Utopia which I wish our own country would imitate —though I don't really expect it will.

End of Book Two

* * * * *

THE END OF THE AFTERNOON DISCOURSE OF
RAPHAEL HYTHLODAY ON THE LAWS AND
CUSTOMS OF THE ISLAND OF UTOPIA
HITHERTO KNOWN BUT TO FEW, AS
REPORTED BY THE MOST
DISTINGUISHED AND
MOST LEARNED MAN,
MR. THOMAS MORE,
CITIZEN AND SHERIFF OF LONDON

FINIS

* * * *

Backgrounds

Communism

The communism of More's *Utopia* has so often been dismissed as an individual quirk of his thinking that it has seemed worthwhile to set down here a few instances of communist advocacy or fantasy from antiquity and the Middle Ages, from pagan and Christian sources. Because Ovid gave such classic form to the legend of the Age of Gold, which goes back at least to Hesiod (who wrote in the eighth century B.C.), he has been promoted out of chronological order to head the list that follows.

It is, undeniably, a list of uneasy bedfellows. People who gave expression to "communist views" often differed sharply in the sort of syntax that they used to frame those views. A man who says all things *used to be* held in common isn't necessarily saying all things *ought to be* held in common, or *will someday again be* held in common. Very few of those who say *things* should be held in common will go as far as Plato in maintaining that *women and children*, too, should be in common. Even when the formula is identical—all things should be held in common—the motivation may be wholly different: those who want to free each person from the tyranny of things don't mean what is meant by those who want to get more and more things for everyone, particularly themselves. So a roster of these early "communist" thinkers doesn't constitute in any sense a tradition. All it suggests is that More's basic idea in *Utopia* was firmly domesticated in Western thought—that it had cropped up recurrently over the centuries, in response to various needs and impulses.

What is peculiar about More is simply the wide range of contexts within which his brand of communism can be placed. *Utopia* has something in common, as it is strict and austere, with Plato's *Republic*; but it is touched also with the dream of the New Jerusalem as it culminated in the ghastly commune of John Bockelson (Jack of Leyden) at Münster, where the saints tried to set up the kingdom of God with fire and sword; and it is not altogether removed from such nostalgic fantasies as the Golden Age and Cloud-Cuckoo Land. The puzzle lies there, in an ordering of affinities. But it shouldn't distract us from the really distinctive tone of More's book, a tone which isn't doctrinaire or dogmatic at all and probably cannot be traced to any literary or philosophical predecessor. The *Utopia* is a municipal administrator's book; it delights in social gadgets which can be made to function for everyone's comfort; its ideal is the balanced budget, the neat operation. Waste is something that disturbs More deeply—waste of physical resources, waste of human potential. His communist state is different from most of its predecessors—to which it nonetheless owes a great deal—in being efficiency-minded. Socialism will not take on this particular tone again, at least not in England, till the advent of the Fabian Socialists in the late nineteenth century. It is a set of values magnificently summarized by George Bernard Shaw in one brief, ringing slogan: "The love of economy is

the root of all virtue." Put alongside its original and apparent opposite,
"The love of money is the root of all evil," that phrase goes a good way
toward defining the special tone of More's *Utopia* as contrasted with its
predecessors.

OVID

(*First Century* B.C.–*First Century* A.D.)

The myth of the Golden Age, from which man sprang and to which he
may someday hope to return, is practically immemorial; as it has no point
of origin, it has no fixed limits, significance, or precise definition. For example, Ovid, who under his slick, civilized Augustan surface had a deep feeling
for the distant past, gave one memorable expression to the myth in the first
book of his *Metamorphoses*. But, like other parts of that radiant poem, the
tale of the Golden Age spread and had repercussions far beyond what Ovid
himself could have visualized. Viewed from a Christian perspective, the Age
of Gold transformed itself almost automatically into the Garden of Eden or
the community of the saints. Long before Freud, psychological interpreters
had no difficulty in reading it as nostalgia for the womb; and messianic rev-
olutionaries, by simply transferring it to the other end of the historical
time-scale, have easily converted it to the classless society or the New Jerusalem. Ovid himself would have been quite as amazed at these develop-
ments as at the notion that his poem had influenced Sir Thomas More's
Utopia. But it did—not so much directly and specifically, as through a diffused and pervasive atmosphere of thought that identified a life of innocence, equality, and closeness to nature as the first and last state of man.

[The Golden Age]†

The age was formed of gold; in those first days
No law or force was needed; men did right
Freely; without duress they kept their word.
No punishment or fear of it; no threats
Inscribed on brazen tablets; no crowds crawled
Beseeching mercy from a lofty judge;
For without law or judge all men were safe.
High on its native hills the pine tree stood,
Unlopped as yet, nor yet compelled to cross
Ocean's wide waves, and help men leave their homes.
Towns had no moats; no horns of winding brass
Nor trumpets straight, nor swords nor shields existed.
The nations dozed through ages of soft time,
Safe without armies; while the earth herself,
Untouched by spade or plowshare, freely gave,
As of her own volition, all men needed:

† Book I, lines 89–136 (R.M.A.).

And men were well content with what she gave
Unforced and uncompelled; they found the fruit
Of the arbutus bush, and cornel-cherries,
Gathered wild berries from the mountain-sides,
Eating ripe fruit plucked from the thorny canes,
And acorns as they fell from Jove's wide oak.
Spring lasted all year long; the warm west wind
Played gently over flowers sprung from no seed:
Soon too the untilled earth brought forth profuse
Her crops of grain; and fields, uncultivated,
Whitened beneath their stalks of bearded wheat.
Streams flowed profuse, now milk, now nectar, and
The living oak poured streams of golden honey.

    Later, with Saturn sent to gloomy Hell,
Jove ruled the world; the Age of Silver came,
Worse than the Age of Gold, though not so bad
As was to be the Age of yellow Brass.
Jove cut the old spring short and turned the year
To the four changing seasons, winter, spring
(Brief now), hot summer, and contrarious fall.
Then first the air burnt white with summer heat,
And icicles hung down, gripped by the winds:
Then men first sought out homes; they lived before
In caves, or else in thickets, where they wove
Together twigs and withes with strips of bark.
Then first the seeds of grain were set in rows,
And bullocks groaned, under the heavy yoke.

    Third of the ages came the Age of Bronze,
Harder of mind, quicker to savage arms,
But not yet brutal. Last was the Age of Iron.
Evil at once broke forth; from such coarse stuff
Modesty, truth, and faith withdrew; their place
Was filled by tricks, deceitful plots, brute force,
Treachery, and the shameful lust for gain.

    Sails now spread to the winds—at first, the sailors
Knew little of their use—while keels of wood
That long had stood on lofty mountain-tops,
Now leaped exultantly over strange waves.
And now the ground itself, which once had been
Common to all, like sunlight and the air,
Fell under the surveyor's drawn-out lines. * * *

PLATO

(*Fourth Century* B.C.)

Though many stories are told of Plato's hostility to private property (More
alludes to one of them in the *Utopia*, above, p. 31), his ideal commonwealth is a mixed community which allows property to the inferior citizens,

but denies it to the caste of ruling "guardians." These are the philosopher-warrior-kings of the ideal state, with whose training Plato is primarily concerned: the subjects over whom they rule have little to do but obey.

Guardians are to be trained from youth on a deliberate lie or myth, the first element of which informs them that they are not children of particular fathers or mothers, but rather children of the land herself, to whom they owe absolute loyalty. They will also be told (by a peculiar socializing of the myth of the four ages of man) that they are the golden or at least the silver people—the lower castes over whom they rule are mere creatures of brass or iron. Partly as a way of fostering this myth, the guardians and their chosen women will consort strenuously and promiscuously together, and the children will be removed to crèches as soon as they are born. Thus no child will ever know its own mother or father, and no dynasty founded on wealth or kinship will ever be in danger of springing up. Far removed from these common temptations of ordinary humanity, the guardians—strenuous athletes of the ideal, shock-troops of the mind—will be able to bring perfect disinterested justice to the state over which they rule.

As usual, Socrates is the main speaker of this dialogue; his interlocutors (except for the furious Thrasymachus, who doesn't appear in this section) are even paler and more colorless than is customary. At the beginning of this excerpt, Socrates is expounding the myth on which he will have the guardians raised.

[The Guardians]†

Citizens, we shall say to them in our tale, you are brothers, yet God has framed you differently. Some of you have the power of command, and in the composition of these he has mingled gold, wherefore also they have the greatest honor; others he has made of silver, to be auxiliaries; others again who are to be husbandmen and craftsmen he has composed of brass and iron; and the species will generally be preserved in the children. But as all are of the same original stock, a golden parent will sometimes have a silver son, or a silver parent a golden son. And God proclaims as a first principle to rulers, and above all else, that there is nothing which they should so anxiously guard, or of which they are to be such good guardians, as of the purity of the race. They should observe what elements mingle in their offspring; for if the son of a golden or silver parent has an admixture of brass and iron, then nature orders a transposition of ranks, and the eye of the ruler must not be pitiful toward the child because he has to descend in the scale and become a husbandman or artisan, just as there may be sons of artisans who having an admixture of gold or silver in them are raised to honor, and become guardians or auxiliaries. For an oracle says that when a man of brass or iron guards the State, it will be destroyed. Such is

† From Plato, *The Republic*, Book III, tr. Benjamin Jowett, III, 3rd Edition (London: Oxford University Press, 1892), pp. 104–6.

the tale; is there any possibility of making our citizens believe in it?

Not in the present generation, he replied; there is no way of accomplishing this; but their sons may be made to believe in the tale, and their sons' sons, and posterity after them. * * *

Then now let us consider what will be their way of life, if they are to realize our idea of them. In the first place, none of them should have any property of his own beyond what is absolutely necessary; neither should they have a private house or store closed against anyone who has a mind to enter; their provisions should be only such as are required by trained warriors, who are men of temperance and courage; they should agree to receive from the citizens a fixed rate of pay, enough to meet the expenses of the year and no more; and they will go to mess and live together like soldiers in a camp. Gold and silver we will tell them that they have from God; the diviner metal is within them, and they have therefore no need of the dross which is current among men, and ought not to pollute the divine by any such earthly admixture; for that commoner metal has been the source of many unholy deeds, but their own is undefiled. And they alone of all the citizens may not touch or handle silver or gold, or be under the same roof with them, or wear them, or drink from them. And this will be their salvation, and they will be the saviours of the state. But should they ever acquire homes or lands or moneys of their own, they will become good housekeepers and husbandmen instead of guardians, enemies and tyrants instead of allies of the other citizens; hating and being hated, plotted and being plotted against, they will pass their whole life in much greater terror of internal than of external enemies, and the hour of ruin, both to themselves and to the rest of the state, will be at hand. For all which reasons, may we not say that thus shall our state be ordered, and that these shall be the regulations appointed by us for our guardians concerning their houses and all other matters?

Yes, said Glaucon.

THE ACTS OF THE APOSTLES

(*First Century* A.D.)

In the Acts of the Apostles, Chapter Four, five verses are devoted to describing the general way of life of the primitive Christians. As the verses themselves emphasize, the spirit of God was strongly on the little community of about a hundred and twenty souls, from whom the entire body of the Christian Church was to grow. In many matters where Christ left no explicit commandments, later ages assumed that he meant the example set by these earliest Christians to prevail. What they did was sanctified not only by proximity to the founder of the religion, but by the Church's subsequent triumph. The practices of the primitive Church must have had divine blessing, since that church overcame persecution and spread so rapidly through the world.

Later, after its triumph, when the Church turned to pride and worldliness, legalism and formalism, the example of the first apostles was invoked in behalf of a return to a community with more spiritual fervor and greater economic equality; and these five verses became potent texts to be invoked by popular preachers and self-appointed prophets throughout the Middle Ages and the Renaissance. We quote from the King James version.

[The Christian Community]

31. And when they had prayed, the place was shaken where they were assembled together; and they were all filled with the Holy Ghost, and they spake the word of God with boldness.

32. And the multitudes of them that believed were of one heart and of one soul: neither said any of them that aught of the things which he possessed was his own; but they had all things common.

33. And with great power gave the apostles witness of the resurrection of the Lord Jesus: and great grace was upon them all.

34. Neither was there any among them that lacked: for as many as were possessors of lands or houses sold them, and brought the prices of the things that were sold,

35. And laid them down at the apostles' feet: and distribution was made unto every man according as he had need.

LUCIAN OF SAMOSATA

(*Second Century* A.D.)

Lucian's "Saturnalian Letters" are addressed to Cronus or Saturn, the father and predecessor of Zeus, on the occasion of his particular festival, the Saturnalia. This was a seven-day festival falling just about the same time as Christmas, in the latter part of December. During the festival all schools were closed, no battles were fought, and no punishments were inflicted; distinctions of rank were abolished, slaves and servants sat at tables alongside their masters, and gifts were exchanged, particularly wax tapers and clay dolls. Behind all these observances lies the myth that Saturn's age was an Age of Gold, when life was simpler, men were better, and nature, as the common heritage of the human race, shared out its blessings equally to all.

Lucian, who was a cynical Syrian rhetorician, doesn't take any of this mythology very seriously. He writes to Saturn, asking that the abuses of his festival be corrected—that the rich be made truly generous and the ideals of the Age of Gold be brought somewhat closer to reality. But his letter suffers the usual fate of such communications in the modern world—Saturn says it doesn't come within the mandate of his department, and shuffles it off to Zeus, who will no doubt conveniently mislay it. Still, though it's only a joke, the occasion provides Lucian with a chance to revive that dream of the Golden Age in which nobody had too much and everybody had what he needed—when there wasn't very much, but everybody had as much as anybody else, and nobody needed more than he had.

[Saturn's Age]†

I to Cronus, Greeting:

* * *

Now the poets inform me that in the old days when you were king it was otherwise with men; earth bestowed her gifts upon them unsown and unploughed, every man's table was spread automatically, rivers ran wine and milk and honey. Most wonderful of all, the men themselves were gold, and poverty never came near them. As for us, we can hardly pass for lead; some yet meaner material must be found. In the sweat of our face the most of us eat bread. Poverty, distress, and helplessness, sighs and lamentations and pinings for what is not, such is the staple of man's life, the poor man's at least. All which, believe me, would be much less painful to us, if there were not the felicity of the rich to emphasize it. They have their chests of gold and silver, their stored wardrobes, their slaves and carriages and house property and farms, and, not content with keeping to themselves their superfluity in all these, they will scarce fling a glance to the generality of us.

Ah, Cronus, there is the sting that rankles beyond endurance—that one should loll on cloth of finest purple, overload his stomach with all delicacies, and keep perpetual feast with guests to wish him joy, while I and my like dream over the problematic acquisition of a sixpence to provide us a loaf white or brown, and send us to bed with a smack of cress or thyme or onion in our mouths. Now, good Cronus, either reform this altogether and feed us alike, or at the least induce the rich not to enjoy their good things alone; from their bushels of gold let them scatter a poor pint among us; the raiment that they would never feel the loss of though the moth were to consume it utterly, seeing that in any case it must perish by mere lapse of time, let them devote to covering our nakedness rather than to propagating mildew in their chests and drawers.

Further let them entertain us by fours and fives, and not as they now do, but more on principles of equality; let us all share alike.

† From "Saturnalian Letters" I and II in the *Works of Lucian*, tr. H. W. Fowler and F. G. Fowler (London: Oxford University Press, 1905), IV, pp. 117–21.

The way now is for one to gorge himself on some dainty, keeping
the servant waiting about him till he is pleased to have done; but
when it reaches us, as we are in the act of helping ourselves it is
whisked off, and we have but that fleeting glimpse of the entrée or
fag-end of a sweet. Or in comes a sucking-pig; half of it, including
the head, falls to the host; the rest of us share the bones, slightly
disguised. And pray charge the butlers not to make us call unto
seven times, but bring us our wine when we ask for it first; and let
it be a full-sized cup and a bumper, as it is for their masters. And
the same wine, please, for every one at table; where is the legal
authority for my host's growing mellow on the choicest bouquet
while my stomach is turned with mere must?

These things if you correct and reform, you will have made life
life, and your feast a feast. If not, we will leave the feasting to
them, and just kneel down and pray that as they come from the
bath the slave may knock down and spill their wine, the cook
smoke their sauce and absent-mindedly pour the pea-soup over the
caviare, the dog steal in while the scullions are busy and make away
with the whole of the sausage and most of the pastry.

Cronus to his well-beloved me, Greeting:

My good man, why this absurdity of writing to me about the
state of the world, and advising redistribution of property? It is
none of my business; the present ruler must see to that. It is an odd
thing you should be the only person unaware that I have long abdi-
cated; my sons now administer various departments, of which the
one that concerns you is mainly in the hands of Zeus; my own
charge is confined to draughts and merry-making, song and good
cheer, and that for one week only. As for the weightier matters you
speak of, removal of inequalities and reducing of all men to one
level of poverty or riches, Zeus must do your business for you. * * *

ST. AMBROSE

(*Fourth Century* A.D.)

Since Christianity began, many preachers have had occasion, or made it, to
denounce the evildoing of the rich; few have been so unbridled in their invective as Saint Ambrose of Milan, the mentor and friend of Saint Augustine.
From a set of sermons preached on the theme of "Naboth's Vineyard" and
later assembled into a single consecutive passage, A. O. Lovejoy has pieced
together the following passages. The original source is that collection of
writings of the "Church fathers" edited by Migne and known to scholars as

"MPL" (Migne, *Patrilogia Latina*) XIV 767–72, 784. Lovejoy's essay, "The Communism of Saint Ambrose," may be found among *Essays in the History of Ideas*, by Arthur O. Lovejoy.

Naboth's Vineyard†

How far, ye rich, will you carry your insane cupidity? ✳ ✳ ✳ Why do you reject nature's partnership of goods, and claim possession of nature for yourselves? The earth was established to be in common for all, rich and poor; why do ye rich alone arrogate it to yourselves as your rightful property? Nature knows no rich, since she brings forth all men poor. For we are born without clothes and are brought forth without silver or gold. Naked she brings us to the light of day, and in want of food and covering and drink; and naked the earth receives back what she has brought forth, nor can she stretch men's tombs to cover their possessions. A narrow mound of turf is enough for rich and poor alike; and a bit of land of which the rich man when alive took no heed now takes in the whole of him. Nature makes no distinction among us at our birth, and none at our death. All alike she creates us, all alike she seals us in the tomb. Who can tell the dead apart? Open up the graves, and, if you can, tell which was a rich man. ✳ ✳ ✳

But why do you think that, even while you live, you have abundance of all things? Rich man, you know not how poor you are, how destitute you would seem even to yourself, who call yourself wealthy. The more you have, the more you want; and whatever you may acquire, you nevertheless remain as needy as before. Avarice is inflamed by gain, not diminished by it. ✳ ✳ ✳

You crave possessions not so much for their utility to yourself, as because you want to exclude others from them. You are more concerned with despoiling the poor than with your own advantage. You think yourself injured if a poor man possesses anything which you consider a suitable belonging for a rich man; whatever belongs to others you look upon as something of which you are deprived. Why do you delight in what to nature are losses? The world, which you few rich men try to keep for yourselves, was created for all men. For not alone the soil, but the very heaven, the air, the sea, are claimed for the use of the few rich. . . . Do the angels in heaven, think you, have their separate regions of space, as you divide up the earth by fixed boundaries? ✳ ✳ ✳

How many men are killed to procure the means of your enjoyment! A deadly thing is your greed, and deadly your luxury. One

† From Arthur O. Lovejoy, *Essays in the History of Ideas*, (Baltimore: Johns Hopkins University Press, 1948), pp. 299–300. Copyright 1948 by The Johns Hopkins University Press. Reprinted by permission of the publisher.

man falls to death from a roof, in order that you may have your big granaries. Another tumbles from the top of a high tree while seeking for certain kinds of grapes, so that you may have the right sort of wine for your banquet. Another is drowned in the sea while making sure that fish or oysters shall not be lacking on your table. Another is frozen to death while tracking hares or trying to catch birds with traps. Another is beaten to death before your eyes, if he chances to have displeased you, and your very viands are bespattered with his blood. * * *

Do you think your great halls (*atria*) exalt you—when they ought rather to cause you remorse because, though they are big enough to take in multitudes, they shut out the voice of the poor? Though, indeed, nothing is gained by your hearing their voice if, when you hear it, you do nothing about it. In fine, does not your very dwelling-place admonish you of your shame, in that in building it you wished to show that your riches surpass [those of others]— and yet you do not succeed? You cover walls, but you leave men bare. Naked they cry out before your house, and you heed them not: a naked man cries out, but you are busy considering what sort of marbles you will have to cover your floors. A poor man asks for money, and does not get it; a human being begs for bread, and your horse champs a golden bit. You gratify yourself with costly ornaments, while other men go without food. How great a judgment, O rich man, do you draw down upon yourself! The people go hungry, and you close your granaries; the people weep, and you turn your finger-ring about. Unhappy man, who have the power but not the will to save so many souls from death: the cost of the jewel in your ring would have sufficed to save the lives of a whole people.

JEAN FROISSART

(Fourteenth Century)

[John Ball's Rebellion]†

* * * In the mean season while this treaty was, there fell in England great mischief and rebellion of moving of the common people, by which deed England was at a point to have been lost without

† From *The Chronicles of Jean Froissart* in Lord Berners' Translation, selected, edited, and introduced by Gillian and William Anderson (Carbondale, Ill.: Southern Illinois University Press, 1963), pp. 160–162 (Volume I, Chapter 381).

recovery. There was never realm nor country in so great adventure as it was in that time, and all because of the ease and riches that the common people were of which moved them to this rebellion; as sometime they did in France, the which did much hurt, for by such incidents the realm of France hath been greatly grieved. It was a marvellous thing and of poor foundation that this mischief began in England, and to give ensample to all manner of people, I will speak thereof as it was done, as I was informed, and of the incidents thereof.

There was a usage in England and yet is in divers countries, that the nobleman hath great franchises over the commons and keepeth them in service, that is to say, their tenants ought by custom to labour the lords' lands, to gather and bring home their corns, and some to thresh and to fan, and by servage to make their hay, and to hew their wood and bring it home. All these things they ought to do by servage, and there be more of these people in England than in any other realm. Thus the noblemen and prelates are served by them and specially in the counties of Kent, Essex, Sussex and Bedford. These unhappy people of these said countries began to stir, because they said they were kept in great servage, and in the beginning of the world they said there were no bondmen, wherefore they maintained that none ought to be bond, without he did treason to his lord, as Lucifer did to God. But they said they could have no such battle,[1] for they were neither angels nor spirits, but men formed to the similitude of their lords, saying, why should they then be kept so under like beasts, the which they said they would no longer suffer, for they would be all one; and if they laboured or did anything for their lords, they would have wages therefor as well as other. And of this imagination was a foolish priest in the country of Kent, called John Ball, for the which foolish words he had been three times in the Bishop of Canterbury's prison. For this priest used oftentimes on the Sundays after mass, when the people were going out of the minster, to go into the cloister and preach and made the people to assemble about him, and would say thus, 'Ah! ye good people, the matters goeth not well to pass in England, nor shall not do till everything be common, and that there be no villeins nor gentlemen, but that we may be all united together, and that the lords be no greater masters than we be. What have we deserved, or why should we be kept thus in servage? We be all come from one father and one mother, Adam and Eve: whereby can they say or show that they be greater lords than we be, saying by that they cause us to win and labour for that they dispend? They are clothed in velvet and camlet furred with grise, and we be ves-

---

1. Lord Berners' text had 'bataille' instead of 'taille'—nature [the Andersons' note].

tured with poor cloth. They have their wines, spices and good bread, and we have the drawing out of the chaff, and drink water. They dwell in fair houses, and we have the pain and travail, rain and wind in the fields; and by that that cometh of our labours they keep and maintain their estates. We be called their bondmen, and without we do readily them service, we be beaten; and we have no sovereign to whom we may complain, nor that will hear us nor do us right. Let us go to the king, he is young, and show him what servage we be in, and show him how we will have it otherwise, or else we will provide us of some remedy. And if we go together all manner of people that be now in any bondage will follow us, to the intent to be made free, and when the king seeth us we shall have some remedy, either by fairness or otherwise.' Thus John Ball said on Sundays when the people issued out of the churches in the villages, wherefore many of the mean people loved him, and such as intended to no goodness said how he said truth. And so they would murmur one with another in the fields and in the ways as they went together, affirming how John Ball said truth.

The Archbishop of Canterbury, who was informed of the saying of this John Ball, caused him to be taken and put in prison a two or three months to chastise him. Howbeit it had been much better at the beginning that he had been condemned to perpetual prison, or else to have died, rather than to have suffered him to have been again delivered out of prison: but the bishop had conscience to let him die. And when this John Ball was out of prison, he returned again to his error as he did before. Of his words and deeds there were much people in London informed, such as had great envy at them that were rich and such as were noble. And then they began to speak among them and said how the realm of England was right evil governed, and how that gold and silver was taken from them by them that were named noblemen. So thus these unhappy men of London began to rebel and assembled together, and sent word to the foresaid countries that they should come to London, and bring their people with them, promising how they should find London open to receive them and the commons of the city to be of the same accord, saying how they would do so much to the king that there should not be one bondman in all England.

This promise moved so them of Kent, of Essex, of Sussex, of Bedford, and of the countries about, that they rose and came towards London to the number of sixty thousand. And they had a captain called Water Tyler and with him in company was Jack Straw and John Ball. These three were chief sovereign captains, but the head of all was Water Tyler and he was indeed a tiler of houses, an ungracious patron.

When these unhappy men began thus to stir, they of London,

except such as were of their band, were greatly afraid. Then the Mayor of London and the rich men of the city took counsel together, and when they saw the people thus coming on every side, they caused the gates of the city to be closed and would suffer no man to enter into the city. But when they had well imagined, they advised not so to do, for they thought they should thereby put their suburbs in great peril to be burnt, and so they opened again the city; and there entered in at the gates in some place a hundred, two hundred, by twenty and by thirty. And so when they came to London they entered and lodged, and yet of truth the third part of these people could not tell what to ask or demand, but followed each other like beasts, as the shepherds did of old time, saying how they would go conquer the Holy Land, and at last all came to nothing. In likewise these villains and poor people came to London a hundred mile off, sixty mile, fifty mile, forty mile and twenty mile off, and from all countries about London, but the most part came from the countries before named. And as they came they demanded ever for the king. The gentlemen of the countries, knights and squires, began to doubt, when they saw the people began to rebel, and though they were in doubt, it was good reason: for a less occasion they might have been afraid. So the gentlemen drew together as well as they might.

The Humanist Circle: Letters

In his prefatory letter to Peter Giles, More mentions a certain churchman of his acquaintance who was trying to arrange with his ecclesiastical superiors to be sent as a missionary to the Utopians. Whether this story is serious or a joke (and if it is a joke, whoever cracked it), it certainly contains a truth: the verisimilitude of *Utopia* did impose on some readers, just as the verisimilitude of *Gulliver's Travels* was to do some two hundred years later. People took the story literally; they assumed that Utopia was a real place, and that Raphael Hythloday had visited it. Partly this was the result of More's straight-faced narrative technique; partly also it was the result of an informal, improvised conspiracy.

More was favored in imposing the *Utopia* on the general public as an actual story of a real place because the humanists of northern Europe formed such a tight and, on the whole, congenial network of personal acquaintances, with Erasmus at their center. More himself wrote a pair of prefatory letters to Peter Giles; under the urging of Erasmus, Peter Giles wrote a letter to the distinguished Jerome Busleiden, confirming More's story and adding a few "authentic"—or, at least, easily fabricated—particulars. Busleiden, a rather heavy-minded man, got the point, and carefully refrained, in his reply to More, from asking any difficult questions. Gerardus Noviomagus and Cornelius Graphaeus, Dutch humanists, wrote commendatory verses; Guillaume Budé wrote about the *Utopia* to Thomas Lupset; Erasmus wrote to the printer John Froben at Basle; and Joannes Paludanus of the University of Louvain wrote a letter to Peter Giles and a set of verses on the *Utopia*. Most of these letters and academic verses were reprinted with More's fantasy, in one edition or another; they formed a garland of humanist testimonials around the work. And while not all of them lent explicit support to the hoax, none of them was so crude as explicitly to question it. More's part in this bewildering epistolary roundabout was characteristically playful and evasive, his chief concern being to prevent the book from being taken too seriously by either naive or pedantic readers. Some contemporary criticism has called Hythloday's tale the real core of the book, viewing the "dialogue of counsel" as the first layer of protective coloration and camouflage and the ironic letters to Peter Giles as the second. More seems thus to be protecting himself from his own thought, as an oyster protects itself from an irritating grain of sand, with successive overlayers. Here, for better or worse, is at least one metaphor for the functioning of literature. Peter R. Allen has written for *Studies in the Renaissance*, X (1963), 91–107, an account of the prefatory letters and verses and their function.

Quite apart from this intricate epistolary interchange, we reprint a long excerpt from an even longer letter addressed by Erasmus to Ulrich von

Hutten, a German humanist, in July 1519. Erasmus was simply trying to describe his friend More to a man who had never met him; the result is one of the warmest and most affectionate documents of the age.

Thomas More to Peter Giles†

My very dear Peter Giles, I am almost ashamed to be sending you after a full year's time this little book about the Utopian state which I'm sure you expected in less than six weeks. For, as you were well aware, I faced no problem in finding my materials, and had no reason to labor over the arrangement of them. All I had to do was repeat what you and I together heard Raphael describe. There was no occasion, either, for fine or far-fetched language, since what he said, being extempore and informal, couldn't be couched in fancy terms. And besides, as you know, he's a man better versed in Greek than in Latin; so that my language would be nearer the truth, the closer it approached to his casual simplicity. Truth in fact is the only quality at which I should have aimed, or did aim, in writing this book.

I confess, friend Peter, that having all these materials ready to hand made my own contribution so slight that there was hardly anything at all for me to do. Thinking up a topic like this from scratch and disposing it in proper order might have demanded a lot of time and work even if a man were gifted with talent and learning. And then if the matter had to be set forth with eloquence, not just bluntly and factually, there's no way I could have done that, however hard I worked, for however long a time. But now when I was relieved of all these problems, over which I could have sweated forever, there was nothing for me to do but simply write down what I had heard. Well, little as it was, that task was rendered almost impossible by my many other obligations. Most of my day is given to the law—listening to some cases, pleading others, compromising others, and deciding still others. I have to visit this man because of his official position and that man because of his lawsuit; and so almost the whole day is devoted to other people's business and what's left over to my own; and then for myself—that is, my studies—there's nothing left.

For when I get home, I have to talk with my wife, chatter with my children, and consult with the servants. All these matters I consider part of my business, since they have to be done unless a man wants to be a stranger in his own house. Besides, a man is bound to bear himself as agreeably as he can toward those whom nature or chance or his own choice has made the companions of his life. But

† Text from J. H. Lupton, ed., *Utopia* (Oxford: Oxford University Press, 1895), pp. 1–12 (tr. R.M.A.).

of course he mustn't spoil them either with his familiarity, or by overindulgence turn the servants into his masters. And so, amid these concerns, the day, the month, and the year slip away.

What time do I find to write, then? especially since I still have taken no account of sleeping or even of eating, to which many people devote as much time as to sleep itself, which devours almost half of our lives. My own time is only what I steal from sleeping and eating. It isn't very much, but it's something, and so I've finally been able to finish our *Utopia*, even though belatedly, and I'm sending it to you now. I hope, my dear Peter, that you'll read it over and let me know if you find anything that I've overlooked. Though I'm not really afraid of having forgotten anything important—I wish my judgment and learning were up to my memory, which isn't half bad—still, I don't feel so sure of it that I would swear I've missed nothing.

For my servant John Clement has raised a great doubt in my mind. As you know, he was there with us, for I always want him to be present at conversations where there's profit to be gained. (And one of these days I expect we'll get a fine crop of learning from this young sprout, who's already made excellent progress in Greek as well as Latin.) Anyhow, as I recall matters, Hythloday said the bridge over the Anyder at Amaurot was five hundred paces long; but my John says that is two hundred paces too much—that in fact the river is barely three hundred paces wide there. So I beg you, consult your memory. If your recollection agrees with his, I'll yield to the two of you, and confess myself mistaken. But if you don't recall the point, I'll follow my own memory and keep my present figure. For, as I've taken particular pains to avoid untruths in the book, so I'd rather make an honest mistake than say what I don't believe. In short, I'd rather be truthful than correct.

But the whole matter can be cleared up if you'll ask Raphael about it—either directly, if he's still in your neighborhood, or else by letter. And I'm afraid you must do this anyway, because of another problem that has cropped up—whether through my fault, or yours, or Raphael's, I'm not sure. For it didn't occur to us to ask, nor to him to say, in what area of the New World Utopia is to be found. I wouldn't have missed hearing about this for a sizable sum of money, for I'm quite ashamed not to know even the name of the ocean where this island lies about which I've written so much. Besides, there are various people here, and one in particular, a devout man and a professor of theology, who very much wants to go to Utopia. His motive is not by any means idle curiosity, but rather a desire to foster and further the growth of our religion, which has made such a happy start there. To this end, he has decided to arrange to be sent there by the Pope, and even to be named Bishop to the Utopians. He feels no particular scruples about intriguing for this post, for he considers it a holy project, rising not from motives of glory or gain, but simply from religious zeal.

Therefore I beg you, my dear Peter, to get in touch with Hythlo-day—in person if you can, or by letters if he's gone—and make sure that my work contains nothing false and omits nothing true. It would probably be just as well to show him the book itself. If I've made a mistake, there's nobody better qualified to correct me; but even he cannot do it, unless he reads over my book. Besides, you will be able to discover in this way whether he's pleased or annoyed that I have written the book. If he has decided to write out his own story for himself, he may be displeased with me; and I should be sorry, too, if, in publicizing Utopia, I had robbed him and his story of the flower of novelty.

But to tell the truth, I'm still of two minds as to whether I should publish the book or not. For men's tastes are so various, the tempers of some are so severe, their minds so ungrateful, their tempers so cross, that there seems no point in publishing something, even if it's intended for their advantage, which they will receive only with contempt and ingratitude. Better simply to follow one's own natural inclinations, lead a merry, peaceful life, and ignore the vexing problems of publication. Most men know nothing of learning; many despise it. The clod rejects as too difficult whatever isn't cloddish. The pedant dismisses as mere trifling anything that isn't stuffed with obsolete words. Some readers approve only of ancient authors; most men like their own writing best of all. Here's a man so solemn he won't allow a shadow of levity, and there's one so insipid of taste that he can't endure the salt of a little wit. Some dullards dread satire as a man bitten by a hydrophobic dog dreads water; some are so changeable that they like one thing when they're seated and another when they're standing.

Those people lounge around the taverns, and as they swill their ale pass judgment on the intelligence of writers. With complete assurance they condemn every author by his writings, just as they think best, plucking each one, as it were, by the beard. But they themselves remain safely under cover and, as the proverb has it, out of harm's way. No use trying to lay hold of them; they're shaved so close, there's not so much as the hair of an honest man to catch them by.

Finally, some men are so ungrateful that even though they're delighted with a work, they don't like the author any better because of it. They are like rude, ungrateful guests who, after they have stuffed themselves with a splendid dinner, go off, carrying their full bellies homeward without a word of thanks to the host who invited them. A fine task, providing at your own expense a banquet for men of such finicky palates, such various tastes, and such rude, ungracious tempers.

At any rate, my dear Peter, will you take up with Hythloday the matter I spoke of? After I've heard from him, I'll take a fresh look at the whole matter. But since I've already taken the pains to write up the subject, it's too late to be wise. In the matter of publication, I hope we can have Hythloday's approval; after that, I'll follow the advice of my friends—and especially yours. Farewell, my dear Peter Giles. My regards to your excellent wife. Love me as you have always done; I remain more fond of you than ever.

Peter Giles to Jerome Busleiden†

Most distinguished Busleiden, the other day Thomas More (who, as you very well know from your long acquaintance with him, is one of the great ornaments of our age) sent me his *Island of Utopia*. It is a place, known so far to only a few men, but which should be studied by many, as going far beyond Plato's Republic. It is particularly interesting because it has been so vividly described, so carefully discussed, and so acutely analyzed by a man of such great talents. As often as I read it, I seem to see even more than I heard from the actual mouth of Raphael Hythloday—for I was present at his discourse, along with More. As a matter of fact, Hythloday himself showed no mean rhetorical gifts in setting forth his topic; it was perfectly plain that he wasn't just repeating what he had heard from other people, but was describing exactly what he had seen with his own eyes and experienced in his own person, over a long period of time. I consider him a man with more knowledge of nations, peoples, and business than even the famous Ulysses. Such a man as this has not, I think, been born in the last eight hundred years; by comparison with him, Vespucci seems hardly to have seen anything.[1] Apart from the fact that we naturally describe what we have seen better than what we have just heard about, the man had a particular skill in explaining the details of a subject. And yet when I contemplate the same matters as sketched by More's pen, I am so affected by them that I sometimes seem to be living in Utopia itself. I can scarcely believe, by heaven, that Raphael saw as much in the five years he lived on the island as can be seen in More's

† The obvious man to whom *Utopia* should have been dedicated was Erasmus. But Erasmus, who had already published the *Praise of Folly*, was too well known as a joker to sponsor the *Utopia*—it would have been giving away the spoof too cheaply. So Erasmus wrote to Peter Giles (on 17 October 1516), instructing him to send a copy of the manuscript to Jerome Busleiden, of whom more below. Giles, taking his cue from More's first letter to him, elaborated the hoax by inventing circumstances to explain the vagueness of Utopian geography, fabricating a special Utopian alphabet, and actually composing some limping verses in "Utopian." Text from Lupton, ed., *Utopia*, pp. xcv-c (tr. R.M.A.).

1. Amerigo Vespucci, Florentine explorer of America.

description. That description contains, in every part of it, so many wonders that I don't know what to marvel at first or most. Perhaps it should be the accuracy of his memory, which could recite almost word for word so many different things that he had heard only once; or else perhaps his good judgment, which traced back to secret sources of which the common man is completely ignorant both the fortunate and unfortunate events that afflict a commonwealth. Or finally I might marvel at the nerve and fluency of his language, in which, while preserving a pure Latin style, he has expressed incisively and comprehensively a great many matters of important policy. This is all the more remarkable in a man distracted, as he is, by a mass of public business and private concerns. But of course none of these remarks will surprise you, most erudite Busleiden, since you have already learned from your intimate conversations with him to appreciate the more-than-human, the almost-divine genius of the man.

For the rest, I can add nothing to what he has written. There is, indeed, a little scrap of verse, written in the Utopian tongue, which Hythloday showed to me after More had gone away. I've prefixed to it an alphabet of the Utopian tongue, and added a few little notes in the margins.

As for More's difficulties about locating the island, Raphael did not try in any way to suppress that information, but he mentioned it only briefly and in passing, as if saving it for another occasion. And then an unlucky accident caused both of us to miss what he said. For while Raphael was speaking of it, one of More's servants came in to whisper something in his ear; and though I was listening, for that very reason, more intently than ever, one of the company, who I suppose had caught cold on shipboard, coughed so loudly that some of Raphael's words escaped me. But I will never rest till I have full information on this point, not just the general position of the island, but its exact latitude—provided only our friend Hythloday is safe and alive.

For we hear various stories about him, some people asserting that he died on the way home, others that he got home but didn't like the way things were going there, retained his old hankering for Utopia, and so made his way back to that part of the world.

It's true, of course, that the name of this island is not to be found among the old cosmographers, but Hythloday himself had a simple answer for that. For, he said, either the name that the ancients gave it has changed over the ages, or else they never discovered the island at all. Nowadays we find all sorts of lands turning up which the old geographers never mentioned. But what's the point of piling up these arguments authenticating the story, when we already have it on the word of More himself?

His uncertainty about having the book published, I attribute to his modesty, and very creditable it is. But on many scores, it seemed to me a work that should not be suppressed any longer; on the contrary, it deserved to be sent forth into the hands of men, especially under the powerful protection of your name. Nobody knows More's good qualities better than you do, and no man is better suited than you to serve the commonwealth with good counsels. At this work you have labored for many years, earning the highest praise for wisdom as well as integrity. Farewell, then, you Maecenas[2] of learning, and ornament of our era.

Antwerp, 1 November 1516

2. Maecenas was the patron of Virgil, Horace, and other Roman writers.

VTOPIENSIVM ALPHABETVM. 13

a b c d e f g h i k l m n o p q r s t u x y

Ó⊖⊕⊙⊖⊙Ɔငᴖⵉⴲᐃ⅃ᒋᒋ⅂ℸⵔⵒⵕⵕⵔⵔ

TETRASTICHON VERNACVLA VTO-
PIENSIVM LINGVA.

Vtopos   ha   Boccas   peula   chama.

polta   chamaan

Bargol   he   maglomi   baccan

foma   gymnofophaon

Agrama   gymnofophon   labarem

bacha   bodamilomin

Voluala   barchin   heman   la

lauoluola   dramme   pagloni.

HORVM VERSVVM AD VERBVM HAEC
EST SENTENTIA.

Vtopus me dux ex non infula fecit infulam.
Vna ego terrarum omnium abſcҩ philoſophia.
Ciuitatem philoſophicam expreſſi mortalibus.
Libenter impartio mea, non grauatim accipio meliora.

b ;

Me, once a peninsula, Utopus the king made an island.
Alone among all the nations, and without complex abstractions,
I set before men's eyes the philosophical city.
What I give is free: what is better I am not slow to take from others.

Jerome Busleiden to Thomas More†

For you, my most distinguished friend More, it was not enough to devote all your care, labor, and energy to the interest and advantage of individuals: such is your goodness and liberality that you must bestow them on the public at large. You saw that this goodness of yours, however great it might be, would deserve more favor, achieve higher renown, and aim at greater glory, the more widely it was diffused, the more people shared in it and were benefited by it. This is what you've always tried to do on other occasions, and now by a singular stroke of luck you've attained it again—I mean by that "afternoon's discussion" which you've described and now published, about the right and proper constitution of the Utopian republic—a topic of which all people are now eager to hear.

It is a delightful description of a wonderful institution, replete with profound erudition and a consummate knowledge of human affairs. Both qualities meet in this work so equally and so congenially that neither yields to the other, but both contend on an even footing. You enjoy such a wide range of learning and such profound experience that whatever you write comes from full experience, and whatever decisions you take carry a full weight of learning. A rare and wonderful happiness! and all the more remarkable in that it withdraws itself from the multitude and imparts itself only to the few—to such, above all, as have the candor to wish, the erudition to understand, and the authority to judge in the common interest as honorably, accurately, and practically as you do now. For you clearly don't consider yourself born for yourself alone, but for the whole world; and so by this splendid work, you have undertaken to place the whole world in your debt.

You could hardly have accomplished this end more effectually and correctly than by setting forth a pattern, a perfect formula for rational men, in the shape of an ideal commonwealth. And the world has never seen one more perfect than yours, more solidly established or more desirable. It far surpasses the many celebrated

---

† Busleiden, to whom Giles addressed his letter of 1 November 1516, was an elderly man, well known in the world, wealthy and substantial. Among other offices, he was provost of Aire; treasurer of Saint Gudule's in Brussels; canon of Mechlin, Mons, and Liège; Archdeacon of Brussels and Cambray; Master of Requests; and Counsellor to Charles, Prince of Castille. During his embassy on the Continent, More had met Busleiden and had much admired his splendid house at Mechlin, as well as his impressive collection of antique coins. Poems on these topics are found among More's *Epigrams*. On the other hand, if we can judge from the few scraps of his remaining writing, Busleiden was more of a pompous rhetorician than a wit—an impressive figurehead, but perhaps also something of a stuffed shirt. The feature of *Utopia* which most impressed him was its communism; and he praised it as a pattern for all the nations in the world. The categorical assurance of this judgment strikes us as odd, given Busleiden's lordly way of life; and perhaps it worried More too—as we shall see. Text from Lupton, pp. 318–19 (tr. R.M.A.).

states of which so much has been said, those of Sparta, Athens, and Rome. Had they been founded under the same auspices as your commonwealth, with the same institutions, laws, regulations, and customs, certainly they would not now be lying flat, level with the ground, and extinguished—alas! beyond all hope of rebirth. On the contrary, they would now be intact, fortunate and prosperous, leading a happy existence—mistresses of the world, besides, and dividing a far-flung empire, by land and by sea.

Feeling pity for the wretched fate of these commonwealths, you feared lest others, which now hold supreme power, should undergo the same fate; so you drew the portrait of a perfect state, one which devoted its energies less to setting up perfect laws than to putting the very best men in charge of administering them. And in this they are absolutely right; for without good rulers, even the best laws (if we take Plato's word for it) would be nothing but dead letters. Such rulers as these serve above all as models of probity, specimens of good conduct, images of justice, and patterns of virtue for the guidance of any well-established commonwealth. What is needed is prudence in the rulers, courage in the military, temperance in the private citizenry, and justice among all men.

Since the state you praise so lavishly is clearly formed on these principles, no wonder if it seems not only a challenge to other nations but an object of reverence to all the peoples, and an achievement to be celebrated among future generations. Its great strength lies in the fact that all squabbles over private property are removed, and no one has anything of his own. Within the society all men have everything in common, and thus every action and each decision, whether public or private, trifling or important, is not directed by the greed of the many or the lusts of the few, but aims at upholding a single uniform rule of justice, equality, and community solidarity. All things being thus tightly bound to a single aim, there is bound to be a clean sweep of everything that might serve as torch, kindling, or fuel for the fires of ambition, luxury, injury, and wrong. These are vices into which even decent men are sometimes pushed against their will, and to their own incomparable loss, by private property or lust for gain or that most pitiful of emotions, ambition. From these sources rise quarrels, clashes, and wars worse than civil, which not only overthrow the flourishing state of supremely happy republics, but cause their previous glories, their splendid trophies, rich prizes, and proud spoils to be utterly defaced.

If my thoughts on this point should be less than absolutely convincing, only consider the swarm of perfectly reliable witnesses I can call to my support—I mean the many great cities destroyed, the states crushed, the republics beaten down, the towns burnt up. Not only have they disappeared without a trace—not even their names are preserved by any history, however far back it reaches.

Whatever our states may be now, in the future they will succeed in escaping these terrible downfalls, disasters, and devastations of war only if they adapt themselves to the good Utopian pattern and don't swerve from it, as people say, by a hair's breadth. If they act so, the result will fully convince them how much they have profited by the service you have done them; especially since, by your help, they will have learned to keep their republic healthy, unharmed, and victorious. Their debt to you will be no less than that owed to men who have saved not just one citizen of a state, but the entire state itself, from danger.

Farewell for now. May you continue to prosper, ever contriving, carrying out, and completing new plans which will bring long life to your country, and to yourself immortality. Farewell, most learned and humane More, supreme ornament of your Britain and of this world of ours. From my house at Mechlin, 1516.

Guillaume Budé[†]

To His English Friend Thomas Lupset, Greeting:

I owe you many thanks, my learned young friend Lupset, for having sent me Thomas More's *Utopia*, and so drawn my attention to what is very pleasant, and likely to be very profitable, reading.

It is not long ago since you prevailed upon me (your entreaties seconding my own strong inclination) to read the six books of Galen *On the preservation of the Health*, to which that master of the Greek and Latin tongues, Dr. Thomas Linacre,[1] has lately rendered the service—or rather, paid the compliment—of translating them from the extant originals into Latin. So well has the task been performed, that if all that author's works (which I consider worth all other medical lore put together) be in time translated, the want

[†] In 1517, Thomas Lupset was no more than twenty-two years old. While study-ing in Paris, he had been acting as agent for his humanist friends, reading proof in a publishing house and, in the case of the second edition of *Utopia*, serving as publicity man. In this capacity, he evi-dently sent a copy of the book to Budé (or Budaeus, as he wrote it in Latin), who was a classical scholar of distin-guished reputation. Like Busleiden, he was a man of considerable personal property; and like Busleiden, he turned out to be enchanted with the idea of communism. More, who had been uneasy from the beginning over the reception of

his book would find, must have been startled to find that the most radical fea-ture of his ideal commonwealth was pre-cisely what appealed most to these learned, conservative, and aristocratic men. Budé's letter to Lupset was printed with the second edition. The translation is that of J. H. Lupton in his edition of the *Utopia* (Oxford, 1895), pp. lxxx–xcii but with his footnotes replaced by those of R.M.A.
1. Thomas Linacre (1460–1524) was ed-ucated abroad, imbibed freely of the "new learning," and became the founder and first president of the Royal College of Physicians.

of a knowledge of Greek is not likely to be seriously felt by our schools of medicine.

I have hastily skimmed over that work, as it stands in Linacre's papers (for the courteous loan of which, for so long a time, I am very greatly indebted to you) with the result that I deem myself much benefited by the perusal. But I promise myself still greater profit when the book itself, on the publication of which at the presses of this city you are now busily engaged, shall have appeared in print.

While I thought myself already under a sufficient obligation to you on this account, here you have presented to me More's *Utopia*, as an appendix or supplement to your former kindness. He is a man of the keenest discernment, of a pleasant disposition, well versed in knowledge of the world. I have had the book by me in the country, where my time was taken up with running about and giving directions to workpeople (for you know something, and have heard more, of my having been occupied for more than a twelvemonth on business connected with my country-house); and was so impressed by reading it, as I learnt and studied the manners and customs of the Utopians, that I well-nigh forgot, nay, even abandoned, the management of my family affairs. For I perceived that all the theory and practice of domestic economy, all care whatever for increasing one's income, was mere waste of time.

And yet, as all see and are aware, the whole race of mankind is goaded on by this very thing, as if some gadfly were bred within them to sting them. The result is that we must needs confess the object of nearly all legal and civil qualification and training to be this: that with jealous and watchful cunning, as each one has a neighbour with whom he is connected by ties of citizenship, or even at times of relationship, he should be ever conveying or abstracting something from him; should pare away, repudiate, squeeze, chouse, chisel, cozen, extort, pillage, purloin, thieve, filch, rob, and—partly with the connivance, partly with the sanction of the laws—be ever plundering and appropriating.

This goes on all the more in countries where the civil and canon law, as they are called, have greater authority in the two courts. For it is evident that their customs and institutions are pervaded by the principle, that those are to be deemed the high-priests of law and equity, who are skilled in *caveats*—or *capiats*, rather;[2] men who hawk at their unwary fellow-citizens; artists in formulas, that is, in gudgeon-traps; adepts in concocted law; getters up of cases; jurisconsults of a controverted, perverted, inverted *jus*.[3] These are the only

2. *Caveats*: warnings; *capiats*: permissions to take.   3. *Jus*: law.

fit persons to give opinions as to what is fair and good; nay, what is far more, to settle with plenary power what each one is to be allowed to have, and what not to have, and the extent and limit of his tenure. How deluded must public opinion be to have determined matters thus!

The truth is that most of us, blind with the thick rheum of ignorance in our eyes, suppose that each one's cause, as a rule, is *just*, in proportion to its accordance with the requirements of the *law*, or to the way in which he has based his claim on the *law*. Whereas, were we agreed to demand our rights in accordance with the rule of truth, and what the simple Gospel prescribes, the dullest would understand, and the most senseless admit, if we put it to them, that, in the decrees of the canonists, the divine law differs as much from the human; and, in our civil laws and royal enactments, true equity differs as much from law; as the principles laid down by Christ, the founder of human society, and the usages of His disciples, differ from the decrees and enactments of those who think the *summum bonum* and perfection of happiness to lie in the moneybags of a Croesus or a Midas.[4] So that, if you chose to define Justice now-a-days, in the way that early writers liked to do, as the power who assigns to each his due, you would either find her non-existent in public, or, if I may use such a comparison, you would have to admit that she was a kind of kitchen stewardess: and this, alike whether you regard the character of our present rulers, or the disposition of fellow-citizens and fellow-countrymen one towards another.

Perhaps indeed it may be argued, that the law I speak of has been derived from that inherent, world-old justice called *natural* law; which teaches that the stronger a man is, the more he should possess; and, the more he possesses, the more eminent among his countrymen he ought to be: with the result that now we see it an accepted principle in the law of nations, that persons who are unable to help their fellows by any art or practice worth mentioning, if only they are adepts in those complicated knots and stringent bonds, by which men's properties are tied up (things accounted a mixture of Gordian knots and charlatanry, with nothing very wonderful about them, by the ignorant multitude, and by scholars living, for the sake of recreation or of investigating the truth, at a distance from the courts),—that these persons, I say, should have an income equal to that of a thousand of their countrymen, nay, even of a whole state, and sometimes more than that; and that they should then be greeted with the honourable titles of wealthy

4. Proverbial rich men of antiquity.

men, thrifty men, makers of splendid fortunes. Such in truth is the age in which we live; such our manners and customs; such our national character. These have pronounced it lawful for a man's credit and influence to be high, in proportion to the way in which he has been the architect of his own fortunes and of those of his heirs: an influence, in fact, which goes on increasing, according as their descendants in turn, to the remotest generation, vie in heaping up with fine additions the property gained by their ancestors; which amounts to saying, according as they have ousted more and more extensively their connections, kindred, and even their blood relations.

But the founder and regulator of all property, Jesus Christ, left among His followers a Pythagorean communion and love; and ratified it by a plain example, when Ananias was condemned to death for breaking this law of communion.[5] By laying down this principle, Christ seems to me to have abolished, at any rate among his followers, all the voluminous quibbles of the civil law, and still more of the later canon law; which latter we see at the present day holding the highest position in jurisprudence, and controlling our destiny.

As for the island of Utopia, which I hear is also called *Udepotia*,[6] it is said (if we are to believe the story), by what must be owned a singular good fortune, to have adopted Christian usages both in public and in private; to have imbibed the wisdom thereto belonging; and to have kept it undefiled to this very day. The reason is, that it holds with firm grip to three divine institutions:— namely, the absolute equality, or, if you prefer to call it so, the civil communication, of all things good and bad among fellow-citizens; a settled and unwavering love of peace and quietness; and a contempt for gold and silver. Three things these, which overturn, one may say, all fraud, all imposture, cheating, roguery, and unprincipled deception. Would that Providence, on its own behalf, would cause these three principles of Utopian law to be fixed in the minds of all men by the rivets of a strong and settled conviction. We should soon see pride, covetousness, insane competition, and almost all other deadly weapons of our adversary the Devil, fall powerless; we should see the interminable array of law-books, the work of so many excellent and solid understandings, that occupy men till the very day of their death, consigned to bookworms, as mere hollow and empty things, or else given up to make wrapping-paper for shops.

5. Ananias sold a property and gave the Apostles only part of the price, instead of the whole gain, as he should have done. See Acts. v.1–7.

6. *Utopia* = "Noplace"; *Udepotia* = "Neverplace." Playing a third change on the name, some of the commendatory verses written on More's book turned Utopia into *Eutopia* = "Goodplace."

Good heavens! what holiness of the Utopians has had the power of earning such a blessing from above, that greed and covetousness have for so many ages failed to enter, either by force or stealth, into that island alone? that they have failed to drive out from it, by wanton effrontery, justice and honour?

Would that great Heaven in its goodness had dealt so kindly with the countries which keep, and would not part with, the appellation they bear, derived from His most holy name! Of a truth, greed, which perverts and sinks down so many minds, otherwise noble and elevated, would be gone from hence once for all, and the golden age of Saturn would return. In Utopia one might verily suppose that there is a risk of Aratus and the early poets having been mistaken in their opinion, when they made Justice depart from earth, and placed her in the Zodiac.[7] For, if we are to believe Hythloday, she must needs have stayed behind in that island, and not yet made her way to heaven.

But in truth I have ascertained by full inquiry, that Utopia lies outside the bounds of the known world. It is in fact one of the Fortunate Isles, perhaps very close to the Elysian Fields; for More himself testifies that Hythloday has not yet stated its position definitely. It is itself divided into a number of cities, but all uniting or confederating into one state, named Hagnopolis;[8] a state contented with its own customs, its own goods, blest with innocence, leading a kind of heavenly life, on a lower level indeed than heaven, but above the defilements of this world we know, which amid the endless pursuits of mankind, as empty and vain as they are keen and eager, is being hurried in a swollen and eddying tide to the cataract.

It is to Thomas More, then, that we owe our knowledge of this island. It is he who, in our generation, has made public this model of a happy life and rule for leading it, the discovery, as he tells us, of Hythloday: for he ascribes all to him. For while Hythloday has built the Utopians their state, and established for them their rites and customs; while, in so doing, he has borrowed from them and brought home for us the representation of a happy life; it is beyond question More, who has set off by his literary style the subject of that island and its customs. He it is who has perfected, as by rule and square, the City of the Hagnopolitans itself, adding all those touches by which grace and beauty and weight accrue to the noble work; even though in executing that work he has claimed for himself only a common mason's share. We see that it has been a matter

7. Aratus of Soli wrote a Greek poem on astronomy, *Phaenomena;* he lived in the third century B.C.

8. From the Greek, "City of the Saints."

of conscientious scruple with him, not to assume too important a part in the work, lest Hythloday should have just cause for complaint, on the ground of More having plucked the first flowers of that fame, which would have been left for him, if he had himself ever decided to give an account of his adventures to the world. "He was afraid, of course, that Hythloday, who was residing of his own choice in the island of Udepotia, might some day come in person upon the scene, and be vexed and aggrieved at this unkindness on his part, in leaving him the glory of this discovery with the best flowers plucked off. To be of this persuasion is the part of good men and wise."[9]

Now while More is one who of himself carries weight, and has great authority to rest upon, I am led to place unreserved confidence in him by the testimony of Peter Giles of Antwerp. Though I have never made his acquaintance in person—apart from recommendations of his learning and character that have reached me—I love him on account of his being the intimate friend of the illustrious Erasmus, who has deserved so well of letters of every kind, whether sacred or profane; with whom personally I have long corresponded and formed ties of friendship.

Farewell, my dear Lupset. Greet for me, at the first opportunity, either by word of mouth or by letter, Linacre, that pillar of the British name in all that concerns good learning; one who is now, as I hope, not more yours than ours. He is one of the few whose good opinion I should be very glad, if possible, to gain. When he was himself known to be staying here, he gained in the highest degree the good opinion of me and of Jehan Ruelle, my friend and the sharer in my studies.[1] And his singular learning and careful industry I should be the first to look up to and strive to copy.

Greet More also once and again for me, either by message, as I said before, or by word of mouth. As I think and often repeat, Minerva has long entered his name on her selectest album; and I love and revere him in the highest degree for what he has written about this isle of the New World, Utopia.

In his history our age and those which succeed it will have a nursery, so to speak, of polite and useful institutions; from which men may borrow customs, and introduce and adapt them each to his own state. Farewell.

From Paris, the 31st of July.[2]

---

9. The passage within quotes is in Greek in the original.
1. Ruelle, like Linacre, was a scholar-physician.

2. The year, 1517, is understood. The second edition appeared sometime in the fall and winter of 1517–18.

Thomas More to Peter Giles†

My dear Peter, I was absolutely delighted with the opinion of that very sharp man whom you know. He posed this dilemma about my *Utopia*: if the story is put forward as true, he said, then I see a number of absurdities in it; but if it's a fable, then it seems to me that in various respects More's usual good judgment is at fault. I suspect this fellow of being learned, and I see that he's a friend; but whoever he is, my dear Peter, I'm much obliged to him. By this frank opinion of his, he has pleased me more than anyone else since the book was published.

For in the first place, either out of devotion to me or interest in the subject itself, he seems to have borne up under the burden of reading the book all the way through—and that not perfunctorily or hastily, the way priests read the hours—those, at least, who read them at all.[1] No, he read slowly and attentively, noting all the particular points. Then, having singled out certain matters for criticism, and not very many, as a matter of fact, he gives careful and considered approval to the rest. And finally, in the very expressions he uses to criticize me, he implies higher praises than some of those who have put all their energies into compliment. It's easy to see what a high opinion he has of me when he expresses disappointment over reading something imperfect or inexact—whereas I don't expect, in treating so many different matters, to be able to say more than one or two things which aren't totally ridiculous.

Still, I'd like to be just as frank with him as he was with me; and in fact, I don't see why he should think himself so keen (so "spirituel," as the Greeks would say), just because he's discovered some absurdities in the institutions of Utopia, or caught me putting forth some half-baked ideas about the constitution of their state. Isn't there something absurd in the institutions of most other states elsewhere in the world? and haven't most of the philosophers who've written about the state, its ruler, and even the office of a private citizen, managed to say something that needs correcting?

† Reprinted by permission of Yale University Press from St. Thomas More, *Utopia*, edited by Edward Surtz, S.J., and J. H. Hexter (New Haven: Yale University Press, 1965) pp. 248–252. Copyright © 1965 by Yale University. Translated by R.M.A. The second letter of More to Peter Giles appeared only in the second edition of *Utopia* (Paris, 1517–18). Like the first, it deprecates (under the pretext of defending) the seriousness with which Hythloday's narration is to be taken. One may speculate that the persons who praised More too highly, and too clumsily, may have been Busleiden or Budé, both of whom had been surprisingly emphatic in endorsing the idea of community property. More evidently preferred to retain some ironic reservations, or at least room for ironic maneuver; and his relief at finding a more critical reader (whoever he was) breathes through this second epistle.

1. Priests read assigned prayers on the hours, with varying degrees of enthusiasm, according to More.

But when he wonders whether *Utopia* is true or a fiction, then I find *his* judgment, in turn, sorely at fault. It's perfectly possible that if I'd decided to write about a republic, and a fable of this sort had occurred to me, I might have spread a little fiction, like so much honey, over the truth to make it more acceptable. But I would certainly have tempered the fiction so that, while it deceived the common folk, it also tipped the wink to the learned, who were capable of seeing through it. So, if I'd done nothing but give special names to the prince, the river, the city, and the island, which hinted to the learned that the island was nowhere, the city was a phantom, the river was waterless, and the prince had no people, that would not have been hard to do, and would have been a good deal more clever than what I actually did. Unless I had a historian's devotion to fact, I am not so stupid as to have used those barbarous and senseless names of Utopia, Anyder, Amaurot, and Ademus.

Still, my dear Giles, I see some people are so suspicious that what we naive fellows have written down of Hythloday's account can hardly find any credence at all with these circumspect and sagacious persons. I'm afraid my personal reputation, as well as my authority as a historian, may be threatened by this skepticism; so it's a good thing that I can defend myself by saying, as Terence's Mysis says about Glycerium's boy, to confirm his legitimacy: "Praise be to God there were some free women present when I gave birth."[2] And so it was a good thing for me that Raphael told his story not just to you and me, but to a great many perfectly respectable and serious-minded men. Whether he told them more things, and more important things, than he told us, I don't know; but he certainly told them just as much as he did us.

Well, if these doubters won't believe such witnesses, let them consult Hythloday himself, for he is not yet dead. I heard only recently from some travelers coming out of Portugal that on the first of last March he was as healthy and vigorous a man as he ever was. Let them get the truth from him—dig it out of him with questions, if they want. I only want them to understand that I'm responsible for my own work, and my own work alone, not for somebody else's good faith.

Farewell, my dearest Peter, to you, your lovely wife, and your delightful little girl. My wife wishes them long life and the best of health.

2. Terence, *The Lady of Andros*, ll.771–72.

Erasmus to Ulrich von Hutten†

Most illustrious Hutten, your love, I had almost said your passion for the genius of Thomas More,—kindled· as it is by his writings, which, as you truly say, are as learned and witty as anything can possibly be,—is, I assure you, shared by many others; and moreover the feeling in this case· is mutual; since More is so delighted with what you have written, that I am myself almost jealous of you. It is an example of what Plato says of that sweetest wisdom, which excites much more ardent love among men than the most admirable beauty of form. It is not discerned by the eye of sense, but the mind has eyes of its own, so that even here the Greek saying holds true, that out of Looking grows Liking; and so it comes to pass that people are sometimes united in the warmest affection, who have never seen or spoken to each other. And, as it is a common experience, that for some unexplained reason different people are attracted by different kinds of beauty, so between one mind and another, there seems to be a sort of latent kindred, which causes us to be specially delighted with some minds, and not with others.

As to your asking me to paint you a full-length portrait of More, I only wish my power of satisfying your request were equal to your earnestness in pressing it. For to me too, it will be no unpleasant task to linger awhile in the contemplation of a friend, who is the most delightful character in the world. But, in the first place, it is not given to every man to be aware of all More's accomplishments; and in the next place, I know not whether he will himself like to have his portrait painted by any artist that chooses to do so. For indeed I do not think it more easy to make a likeness of More than of Alexander the Great, or of Achilles; neither were those heroes more worthy of immortality. The hand of an Apelles is required for such a subject, and I am afraid I am more like a Fulvius or a Rutuba than an Apelles.[1] Nevertheless I will try to draw you a sketch, rather than a portrait, of the entire man, so far as daily and domestic intercourse has enabled me to observe his likeness and retain it in my memory. But if some diplomatic employment should ever bring you together, you will find out, how poor an artist you have chosen for this commission; and I am afraid you will think me

† Three years after the first publication of *Utopia*, Ulrich von Hutten, author of the satirical *Letters of Obscure Men*, asked Erasmus about Thomas More, whom he admired but had never met. The sketch which Erasmus wrote in response to this request needs no further introduction. From *Epistles of Erasmus*, tr. Francis M. Nichols (London: Longmans, Green, 1917), III, 387–99. Footnotes are those of R.M.A., unless credited to Nichols.
1. In the passage of Horace here alluded to (Sat. II. vii. 96), Fulvius and Rutuba are generally understood to be the names of gladiators, depicted in a popular hand-bill. But Erasmus appears to interpret them as the names of humble artists dealing with such common-place subjects. [Nichols's note.]

guilty of envy or of wilful blindness in taking note of so few out the many good points of his character.

To begin with that part of him which is least known to you,—in shape and stature More is not a tall man, but not remarkably short, all his limbs being so symmetrical, that no deficiency is observed in this respect. His complexion is fair, his face being rather blonde than pale, but with no approach to redness, except a very delicate flush, which lights up the whole. His hair is auburn inclining to black, or if you like it better, black inclining to auburn; his beard thin, his eyes a bluish grey with some sort of tinting upon them. This kind of eye is thought to be a sign of the happiest character, and is regarded with favour in England, whereas with us black eyes are rather preferred. It is said, that no kind of eye is so free from defects of sight. His countenance answers to his character, having an expression of kind and friendly cheerfulness with a little air of raillery. To speak candidly, it is a face more expressive of pleasantry than of gravity or dignity, though very far removed from folly or buffoonery. His right shoulder seems a little higher than his left, especially when he is walking, a peculiarity that is not innate, but the result of habit, like many tricks of the kind. In the rest of his body there is nothing displeasing,—only his hands are a little coarse, or appear so, as compared with the rest of his figure. He has always from his boyhood been very negligent of his toilet, so as not to give much attention even to the things, which according to Ovid are all that men need care about.[2] What a charm there was in his looks when young, may even now be inferred from what remains; although I knew him myself when he was not more than three and-twenty years old; for he has not yet passed much beyond his fortieth year. His health is sound rather than robust, but sufficient for any labours suitable to an honourable citizen; and we may fairly hope, that his life may be long, as he has a father living of a great age, but an age full of freshness and vigour.

I have never seen any person less fastidious in his choice of food. As a young man, he was by preference a water-drinker, a practice he derived from his father. But, not to give annoyance to others, he used at table to conceal this habit from his guests by drinking, out of a pewter vessel, either small beer almost as weak as water, or plain water. As to wine, it being the custom, where he was, for the company to invite each other to drink in turn out of the same cup, he used sometimes to sip a little of it, to avoid appearing to shrink from it altogether, and to habituate himself to the common practice. For his eating he has been accustomed to prefer beef and salt

2. Ovid, *de Arte Amandi*, lib. i. 514, "recommends that the toga fit properly, have no holes in it, etc." [Nichols's note; quoted portion of note translated by R.M.A.]

meats, and household bread thoroughly fermented, to those articles of diet which are commonly regarded as delicacies. But he does not shrink from things that impart an innocent pleasure, even of a bodily kind, and has always a good appetite for milk-puddings and for fruit, and eats a dish of eggs with the greatest relish.

His voice is neither loud nor excessively low, but of a penetrating tone. It has nothing in it melodious or soft, but is simply suitable for speech, as he does not seem to have any natural talent for singing, though he takes pleasure in music of every kind. His articulation is wonderfully distinct, being equally free from hurry and from hesitation.

He likes to be dressed simply, and does not wear silk, or purple, or gold chains, except when it is not allowable to dispense with them. He cares marvellously little for those formalities, which with ordinary people are the test of politeness; and as he does not exact these ceremonies from others, so he is not scrupulous in observing them himself, either on occasions of meeting or at entertainments, though he understands how to use them, if he thinks proper to do so; but he holds it to be effeminate and unworthy of a man to waste much of his time on such trifles.

He was formerly rather disinclined to a court life and to any intimacy with princes, having always a special hatred of tyranny and a great fancy for equality; whereas you will scarcely find any court so well-ordered, as not to have much bustle and ambition and pretence and luxury, or to be free from tyranny in some form or other. He could not even be tempted to Henry the Eighth's court without great trouble, although nothing could be desired more courteous or less exacting than this Prince. He is naturally fond of liberty and leisure; but as he enjoys a holiday when he has it, so whenever business requires it, no one is more vigilant or more patient.

He seems to be born and made for friendship, of which he is the sincerest and most persistent devotee. Neither is he afraid of that multiplicity of friends, of which Hesiod disapproves.[3] Accessible to every tender of intimacy, he is by no means fastidious in choosing his acquaintance, while he is most accommodating in keeping it on foot, and constant in retaining it. If he has fallen in with anyone whose faults he cannot cure, he finds some opportunity of parting with him, untying the knot of intimacy without tearing it; but when he has found any sincere friends, whose characters are suited to his own, he is so delighted with their society and conversation, that he seems to find in these the chief pleasure of life, having an absolute distaste for tennis and dice and cards, and the other games with which the mass of gentlemen beguile the tediousness of Time.

3. Hesiod, the father of Greek didactic poetry, flourished in the eighth century B.C.; his *Works and Days* is full of this sort of practical advice.

It should be added that, while he is somewhat neglectful of his own interest, no one takes more pains in attending to the concerns of his friends. What more need I say? If anyone requires a perfect example of true friendship, it is in More that he will best find it.

In company his extraordinary kindness and sweetness of temper are such as to cheer the dullest spirit, and alleviate the annoyance of the most trying circumstances. From boyhood he was always so pleased with a joke, that it might seem that jesting was the main object of his life; but with all that, he did not go so far as buffoonery, nor had ever any inclination to bitterness: When quite a youth, he wrote farces and acted them. If a thing was facetiously said, even though it was aimed at himself, he was charmed with it, so much did he enjoy any witticism that had a flavour of subtlety or genius. This led to his amusing himself as a young man with epigrams, and taking great delight in Lucian. Indeed, it was he that suggested my writing the *Moria*, or Praise of Folly,[4] which was much the same thing as setting a camel to dance.

There is nothing that occurs in human life, from which he does not seek to extract some pleasure, although the matter may be serious in itself. If he has to do with the learned and intelligent, he is delighted with their cleverness, if with unlearned or stupid people, he finds amusement in their folly. He is not offended even by professed clowns, as he adapts himself with marvellous dexterity to the tastes of all; while with ladies generally, and even with his wife, his conversation is made up of humour and playfulness. You would say it was a second Democritus, or rather that Pythagorean philosopher, who strolls in leisurely mood through the market-place, contemplating the turmoil of those who buy and sell. There is no one less guided by the opinion of the multitude, but on the other hand no one sticks more closely to common sense.

One of his amusements is in observing the forms, characters and instincts of different animals. Accordingly there is scarcely any kind of bird, that he does not keep about his residence, and the same of other animals not quite so common, as monkeys, foxes, ferrets, weasels and the like. Beside these, if he meets with any strange object, imported from abroad or otherwise remarkable, he is most eager to buy it, and has his house so well supplied with these objects, that there is something in every room which catches your eye, as you enter it; and his own pleasure is renewed every time that he sees others interested.

When of a sentimental age, he was not a stranger to the emotions of love, but without loss of character, having no inclination to press his advantage, and being more attracted by a mutual liking than by any licentious object.

---

4. *Moria* is Greek for "folly"; Erasmus wrote the *Praise of Folly* in More's house (1509).

He had drunk deep of good letters from his earliest years; and when a young man, he applied himself to the study of Greek and of philosophy; but his father was so far from encouraging him in this pursuit, that he withdrew his allowance and almost disowned him, because he thought he was deserting his hereditary study, being himself an expert professor of English law. For remote as that profession is from true learning, those who become masters of it have the highest rank and reputation among their countrymen; and it is difficult to find any readier way to acquire fortune and honour. Indeed a considerable part of the nobility of that island has had its origin in this profession, in which it is said that no one can be perfect, unless he has toiled at it for many years. It was natural that in his younger days our friend's genius, born for better things, should shrink from this study; nevertheless, after he had had a taste of the learning of the schools, he became so conversant with it, that there was no one more eagerly consulted by suitors; and the income that he made by it was not surpassed by any of those who did nothing else; such was the power and quickness of his intellect.

He also expended considerable labour in perusing the volumes of the orthodox fathers; and when scarcely more than a youth, he lectured publicly on the *De Civitate Dei* of Augustine[5] before a numerous audience, old men and priests not being ashamed to take a lesson in divinity from a young layman, and not at all sorry to have done so. Meantime he applied his whole mind to religion, having some thought of taking orders, for which he prepared himself by watchings and fastings and prayers and such like exercises; wherein he showed much more wisdom than the generality of people, who rashly engage in so arduous a profession without testing themselves beforehand. And indeed there was no obstacle to his adopting this kind of life, except the fact, that he could not shake off his wish to marry. Accordingly he resolved to be a chaste husband rather than a licentious priest.

When he married, he chose a very young girl, a lady by birth, with her character still unformed, having been always kept in the country with her parents and sisters,—so that he was all the better able to fashion her according to his own habits. Under his direction she was instructed in learning and in every kind of music, and had almost completely become just such a person as would have been a delightful companion for his whole life, if an early death had not carried her away. She had however borne him several children, of whom three girls, Margaret, Alice and Cecily, and one boy, John, are still living.

More did not however long remain single, but contrary to his friends' advice, a few months after his wife's death, he married a

---

5. Saint Augustine, *The City of God.*

widow, more for the sake of the management of his household, than to please his own fancy, as she is no great beauty, nor yet young, *nec bella admodum nec puella,* as he sometimes laughingly says, but a sharp and watchful housewife; with whom nevertheless he lives, on as sweet and pleasant terms as if she were as young and lovely as any one could desire; and scarcely any husband obtains from his wife by masterfulness and severity as much compliance as he does by blandishments and jests. Indeed, what more compliance could he have, when he has induced a woman who is already elderly, who is not naturally of a yielding character, and whose mind is occupied with business, to learn to play on the harp, the viol, the spinet and the flute, and to give up every day a prescribed time to practice? With similar kindness he rules his whole household, in which there are no tragic incidents, and no quarrels. If anything of the kind should be likely, he either calms it down, or applies a remedy at once. And in parting with any member of his household he has never acted in a hostile spirit, or treated him as an enemy. Indeed his house seems to have a sort of fatal felicity, no one having lived in it without being advanced to higher fortune, no inmate having ever had a stain upon his character.

It would be difficult to find any one living on such terms with a mother as he does with his step-mother. For his father had brought in one stepmother after another; and he has been as affectionate with each of them as with a mother. He has lately introduced a third, and More swears that he never saw anything better. His affection for his parents, children and sisters is such, that he neither wearies them with his love, nor ever fails in any kindly attention.

His character is entirely free from any touch of avarice. He has set aside out of his property what he thinks sufficient for his children, and spends the rest in a liberal fashion. When he was still dependent on his profession, he gave every client true and friendly counsel with an eye to their advantage rather than his own, generally advising them, that the cheapest thing they could do was to come to terms with their opponents. If he could not persuade them to do this, he pointed out how they might go to law at least expense; for there are some people whose character leads them to delight in litigation.

In the city of London, where he was born, he acted for some years as judge in civil causes. This office, which is by no means burdensome,—inasmuch as the Court sits only on Thursday before dinner,—is considered highly honorable; and no judge ever disposed of more suits, or conducted himself with more perfect integrity. In most cases he remitted the fees which are due from the litigants, the practice being for the plaintiff to deposit three groats before the hearing, and the defendant a like sum, and no more being allowed to be exacted. By such conduct he made himself extremely popular in the city.

He had made up his mind to be contented with this position, which was sufficiently dignified without being exposed to serious dangers. He has been thrust more than once into an embassy, in the conduct of which he has shown great ability; and King Henry in consequence would never rest until he dragged him into his court. 'Dragged him,' I say, and with reason; for no one was ever more ambitious of being admitted into a court, than he was anxious to escape it. But as this excellent monarch was resolved to pack his household with learned, serious, intelligent and honest men, he especially insisted upon having More among them,—with whom he is on such terms of intimacy that he cannot bear to let him go. If serious affairs are in hand, no one gives wiser counsel; if it pleases the King to relax his mind with agreeable conversation, no man is better company. Difficult questions are often arising, which require a grave and prudent judge; and these questions are resolved by More in such a way, that both sides are satisfied. And yet no one has ever induced him to accept a present. What a blessing it would be for the world, if magistrates like More were everywhere put in office by sovereigns!

Meantime there is no assumption of superiority. In the midst of so great a pressure of business he remembers his humble friends; and from time to time he returns to his beloved studies. Whatever authority he derives from his rank, and whatever influence he enjoys by the favour of a powerful sovereign, are employed in the service of the public, or in that of his friends. It has always been part of his character to be most obliging to every body, and marvellously ready with his sympathy; and this disposition is more conspicuous than ever, now that his power of doing good is greater. Some he relieves with money, some he protects by his authority, some he promotes by his recommendation, while those whom he cannot otherwise assist are benefited by his advice. No one is sent away in distress, and you might call him the general patron of all poor people. He counts it a great gain to himself, if he has relieved some oppressed person, made the path clear for one that was in difficulties, or brought back into favour one that was in disgrace. No man more readily confers a benefit, no man expects less in return. And successful as he is in so many ways,—while success is generally accompanied by self-conceit,—I have never seen any mortal being more free from this failing.

I now propose to turn to the subject of those studies which have been the chief means of bringing More and me together. In his first youth his principal literary exercises were in verse. He afterwards wrestled for a long time to make his prose more smooth; practising his pen in every kind of writing in order to form that style, the character of which there is no occasion for me to recall, especially to you, who have his books always in your hands. He took the greatest pleasure in declamations, choosing some disputable subject, as involving a keener exercise of mind. Hence, while still a youth, he attempted a dialogue, in which he carried the defence of Plato's community even to the matter of wives! He wrote an answer to Lucian's *Tyrannicide*, in which argument it was his wish to have me for a rival, in order to test his own proficiency in this kind of writing.

He published his *Utopia* for the purpose of showing, what are the things that occasion mischief in commonwealths; having the English constitution especially in view, which he so thoroughly knows and understands. He had written the second book at his leisure, and afterwards, when he found it was required, added the first off-hand. Hence there is some inequality in the style.

It would be difficult to find any one more successful in speaking *ex tempore*, the happiest thoughts being attended by the happiest language; while a mind that catches and anticipates all that passes, and a ready memory, having everything as it were in stock, promptly supply whatever the time, or the occasion, demands. In disputations nothing can be imagined more acute, so that the most eminent theologians often find their match, when he meets them on their own ground. Hence John Colet, a man of keen and exact judgment, is wont to say in familiar conversation, that England has only one genius, whereas that island abounds in distinguished intellects.

However averse he may be from all superstition, he is a steady adherent of true piety; having regular hours for his prayers, which are not uttered by rote, but from the heart. He talks with his friends about a future life in such a way as to make you feel that he believes what he says, and does not speak without the best hope. Such is More, even at Court; and there are still people who think that Christians are only to be found in monasteries! Such are the persons, whom a wise King admits into his household, and into his chamber; and not only admits, but invites, nay, compels them to come in. These he has by him as the constant witnesses and judges of his life,—as his advisers and travelling companions. By these he rejoices to be accompanied, rather than by dissolute young men or by fops, or even by decorated grandees, or by crafty ministers, of whom one would lure him to silly amusements, another would incite him to tyranny, and a third would suggest some fresh schemes for plundering his people. If you had lived at this Court, you would, I am sure, give a new description of Court life, and cease to be *Misaulos*;[6] though you too live with such a prince, that you cannot wish for a better, and have some companions like Stromer and Copp, whose sympathies are on the right side. But what is that small number compared with such a swarm of distinguished men as Mountjoy, Linacre, Pace, Colet, Stokesley, Latimer, More, Tunstall, Clerk, and others like them, any one of whose names signifies at once a world of virtues and accomplishments? However, I have no mean hope, that Albert, who is at this time the one ornament of our Germany, will attach to his household a multitude of persons like himself, and set a notable example to other princes; so that they may exert themselves in their own circles to do the like.[7]

6. A hater of courts.
7. The letter trails off in gossip and compliments; the portrait of More is complete.

Criticism

Essays and Studies

A Note on the First Four Essays

Four contrasting books on *Utopia* frame the discussion which, over the last century, has sprung up around More and his erudite little joke. The very presence of Karl Kautsky among the students of More is an occasion for surprise; for he was not a man of letters, not a medieval historian, not a Catholic apologist, not even an Englishman—and thus seems to have none of those titles which would "justify" an interest in More. He was a practical and practicing communist, born in Austria and active all his life in the vigorous internecine squabbling that seems natural to communist sects. He served as secretary to Friedrich Engels; and as editor (posthumous) to Karl Marx, assembling from notes the last volume of *Das Kapital*; he was the intimate of the German Spartacist (communist) leaders Karl Liebknecht and Rosa Luxemburg. During a long and active life, he produced numerous volumes, the character of which can be estimated from their titles: *Karl Marx' ökonomische Lehren* (1887), *Geschichte des Sozialismus* (1894), *Die soziale Revolution* (1902), *Der Weg zur Macht* (1909), and *Die materialistische Geschichtsauffassung* (1927). But apparently the beatification of More by Pope Leo XIII in 1886 stirred latent chords of sympathy in Kautsky, for just two years later he produced his own full-length study of More and his *Utopia*.

As might be expected, Kautsky's interest in More was as a precursor of socialism; and he made the most, as might also be expected, of everything in More's life and writings that could be turned to serve this frankly polemical and partisan purpose. R. W. Chambers's biography of More, on the other hand, served the contrasting ideology, though less explicitly. It too was inspired by an act of the Catholic Church. Four hundred years after More's execution, Pope Pius XI, in 1935, declared him a saint and officially canonized him. Though Chambers was himself an Anglican, not a Catholic, he arranged for publication of his biography to coincide with the canonization of his subject; and the ideological bias of the book, as Kautsky would call it, is strongly Catholic. Chambers's volume makes, in fact, only the barest mention of Kautsky; but there can be no question that the later writer knew the work of his predecessor and pointed many of his arguments directly against the positions assumed by Kautsky. For Chambers, More is not the precursor of socialism at all; he is the spokesman of a medieval and a monastic way of life. The contrast between the two views couldn't be sharper.

During the late 1940s, Russell Ames and J. H. Hexter carried the dispute forward, while at the same time edging on both sides toward a safer middle ground. Their books were written consecutively, though at no great interval of time, when both were teaching at Queens College in New York City; there was some mutual polemic, though it is greatly softened in the final versions of both books. Essentially Ames, while accepting Kautsky's premises, qualifies his conclusions by proposing More as a liberal bourgeois criticizing feudal cruelties and irrationalities. Hexter, while softening Chambers's insistence on the monastic and illiberal character of the *Utopia*, still urges that the essential emphasis of More's book falls on the need for reform of the conscience. This is not Hexter's last word on the subject, and an inquisitive reader should compare his introduction to the edition of *Utopia* in Volume IV of the Yale University Press edition. Still, the contrast between Ames and Hexter is nearly as sharp as that between Kautsky and Chambers. The reader will decide for himself which presents the More, or the *Utopia*, that best answers to his own reading of the book and of the author's life.

KARL KAUTSKY

The Roots of More's Socialism†

As a Humanist and a politician, More was in the front rank of his contemporaries, as a Socialist he was far ahead of them all. His political, religious, and Humanist writings are to-day only read by a small number of historians. Had he not written *Utopia* his name would scarcely be better known to-day than that of the friend who shared his fate, Bishop Fisher of Rochester.[1] His socialism made him immortal.

Whence originated this socialism?

Unlike the historians of the idealistic school, we do not believe in a Holy Spirit which illumines minds and fills them with ideas, to which the political and economic development adapts itself. We rather start from the assumption that the contradictions and antagonisms which the economic development creates in society stimulate thought and provoke investigations by men who are favourably situated to prosecute such researches, so that they may understand what is going on before their eyes and remove the suffering which contemporary conditions entail. In this way arise political and social ideas which influence contemporary thought, or at least, particular classes, in the degree that they respond to the actual conditions, and which are correct so far as they coincide with the interests of the aspiring classes.

So it comes about that certain ideas are only operative under certain conditions, that ideas which at one time encounter indifference and even scorn are taken up with enthusiasm, and often without

† From Karl Kautsky, *Thomas More and His Utopia*, tr. H. J. Stenning (New York, 1927), pp. 159–171 (Part III, Chapter 1, Section 1). First German edition 1888. Copyright 1927 by International Publishers Co., Inc. Reprinted by permission of the publisher. Footnotes are by R.M.A.
1. Like More, John Fisher refused to swear to the king's supremacy, and like More he was beheaded in 1535.

strict verification, a few decades later. Idealist historians are unable to explain why this is so; they are therefore obliged in the last resort to seek refuge in God, in a mystery, like all idealist philosophers; it is the "time spirit" which decides whether or not an idea shall achieve social validity.

The materialist conception of history alone explains the influence of particular ideas. It is not concerned to deny that every age has its particular ideas which condition it, and that these ideas form the dynamics of social development. It does not, however, stop at this point, but proceeds to investigate the forces which set the machinery in motion, and these it finds in the material conditions.

It is clear that ideas must be fermenting for some time before they can exercise any influence on the masses. There is a tendency to reproach the masses with running after novelties, whereas the truth is that they cling most obstinately to the old. The antagonism of the new economic conditions to the transmitted conditions and the ideas which accord therewith must be fairly pronounced before it penetrates to the mind of the masses. Where the acumen of the investigator perceives unbridgable antagonisms of classes, the average man sees only accidental personal disputes; where the investigator sees social evils which could only be removed by social transformations, the average man consoles himself with the hope that times are only temporarily bad and will soon improve. We are not speaking of the members of classes on the decline, most of whom will not face facts, but have in mind the nascent classes, whose interests it is to see, but who cannot see until they bump right up against the new conditions. Their ideas also were conditioned by the newly developing material conditions, but these conditions were not yet sharply defined enough to render the aspiring classes accessible to these ideas.

But a thinker who takes his stand on the material conditions may be a whole epoch in advance of his time, if he perceives a newly evolving mode of production and its social consequences not only sooner than most of his contemporaries, but straining far into the future, also glimpses the more rational mode of production into which it will develop.

Thomas More is one of the few who have been capable of this bold intellectual leap; at a time when the capitalist mode of production was in its infancy, he mastered its essential features so thoroughly that the alternative mode of production which he elaborated and contrasted with it as a remedy for its evils, contained several of the most important ingredients of Modern Socialism. The drift of his speculations, of course, escaped his contemporaries, and can only be properly appreciated by us to-day. Despite the immense economic and technical transformations of the last three hundred years, we find in *Utopia* a number of tendencies which are still operative in the Socialist Movement of our time.

Our first enquiry pertains to the causes of such an extraordinary phenomenon. If we are not to resort to spiritism and clairvoyance, there must have been a peculiar chain of circumstances which inclined More alone in his age towards socialist theories—Münzer's socialism was of a character quite different from More's and cannot therefore be taken into account.[2]

Despite the fact that, for obvious reasons, none of More's biographers has dealt with this question and that More himself gives us but few hints, we think we are able to indicate at least some of these causes, partly personal, partly of a local nature, which in conjunction with the general situation as we have sketched it in the first part, explain why Socialism found a theoretical expression earlier than Capitalism.

These circumstances are, put shortly, More's personal character, his philosophical training, his activity in practical affairs, and the economic situation of England.

More's personal character may indeed be regarded as one of the causes of his Socialism. Erasmus tells us how amiable, helpful, and full of sympathy with the poor and oppressed More was: he called him the protector of all the poor.

Only in the northern countries of Western Europe were the material conditions in the sixteenth century favourable to the formation of such a disinterested character. In the mercantile republics of Italy, as in the Courts of the Romance monarchies,[3] egotism, the grand feature of the new mode of production, reigned absolutely; it reigned openly, boldly, full of revolutionary defiance. It was a vast egotism, quite different from the cowardly, mendacious, despicable egotism of to-day, which hides itself behind conventional hypocrisy.

Generally speaking, in the towns of England and Germany, entirely different economic conditions prevailed from those in the Italian towns, and to a lesser degree in the towns of France and Spain. Agriculture, together with the Mark constitution,[4] still formed to a great extent the basis even of the urban mode of production; the separation of the country from the town was nowhere completely defined.

"As late as the year 1589, the Duke of Bavaria recognised that the burghers of Munich could not exist without commons. Tillage of the soil must then have been a chief support of the citizens" (L.L. v. Maurer).

At the commencement of the sixteenth century the primitive

2. Thomas Münzer, German religious enthusiast, who after polemicizing against Luther perished in the Peasants' War.
3. The French monarchy, and lesser monarchies associated with it.

4. The so-called Mark System allowed small groups of freemen to hold and cultivate land in common.

agrarian communism still existed in England. It had survived under cover of feudalism, and only then began to yield place to another system of agriculture. The features which corresponded to primitive communism still existed, especially among the lower population, and we meet them in More only slightly glossed over with the Humanistic and courtier traits and the self-censure which the conditions imposed upon him. In his serenity, tenacity, unyieldingness, selflessness, and helpfulness we see the impress of all the characteristics of communistic "Merry England."

But sympathy with the poor does not make one a socialist, although without that sympathy no one is likely to become a socialist. In order that socialist sentiments and ideas should grow out of this interest, it must be conjoined with a special economic situation, the existence of a working proletariat as a permanent mass phenomenon, and on the other hand profound economic insight.

The existence of a proletariat of vagabonds creates benevolence and induces almsgiving, but does not produce a socialism of the modern variety.

Now in More's time England was much favoured with respect to the economic development, much more so than, for example, Germany. In respect of the opportunity to appreciate it More's position was almost unique in the northern countries. The only persons who had then learnt to think scientifically and methodically, to generalise, and who were, therefore, capable of formulating a theoretical socialism, were the Humanists. Now in the northern countries Humanism was an exotic growth, in which no class had a special interest. While the Humanists in Italy were busily engaged in active affairs, and therefore gave expression to the economic and political tendencies of their time and country, the great majority of German Humanists were merely schoolmasters with no glimmering of practical affairs, who, instead of delving into the past for weapons in the struggles of the present, stood aloof from those struggles and retired to their studies, in order to live wholly in the past.

Germany's development did not tend to close the gap between science and life. On the contrary, the rudeness, the barbarism, the boorishness into which Germany sank to an increasing extent after the sixteenth century, and from which she did not emerge until the beginning of the eighteenth century, rendered the maintenance of science in Germany possible only by its being completely divorced from active life.

The fundamental cause of Germany's decay resided in the alteration of the trade routes after the end of the fifteenth century, which not only impeded the economic development in Germany, but transformed it for some time into economic retrogression.

The discoveries of the Portuguese in the second half of the fifteenth century opened a sea route to India. At the same time the old communications with the East through Asia Minor and Egypt were interrupted by the invasions of the Turks, while the caravan routes from Central Asia had previously been closed in consequence of local upheavals.

This paralysed not only the trade of the Mediterranean seaboard, but also that of the towns on the great German waterways, which, besides being the intermediaries of the trade between Italy and the North, traded with the East on their own account by other routes —via Trebizond and the Black Sea as well as the land route over Russia. The total effect of these changes was to sever the arteries of the German towns, especially of the Hansa towns on the Baltic and the towns in Southern Germany, Nuremberg, Augsburg, etc.

The towns on the Rhine and on the estuaries of the North Sea suffered less, but the trade which they supported was insignificant and its direction had changed. It flowed not from East to West, from South to North, but contrariwise.

Antwerp became for the sixteenth century what Constantinople had been in the fourteenth century and what London was to become in the eighteenth century: the centre of world trade, the focus of the treasures of the East, to which the Americas were now added, whence they were poured out over the whole of Europe.

The proximity of Antwerp inevitably exercised the most stimulating effect upon the commerce of England, and especially of London. And even in More's time England strove to acquire overseas possessions, although as yet without any great success. England's commerce increased as Germany's declined.

Out of mercantile the beginnings of industrial capital were already beginning to develop. Englishmen began to manufacture wool in their own country after the Flemish example, and even in the time of Henry VIII complaints were heard of the decay of independent handicraft in wool-combing. In Richard III's time, Italian merchants in England were accused (An Act touching the merchants of Italy) of buying up large quantities of wool and employing the weavers to prepare it.

But in the England of More the beginnings of the capitalist mode of production in agriculture were much more perceptible than these nuclei of industrial capital. It is one of England's most remarkable peculiarities that capitalism developed there earlier in agriculture than in industry.

The causes of this have already been indicated: they are to be traced to the quality of English wool, which made it a much-sought-after raw material for woolen manufactures.

Next to wool, timber and fuel were important agricultural products in England, in view of the growth of the towns, as was barley for the Flemish breweries. The demand for wool grew in the degree that manufactures on the one hand, and the means of transport on the other, developed. At the outset English wool found its chief market in the Netherlands, but at the end of the fifteenth century it was being exported both to Italy and to Sweden. Among other things, this may be inferred from two commercial treaties which Henry VII concluded with Denmark and Florence in 1490.

As the market grew, the merchants and great landowners of England redoubled their efforts to extend wool production. The landowners found the simplest way of doing this was to claim for themselves the common lands which the peasants had a right to use. Thus the peasant was more and more deprived of the opportunity of keeping cattle, his entire business fell into disorder, and financial ruin overtook him. Then the great landowner's land hunger grew more quickly than the peasant was "freed" from the soil. All kinds of expedients were adopted. Not merely individual peasants, but sometimes the inhabitants of entire villages and even small townships were expelled, to make room for sheep.

So long as the landlords themselves farmed their estates, or, as happened for a short period, leased portions of them to tenants, to whom they advanced the necessary agricultural plant, cattle, etc., the expansion of their property was always limited by the plant and stock which the landlord possessed. There was no point in extending his property unless he was able at the same time to add to his plant and stock. This limit melted away and the land hunger of the great landowners knew no bounds with the arrival of the capitalist farmer, who used his own capital to employ wage workers to cultivate the land which he leased. This class arose in England in the last third of the fifteenth century. It rapidly increased in the sixteenth century, in consequence of the unexampled profits which it then made, and which not only accelerated the accumulation of capital, but also attracted capitalists from the towns.

The rise of profits is to be especially attributed to the depreciation of gold and silver which was caused by the immense transfers of the precious metals from America to Europe; the effect of this monetary depreciation may well have been accentuated by the currency debasement of princes.

In the course of the sixteenth century the prices of agricultural products rose by 200 to 300 per cent. in consequence of the currency depreciation. Rents, on the other hand, were slow in rising, as the leases ran for long terms and did not keep pace with the prices of agricultural products. Therefore they fell actually if not nominally.

The farmers' profits grew at the expense of rents.

This not only increased the number of farmers and the amount of their capital, but also formed a fresh incentive for the large landowners to extend their estates, in order to make good their losses in this way.

The consequence was a rapid impoverishment of the small peasants. A concurrent phenomenon was the dispersal of the feudal bands of retainers, to which we have made reference in the first part

The retainers were in any case a burden for the working people. Where they remained in existence, they were a burden on the peasants who were obliged to support them. Where they were broken up, they became a scourge to the wage earners, by swelling the ranks of the unemployed.

The fourteenth and fifteenth centuries were the Golden Age for the peasants and wage workers of England.

At the end of this epoch they were both suddenly plunged into deepest poverty. The number of workless swelled to terrible dimensions. The most gruesome punishments were not, of course, calculated either to diminish their numbers or to restrain them from crime: punishment for crime was uncertain, but sure was the punishment for abstention from crime: starvation.

Not much better than the situation of the workless was that of the propertyless workers, who then began to form a numerous class in agriculture. What parliamentary legislation had only incompletely achieved in the preceding two centuries was easily attained in the sixteenth century by the oppressive weight of the reserve army of the workless. Real wages diminished, and labour time was extended.

Food prices rose by 300 per cent., wages only by 150 per cent. From More's time onwards began that steady decay of the English workers in town and country, whose position reached its lowest level in the last quarter of the eighteenth and the first quarter of the nineteenth century, after which it improved, at least for certain sections, owing to trade union organisation.

Wages fell along with rents, profits grew, and so did capitalism.

When capitalism first invades industry and then turns to agriculture, it seems at the onset to wear a benevolent aspect. It must aim at a constant extending of the market, of production, while the importation of labour-power proceeds but slowly. In its early stages, such an industry is always complaining of the lack of labour-power. Capitalists must outbid handicraftsmen and peasants in order to entice away from them their journeymen and bondsmen: wages rise.

In this way capitalism began in many countries; it was hailed as a blessing. Not so in England, where it first invaded and revolutionised agriculture. Improvements in methods of cultivation made many workers superfluous. Capitalism in agriculture meant the direct setting-free of workers. In England this process of setting-free proceeded in its severest forms, at a time when industry was developing but slowly and required only small supplies of labour-power; least of all, the ignorant country labourer.

And hand in hand with the separation of the workers from the land, from their means of production, a rapid concentration of landed property into a few hands was going on.

Nowhere else in Europe, therefore, were the unfavourable reactions of the capitalist mode of production upon the working classes so immediately obvious as in England; nowhere did the unhappy workers clamour so urgently for assistance.

That such an economic situation should cause a man of More's character to reflect and to cast about for means of alleviating the intolerable conditions is what we should expect.

More was not the only person who sought for and propounded such expedients. From numerous writings of that time, from numerous Acts of Parliament we may perceive how deep was the impression made by the economic revolution then proceeding, and how generally the shabby practices of the landlords and their tenants were condemned.

But none of those who put forward remedies had a wider outlook, to none of them came the conviction that the sufferings incident to the new mode of production could only be ended by a transition to another and higher mode of production; none of them, save More, was a Socialist.

A theory of Socialism could only arise within the realm of Humanism. As a Humanist, More learned to think methodically and to generalise. As a Humanist he was enabled to look beyond the horizon of his time and his country; in the writings of classical antiquity he became acquainted with social conditions different from those of his own time. Plato's ideal of an aristocratic-communist community must have prompted him to imagine social conditions which, being the opposite of those existing, were free from their concomitant poverty. Plato's authority must have encouraged him to regard such a community as more than a mere figment of the imagination, and to set it up as a goal which humanity should strive to attain.

In so far was Humanism favourable to More's development. But the situation in England was, in a scientific respect, similar to that in Germany: English Humanism remained an imported, exotic growth, without roots in the national life, a mere academic affair. Had More been a mere Humanist, he would hardly have attained to Socialism. We know, however, that More's father, much to the regret of Erasmus and his other Humanist friends, soon tore him away from his studies, in order to put him to the study of law and then to launch him on a practical career. We know in what close relationship More stood to the London merchants, how he was entrusted with the care of their interests on every important occasion. The majority of the positions which More filled impelled him to deal with economic questions; the fact that he was appointed to these posts also proves that he was regarded as an expert in economic matters.

We know that he was a popular advocate, that in 1509 he was appointed Under-Sheriff, in which position he had sufficient opportunity to gain an insight into the economic life of the people. We have also mentioned several missions of which he was a member, for the conduct of commercial negotiations. The first was to Bruges in 1515. In the same year Parliament appointed him a Commissioner of Sewers. His second mission was to Calais in 1517, in order to compose disputes between English and French merchants. In 1520 we find him on a mission to Bruges, to settle disputes between English merchants and the Hansa. Then he became Treasurer, and, in 1523, Speaker in the Commons, both positions presupposing experience in financial matters, and shortly afterwards Chancellor of the Duchy of Lancaster: truly, if anybody had an opportunity to become acquainted with the economic life of his time, it was More. And he became acquainted with it from the most modern standpoint that was then possible, from that of the English merchant, for whom world trade was then opening up. In our view, this close connection of More with mercantile capital cannot be too strongly emphasised. To this we attribute the fact that More thought on modern lines, that his Socialism was of a modern kind.

We believe that we have disclosed the most essential roots of More's Socialism: his amiable character in harmony with primitive communism; the economic situation of England, which brought into sharp relief the disadvantageous consequences of capitalism for the working class; the fortunate union of classical philosophy with activity in practical affairs—all these circumstances combined must have induced in a mind so acute, so fearless, so truth-loving as More's an ideal which may be regarded as a foregleam of Modern Socialism.

R. W. CHAMBERS†

The Meaning of *Utopia*

An ex-Cabinet minister is still alive who dates his political career from the accidental purchase of a copy of *Utopia* at a second-hand bookstall. One of his colleagues in the Cabinet has written of

† From R. W. Chambers, *Thomas More*, (London: Jonathan Cape, 1953), pp. 125–132, 135–137, and 143–144. Reprinted by permission of Jonathan Cape Ltd. on behalf of the Estate of R. W. Chambers. References to the text of Utopia have been changed to reflect the paging of this edition. Chambers's notes are marked as his; others are by R.M.A.

Utopia, that no treatise is better calculated to nourish the heart of a Radical. *Utopia* has become a text-book of Socialist propaganda. It did more to make William Morris a Socialist than ever Karl Marx did.[1] All this testifies to its abiding power; yet we must never think of More as writing it for Nineteenth-Century Radicals or Twentieth-Century Socialists. Even he could not do that.

The first step to an appreciation of *Utopia* is to understand how it must have struck a scholar in the early Sixteenth Century. That is a difficult task, yet not an impossible one; and if we would understand More himself, it is a task which we must undertake.

We shall then find, I think, that few books have been more misunderstood than *Utopia.* It has given the English language a word 'Utopian' to signify something visionary and unpractical. Yet the remarkable thing about *Utopia* is the extent to which it adumbrates social and political reforms which have either been actually carried into practice, or which have come to be regarded as very practical politics. Utopia is depicted as a sternly righteous and puritanical State, where few of us would feel quite happy; yet we go on using the word 'Utopia' to signify an easy-going paradise, whose only fault is that it is too happy and ideal to be realized. *Utopia* is the first of a series which we have christened 'Ideal Commonwealths'. Some of these, for example William Morris' *News from Nowhere,* really *are* ideal. They are 'Utopian' in the current sense, that is to say, they are quite unpractical fancies of what this world might be like if the dreamer could shatter it to bits, and then remould it nearer to the heart's desire. For instance, in *News from Nowhere* we might be sure that the Divine Worship of the citizens would be Morris' ideal. If he gives them no Divine Worship, that also tells its tale. Now, More does not make his Utopians Christian. So modern scholars have argued: 'Utopia is an ideal commonwealth; *argal* More thought the vague deism of his Utopians more ideal than the popular religious beliefs of his time.'

Such argument might be reasonable if *Utopia* were a modern 'Ideal Commonwealth'. But we must never forget that More's education fell not in the Nineteenth but in the Fifteenth Century. To a man educated in that century, the distinction was obvious between the virtues which might be taught by human reason alone, and the further virtues taught by Catholic orthodoxy. It was part of the medieval system to divide the virtues into the Four Cardinal Virtues (to which the heathen might attain) and the Three Christian Virtues. The Four Cardinal Virtues—Wisdom, Fortitude, Temperance, and Justice—are the foundation of Plato's common-

1. William Morris (1834–96), among his many other diverse activities, was a socialist agitator. *News from Nowhere,* his brief tract, is Marxism with a thick overlay of nostalgia for the medieval.

wealths, as outlined in the *Republic* and the *Laws*.[2] These virtues were taken into the medieval system—part of the immense debt it owes to Greek philosophy. The Three Christian Virtues—Faith, Hope, and Charity—come of course from St. Paul's *First Epistle to the Corinthians*. Four and Three make Seven—the Perfect Number, which was extremely comforting. The perfect Christian character must comprise all seven. But the four heathen virtues were sufficient to ensure that a man or a State might be a model of conduct in secular matters. In Dante's *Divine Comedy* Virgil represents Philosophy, Reason, Human Wisdom. He is able to rescue Dante from the dark wood (although he was one of those who had not the three sacred virtues) because he knew and followed the four other virtues without fault. So Virgil can guide Dante till he meets Beatrice, but can go no further.

For a pattern of a State, Dante turns to Heathen Rome or to Heathen Greece. And it is not because of his deep learning that Dante does this. Our great English medieval poet, William Langland, the author of *Piers Plowman*, had but a commonplace education, but his system is similar. *Do Well* is the virtue of secular life, and the examples of it are the great non-Christian philosophers and rulers: Aristotle, Solomon, Socrates, Trajan. *Do Better* and *Do Best* represent forms of Christian virtues. And so More's friend, Busleiden, in his introductory letter to *Utopia*, tells us that the perfect commonwealth must unite 'Wisdom in the ruler, Fortitude in the soldiers, Temperance in private individuals, and Justice in all'.

In basing his *Utopia* upon these four heathen virtues, More is following medieval tradition; further, he is following his great examples, Plato's *Republic* and *Laws*; but, above all, he makes his satire upon contemporary European abuses more pointed. The virtues of Heathen Utopia show up by contrast the vices of Christian Europe. But the Four Cardinal Virtues are subsidiary to, not a substitute for, the Christian virtues. More has done his best to make this clear. It is not his fault if he has been misunderstood, as the following example will show.

Most of us would agree with Dame Alice in deploring More's extreme austerities.[3] We have seen that, years before *Utopia* was written, she had complained to More's confessor about that shirt of hair. It was no good. It may have been some ten years after *Utopia* was written that, as Roper tells us, More's daughter-in-law, young Anne Cresacre, noticed it:

> My sister More, in the summer as he sat at supper, singly in his doublet and hose, wearing thereupon a plain shirt, without ruff or

2. *Republic*, Book IV; *Laws*, Book XII [Chambers's note].
3. Dame Alice was More's second wife, who strongly objected to her husband's strict principles and ascetic practices.

collar, chancing to spy, began to laugh at it. My wife [Margaret Roper] not ignorant of his manner, perceiving the same, privily told him of it; and he, being sorry that she saw it, presently amended it. He used also sometimes to punish his body with whips, the cords knotted, which was known only to my wife, whom for her secrecy above all other he specially trusted, causing her, as need required, to wash the same shirt of hair.[4]

Now, despite all this, we are told that the Utopians condemn bodily austerities as 'a point of extreme madness, and a token of a man cruelly minded toward himself'.

More's biographers and commentators have been puzzled. Yet the very next sentence of *Utopia* explains the puzzle. The Utopians have only reason to guide them, and they believe that *by man's reason* nothing can be found truer than their view, '*unless any godlier be inspired into man from Heaven*'. The same point is made by More later. There *are* orders of ascetics in *Utopia*: if the ascetics grounded their action on reason the Utopians would mock them; but as they base it on religion, the Utopians honour them and regard them as holy.[5]

We find More, a dozen years later, urging against the Reformers this same doctrine which lies at the root of *Utopia*: 'That Reason is servant to Faith, not enemy.' More argues against the Lutherans that Reason, Philosophy, and even Poetry have their part to play: the Lutherans, who would cast away all learning except the Bible are, says More, 'in a mad mind', and he quotes St. Jerome to prove that pagan Philosophy and Poetry have their use for Christians. By 'Poetry' More of course means any work of the imagination: his Protestant critics deride *Utopia* as 'poetry', and More himself as a 'poet'. When a Sixteenth-Century Catholic depicts a pagan state founded on Reason and Philosophy, he is not depicting his ultimate ideal. Erasmus tells us that More's object was 'to show whence spring the evils of States, with special reference to the English State, with which he was most familiar'. The underlying thought of *Utopia* always is, *With nothing save Reason to guide them, the Utopians do this; and yet we Christian Englishmen, we Christian Europeans ...!*

Just as More scored a point against the wickedness of Christian Europe, by making his philosophers heathen, so Jonathan Swift scored a point against the wickedness of mankind by representing *his* philosophers, the Houyhnhnms, as having the bodies of horses. Yet we do not call Swift inconsistent, because he did live on a diet of oats, or, like poor Gulliver, fall into the voice and manner of horses in speaking. Swift did not mean that all horses are better

4. Roper, *Life of More*, p. 49   5. *Utopia*, above, pp. 54–55 and 83. [Chambers's note].

than all men. He meant that some men are worse than horses.
More did not mean that Heathendom is better than Christianity.
He meant that some Christians are worse than heathen.

Dante and Langland and innumerable medieval writers had said
the same before him. The conviction that life might be nobly lived
on the basis of the four heathen cardinal virtues was one which the
Catholic Middle Ages had inherited from Greek philosophy.

So, naturally, More is interested in the problem which for half a
lifetime tormented Dante and Langland; what will be the fate, in
the next world, of the just heathen, who are an example to us in
the affairs of this world? More's answer is tentative, but he quotes
with approval the 'comfortable saying' of Master Nicholas de Lyra,
the Franciscan, Dante's younger contemporary. Nicholas de Lyra
argued that, though a much fuller faith is demanded from Christians, it suffices for the heathen to have believed 'that God is, and
that He is the rewarder of them that seek Him'; these are, says de
Lyra, 'two points such as every man may attain by natural reason,
holpen forth with such grace as God keepeth from no man'.

And More quoted this,[6] not in his alleged 'emancipated' youth,
but in his last book, the *Treatise upon the Passion*, written in the
Tower, when he had dismissed all worldly affairs, and was awaiting
martyrdom 'for the faith of the Catholic Church'.

What, then, is the attitude of *Utopia* as to these two articles,
which represent, in More's view, the orthodoxy to which a heathen
may attain? King Utopus tolerated all varieties of belief and disbe-
lief, save on these two points; he forbade, 'earnestly and straitly'
that any man should disbelieve in either (1) Divine Providence, or
(2) a future life in which, as the Utopians believed, the just would
be rewarded by God's presence.

So far was this simple creed from appearing lax to More's friends,
that the marginal note (written either by Erasmus or by Peter
Giles) contrasts the Utopian faith in immortality with the laxity
and doubts of many Christians: '*The immortality of the soul, concerning which not a few, though Christians, to-day doubt or dispute.*' But in Utopia, the man who disbelieves either of these articles is not counted as a citizen, or even as a man; he is excluded from
all office, and despised, as being necessarily of a base and vile
nature. To suffer lifelong public contumely, in a land where all life
is lived in public, and where, save as a citizen, a man has and is
nothing, is a punishment which many would feel to be worse than
death. Yet the sceptic may not, publicly, argue in his own defence.
Then comes the sentence which has been so often quoted, out of its
context. In the old translation it runs, 'Howbeit they put him to no

6. *Works*, 1557, p. 1287-8 [Chambers's note].

punishment'. Of course, More did not write such nonsense. What he really says is, 'They do not put him to any bodily punishment' —so long, that is, as he humbly submits to the disgrace and to the silence which his heresies involve.[7] The charge against More of inconsistency rests upon refusing to notice his distinction between liberty to hold an opinion, and liberty to preach that opinion; between a man being in More's phrase ' a heretic alone by himself', and being 'a seditious heretic'.

Bishop Creighton,[8] to prove that More in later life 'put his principles aside', quotes the passage which tells how King Utopus, when settling the Utopian constitution, found many religions prevalent in the land, and ordained that they should all be tolerated. Creighton then omits the passage about Utopus disgracing and muzzling those who held the opinions he thought pernicious. But this passage is vital; for, in the light of it, we find that Utopus did *not* tolerate the preaching of all views, but only of those which he, in his wisdom, thought tolerable. Then Creighton begins to quote again. Even those who held most noxious opinions 'were put to no punishment'. They are put to no bodily punishment, so long as they will submit to being disfranchised, despised, and silenced.

But, as the watchman says to Dogberry, 'How if they will not?'[9] We can tell what would happen *then*, when we remember that, even in the discussion of such opinions as the State allows, any violent or seditious speech is punished in Utopia by banishment or bondage. And, in Utopia, if a man condemned to bondage jibs at his punishment, he is slain out of hand like a wild beast. Suppose that two sceptics, who did not believe the soul of man to be immortal, had discussed, in private, in Utopia, how they could get the law repealed which silenced and disfranchised them. They would have incurred the penalty imposed on those who plot against the fundamental laws of Utopia. And, even for the highest magistrates, that penalty is death.

Still, within these narrow limits, the Utopian has liberty of conscience. He may not spread among the common people a belief which the State thinks harmful, nor may he discuss the most innocent opinions in a way likely to cause sedition and dissension. He may not, in private, discuss any affair of State. But, if he submits to these restrictions, he is left alone; he is not to be terrorized into saying that he believes what he does not believe.

It may be a low ideal of liberty which allows, to a man who holds

---

7. See translation, p. 81 and note 9.
8. Bishop Mandell Creighton, nineteenth-century historian, wrote many books on the early Reformation period in England.

9. The allusion is to Shakespeare's *Much Ado About Nothing*, Act III.

views disapproved by the authorities, freedom of thought only on condition that he does not claim freedom of speech. But that *is* the liberty Utopia allows. I shall try, later, to show how far More stuck to that ideal.

Utopia and the Problems of 1516

But we merely confuse the issues if we use our modern question-begging terminology, and contrast More's alleged 'emancipated youth' with his orthodox old age. If we try to judge it in relation to the early Sixteenth Century, we shall find that *Utopia* is by no means 'emancipated'; it is rather a protest against undue 'emancipation'.

Utopia is, in part, a protest against the New Statesmanship: against the new idea of the autocratic prince to whom everything is allowed. I do not say that it is an impartial protest. The evil counsellors, who are represented in the First Book of *Utopia* egging the prince to despotism, might have replied that their ideal was not necessarily base or sycophantic. Patriots have sometimes seen in tyranny the only force strong enough to make their country great; reformers have sometimes seen in it the only force strong enough to carry through the reformation they desire. But *Utopia* is hostile to it.

Again, *Utopia* is, in part, a protest against the New Economics: the enclosures of the great landowners, breaking down old law and custom, destroying the old common-field agriculture. Here again, we must not suppose that *Utopia* gives us the full story. There was much more in the problem of enclosures than the greed of the great landlord, 'the very plague of his native country'.[10] The up-to-date farmer was also in favour of sweeping away all traces of the older communal husbandry. Thomas Tusser, a humble but practical agriculturist, says:

> Where all things in common do rest,
> Yet what doth it stand ye in stead?[1]

Now, in contrast to this changing world, More depicts a state where "all things in common do rest', and where there is no place for the grabbing superman. More's theoretical *Utopia,* looking back to Plato's *Republic* and to corporate life in the Middle Ages, probably seemed to some contemporaries the reverse of 'progressive'. Cardinal Pole has told of a conversation he had in his youth with Thomas Cromwell. Cromwell ridiculed the *Republic* of Plato,

10. See *Utopia*, above, p. 14.
1. Thomas Tusser published in 1557 "A Hundredth Good Pointes of Husban-
drie," describing in lame but quaint verse the way to make crops grow.

which, after so many centuries, has led to nothing. *He* had a book on statesmanship in manuscript, by a practical modern writer, based on experience. The book which Cromwell offered to lend to Pole, was *The Prince* of Nicholas Machiavelli.[2]

It is noteworthy that the two most potent books on the State written in the Sixteenth Century were written within so few years of each other. Parts of *Utopia* read like a commentary on parts of *The Prince*, as Johnson's *Rasselas* reads like a commentary on Voltaire's *Candide*, though we know that in neither case can the English writer have read his continental predecessor.[3] There is a reason for the coincidence; before *The Prince* was written, ideas used in *The Prince* had been gaining ground. They were the 'progressive' ideas, and we may regard *Utopia* as a 'reaction' against them.[4] Over and over again, in Book I of *Utopia*, Raphael Hythlodaye imagines himself as counseling a prince, telling him what he ought to do, against those who are telling him what he *can* do; and always Raphael admits that these ideas of justice which he has brought from Utopia are opposed to all that the most-up-to-date statesmen of Europe are thinking and doing.

And so, from the point of view of the new age of Machiavellian statesmanship and commercial exploitation, *Utopia* is old-fashioned. The King is to 'live of his own', in medieval wise, and to turn a deaf ear to the counsellors who would make him all-powerful. The big landlords are to have mercy on their tenants, and not to allow them to be sacrificed to economic progress, and the law of supply and demand in the wool market.

* * *

Another leading problem of controversy was the immortality of the soul. Did philosophy and human reason, apart from revelation, teach such immortality? There were philosophers who said 'No'; and, three years before *Utopia* was published, this matter also had come before the Lateran Council.[5] Teachers of philosophy were enjoined to point out how Christian philosophy corrected the views of the heathen on immortality; they were to refute these heathen

2. *Epistolarum*, Pars i, Brescia, 1744, pp. 135–7. An attempt has been made to argue that Pole mistook the book, and that Cromwell really meant to lend him *The Courtier of* Castiglione. (Van Dyke, *Renascence Portraits*, p. 401.) The argument is unconvincing. [Chambers's note].

3. Dr. Johnson published *Rasselas* and Voltaire *Candide*, within a few weeks of each other in 1759; Machiavelli's *Prince* was written in 1513, two years before *Utopia*, though not published till much later.

4. I had written this before reading Her-

mann Oncken's lecture on the *Utopia* (1922), but I am glad to find that I have the support of his authority: *Sitzungsberichte der Heidelberger Akademie, Phil.-Hist. Klasse* (1922), 2, p. 12 [Chambers's note].

5. 19 Dec. 1513: *Concilium Lateranense V, Sessio viii.* See *Conciliorum Omnium tomus XXXIV*, Paris, 1644, pp. 333–5, 557 [Chambers's note]. [The Lateran Council, held in the Roman church of St. John Lateran, was the last of five going under that name. It was in session from 1512 to 1517 (R.M.A.).]

errors, and steps were taken to ensure that the student *in sacris ordi-nibus constitutus*[6] should not spend more than five years upon philosophy and poetry, before diluting them with the safer studies of theology and pontifical law.

Now, let us try and look at *Utopia* from the point of view of 1516. Here is a heathen community, whose religion is founded on philosophy and natural reason. Yet, so far from doubting the immortality of the soul, they base their whole polity upon it. No disbeliever in immortality may be a citizen of Utopia. In life, and in death, every true Utopian has a firm trust in the communion of saints.

So that, in the eyes of More's friends, Erasmus or Peter Giles, *Utopia* is a striking defence of a vital tenet of the Christian faith. More will not tolerate the ambiguous formula: 'As an orthodox Catholic I believe in immortality; as a philosopher I doubt.' Reason and philosophy teach the Utopian to affirm that he is somehow in touch with the souls of the noble dead, mighty overseers whose presence encourages him to do his duty the more courageously.

Thus here we find More in *Utopia* opposing the scepticism of his age, precisely as we have seen him opposing its Machiavellian state-craft. And so thoroughly is *Utopia* a book of the hour, that here again More seems to be making a comment on a book which he had never seen. For it was in the very same November of 1516, in which Peter Giles was writing the dedicatory epistle of *Utopia*, that the professor of Philosophy at Bologna, Pomponazzi, published his famous treatise on the Immortality of the Soul. Pomponazzi submitted to the Church in all matters of faith, but, as a philosopher, he stubbornly upheld his doubt as to the doctrine of immortality.[7]

Therefore More's *Utopia*, among other things, is a contribution to this current controversy. More attacks the enemy in their philosophical camp, and makes his heathen Utopians into unexpected allies of the Catholic faith with regard to this great dogma—and, as we shall see later, with regard to other things as well.

But the imminent problem was monasticism. There was an incompatibility between the declining spirit of the monastic common life, and the rising commercialism of the grasping 'new rich'. Within a quarter of a century commercialism was to destroy monasticism in England. More stands, as it were, at the crossways, and asks, 'Why not destroy commercialism? Is not the spirit of the common life really better worth preserving?' It is significant that *the religious houses are the one European institution which the Utopians are said to approve.* And with reason, for in Utopia,

6. Students studying for holy orders, theology students.
7. The *Tractatus de immortalitate ani-mae* is dated Bologna, 6 Nov. 1516; *Utopia* is dated Antwerp, 1 Nov. 1516 [Chambers's note].

though the rule of celibacy is necessarily absent, the monastic idea is at work. The Utopian State is as sumptuous as many a religious house was. But the Utopian, like the monk or friar, may possess nothing. Everyone in Utopia must wear the common habit (in a letter to Erasmus we shall find More calling it Franciscan).[8] There are four varieties, for men and women, married and unmarried. The cloaks of the Utopians are all of one colour, and that is 'the natural colour of the wool.' Their hours of work, of recreation, the very games they may play, are all regulated. There are no foolish and pernicious games like dice. Instead, the Utopians have two games, one of which is intended to teach mathematics, and the other to teach morals. The Utopians eat in refectories, beginning every dinner and supper by reading something pertaining to good manners and virtue. Talk at table is initiated and directed by the elders, who graciously encourage the younger married people to join in the discussion, by turning it into a kind of oral examination. As for the men below twenty-two and the girls below eighteen: they serve, or else stand by, in marvellous silence, watching their elders eat and talk.

In much of this, More is perhaps joking; it was his way to utter his jests with such a solemn face as to puzzle his own household.[9] But, underneath More's fun, was a creed as stern as that of Dante, just as, underneath his gold chain, was the shirt of hair. And, quite certainly, the ideal of *Utopia* is discipline, not liberty. It is influenced by some of the most severe disciplines the world has ever known. Through Plato's *Republic* it goes back to the barrack life of a Spartan warrior; through More's own experience to the life of a Charterhouse monk.[1] And the discipline of Utopia is enforced rigidly, even ferociously. If the Utopian attempts to break the laws of his native land, there is the penalty of bondage, and, if that fails, of death. We have seen that even to speak of State affairs, except at the licensed place and hour, is punishable in Utopia with death, lest permission to discuss politics might lead to revolution. Has any State, at any time, carried terrorism quite so far?

Many framers of ideal commonwealths have shirked the question of compulsion, by imagining their citizens to have all become moral overnight. More does not choose this easy way. He recognizes that there will be a minority, to whom higher motives do not appeal. For them, there is penal servitude; if that fails, death.

But no great State can be founded on terrorism. For the mass of its citizens, Utopia is founded on religious enthusiasm. Faith in

8. P. S. Allen, ed., *Letters of Erasmus*, II, No. 499 [Chambers's note].
9. Cresacre More, 1726, p. 179; cf. *Works*, 1557, p. 127 [Chambers's note]. Cresacre More was Sir Thomas's great grandson; he compiled a life of his distinguished forebear about the year 1627 (R.M.A.).
1. A Carthusian monk, one attached to an extremely strict order.

God, and in the immortal destiny of the human soul, supplies the driving power which is to quench human passion and human greed.[2] Based on religion, Utopia is supported by a belief in the dignity of manual labour. Even rulers and magistrates, although legally exempt, share in this work as an example to others.[3] So a six-hour day suffices, and the rest of the time is free for those intellectual and artistic pursuits in which, to the Utopians, pleasure consists.[4] But religion is the basis of all.

Now a monk of to-day, Dom Ursmer Berlière, of the Abbey of Maredsous, has pointed out how at the beginning of the Middle Ages, monasticism, as St. Benedict shaped it, gave a pattern to the State. St. Benedict's monastery 'was a little State, which could serve as a model for the new Christian society which was arising from the fusion of the conquered and conquering races—a little State which had for its basis, religion; for its support, the honour given to work; for its crown a new intellectual and artistic culture.' The writer was not thinking of *Utopia*. I do not know if he had ever read it. But, at the end of the Middle Ages, we find More depicting a State founded on just these things: the common life, based on religion; honour given to manual labour; intellectual and artistic culture. However far these things might sometimes be from monastic practice, the writer of *Utopia* could never have approved of the destruction of monasticism; he looked for its reform.

* * *

We can only understand *Utopia* if we remember the Europe for which it was written; at home John Rastell preaching exploration to the More household;[5] abroad the travels of Vespucci in every man's hands; Vespucci, who had found folk holding property in common, and not esteeming gold, pearls, or jewels. (It is important to remember that the Inca empire of Peru, which in more than one detail had a likeness to Utopia, was not known till some fourteen years later; Cortes had not yet conquered Mexico.)

The problem of poverty and unemployment (destined in England to be aggravated by the Dissolution of the Monasteries) was already a European one. Ten years after *Utopia*, More's friend Vives wrote a tract on it.[6] At the root of More's interest in colonization lies his pity for the unemployed labourers:

'Poor silly[7] wretched souls; away they trudge out of their known

---

2. See *Utopia*, above, pp. 80–81.
3. *Ibid.*, pp. 42–43.
4. *Ibid.*, esp. pp. 41, 44.
5. John Rastell was More's brother-in-law.
6. Juan Luis Vives, Spanish humanist, wrote prodigiously on a vast range of subjects.
7. Foolish. The translation of *Utopia* is Ralph Robynson's; cf. above, *Utopia*, p. 14.

and accustomed houses; all their household stuff, being suddenly thrust out, they be constrained to sell it for a thing of naught. And when they have, wandering about, soon spent that, what can they do but steal, and then be hanged, or else go about abegging. Whom no man will set awork, though they never so willingly offer themselves thereto.'

But the fact that *Utopia* belongs to its age does not mean that it is the less epoch-making. Some things which may now seem commonplaces to us were less so then. It may seem quite natural to us that in Utopia there should be no class distinctions. It was less obvious to a scholar of the Renaissance. Plato's Commonwealths had been based on class distinction. In the *Laws* the citizens fall into four classes. In the *Republic*, also, there are classes, although so much attention is given to the warrior class, and their common life, that we almost forget the others. Plato is emphatic that every man should have one job only, and he does not waste words on his artisans, except to urge that they must be experts in their own business, and must stick to it. The Middle Ages inherited the same idea of the State: ploughmen and artisans to labour, clerks to pray and study, knights to fight. But the Utopian citizen does all three things; he labours with his hands, studies in his spare hours, and, though he hates warfare, is, at need, a soldier.

It is noteworthy that, despite his admiration for Greek life and thought, More did not build Utopia after the Hellenic pattern. His free citizens are not a privileged class dependent on slave labour, nor are his bondmen a distinct class. Bondage in Utopia is penal servitude—a humane substitute for the death penalty. The repentant bondman is restored to freedom, the incorrigible bondman is slain. But the citizens themselves are all workers.

Finally the outstanding feature of *Utopia* is implied in the great sentence with which Raphael ends his story:

> When I consider all these commonwealths which nowadays anywhere do flourish, so God help me, I can perceive nothing but a conspiracy of rich men, procuring their own commodities under the name and title of the commonwealth.

The Middle Ages had often been charitable to the poor, and More's age had inherited vast charitable endowments. More altogether approved of these endowments, and, later, we shall find him defending them against the fanaticism of reformers who wished to hand them over to a conspiracy of rich men procuring their own commodities under the title of the commonwealth. But More's claim for *justice* goes far beyond medieval admonitions to charity. Its publication throughout Europe by the printing press marks an epoch.

RUSSELL A. AMES

[More the Social Critic]†

More's *Utopia* expresses the various reforming purposes of the statesman, and the lawyer, the merchant, the humanist, and the man of religion. These purposes were, of course, intertwined and overlapping as well as distinguishable. The middle class, in its inconsistent and only partly conscious campaign against feudalism, had the merchants as its chief economic power and the humanists as its ideological shock troops—with More active in both groups. The *Utopia*, incorporating many views acceptable to the London merchants, presented a program of social reform, and was, first of all, a humanist tract. Its form and spirit owed much to classical literature and to religious tradition, but its substance was contemporary and secular.

The hypothesis may be very seriously projected that the *Utopia* in every detail had a practical meaning in More's day. This is not to say that More was urging his contemporaries immediately to institute in their societies every practice of the Utopians. The hypothesis implies, rather, that those Utopian practices which were fantastic consistently indicated a practical line of conduct which would be understood by sympathetic readers.

R. W. Chambers, in the most notable of recent books on More, shows that many Utopian customs and ordinances directly reflect More's opinions of current problems, particularly religious problems. Chambers believes, however, that More often makes his Utopians do things which are not approved because the Utopians follow reason rather than the imperatives of the Christian religion. It is more accurate to say that even when the Utopians depart from practices acceptable to Christianity, they do so in such a way as to indicate how a sixteenth century European should behave. Chambers feels that "The underlying thought of *Utopia* always is, *With nothing save Reason to guide them, the Utopians do this; and yet we Christian Englishmen, we Christian Europeans . . . !*"[1] This is certainly part of the meaning of Utopia; but it may be better phrased thus: *The Utopians, guided by Reason and also by their basically sound religion, have almost achieved a truly Christian ideal which they live by while we Christians do not.* In short, though More was limited by the necessities of keeping his fiction logical, consistent, and an adequate disguise for his attacks and proposals,

---

† From Russell Ames, *Citizen Thomas More and His Utopia* (Princeton: Princeton University Press, 1949), pp. 8-21. Reprinted by permission of the author. Unmarked notes are by Ames; others are by R.M.A. References to the text of *Utopia* have been changed to reflect the paging of this edition.
1. Chambers, p. 128, above, p. 149.

he makes every effort within this framework to teach social and religious truth. The Utopians "joine unto the reasons of Philosophye certeyne principles taken oute of religion: wythoute the whyche . . . they thynke reason of it selfe weake and unperfecte."[2] The Utopians have more than reason to guide them, and are quite conscious of the fact; their only real difference from Europeans is that they actually follow reason, which leads them closer and closer to Christian religion and to ideal Christian behavior.[3]

The hypothesis outlined above suggests the following type of analysis. Utopian children confess their misdeeds to their parents.[4] This does not mean that More advises English children to stop confessing to priests. It means two quite different things: first, the Utopians, though not in contact with Christianity, by reason and natural religion found their way to confession, and this proves that the confessional as ordained by the church is both a godly and a rational institution; secondly, the Utopian practice suggests that a virtuous Utopian parent is a better confessor than a corrupt European priest, and that the latter had better reform himself. Thus, the institution of confession is upheld, and at the same time reform is advocated. Similarly, when we see that in *Utopia* many religions are permitted, we should not assume that More advocates the dismemberment of European Christianity and the institution of many new religions. More does mean, however, in these years before Luther appeared on his horizon, that true faith will peacefully conquer false ideas, that bigoted repressions may halt that revival of true religion which Colet and Erasmus were attempting, and that it is unchristian for Portuguese gold-hunters to drive Indians into church with the sword. More's general discussion of religion in Utopia is meant to prove, not the superiority of agnosticism to Christianity, but that Christianity has nothing to fear from peace, freedom, and rational criticism.

The meaning of More's apparent advocacy of communism—a question more closely related to the main interest of this study—can be understood through a similar type of analysis. It is improbable, though possible, that More was a practical advocate of communism in England, however much he *may* have been drawn to the theory of it. The lesson of Utopian communism is, however, that economic conditions are the cause of social evils and that the English ruling classes will not make themselves happier and wealthier by overworking, dispossessing, hanging, or failing to employ the poor, or even by exhorting the poor with pious phrases to a better life. In such futile ways they will only impoverish their country. Instead, they

2. From Robynson's translation; see above, *Utopia*, p. 54.
3. Budé wrote that the Utopians "have adopted Christian usages both in public and in private" [Ames's note]. See Budé's letter to Lupset, above, p. 122 (R.M.A.).
4. See *Utopia*, above, p. 86.

must revive husbandry and cloth-working, improve law and government, and extend trade. Most critics of *Utopia* have spent so much time trying to prove either that communism won't work, or that More was not a communist, that they have ignored the immediate and practical significance of his economic criticism.

Many other aspects of the *Utopia* need detailed rather than abstract attention. More the lawyer, as well as More the saint, the humanist, and the statesman, wrote the book. His actual practice as a lawyer clearly led him to the severest criticism of legal trickery and injustice. His legal studies, however probably gave him part of his social ideals. The Roman law, to which he had some attachment as a member of a society of Roman lawyers, did support the claims of absolute monarchy, but it also, in the Justinian code, proposed a harmonious commonwealth of nations[5] which was an ideal of More's both in Utopia and in England. John Rastell, More's brother-in-law, in his preface to a *Book of Assizes* which he printed in 1513, praises the function of good laws as a curb upon greed: "Wealth, power and glory are . . . in themselves evil things, since they cannot be achieved except at the cost of impoverishment, subjection and humiliation. They cannot, for that reason, constitute the commonweal."[6]

Similarly, the influence of primitive Christian communism on *Utopia* has not been emphasized, though *Utopia* itself emphasizes it.[7] The direct effect of the Gospels must have been strong. Even more important was the republican, and more or less radical economic character of northern humanism. From this, which is not the main subject of the present study, probably flows the major influence on *Utopia*.

That the first book refers in a general way to contemporary social evils is, of course, obvious to all readers. That the whole work refers frequently to specific events with which More was often personally acquainted, is not so well known.

Some of the more obvious examples can show how specific these references were. Hythlodaye, telling why he will not take service as an adviser to princes, asked More how the king of France would respond if advised to govern his own land well and give up foreign invasion, and More admitted that the king would not be pleased with the advice.[8] This is no general, classical attack on war but a definite reference to the invasion of Italy by Francis I in the preceding year (1515) which culminated in the victory of Marignano in September. Clearly the advice against invasion applied equally well

5. J. N. Figgis, *Studies of Political Thought from Gerson to Grotius, 1414-1625*, 1931, p. 9. [Ames's note.] The codification of laws achieved under Justinian (482-565) was one of the great and enduring achievements of the late Roman Empire (R.M.A.).
6. Reed, p. 207.
7. See *Utopia* above, pp. 29 and 79.
8. See *Utopia* above, p. 25.

to Henry VIII's invasions of France (1512–1514). Hythlodaye's description of the way kings are advised to get money[9] perfectly describes the recent practices of Henry VII: juggling the value of currency, feigning war and taxing for it, reviving old laws to collect new fines, establishing new regulations to sell exemption from them. Particularly, the attack on the revival of old Crown privileges points to Henry VII's collection of dues for the knighting of his dead son Arthur, which More resisted in the parliament of 1504. It was noted above that shafts directed against Francis I also struck Henry VIII: similarly criticism of Henry VII applied in part to Henry VIII. Both the French and the Utopian practice of bribing and corrupting enemy populations suggested the intrigues of Henry VIII and his minister Dacre, who sowed treason among the Scotch lords. It is reasonable to assume that every item of criticism in *Utopia* recalled to well-informed readers precise events in current history, many of which may not be easy to identify today.

More's connections with the merchants of London, with the Court, and with humanists, kept him familiar also with more remote continental affairs and even with some African, Asian, and American conditions. Reports at this time from Sir Robert Wingfield, English ambassador to the Emperor Maximilian, are rich in references to the politics of eastern Europe, the Turkish threat, and Italian conditions. The direct attack on international intrigues in the first book of *Utopia*,[1] as well as the ironic attack in the second book,[2] were unusually apropos in these two years (1515–1516) when the book was being written. International relations were peculiarly unstable. Peace had just come in 1514 after England's successful wars against France. In 1515 France invaded Italy and won an unexpected victory which sharply changed the balance of forces. The new peace following was of the most fluid character, and the diplomatic correspondence of the time shows that all cats were ready to jump in any direction at any moment.

The influence of foreign events and conditions on Utopia has hardly been mentioned by its students, though Chambers discusses the problem of the unity of Christendom against the Turk, and points out, concerning More's embassy of 1515, that "Everywhere in *Utopia* we can trace the influence of these [Flemish] foreign scholars and foreign men of affairs, as well as of the civilization of the noble Flemish cities."[3] This was probably the most important continental influence, for More did not travel much elsewhere. It is noted by J. H. Lupton, who contrasts London with the towns of Flanders.[4]

---

9. See *Utopia* above, p. 25.
1. See *Utopia* above, pp. 23–25.
2. See *Utopia* above, p. 70.

3. Chambers, p. 120.
4. Lupton, pp. xxix–xxx.

Also important among the influences on *Utopia* were ideals of city and guild life, and a popular English devotion to the common weal. It is surprising that Kautsky, a socialist, neglects these, though he pays general tribute to the liberty-loving sentiments of the English and emphasizes his belief that More, in peculiar English conditions, differed from other humanists in his concern for the people. The youthful radicalism of John Rastell, More's brother-in-law, and his ideal of the commonwealth expressed in legal theory,[5] the common weal advocated by economists like Clement Armstrong[6]— all these, mentioned below, are native parallels to *Utopia*, and express its practical content, rather than its literary form as Plato's *Republic* does.

To summarize the problem of the general character of *Utopia*: rather abstract polemics over religion and communism, divorced from the detailed events of More's experience, have obscured *Utopia's* nature as an effort at practical social reform. The obscurity has been lighted up by Chambers, Seebohm, and Kautsky more than by other writers.

The two best books on More, those by Kautsky and Chambers, may now be given a general criticism. This is none too grateful a task, for the critic's sword is very likely to develop a reverse edge when he also attempts an interpretation of More and his *Utopia*. More's experience was so rich and varied, the society in which he lived so fast changing and contradictory in nature, his book so disguised in meaning, so many-sided, constructed on so many levels of reference, that almost any foolish speculation concerning *Utopia* is likely to have a little truth in it, and almost any well-founded hypothesis is bound to be incomplete and somewhat one-sided. A few claims and excuses can be made for the present study. It does not pretend to exhaust the subject: it does not concentrate on that aspect of *Utopia* which the present writer considers central—its nature as a pamphlet written to promote humanistic, Erasmian social reform. Secondly, this writer is quite certain that he has felt little or no compulsion to dress More in his own political and religious clothing. Lastly, this study consciously employs throughout the weakest of all forms of argument—analogy. The *Utopia* being itself the best evidence of what More was thinking when he wrote it, at the same time hiding much of this thought within many levels of meaning, interpretation must proceed by probability, by hopeful comparisons.

Kautsky's study, *Thomas More and His Utopia*, is the only one which gives full attention to the book as an expression of the views

5. Preface to the *Book of Assizes* (1513).
6. "A Treatise Concerninge the Staple and the Commodities of this Realme" (c. 1519–35), *Tudor Economic Documents*.

of the English middle class, particularly of the London merchants. It is a brilliant work but, unfortunately, little read. Kautsky, in much of his general historical view and in his detailed analysis of *Utopia*, is sound and flexible. Occasionally, however, his generalizations are loose and his applications of them mechanical. On a number of important points new materials and more concrete analysis suggest changes of emphasis, and even reversal of his interpretation.

Most of the faulty generalizations in Kautsky's work are rooted in what this study holds to be a mistaken view of the stage in historical development which England had reached in the early sixteenth century. Kautsky maintains that "In More's time capitalism was just beginning to gain the upper hand over the industry and agriculture of England. Its domination had not lasted long enough to effect a technical revolution. . . ."[7] It will be seen in Chapter I below that this description would probably apply better to the eighteenth century, better certainly to the end of the sixteenth century than to its beginning. Capitalism was yet a long way from *dominating* English society, but Kautsky's belief that it was doing so leads him to see the central conflict of the time as that between capitalism and the workers of England,[8] rather than between feudalism and capitalism.

Perhaps, as well we all tend to do, Kautsky has transferred his own dominant interest in his own time into the life of the past. Whatever the reason for it, his idea that capitalism was dominant and feudalism completely broken[9] causes him to view princely absolutism as almost identical in interests with capital,[1] the humanists as universally supporters of monarchy insofar as they had any political views,[2] the English nobility as completely subservient to the Crown,[3] the London citizens as the chief props of Tudor absolutism and the only rival of its power,[4] etc.

By claiming that the great landowners were at least temporarily helpless—as a result of the Wars of the Roses[5]—Kautsky tends, perhaps unconsciously, to consider the Tudor monarchy a great power in and of itself rather than a fulcrum for pressures, though occasionally he notes the rather feeble influence of various groups on government.[6]

Only one group is said to have had any substantial influence. "In More's time," Kautsky writes, "the citizens of London were a power for which the English kings had more respect than for the Church, the nobles, the peasants, and the country towns," the masters of London were "the actual masters of the country," and the "mer-

7. Kautsky, p. 205.
8. *Ibid.*, pp. 168–69, 171.
9. *Ibid.*, p. 119.
1. *Ibid.*, p. 17.
2. *Ibid.*, p. 99.

3. *Ibid*, pp. 115–16, 118.
4. *Ibid.*, p. 123.
5. *Ibid.*, p. 116.
6. *Ibid.*, pp. 120–24.

chants possessed the greatest power in London."[7] When we add Kautsky's implication that More was the leading representative of the London merchants,[8] More appears almost as the uncrowned king of England.

Of course, Kautsky does not mean to imply just this. He notes that though "the middle classes could not be bribed or intimidated . . . their representatives could; while the king could have members of Parliament who displeased him executed for high treason."[9] Also, he calls the London citizens "the decisive power in the realm *next to* [italics mine] the monarchy."[1] And he does, finally, in a round-about way, suggest that the nobility had decisive power, saying that "in More's time the English nobility and clergy were the submissive servants of the monarchy, to which they imparted an absolute power such as it then possessed in no other country of Europe."[2] Aside from questions of its accuracy in detail, this statement is a paradox lodged at the very center of our problem. A class capable of imparting absolute power cannot, in any logic, actually be feeble and servile. If the English nobility made the Crown more powerful than London, then the nobles were the ruling class, even if not a very strong one, and were as a group, in the last analysis, the masters rather than the servants of monarchy.

However wrong or right Kautsky may be, he has been alone in discussing such fundamental questions as a prelude to interpretation of *Utopia*, and the meaning of *Utopia* waits on our answer to the question of the precise character of European, especially English, society at the time the book was written. . . .

If it is held that the period of absolute monarchy has generally been, almost to its end, feudal rather than capitalist, a number of Kautsky's less sweeping generalizations also become suspect. Emphasis then shifts from merchant and humanist satisfaction with the *status quo* to emphasis upon middle class discontent with monarchy and sympathy with oppressed peasants and craftsmen. At least, this seems the proper emphasis for the "advanced" elements in the middle class, and surely, at the time he wrote *Utopia*, More expressed very advanced ideas which caused Kautsky to say: "We see how revolutionary *Utopia* was. . . ."[3]

It would be a mistake, however, to assume that Kautsky is crudely inconsistent. He is far too conscious of the actual contradictory nature of things for that, and it is difficult to suggest error in his work without ignoring some telling correction of it. Nevertheless, an attempt should be made to correct some of his interpretations—partly to call his study forcefully to the attention of stu-

7. *Ibid.*, p. 121.
8. *Ibid.*, pp. 140, 142.
9. *Ibid.*, p. 124.

1. *Ibid,,* p. 123.
2. *Ibid.*, p. 118.
3. *Ibid.*, p. 242.

dents of More who may have missed it, and partly to warn them of the type of theoretical weakness they may find in it. A few examples follow.

Though Kautsky recognizes that the London citizens were in frequent opposition to the early Tudor Crown, he says that "scarcely any class in the sixteenth century regarded the monarchy as more necessary than did the merchants,"[4] and he says of capital that "order was its most important vital element."[5] Yet later he remarks that "the vital principle of capitalism is free competition . . . and therefore the abolition of caste distinctions."[6] Now it is certainly true that mercantile capitalists needed many of the freedoms which monarchial order established for them, and it is also true that the essence of later, fully developed capitalism was free competition. But to take only one side of this contradiction, then to ignore further contradictions within that side, and to draw from it the basic political views of Thomas More—he was "an opponent of every popular movement and a champion of constitutional monarchy"[7] —is doubtful logic to say the least. It will be seen below that the more merchants loved order, the more they were devoted to and parasitic upon feudalism; that the lesser nobility were more devoted to the Crown than the merchants were; and that the merchants were more jealous of their own order of monopoly within the towns than of the king's order. As for More's politics, Kautsky repeats his opinion toward the end of his book and then partially corrects it: "It is characteristic of More that he could not imagine such a community [Utopia] without a prince. It is true the latter has nothing to do except to avoid coming under suspicion of striving for absolute power."[8] That is, Utopia's prince is not a prince in the Tudor sense, or in much of any other sense. Actually, he is elected by elected representatives of the people; the people themselves nominate him; and he may be deposed legally. If this may be called a species of bourgeois prince, it is so to the point of extinction. And there is, as a matter of fact, good reason to believe that the [prince] of Utopia is a local city official, and that that republic has no monarch at all.

Thus, it may be argued, the theoretical trend of Kautsky's thought drives him into presumable error. Other such interpretations will be discussed in appropriate places below.

Next to Kautsky's, the most valuable modern work on More is that by R. W. Chambers. Chambers, oddly enough, barely mentions Kautsky's book and substantially ignores everything it says, but his comments on *Utopia* are an implied refutation of Kautsky.

4. *Ibid.*, p. 143.
5. *Loc. cit.*
6. *Ibid.*, p. 211.

7. *Ibid.*, p. 206.
8. *Ibid.*, p. 233.

Indeed, the two may be described as precise opposites, both in the form and content of their work. Kautsky sees More as a bourgeois, critical of rising capitalism, who could leap over an era to grasp the essentials of socialism. Chambers sees More as a bourgeois, critical of rising capitalism, who dreamed of reforming society in accord with the best elements of medieval thought and practice. Both approaches are based on substantial particles of truth, but it is the main thesis of this study that More was a bourgeois, critical of rising capitalism and especially of declining feudalism, who hoped to reform society along bourgeois-republican lines in the immediate future, and that to this aim his medieval and socialist ideas were subordinate. Kautsky sees the life and thought of More as contradictory in nature; Chambers sees them as a unity. The underlying social theories in Kautsky's work are clearly stated, but in Chambers' they are not. Kautsky's interest in primarily intellectual and social; Chambers' interest is mainly personal and spiritual. The one writes bald historical exposition, the other charming informative essays and episodes. Kautsky has written a social interpretation of *Utopia*, and Chambers has created a kind of symphony in which the benign character of More is the theme. The reason for these differences is, of course, the fact that life made Kautsky a socialist and Chambers a conservative but tolerant medievalist.

Since Chambers' thought has been influenced by high church and liberal-capitalist English culture, it is not surprising that he tries to reconcile what may be called liberal and authoritarian, progressive and conservative elements in More's life and thought. The reconciliations made are quite plausible, for Chambers' book is scholarly and very skillfully written, and it is hard to resist the charm of his modesty, his generosity to opponents, and his fine idealism.

Chambers does not recognize any conflicts among More's ideas and attitudes, though he mentions many facts which, if made neighbors, fall to quarreling. His purposes, however, declared and implied, demand a harmony among the facts. What, precisely, are these purposes? His undeclared purpose seems to be to prove that More was conservative, medieval, in religion, politics, and economics. His declared purpose is to depict More for non-Catholic readers "not only as a martyr . . . but also as a great European statesman . . . [whose] farsighted outlook was neglected amid the selfish despotisms of his age . . . [and whose] words . . . acts and . . . sufferings were consistently, throughout life, based upon principles which have survived him."[9] It may be noted, incidentally, that these principles are nowhere in the book precisely described, but are only suggested

9. Chambers, p. 15.

by the goodness, kindness, and tolerance which the reader finds on
each page.

Chambers sets himself a difficult task. It seems that he must
prove that More was, in all ways and times, orthodox in his Catholi-
cism, limited by the ideals of the past, yet spacious and prophetic in
his social vision. If Chambers had openly faced certain contradictions in his task, and had made them a part of his hypothesis, his
account of More would be at the same time less rigid and less frag-
mentary and would have in it more of the growth, flow, and struggle of real life. Erasmus said (and Chambers mentions this at the
beginning of his book) that he felt incompetent to portray Thomas
More's many-sided character.

Most controversy concerning More has, however, centered on this
question of his consistency. Liberal historians have found him an
unfortunate example of that perennial phenomenon—the liberal in
youth turned conservative with age—and Chambers has correctly
pointed out that this is nonsense, for More was a good thirty-eight
years old when he wrote *Utopia*. But such historians are able to
point out, in their turn, that More opposed religious coercion in
Utopia and later, as chancellor, not only persecuted heretics but
defended such persecution in theory. Such historians, being philosophical idealists, assume that views should never change, regardless
of changing conditions: if one is against war, he should oppose all
wars; if one is for tolerance, he should tolerate anyone and everything. Chambers, also a philosophical idealist, also believes that one
should not change his views, and claims that More did not. It is
probable, however, that More did change his views on religious tolerance gradually, after 1516, under the pressure of such events as
the rise of Lutheranism, the knights' and peasants' wars in Germany
—with the general decline of reformers' hopes in a period of sharp-
ening social crisis. Chambers seeks to show that More was neither
very liberal in *Utopia* concerning religion and politics nor bigoted
and cruel in later years when he dealt with heretics. These two purposes lead him to some rather extraordinary evasions and confusions
which merit special attention as extreme examples of the central
weakness of a valuable study. The facts in this controversy seem
clear: More did establish full toleration of all religions in Utopia,
punishing only atheists; and he did, later, not only approve but also
bring about the execution of heretics. Chambers, perhaps unconsciously, has blurred and obscured these facts to the point of giving
precisely the opposite *impression* that freedom of religion did not
really exist in Utopia, and that More never harmed a heretic.

That Chambers cannot successfully reconcile, in the person of
More, even the best elements of feudal, capitalist, and socialist

thought—and it must be admitted that More does express something of each in *Utopia* alone—should not blind us to the virtues of
his work. Chambers makes some acute criticisms of those liberal historians who admire Henry VIII, and a whole generation of heartless
pirate capitalists, because of their gifts to "progress" and "freedom." Certainly he was right, in part, in seeing More's social criticism as a medieval protest against a horrifying "New Order." But
More was not a true feudal philosopher, such as we find today in
Lin Yutang or Gandhi.[1] The New Order he opposed was not really
new but a revival, an intensification, a harsh reorganization of the
Old Order—just as fascism, in our day, is a spuriously "new" organization of moribund social forces. Thus it is seen that our basic
criticism of Kautsky and Chambers is the same. From opposed
points of view both see the brutal aspects of rising capitalism as the
object of More's critical thought. An attempt will be made in the
following pages to show that More criticized decadent feudalism in
the interests of the "best" aspects of rising capitalism, medieval and
Renaissance.

J. H. HEXTER

The Roots of *Utopia* and All Evil[†]

We are better equipped to discover what those ends[1] are now
that we know that bond labor, abolition of markets and money,
and restriction of wants by enforced community of consumption are
of a piece with the abolition of private property and profit and with
the obligation to toil—indispensable motifs in the total pattern of
More's best state of the commonwealth. A society where wants are
tightly bound up and where the penal power of the state is made
daily conspicuous by men in heavy gold chains—this is no ideal
society of Modern Socialism. Altogether missing from *Utopia* is that
happy anarchist last chapter of modern socialism intended to justify
all the struggle, all the suffering, all the constraint that we must
undergo in order to reach it. *Utopia* does not end in an eschatologi-
cal dream.

More simply did not believe that all the evil men do can be
ascribed to the economic arrangements of society, and that those

1. Lin Yutang was a homely philosopher
popular in the 1930s. Linking him with
Gandhi is a way of derogating the latter.
(R.M.A.).
† From J. H. Hexter, *More's Utopia:
The Biography of an Idea* (Princeton:
Princeton University Press, 1952), pp.

71–81 (Part II, section 8). Footnotes are
Hexter's except where credited to R.M.A.
References to the text of *Utopia* have
been changed to reflect the paging of
this edition.
1. Hexter has been discussing the ends of
Utopian society, its objectives (R.M.A.).

evils and the very potentiality for evil will vanish when the economic arrangements are rectified and set on a proper footing. More
believed no such thing because in his view of men and their affairs
there was a strong and ineradicable streak of pessimism. More's pessimism was ineradicable because it was part and parcel of his Christian faith. He knew surely, as a profoundly Christian man he had to
know, that the roots of evil run far too deep in men to be destroyed
by a mere rearrangement of the economic organization of society.
His residue of pessimism leads More to provide even "the best state
of the commonwealth" with an elaborate complement of laws dras-
tically limiting the scope given to individual human desires and to
arm its government with extensive and permanent powers of coercion. Although he was convinced that the institutions of the society
that he knew provided the occasions for the evils he saw, he did not
—and as profoundly orthodox Christian he could not—believe that
the evils were totally ascribable to the institutions. His probings led
him to believe that the roots of the evils of sixteenth century
Europe, though nourished in the rich black earth of an acquisitive
society, were moistened by the inexhaustible stream of sin.

Underlying the whole catalogue of evils of his time he finds one
or another of several sins. Luxury, gluttony, envy, vanity, vainglory,
lust, hypocrisy, debauchery, sloth, bad faith and the rest all find an
easy vent in the Christendom he knew, whose institutions seemed
to him as if contrived to activate human wickedness and anesthetize
human decency. Yet More does not give equal attention to all the
kinds of sin; the realm of evil is not a republic of equals. The
Deadly Sins themselves are not on an even footing in the Utopian
Discourse. Gluttony and Anger get short shrift, Envy is there only
as a counterfoil to a deadlier sin, and Lust, that whipping boy of
our feeble latter-day Christianity, receives but a passing glance. The
great triumvirate that rules the empire of evil, are Sloth, Greed, and
Pride.

It is sloth that in More's day leads stout fellows able to work to
enter into the idle bands of serving men; it is sloth that leads them
to fill with drinking, gaming, and brawling the hours they ought to
spend in honest toil.[2] It is sloth, the avoidance of labor, that the
Utopians punish with bondage.[3] Yet although to More's mind idleness was among the most destructive cankers on the social body,
although it preoccupied him as much as any other problem, he did
not blame that idleness wholly on sloth. The lazy good-for-nothing
scum that the great leave in their wake is conjured into being by
the great men themselves, who provide their followers with the
means of debauchery and vice. And it is not sloth but a greater sin

2. See above, *Utopia*, pp. 12–13, 49.   3. See above, *Utopia*, p. 41.

that leads the great men to foster the infection of idleness in the body of the commonwealth.

Even above sloth in the hierarchy of sin lie greed and pride. In dealing with these two paramount sins More's Christian faith stood him in good stead. It provided him with a basic insight into the underlying pattern of evil, a pattern somewhat obscured by our modern climate of opinion. For he did not believe that greed and pride were on a parity with each other as sources of the social ills of his day, or that they offered equal obstacles to the establishment of the Good Society; but at this point it requires special care to read More's meaning right. The best known passage of *Utopia*, the attack on enclosure in the Dialogue section, is directed against the "inordinate and insatiable covetousness" of landlords and engrossers.[4] Much of the Discourse section, moreover, is taken up with variation after variation on a single theme: "The love of money is the root of all evil." Now the inordinate desire for riches is greed or avarice, and from this it would seem to follow almost as a syllogism that greed was what More discovered as a result of his social analysis to be the fount and origin of the sickness of his own society. Yet it is not so. Greed was a sin, revolting enough in More's eyes; but it is not a sufficiently attractive vice to stand alone. Men are impelled to it not by its charms, but, like other animals, by fear of want. "*Why*," Hythloday asks, "*should anyone consider seeking superfluities, when he is certain that he will never lack anything? Indeed in all kinds of living things it is . . . fear of want that creates greed and rapacity.*"[5] It is one of the perverse traits of the regime of private property, where each must make provision for and look after his own, that an amiable regard for his kin continually tempts man to the sin of avarice.[6]

But this sin, certain to beset a pecuniary society, is essentially, a parasite on the insecurity inherent in that kind of society and has no roots of its own. It is sustained rather by the institutional roots of the property system itself. Even the rich, More suggests, realize this, and are "not ignorant how much better it were to lack no necessary thing than to abound with overmuch superfluity, to be rid out of innumerable cares and troubles, than to be *bound down*[7] by great riches."[8] If avarice were the great danger to society the Utopian commonwealth could be instituted along lines far less rigorous and repressive than those More prescribes. But avarice is not all.

4. See above, *Utopia*, p. 14.
5. "For why should it be thought that man would ask more than enough, which is sure never to lack? Certainly, in all kinds of living creatures, . . . fear of lack doth cause covetousness and ravine"; *Nam cur superuacua petiturus putetur is, qui certum habeat nihil sibi un-quam defuturum? Nempe auidum ac rapacem . . . timor carendi facit, in omni animantum genere.* See above, *Utopia*, p. 45.
6. See above, *Utopia*, p. 88.
7. "be besieged with"; *obsideri*
8. See above *Utopia*, p. 90.

Fear of want makes for greed in all living creatures, including man;
in man alone greed has a second set of roots deeper in his nature
even than fear. For men only of God's creatures are greedy out of
"pride alone, which counts it a glorious thing to pass and excel
others in the superfluous and vain ostentation of things."[9] Here, I
think, lies the heart of the matter. Deep in the soul of the society
of More's day, because it was deep in the soul of all men, was the
monster Pride, distilling its terrible poison and dispatching it to all
parts of the social body to corrupt, debilitate, and destroy them.
Take but a single example: Why must the poor in Europe be "wea-
ried from early in the morning to late in the evening with continual
work like laboring and toiling beasts" leading a life "worse than the
miserable and wretched condition of bondmen, which nevertheless
is almost everywhere the life of workmen and artificers?"[1] Human
beings are consigned to this outrageous slavery merely to support
the enormous mass of the idle, and to perform the "vain and superfluous" work that serves "only for riotous superfluity and unhonest
pleasure."[2] What feeds the unhonest pleasure that men derive
from luxuries and vanities, or to use the phrase of a modern moralist, from conspicuous consumption and conspicuous waste? It
is pride. Many men drudge out their lives making vain and needless
things because other men "count themselves nobler for the smaller
or finer thread of wool"[3] their garb is made of, because "they think
the *value*[4] of their own persons is thereby greatly increased. And
therefore the honor, which in a coarse gown they dare not have
looked for, they require, as it were of duty, for their finer gowns'
sake. And if they be passed by without reverence, they take it
angrily and disdainfully."[5] The same sickness of soul shows itself in
"pride in vain and unprofitable honors." "For what natural or true
pleasure doest thou take of another man's bare head or bowed
knees? Will this ease the pain of thy knees or remedy the frenzy of
thy head? In this image of counterfeit pleasure they be of a marvelous madness *who flatter and applaud themselves with the notion of
their own nobility*."[6] It is to support this prideful and conceited
burden to keep idlers in luxury. The great mass of wastrels bearing
down on Christendom are maintained to minister to the pride and
vainglory of the great. Such are "the flock of stout bragging rush-
bucklers,"[7] "the great . . . train of idle and loitering servingmen,"[8]
that "rich men, especially all landed men, which commonly be
called gentlemen and noblemen,"[9] themselves fainéants, "carry

9. See above, *Utopia*, p. 46.
1. See above, *Utopia*, p. 41.
2. See above, *Utopia*, p. 42.
3. See above, *Utopia*, p. 57.
4. "price"; *precii*
5. See above, *Utopia*, p. 57.
6. "which for the opinion of nobility re-

joice much in their own conceit"; *ii qui
nobilitatis opinione sibi blandiuntur ac
plaudunt.* See above, *Utopia*, p. 57.
7. See above, *Utopia*, p. 42.
8. See above, *Utopia*, p. 12.
9. See above, *Utopia*, p. 42.

about with them at their tails."[1] Such too are the armies, maintained by those paragons of pride, the princes of Europe, out of the
blood and sweat of their subjects, to sustain their schemes of mega-
lomaniac self-glorification.[2] Thus seeking in outward, vain, and
wicked things an earthly worship which neither their achievement
nor their inner virtue warrants, Christians lure their fellow men into
the sin of sloth, or subject them to endless labor, or destroy their
substance, their bodies, and their souls too, in futile wars; and over
the waste and the misery, over the physical ruin and the spiritual,
broods the monster sin of pride.

The Utopian Discourse then is based on a diagnosis of the ills of
sixteenth century Christendom; it ascribes those ills to sin, and primarily to pride, and it prescribes remedies for that last most disastrous infection of man's soul designed to inhibit of not to eradicate
it. For our understanding of the Utopian Discourse it is of the
utmost importance that we recognize this to be its theme. Unless
we recognize it, we cannot rescue More from the ideologically motivated scholars of the Left and the Right, both as anxious to capture
him for their own as if he were a key constituency in a close Parliamentary election. According to the Rightist scholars, who have
allowed their nostalgia for an imaginary medieval unity to impede
their critical perceptions, More was one of the last medieval men.
He was the staunch defender of Catholic solidarism represented in
medieval order and liberties, in a stable, agrarian subsistence economy, in guild brotherhood, monastic brotherhood, and Christian
brotherhood against the inchoate growth of modern universal other-
hood, already embodied, or shortly to be embodied in nascent capitalism, the New Monarchy, Protestantism, and Machiavellianism.[3]
On the other hand, the most recent exponent of the *Utopia* as an
exemplification of dialectical materialism has seen More as a fine
early example of the Middle Class Man whose social views are one
and all colored by his antipathy to late medieval feudalism as represented in the enfeebled but still exploitative Church and in the
predatory and decadent feudal aristocracy, making their final rally in
the courts of equally predatory and decadent dynastic warrior
princes.[4]

Both of these formulations—that of the Left and that of the
Right—are subject to a number of weaknesses. They are both based
on conceptions of economic development and social stratification in
the sixteenth century and earlier more coherent than correct, and
largely mythological in many respects. The Leftist scholars by

1. See above, *Utopia*, p. 12.
2. See above, *Utopia*, p. 13.
3. Chambers, passim; Campbell, passim. I borrow the concept of modern "other-hood" from my friend Prof. Benjamin

Nelson, *The Idea of Usury: From Tribal Brotherhood to Universal Otherhood*, The History of Ideas Series, 3.
4. Ames, passim.

regarding More's age from a particular twentieth century perspective, the Rightists by regarding it from what they fondly imagine to be a medieval perspective deprive both More's opinions and his age of the measure of internal cohesion that both in truth possess. But to document these criticisms adequately would require an inordinate amount of space.[5] For the moment it must suffice to point out that from *Utopia* and from the events of More's life, scholarly ideologues both of the Left and of the Right have been able to adduce a remarkable number of citations and facts to support their respective and totally irreconcilable views. Now this paradox is amenable to one of two possible explanations. The first would require us to assume that More's thought was so contradictory, disorderly, and illogical as to justify either of these interpretations or both, although in reason and common sense they are mutually contradictory. But the intellectual coherence and sureness of thought of the Utopian Discourse and the sense of clear purpose that it radiates seem to preclude this resolution of the paradox. The second possibility is that either point of view can be maintained only by an unconscious but unjustifiable underestimate of the weight of the citations and data offered in support of the opposite point of view, but that all the citations and data fall into a harmonious pattern if looked at in a third perspective.

The character of that third possible perspective I have tried to suggest: the Utopian Discourse is the production of a Christian humanist uniquely endowed with a statesman's eye and mind, a broad wordly experience, and a conscience of unusual sensitivity, who saw sin and especially the sin of pride as the cancer of the commonwealth. Now the social critic of any age is bound to direct his most vigorous attack at the centers of power in that age and reserve his sharpest shafts for the men possessing it. For however great the potentialities for evil may be in all men, real present social ills, the social critic's stock in trade, are immediately the consequence of the acts and decisions of the men actually in a position to inflict their wills on the social body. In a pecuniary society enjoying a reasonable measure of internal security and order but subject to great disparities of wealth, the social critic is bound to attack the very rich, because in such a society, where direct violence does not bear all the sway, riches become a most important source of power. This does not necessarily imply that pride is wholly confined to rich and powerful men, although by their possession of and preoccupation with money and power, the two goods most highly prized by

5. I have touched on two aspects of the general problem of sixteenth century society in two recent articles, "The Education of the Aristocracy in the Renaissance," *Journal of Modern History*, 22, 1950, pp. 1–20; and "The Myth of the Middle Class in Tudor England," *Explorations in Entrepreneurial History*, 2, 1949–1950, pp. 128–140.

the wordly, they are sure to be especially vulnerable to that sin. It is more to the point, however, that the pride of the powerful is, by virtue of their power, socially efficacious, since it is armed with the puissance of command. It can get what it wickedly wants. In More's Europe—the illicit violence of lordship almost everywhere having been suppressed by the new monarchs—it was the pride of the rich that did the real wicked work in the world, the work of fraud, oppression, debauchery, waste, rapine, and death. So More's shafts find their target in the rich and the powerful—in the bourgeois usurer, the engrosser, the court minion, the mighty lord of lands and men, the princes of the earth, in the encloser and depopulator whether that encloser was a parvenu grazier-butcher still reeking of the blood of the City shambles or a predacious noble of immaculate lineage or an ancient abbey rich in estates and poor in things of the spirit. These were his target not because together they form a homogeneous social class, for they do not, nor because they are all decadently medieval or all inchoately modern, for they are not all one or all the other, but because their riches and power sustained the empire of pride over the world that More knew and whose social ills he had traced to that center of evils.

Once we recognize that More's analysis of sixteenth century society led him to the conclusion that pride was the source of the greater part of its ills, the pattern of the Utopian commonwealth becomes clear, consistent, and intelligible. In its fundamental structure it is a great social instrument for the subjugation of pride. The pecuniary economy must be destroyed because money is the prime instrument through the use of which men seek to satisfy their yet insatiable pride. It is to keep pride down that all Utopians must eat in common messes, wear a common uniform habit, receive a common education, and rotate their dwelling places. In a society where no man is permitted to own the superfluities that are the marks of invidious distinction, no man will covet them. Above all idleness, the great emblem of pride in the society of More's time, a sure mark to elevate the aristocrat above the vulgar, is utterly destroyed by the common obligation of common daily toil. It is through no accident, through no backwardness of the Tudor economy, that More makes the Utopian commonwealth a land austere and rigorous beyond most of the imaginary societies elaborated by his later imitators. Had he cared only to consider man's material welfare, his creature comfort, it need not have been so. More was a logical man; he knew that to bind up pride on all sides it takes a strait prison, and he did not flinch from the consequences of his diagnosis. As he truly says this "kind of vice among the Utopians can have no place"[6]

6. See above, *Utopia*, p. 46.

Since More does not explicitly speak of pride very often in *Utopia*, my emphasis on its role in his social thought on both the critical and constructive side may seem exaggerated. Let anyone who thinks this is so consider the words with which More draws Hythloday's peroration and the whole Discourse of the best state of a commonwealth to its conclusion: "I doubt not that the respect of every man's private commodity or else the authority of our Saviour Christ . . . would have brought all the world long ago into the laws of this weal public, if it were not that one only beast, the princess and mother of all mischief, Pride, doth withstand and let it. She measureth not wealth and prosperity by her own commodities but by the miseries and incommodities of others; she would not by her good will be made a goddess if there were no wretches left *over whom she might, like a scornful lady, rule and triumph,*[7] over whose miseries her felicity might shine, whose poverty she might vex, torment, and increase by gorgeously setting forth her riches. This hellhound creeps into men's hearts; and plucks them back from entering the right path of life, and is so deeply rooted in men's breasts that she cannot be plucked out."[8]

The disciplining of pride, then, is the foundation of the best state of the commonwealth. And more than that, it is pride itself that prevents actual realms from attaining to that best state.

ROBERT C. ELLIOTT

The Shape of *Utopia*†

More's Utopians are a peace-loving people, but their land was born to controversy. Many claim it: Catholics and Protestants, medievalists and moderns, socialists and communists; and a well-known historian has recently turned it over to the Nazis. Methods of legitimating claims vary widely, although most are necessarily based upon ideological interpretation of More's book. Over the past generation, however, in all the welter of claim and counter-claim, one single interpretation has emerged to dominate the field. H. W. Donner calls it "the Roman Catholic interpretation" of *Utopia*.[1] Its most trenchant, certainly most influential, statement is by R.

7. "whom she might be lady over to mock and scorn"; *quibus imperare atque insultare possit.*
8. See above, *Utopia*, p. 90.
† Robert C. Elliott, "The Shape of Utopia," *English Literary History*, Vol. 30, no. 4 (December 1963), pp. 317–334. Copyright © 1963 by The Johns Hopkins University Press. Reprinted by permission of the publisher. Notes are Elliott's unless credited to R.M.A.; references to *Utopia* have been changed to reflect the paging of this edition.
1. *Introduction to Utopia* (London, 1945), p. 81.

W. Chambers; the interpretation, in brief, amounts to this: "When a Sixteenth-Century Catholic depicts a pagan state founded on Reason and Philosophy, he is not depicting his ultimate ideal. . . . The underlying thought of *Utopia* always is, *With nothing save Reason to guide them, the Utopians do this; yet we Christian Englishmen, we Christian Europeans* . . . !"[2] This statement cuts cleanly through murky tangles of critical debate. It is founded upon awareness of the relation between reason and revelation in Catholic doctrine, and the importance of that relation in making judgments about *Utopia*; it is consonant with everything we know of More and his life. Most recently this interpretation has received powerful support from Edward L. Surtz, S.J., in a number of articles and in his two books on *Utopia*, *The Praise of Pleasure* (Cambridge, Mass., 1957) and *The Praise of Wisdom* (Chicago, 1957). Father Surtz begins and ends both books with versions of the Chambers thesis, which he too calls "the Catholic interpretation of *Utopia*."[3]

The interpretation itself seems to me unassailable, the way of labeling it open to grave question. How far, one is bound to ask, does acceptance of this "Catholic" reading entail the acceptance of other Catholic interpretations which may seem corollary? The problem arises as one reads the work of Father Surtz. In *The Praise of Wisdom*, Father Surtz announced that his intention was to "produce additional evidence, throw more light, modify present interpretations, and draw new conclusions on intriguing but vexing problems" (p. viii). The book and its companion volume fulfill splendidly this aim. But it is also true that in both books Father Surtz arrives at Catholic interpretations of various issues in the *Utopia* which seem to me—and, I would assume, to a good many others— quite unacceptable. One admires the frankness with which he admits the perplexities, even the irritations, he has encountered in dealing with prickly religious and moral sentiments expressed in *Utopia*, but one cannot accept—even as satisfactory explanation— the way he has dealt with some of them.

To be specific: the Utopians notoriously recommend euthanasia for the incurably ill. There is no equivocation on this point in the text. As Raphael Hythloday reports matters, the Utopians believe that a man whose life has become torture to himself will be—and should be—glad to die; in these extreme cases the priests and magistrated exhort the patient to take his own life.[4] Responding to this passage, Father Surtz deals roundly with the Utopians: they "need to be set straight by Christian revelation on this point" (*Praise of Wisdom*, p. 91). Similarly, some Utopians "err," he writes "in the

2. Raymond W. Chambers, *Thomas More* (London, 1935), p. 128. See above, p. 151.
3. "Interpretations of *Utopia*," *Catholic* *Historical Review*, XXXVIII (1952), 168 and note 52.
4. See above, *Utopia*, p. 65.

maintenance of an extreme view of immortality," for they think the souls of even brute animals are immortal (pp. 77–78). Because divorce is allowed in Utopia, Father Surtz scolds the inhabitants for violating the natural law "which is obligatory on all men, Christian and non-Christian, including the Utopians" (p. 247). Mistakes like these would have become evident to the Utopians had they "been fortunate enough to possess supernatural revelation" (p. 11).

This way of dealing with religious questions in Utopia is not only to number Lady Macbeth's children but to spank them as well. Perhaps it is a tribute to More's creative powers that Father Surtz should treat the Utopians as though they were subject to judgments of the same order as persons who actually live. "In his heart," he writes of Raphael Hythloday and his attitude toward Utopian communism, "he realizes that, given the general run of Christians, his commonwealth, like the republic of Plato, will never exist in the Christian West" (*Praise of Pleasure*, p. 181). But Hythloday has no heart, and it is no good looking behind his words to concealed or unacknowledged meanings: Hythloday *is* only the words that the words of Thomas More say he speaks. Father Surtz's argument against Hythloday on Utopian communism is undoubtedly cogent from a doctrinal point of view, but it has little to do with the literary work in which the ideas on communism exist.

The major problem is one of method. Father Surtz seeks to discover More's "real intent and thought." In the last chapter of *The Praise of Pleasure* he writes that his method is "to study each problem by itself in the light of all his letters and writings and against the background of antecedent and contemporary literature and philosophy." In the Preface to *The Praise of Wisdom* he says that he examines the "pertinent sections in the *Utopia* point by point . . . to determine the relation of each point to fifteenth-century and sixteenth-century formulations of Catholic teaching." The result of the method is that we are given an admirable historical, philosophical, and religious context for the many vexed issues that arise in *Utopia*. Three chapters on communism in *The Praise of Pleasure*, for example, provide a comprehensive account of classical, scriptural, patristic, and humanist attitudes toward the matter. All the major issues of *Utopia* are thus "placed." We are given no sense, however, that these questions exist, not as abstract political, religious, or philosophical propositions, but as constitutive elements in a work of art. What is wanted instead of the Catholic interpretation of communism is an interpretation of *Utopia* that will show us how the question of communism is incorporated into the total structure of the work. Father Surtz is aware of a problem of literary interpretation; he recognizes the ironic structure of *Utopia*—in fact, he deplores it. "Unfortunately," he writes, "for purposes of satire or irony, he [More] has introduced into his 'philosophical city' institutions which impart an air of realism but which he himself terms silly or even absurd. Correct interpretation becomes troublesome and elusive" (*Praise of Pleasure*, p. 193). The *Utopia*, by virtue of what it *is*, becomes an obstacle to Father Surtz's purpose. Something is radically wrong.

Clearly we need, not the Catholic or the Marxist or the city-planner interpretation of *Utopia*, so much as we need an interpretation that will tell us what *Utopia* is, that will place it with respect to the literary conventions which give it form and control its meaning. In one sense, of course, *Utopia* made its own conventions: it is the beginning, it creates its own genre. More was like Adam in the Garden of Eden: his use of the name was constitutive; he named the thing and that is what it was.

But in another sense the Adamic form was hardly new at all. Its structure, its use of characters, its rhetorical techniques, its purpose, its subject, its tone—all these accord with the conventions of a liberary genre firmly, if ambiguously, fixed in literary history. *Utopia* has the shape and the feel—the form—of satire. It is useful to think of it as a prose version with variations of the formal verse satire composed by Horace, Persius, and Juvenal. If we approach it in this way, we shall be able to adjust our expectations and our ways of interpreting and evaluating to conform to the laws of the country to which *Utopia* belongs.

We can establish the general shape of *Utopia* by putting together two comments of More's contemporaries. "If you have not read More's Utopia," writes Erasmus to his friend William Cop, "do look out for it, whenever you wish to be amused, or rather I should say, if you ever want to see the sources from which almost all the ills of the body politic arise."[5] The second comment is from Jerome Busleiden's letter to More, published with the *Utopia*: You have done the whole world inestimable service, he writes, "by delineating . . . an ideal commonwealth, a pattern and finished model of conduct, than which there has never been seen in the world one more wholesome in its institution, or more perfect, or to be thought more desirable" (above, p. 117). Here are the two sides of *Utopia*: the negative, which exposes in a humorous way the evils affecting the body politic; the positive, which provides a normative model to be imitated. "O holy commonwealth, which Christian ought to emulate" (*O sanctam rempublicam, et uel Christianis imitandam*), reads a marginal comment on the text by either Erasmus or Peter Giles (Lupton ed., p. 169). This general negative-positive structure is of course common enough in many forms of discourse. St. Augus-

5. Epistle 519 in *The Epistles of Erasmus*, trans. Francis M. Nichols (New York, 1962), II, 503.

tine very consciously organized *The City of God* this way: the first ten books attacking erroneous beliefs, the last twelve establishing his own position, with destructive and constructive elements working through both parts. Sermons are often put together on this principle, as are literary-moral forms like the beast fable in which the greedy fox comes to a bad and instructive end. But for our purposes it is significant that this too is the characteristic skeletal shape of the formal verse satire as it was written by Horace, Persius, and Juvenal. The Roman satire divides readily into two disproportionate elements: Part A (as Mary Claire Randolph has called it) in which some aspect of man's foolish or vicious behavior is singled out for exposure and dissection, and Part B, which consists (whether explicitly or implicitly) of an admonition to virtue and rational behavior.[6] It establishes the standard, the "positive," against which vice and folly are judged.

Utopia and Roman satire have this general structural outline in common, but many other canonical elements as well. So true is this that one must read the *Utopia* with an eye—and an ear—to complexities of the kind one finds in Horace and Alexander Pope, testing the voices of the speakers against the norms of the work, weighing each shift of tone for possible moral implication. The meaning of the work as a whole is a function of the way those voices work with and against each other: a function of the pattern they form.

More knew ancient satire well. Lucian was one of his favorite authors: "If . . . there was ever anyone who fulfilled the Horatian precept and combined delight with instruction, I think Lucian certainly stood *primus inter pares* ["first among equals"—R.M.A.] in this respect," he wrote in the dedicatory epistle prefacing the translation into Latin of some of Lucian's dialogues that he and Erasmus collaborated on.[7] The Latin satirists were part of the literary ambiance in which More moved most freely; he often quotes from them, and it is clear that he had given a good deal of thought to certain problems having to do with satire as a form. When the Louvain theologian Martin Dorp attacked Erasmus' *Praise of Folly*, More replied in a long letter in which he defends the *Folly* with arguments drawn from the *apologiae* of the Roman satirists and from

6. "The Structural Design of the Formal Verse Satire," *Philological Quarterly*, XXI (1942), 368–74 Cf. A. Cartault: "Les satires morales d'Horace contiennent une partie de destruction et une partie de construction; en d'autres termes une partie satirique et une partie proprement morale. Ce sont deux faces de la même oeuvre, mais elles sont étroitement soudées entre elles; on peut les distinguer, non les séparer." *Etude sur les Satires d'Horace* (Paris, 1899), p. 347. ["The moral satires of Horace contain one destructive and one constructive part; in other words, one part is satiric and one is, properly speaking, moral. They are two aspects of the same work, but intimately connected with one another; though you can distinguish them, you cannot separate them."—tr. R.M.A.]

7. Translation by C. R. Thompson in his *The Translations of Lucian by Erasmus and St. Thomas More* (Ithaca, 1940), pp. 24–25.

St. Jerome's justification of his own satire. More's letter, together with the dedicatory essay to him in the *Praise of Folly* and Erasmus' own epistolary *apologia* written to the same Martin Dorp (who in real life played the conventional role of the *adversarius* in satire), form an elaborate compendium of arguments satirists have always used to justify their ambiguous art.[8]

The *Utopia*, like many formal verse satires, is "framed" by an encounter between a satirist and an adversary. Just as "Horace" gets entangled in talk with his intolerable bore, or engages in dialogue with his learned friend Trebatius, or "Juvenal" joins Umbricius on the way out of Rome,[9] so "More" encounters Raphael Hythloday who is to carry the burden of the long conversation in the garden in Antwerp. "More's" role is that of interlocutor and adversary; the satirist-narrator is Raphael Hythloday whose tale is prose but nonetheless Roman in purpose and in form.

This is particularly apparent in the first book. At one point a query by "More" leads Hythloday into reminiscence about his stay years before with Cardinal Morton in England. He recalls a foolish argument that developed at table one day between a jesting scoffer who was accustomed to play the fool and an irascible friar. The fool, says Hythloday, having delivered himself of some sharp gibes at the venality of monks, and finding his railing well received, made an equally sharp thrust at the friar, to the delight of the assembled company. The friar, "being thus touched on the quick, and hit on the gall (*italo perfusus aceto*) so fret, and fumed, and chafed at it, and was in such a rage, that he could not refrain himself from chiding, scolding, railing, and reviling. He called the fellow ribald, villain, javel, back-biter, and the child of perdition, citing therewith terrible threatenings out of Holy Scripture. Then the jesting scoffer began to play the scoffer indeed, and verily he was good at that . . ." (above, pp. 20–21). The climax of the row came when the friar threatened to invoke the curse of Elisha against the fool and to excommunicate him. With that, Cardinal Morton intervened, says Hythloday, to end the grotesque little episode.

Hythloday apologizes twice for telling this story; and although it

8. For a study of the conventional *apologia*, see Lucius R. Shero, "The Satirist's *Apologia*," *Classical Studies*, Series No. II, Univ. of Wisconsin Studies in Language and Literature, No. 15 (Madison, 1922), pp. 148–67. More's letter is in *St. Thomas More: Selected Letters*, trans. Elizabeth F. Rogers (New Haven, 1961), pp. 40, 42, 55–61. Erasmus' letter is Epistle 337 in *Opus Epistolarum Des. Erasmi Roterodami*, ed. P. S. Allen and others (1906–58), II, 90–114. For St. Jerome, see *Select Letters*, trans. F. A. Wright (Cambridge, 1954), Letters XXII, 32; XL; LII, 17. Good discussions of Jerome as satirist are in John Peter, *Complaint and Satire in Early English Literature* (Oxford, 1956), pp. 15 ff.; David S. Wiesen, "St. Jerome as a Satirist," (Harvard University diss., 1961).

9. The reference is to Horace, *Satires*, I.9, and II.1; and to Juvenal, Satire III. These are the two great models of Roman satire. Names in quotation marks imply that the reference is not to an actual person but to a literary mask or representation of him (R.M.A.).

has some slight relevance to Hythloday's major theme and a bur-
lesque-show quality of humor about it, it is not immediately apparent why More includes it. Certain elements in the scene, however
—the spiraling invective, the character of contest and performance,
of flyting, the threat of a fatal curse—are of the primitive stuff from
which formal satire developed: the underwood of satire, Dryden
called it.[1] But in addition to genetic sanctions, More had excellent
literary precedent for the scene. It is modeled on Horace's *Satires*, I,
7, which consists largely of a contest in scurrility between a witty
half-Greek trader and a "foul and venomous" Roman. (It is also
very like the wit-contest in *Satires*, I, 5 ["The Journey to
Brundisium"], between Sarmentus the jester and the buffoon Mes-
sius Cicirrus, which so delighted "Horace," "Maecenas," and
"Virgil.") A marginal note to the Latin text of *Utopia* calls attention to More's use of the phrase *perfusus aceto* ["sprinkled with
vinegar"—R.M.A.] from Horace's satire, thus making explicit the
relation between the two scenes. Horace's poem ends with a pun,
More's episode with the discomfiture of the foolish friar. His satire
is the sharper.

Immediately before this scene Hythloday had been engaged (he
tells "More" and "Giles") in a more serious contest with a lawyer
at Cardinal Morton's table. The lawyer praised the rigors of English
justice which loads twenty thieves at a time on one gallows. Hythloday, radically disagreeing, attacked the severity of the punishment
and the social conditions which drive men to theft. A single passage
from this dialogue-within-a-dialogue is enough to establish Hythloday's superb talent as satirist. He speaks:

> There is another [necessary cause of stealing], which, as I sup-
> pose, is proper and peculiar to you Englishmen alone.
> What is that? quoth the cardinal.
> Forsooth, my lord, quoth I, your sheep that were wont to be so
> meek and tame and so small eaters, now, as I hear say, be become
> so great devourers and so wild, that they eat up and swallow
> down the very men themselves. They consume, destroy, and
> devour whole fields, houses, and cities. For look in what parts of
> the realm doth grow the finest and therefore dearest wool, there
> noblemen and gentlemen, yea and certain abbots, holy men no
> doubt, not contenting themselves with the yearly revenues and
> profits that were wont to grow to their forefathers and predeces-
> sors of their lands, nor being content that they live in rest and
> pleasure nothing profiting, yea, much annoying the weal-public,
> leave no ground for tillage. They enclose all into pastures; they

1. "Essay on Satire," *Works*, ed. Scott,
Saintsbury (Edinburgh, 1887), XIII, 47.
For discussion of the primitive materials
out of which literary satire grew, see

Robert C. Elliott, *The Power of Satire:
Magic, Ritual, Art* (Princeton, 1960),
Chaps. I, II, and pp. 158–59.

throw down houses; they pluck down towns, and leave nothing standing but only the church to be made a sheep-house.

Here are characteristic devices of the satirist, dazzlingly exploited: the beast fable compressed into the grotesque metaphor of the voracious sheep;[2] the reality-destroying language which metamorphoses gentlemen and abbots into earthquakes, and a church into a sheep barn; the irony coldly encompassing the passion of the scene. Few satirists of any time could improve on this.

Hythloday is expert in his role, which means, of course, that More is expert in his. It does not mean that More's satire and his values are identical with those of the character he created. The interesting and delicate critical question throughout *Utopia* is to determine where possible the relation between the two. To what degree does Thomas More share in the negative criticism of Raphael Hythloday and in the standards of excellence (Part B of Hythloday's satire) which he voices from time to time? The problem would seem to be simplified by the fact that More is himself a character—a real character in a real garden—in the dialogue; he argues with Hythloday, agrees with many things he says, disagrees with others, and in general conducts himself in such a way that we inevitably tend to identify "More" with More, the sentiments uttered by "More" in the dialogue in the garden with those actually held by the emissary from London. "For, when, in any dialogue," writes R. W. Chambers, "More speaks in his own person, he means what he says. Although he gives the other side a fair innings, he leaves us in no doubt as to his own mind" (*More*, p. 155). A great many critics have agreed with Chambers.

It is a dangerous assumption. More dealt habitually in irony: Beatus Rhenanus once characterized him as "every inch pure jest,"[3] and no one in life knew quite how to take him. "But ye use . . . to loke so sadly when ye mene merely," More has a friend say in a dialogue, "that many times men doubte whyther ye speke in sporte, when ye mene good ernest."[4] It is unreasonable to assume that he could not be similarly mercurial in *Utopia*. Lucian and Horace, appearing as characters in their own dialogues, sometimes come croppers themselves, end up as butts of their own satire. More's capacities are similar. I see no way of resolving the cruxes in *Utopia* which have caused so much controversy except by avoiding a priori judgments and listening to the voices as they speak.

2. Marx quoted the passage in *Capital*; see the translation of the 4th. ed. by Eden and Cedar Paul (London, 1928), p. 797, note.
3. Thomas More, *Latin Epigrams*, trans. Leicester Bradner and Charles A. Lynch (Chicago, 1953), p. 126. More suppressed this characterization (which appears in the letter prefacing the Epigrams) in the 3rd ed. of 1520; see *Epigrams*, p. xvi. ["Beatus Rhenanus" was the Latin pen-name of a Dutch humanist well known to Erasmus and More—R.M.A.]
4. "A Dialogue Concernynge Heresyes," *Works*, ed. William Rastell (London, 1557), p. 127.

In the governing fiction of *Utopia* "More" is much taken with his new friend whose eloquence is remarkably persuasive; but on two major matters they disagree, and in Book I they argue their respective positions. The points at issue are, first, "More's" conviction that it is the duty of a philosopher like Hythloday to take service in a prince's court so that his wise counsel may benefit the commonwealth; and, second, Hythloday's contention that "where possessions be private, where money beareth all the stroke, it is hard and almost impossible that there the weal-public may justly be governed and prosperously flourish" (above, *Utopia*, p. 30)—in short, his argument for communism. Neither argument is conclusive in Book I, but for different reasons.

The Dialogue of Counsel (as J. H. Hexter calls it) is inconclusive because opponents, arguments, and rhetoric are evenly matched.[5] In many formal satires the interlocutor is a mere mechanism, set up to launch opinions for the satirist to shoot down. Not so here. "More" invokes Platonic doctrine as he urges upon Hythloday his duty to join the court of a king. Hythloday responds by creating hypothetical examples showing the folly of a moral man's attempting to influence the immoral counsels which prevail at European courts. But, says "More," a sense of decorum is necessary: counsel tempered to the possibilities available, the ability to take a part in the play actually in hand. "You must not forsake the ship in a tempest because you cannot rule and keep down the winds . . . you must with a crafty wile and subtle train study and endeavour yourself, as much as in you lieth, to handle the matter wittily and handsomely for the purpose; and that which you cannot turn to good, so to order it that it be not very bad. For it is not possible for all things to be well unless all men were good, which I think will not be yet this good many years" (above, *Utopia*, pp. 29–31).[6]

Both arguments are coherent, eloquent, persuasive; they meet head-on, as they were to meet 150 years later in the confrontation of Alceste and Philinte in Molière's *Misanthrope*; as they have met many times in life and literature, with inconclusive results. From the text of *Utopia* itself it is impossible to say who "wins" in the Dialogue of Counsel. Not long after it was written, More was in the service of Henry VIII; and it is even possible that this dialogue was composed as a move in a complex political game; or perhaps it is better to think of it, with David Bevington, as a dialogue of More's mind with itself.[7] In any case, More's action in life has no necessary bearing on the debate conducted so brilliantly in the hypothetical realm of his book.

5. *More's Utopia* (Princeton, 1952), pp. 96–138.
6. Cf. Horace, *Satires*, II, 1, l. 59; Persius, *Satires*, I, 1. 120; Juvenal, *Satires*, I, ll. 30, 79.

7. "The Dialogue in Utopia," *Studies in Philology*, LVIII (1961), 496–509.

The argument over communism is inconclusive in Book I for a different reason. Hythloday claims the authority of Plato when he says that only if all things are held in common can there be established a justly governed and prosperous commonwealth. "More" disagrees and in four bare sentences advances the classical objections to communism: it destroys initiative, encourages dependence on others and hence sloth, is conducive to sedition, bloodshed, and the destruction of authority. But, responds Hythloday (in the perennially effective gambit of utopian fiction), you have not seen Utopia! If you had lived there for five years as I did, "you would grant that you never saw people well ordered but there" (above, *Utopia*, p. 32). A good deal of Book II is, in effect, an answer to "More's" objections; and in this sense the dialogue continues, to be concluded only at the end of the tale.

Throughout Book I Raphael Hythloday's concentration is on those things which, in Erasmus' words, cause commonwealths to be less well off than they should be; this is consistent with his role as satirist. He exposes evil, bares the sources of corruption, as in his Juvenalian outburst against "that one covetous and insatiable cormorant and very plague of its native country," who may enclose thousands of acres of land, forcing the husbandmen and their families out onto the road, into beggary, theft, thence to the gallows (above, *Utopia*, pp. 14–15). Hythloday lays about him fiercely, but as he opens up one social problem after another he suggests remedies, balancing off the negative criticism with positive suggestion. On the enclosure question he exhorts to action: "Cast out these pernicious abominations; make a law that they which plucked down farms and towns of husbandry shall re-edify them. . . . Suffer not these rich men to buy up all to engross and forestall, and with their monopoly to keep the market alone as please them. Let . . . husbandry and tillage be restored . . ." (above, *Utopia*, p. 16). In the argument with the lawyer over the treatment of thieves ("What can they then else do but steal, and then justly pardy be hanged?"), he recommends for England the ways of the Polylerites, which he describes in detail. Within one frame of reference these are the positives—the standards—of Hythloday the satirist; and as they seem convincing to "Cardinal Morton," there is good reason to believe that Thomas More approves.

Hythloday realizes, however, that these positives, important as they may be in the circumstances of the moment, are mere palliatives. In his view, as long as private property exists it will be impossible to remove from "among the most and best part of men the heavy and inevitable burden of poverty and wretchedness" (above, *Utopia*, p. 30). To be sure, mitigating laws can be passed, and he lists a number of possibilities; but this would be only to "botch up for a time" a desperately sick body; no cure is possible "whiles every man is master of his own to himself" (above, *Utopia*, pp 31–32). Hythloday is no man for half measures; his true positive, the standard to which he is passionately committed, is that of full cure. The necessary condition of cure in his view is community of property. "More," we know, flatly disagrees, and the burden of proof is left to Hythloday. Book II is the statement of his case.

The statement is largely expository and, until the very end, notably undramatic (an unhappy characteristic of most comparable statements, obligatory in subsequent literary utopias). Book II is still satiric, as we shall see, but it is as though the normal proportions of satire were here reversed, with Part B—the positives—in preponderance. Hythloday makes some pretense of being objective in his discussion of the institutions of Utopia ("we have taken upon us to shew and declare their laws and ordinances, and not to defend them" [above, *Utopia*, p. 61]), but his enthusiasm overwhelms objectivity. Only occasionally does he express any reservation, as when he remarks that the Utopians seem almost too much inclined to the opinion of those who place the felicity of man in pleasure (but then "pleasure" is scrupulously and favorably defined [above, *Utopia*, p. 56 ff.]), or as when he and his fellows laugh at the custom according to which a Utopian wooer and his lady see each other naked before marriage. Although Hythloday finds this a "fond and foolish" practice, the arguments advanced by the Utopians (as reported by Hythloday) are most persuasive, so that the thrust of the rhetoric in the passage favors the custom, while Hythloday condemns it. This is a clear point at which the norms of the work itself are not in accord with Hythloday's standards. His disclaimer works as a double ironic shield for Thomas More: "I am not Hythloday, and besides, he is against it; he says so." Still, *Utopia* argues for the practice.[8]

Except for this, however, Hythloday's tale is of a realm that he finds ideal, where laws, customs, and institutions are designed to foster the good, and to suppress the wickedness, in man. Utopians are not perfect people, but their commonwealth is rationally conducted so that in nearly every point the Utopian achievement is a reproach to the nations of Europe. Chambers' comment is worth repeating: "The underlying thought of *Utopia* always is, *With*

8. The *Utopia* is a textbook on the use of irony as protective device. "Utopia" ("nowhere"), "Hythloday" ("purveyor of nonsense"), many of the place names bearing comparable significance act as formal disclaimers encompassing the harsh truths told in the work. In ."A Dialogue Concernynge Heresyes," More mocks some of these devices while elaborately using them: "More" is discussing problems of heresy with the messenger from a friend. The messenger insists that what he says is not his opinion but what he has heard others say. But "More" forgets: "And first wher ye saie. Nay quod he where thei say. Well quod I, so be it, where they say. For here euer my tong trippeth." *Works*, ed. Rastell, p. 124.

*nothing save Reason to guide them, the Utopians do this; and yet
we Christian Englishmen, we Christian Europeans . . . !"* In this
sense the very presentation of Utopian life has a satiric function in
so far as it points up the discrepancy between what is and what
ought to be.

Hythloday has a great deal of explanation to get through in Book
II, and perhaps it is inevitable that the expository tone dominates
his discourse. Still, that preoccupation does not force him to abandon his role as overt satirist. At times, while discussing the way of
life of the Utopians he thinks of Europe and becomes hortatory, as
though preaching to an audience rather than addressing "More" or
"Giles." What shall I say, he asks, of misers who hide their gold?
"And whiles they take care lest they shall lose it, do lose it indeed.
For what is it else, when they hide it in the ground, taking it both
from their own use and perchance from all other men's also? And
yet thou, when thou hast hid thy treasure, as one out of all care
hoppest for joy" (above, *Utopia*, p. 58). (*et tu tamen abstruso the-
sauro, uelet animi iam securus, laetitia gestis.* [Lupton ed., p.
198].) We are not to think here of "More" or "Giles" dancing in
delight after digging his gold into the ground; the shift in person is
to the indefinite "thou" (*tu*) of an audience "out there." Passages
like these have the feel of medieval complaint, although in the
sudden shift of person and the moralistic utterance they are completely in character with many Roman satires: some of Persius,' for
example, or Horace's *Satires*, II, 3, 11. 122ff. which is on exactly
the same theme.

Another variation of the satirist's tone is sounded when Hythloday speaks of the extraordinary learning of the Utopians who, without having heard of the Greeks, knew all that the Greeks knew of
music, logic, and mathematics. "But," he adds, "as they in all
things be almost equal to our old ancient clerks, so our new logicians in subtle inventions have far passed and gone beyond them.
For they have not devised one of all those rules of restrictions,
amplifications, and suppositions, very wittily invented in the small
logicals which here our children in every place do learn" (above,
Utopia, p. 54). The voice is suddenly that of the ingénu, of Gulliver speaking 200 years before his time, but with this difference:
Gulliver would believe what he said, whereas Hythloday is ironic.

He can use the technique lightly, as above, or with a bitter, driving, daring intensity. He is explaining that the Utopians do not
enter into treaties with their neighbors because treaties are often
broken in their part of the world. It is not so in Europe, says Hythloday: "especially in these parts where the faith and religion of
Christ reigneth, the majesty of leagues is everywhere esteemed holy
and inviolable, partly through the justice and goodness of princes,

and partly at the reverence and motion of the head bishops. Which, like as they make no promise themselves but they do very religiously perform the same, so they exhort all princes in any wise to abide by their promises, and them that refuse . . . they compel thereto. And surely they think well that it might seem a very reproachful thing if, in the leagues of them which by a peculiar name be called faithful, faith should have no place" (above, *Utopia,* p. 70). Again, the echoes set up in one's ears are from a later traveler to Utopia, whose praise of things European withered what it touched. His predecessor Hythloday, is using with exemplary skill the ancient rhetorical trick of blame-by-praise. As Alexander Pope puts it: "A vile encomium doubly ridicules."

This is superb; but the account of Utopia is enlivened only intermittently by such flashes—or by sudden bits of internal dialogue, so characteristic of Roman satire, like that between the mother and child on the sumptuous dress of the visiting Anemolians (above, *Utopia,* p. 52). The Utopians seem to be a fairly sober lot, although they are delighted with the works of Lucian that Hythloday has brought with him, and (like More) they take much pleasure in fools. Their sense of the satiric is more likely to be expressed in concrete than in verbal ways: they fetter their bondsmen with chains of gold, creating thus an image of the world.

At the end of his discourse, Hythloday summons his forces for summary and justification. Pulling together the major themes, he turns to "More" with a powerful and eloquent defense of the Utopian commonwealth ("which alone of good right may take upon it the name") and of communism ("though no man have anything, yet every man is rich"). From this he moves into outraged criticism of the ways of the world in Europe: the pampering of useless gentlemen, "as they call them," in savage contrast to the inhuman treatent of "plowmen, colliers, labourers, carters, ironsmiths, and carpenters, without whom no commonwealth can continue" (above, *Utopia,* p. 89); the codification of injustice into law which is used to mulct the poor. "Therefore, when I consider and weigh in my mind all these commonwealths which nowadays anywhere do flourish, so God help me, I can perceive nothing but a certain conspiracy of rich men procuring their own commodities under the name and title of the commonwealth. They invent and devise all means and crafts, first how to keep safely, without fear of losing, that they have unjustly gathered together, and next how to hire and abuse the work and labour of the poor for as little money as may be" (above, *Utopia,* p. 89). Christ counseled that all things be held in common, and the whole world would have come long ago to the laws of the Utopians were it not for that "one only beast, the princess and mother of all mischief, Pride" (above, *Utopia,* p. 90).

Hythloday's tone at the end of his tale is that of prophet or hero —his final variation on the scale of tones available to the satirist. It would be idle to look for a source; many satirists and many writers of complaint have sounded the same trumpet: Juvenal, St. Jerome, Piers Plowman, great medieval preachers like the Dominican John Bromyard, of whom G. R. Owst writes.[9]

But the heroic note is not the last note sounded. A final paragraph remains, bracketing Hythloday's peroration, winding up the debate on communism, reasserting by its very form the relation of *Utopia* to Roman satire—and, indeed, to a whole body of literature which distinguishes between exoteric and esoteric teaching. Nothing could be more deft than the way "More" excuses himself to the reader for not having voiced his objections to some of the Utopian laws: Hythloday was tired after his long discourse, and, besides, it was not certain he could abide opposition. "More" contents himself, before leading his friend into supper, with praising the Utopian institutions and Hythloday's account of them; and in enigmatic comment he admits that while he can not agree with all that has been said, there are many things "in the Utopian weal-public which in our cities I may rather wish for than hope for."

"More" leaves with us, however, a statement of the reservations which he withheld from Hythloday—reservations about certain laws and institutions of Utopia founded, in his view, "of no good reason" (the Latin *perquam absurde* ["quite absurd"—R. M. A.] is considerably stronger). Among these are their methods of waging war and their religious customs, but chiefly in his mind is "the principal foundation of all their ordinances," the "community of their life and living without any occupying of money." "More" makes clear his objection: by doing away with money, "the true ornaments and honours, as the common opinion is, of a commonwealth, utterly be overthrown and destroyed." What, in this view, are the true ornaments and honours of a commonwealth? They are "nobility, magnificence, worship (*splendor*), honour, and majesty." Of course we smile: this cannot be Thomas More speaking, whose heretical opinions about magnificence are well known. This is "More," a *persona* he has created for complex purposes of his own —a *persona* who suddenly adopts the values held dear by "common opinion": nobility, magnificence, and the rest are the true ornaments of a commonwealth. But, as Father Surtz admirably says, "the whole purpose of *Utopia* has been to prove that those are *not* the qualities which should distinguish a commonwealth."[1] Unless the whole satiric thrust of *Utopia* has failed for us (as the thrust of

9. *Literature and Pulpit in Medieval England* (New York, 1961), pp. 300 ff. 1. *Praise of Pleasure*, p. 183. Father Surtz is one of very few commentators to see the point of this, but he allows it no significance, no qualifying effect on the meaning of "More's" disclaimer.

Hythloday's discourse has apparently failed for "More"), we must recognize that at this point "More" becomes a gull.

The formal situation here is like that sometimes found in Roman satire. "More" is precisely in the case of "Horace" (*Satires*, II, 3), who, after listening in silence to Damasippus' long Stoic discourse on the theme, Everyone save the wise man is mad, loses his temper at the end, thus neatly placing himself outside the category of the sane. "Horace," like "More," is undercut by his creator.[2]

The effect of this in *Utopia* is complex. In Book I "More" advanced cogent reasons for opposing the principle of communism advocated by Hythloday. Book II, while it covers a good deal of ground, is fundamentally an answer to "More's" objections: Hythloday's peroration points this up. "More" remains unconvinced, but the reasons he gives, *perquam absurde*, make no sense. His disclaimer is in effect nullified by the comically ineffective way he misses the point.[3] Where does this leave us? It leaves Hythloday riding high, his arguments unanswered, his eloquence ringing in our ears. Perhaps we have been deafened a bit—or frightened. Jerome Busleiden wrote that the commonwealth of Utopia was not only an object of reverence to all nations and "one for all generations to tell of," but also "an object of fear to many" (see above, p. 118).

And what of Thomas More, that man whose imagination pushed at the limits of the licit, and who wore a hair shirt? I think it very doubtful that we can ever know what he, in his many conflicting roles of philosopher, moralist, religious polemicist, man of great affairs—what this man "really" believed about communism.[4] Of Thomas More, author of *Utopia*, we can speak with confidence. The idea attracted him strongly. If by nothing else, he makes this plain in the way that, at the climactic point of the dialogue, he disclaims the attraction: by deliberately and unmistakably undercutting "More." The best evidence, of course, is in what he gives to Raphael Hythloday: the powerful criticism rooted in the realities of England; then the moral fervor and the compelling force of his eloquence as he argues for the institutions which make Utopia the best of all commonwealths. In a technical sense, "More's" early objec-

2. Cf. Horace, *Satires*, II, 7. More would have known the same technique in Lucian. He translated *The Cynic*, for example, in which "Lycinus" (a transparent covername for Lucian) ridicules a Cynic and ends up badly worsted in debate. (The point is not affected by the fact that Lucian's authorship of *The Cynic* is in question).
3. Marie Delcourt, in her ed. of *L'Utopie* (Paris, 1936), p. 207, note, says that as a precaution, "More désavoue sa propre création," although "on ne sent . . . aucune conviction réelle."

["More disavows his own creation, though one feels no real conviction" (tr. R. M. A.).] A plain disavowal would have been simple; as it is, it turns back on itself. It should be added that, technically, "More's" dubieties stand about the Utopians' methods of warfare, religious practices, and other laws; his disclaimer is absurd, that is, only in its application to communism.
4. For a discussion of his relevant expressions of opinion outside the *Utopia*, see Surtz, *Praise of Pleasure*, pp. 184–90.

tions to communism are never met—how could they be? Hythloday simply points to Utopia and says, Look, it works! But we quickly forget the flimsiness of this "proof," if we have ever noticed it, as we are swept along by the passion of a man who has seen a vision and come back to tell of it. *Utopia* argues for the ideal of communism by the best test available: More has given to Raphael Hythloday all the good lines.[5]

Thus the shape of *Utopia* is finished off, enigmatically but firmly, in the terms Hythloday provides. This reading of the work of course conflicts with the readings of Chambers, Father Surtz, and others in certain important respects; but it need not conflict with that fundamental interpretation of theirs cited at the beginning of this essay: "When a Sixteenth-Century Catholic depicts a pagan state founded on Reason and Philosophy, he is not depicting his ultimate ideal." It depends on the focus of interest. If we are interested in Thomas More as a man, his beliefs, his values, rather more than we are interested in *Utopia* as a thing in itself, then we must unquestionably posit a third standard, a third norm—one barely hinted at in the work. Two standards can be derived from within *Utopia* itself. The first is on the level of reform within existing institutions: laws to enforce the rebuilding of devastated farms and towns, the restriction of monopoly, provision of work for the idle, limitations on the power of the rich and the wealth of the king, etc. The second and higher standard is the ideal of the work itself, so to speak: Utopia, the model commonwealth, the only one worthy of the name. But if we go outside the *Utopia* to think of Thomas More's ideal, we must think of one far higher yet. Father Surtz cites the appropriate passage. For More, the ultimate ideal would be "the holy city, New Jerusalem, coming down out of heaven from God" (Revelation, XXI, 2).

ROBERT M. ADAMS

The Prince and the Phalanx

The Prince by Machiavelli and *Utopia* by Sir Thomas More constitute a pair of contemporary cross-European books (like Voltaire's *Candide* and Dr. Johnson's *Rasselas*) which are linked indissolubly together by a bond more subtle and interesting than that of influ-

5. Cf. Russell A. Ames, *Citizen Thomas More and His Utopia* (Princeton, 1949), who says that it should be no more necessary to prove that Hythloday speaks for More than to prove that the King of Brobdingnag speaks for Swift. "In general, it should be obvious that no satirist will persuasively present at length major views with which he disagrees" (p. 56).

ence. Machiavelli wrote in 1513, but his manuscript was not published till 1532; however widely it circulated in manuscript during the early sixteenth century, it could hardly have traveled fast enough to be in More's hands when he wrote the *Utopia* during the years 1515 and 1516, or before he published it in the latter year.

Both books arose out of a common and rather peculiar set of circumstances: their authors had been employed by national governments in diplomatic and administrative roles not traditionally assumed by men of their social class. Bourgeois of their sort might well make municipal counsellors or mayors; they did not very often serve as ambassadors and intimate advisers to those holding supreme power in the state. Such posts traditionally went to men of noble rank, large possessions, independent wealth, and independent power —to barons and lords, in a word. Such power as More and Machiavelli could wield, in England and Florence, rose entirely from their personal qualities and attainments. They had no rank; they had no power of their own; they had no money. They had a claim on the ruler's attention, just as civil servants do—on the score of expertise. They knew something of human law, something of human history; but mostly, because they had experience of business and politics, they knew the way of the world. Traditional moral advice the ruler could get where he had traditionally got it—from the Church. Military advice he could get, when he needed it, from military men— barons or *condottieri*.[1] But in the business of business, of bargaining and diplomacy, clever men are certainly of the greatest use to a ruler. The only question is to decide who's clever: for almost every man of a certain age thinks himself a sagacious and understanding fellow. The relation of Machiavelli and More to their employers depended throughout on an intangible—the confidence on which their professional life depended was something they had to create as they went along.

Nothing could conceivably be more precarious than the position of these middle-class advisers, weak in themselves, who undertook to become, ambiguously, servants and directors of the strong. The contemporary situation that most resembles this one is the relation which prevails in the advertising business between the account executive and his client. At a whim, by a word, the latter can fire or replace the former. Yet as long as he retains the client's confidence, the account executive controls immense power, immense sums of money. When he is good, he is very, very good; and when he is bad, he is horrid.

For most of his political life, Machiavelli worked in service to the Florentine republic; he found it exasperatingly timid, indecisive,

---

1. *Condottieri* were the professional soldiers of the Italian Renaissance—powerful leaders, who often had their own companies of soldiers.

and inefficient. When the republic went to smash, in September 1512, he wasted no time in weeping over cracked eggs. His most famous book was written immediately after the catastrophe; it deals with the functions of a prince and is dedicated to a prince, on the assumption that a prince will be in power. There can be no question that the republican form of government was the one Machiavelli overwhelmingly preferred; but when the choice he was offered was a prince or nothing, he chose to use the powers of a prince, such as they were, for the preservation and well-being, so far as possible, of the state. Even in *The Prince*, dedicated to members of the Medici family (traditional enemies of the Florentine Republic), Machiavelli makes no real effort to conceal his republican sympathies. His prince is welded to the people with bonds of self-interest, if only because they are the popular militia on whom his power wholly depends. Machiavelli counts on his prince chiefly to provide that decision and long-range planning in which all his experience showed republics were fatally deficient. As for More, from the beginning amply aware of the problems involved in directing princes, his fantasy ran not only to republicanism but to communism and the rule of reason. This may have been simply reaction to an experience of royal tyranny which in 1515–16 must have been embodied in Henry VII more than Henry VIII. But the rigorous collectivism of the Utopians was not simply anti-monarchical; it was a way of enforcing the control of reason over man's appetitive nature. For the appetitive nature of which More had had most terrible and intimate experience involved men of privilege, among whom the prince himself was inevitably prominent. Thus each man put his faith in a system dominated by the ruler of whom he had had least disillusioning experience.

In one of those brilliant, casual metaphors that he throws off so lightly, Machiavelli says (in Chapter XVIII of *The Prince*) that Homer represents the centaur Chiron as the tutor of Achilles and other princes, in evidence that the prince must learn to use two natures, the human and the bestial, in order to hold power.[2] On one level he must seem to be, and may even actually be, concerned with equity and truth; on another level, it's his own survival and that of his people that he must look out for. The priority of these two levels is determined by brutal practicality. Before the ruler of a state can try to be just, he must first survive; to survive, he must often be unjust. To say the least, this imposes extraordinary burdens on the character of the ruler, whoever he may be. The qualities of

2. So far as I can tell, this interpretation of Chiron is original with Machiavelli: though centaurs always unite two natures, Chiron particularly is traditionally described as gentle and humane, expert in music and medicine as well as warfare. But the application to royalty and its special problems doesn't seem to have any precedent in mythology.

jungle survival—strength and cunning, ferocity and guile, ruthless-
ness and trickery, or whatever other hateful complements the vocab-
ulary allows—are not accidental corruptions of the ruler's nature;
they are inherent in the job, they are primary. Yet this is the very
person we must trust to embody reason, and to enforce it. "Enforce"
suggests extra complications. For reason by itself enforces nothing;
at best it is a guide, and mostly only a check. The only force that
controls one passion is another. The human and rational side of the
ruler cannot control the bestial side without using bestial energies
to do it. It's a secondary question whether we place the burden of
this frightful moral impasse on the shoulders of one man specially
trained to bear it, or divide it among the citizens at large, trusting
them to shame one another (and spy or terrify one another, if necessary) into conformity. The difference between these arrangements
is the difference between Machiavelli and More.

An important element in the comparison is the extraordinary sim-
plification that More silently achieves for his Utopians by abolishing, for all practical purposes, time and space. Time is abolished for
the Utopians in the sense that they have almost no history, and
what little they have is almost without consequences. In 1,760 years
of recorded time, we learn of only two events—the shipwreck of a
vessel carrying Roman and Egyptian passengers, some 1,200 years
ago, and a "recent" war between the Alaopolitans and the Nephelogetes, in which the Utopians took part on the side of the former,
without any consequences for themselves of which we hear. Space is
abolished in that the Utopians live on an island amply protected
against outsiders, with few neighbors and those few conveniently
disposed to appear when needed and to disappear, for centuries or
millennia, when not needed. (The warlike Zapoletes are particularly
well programmed for Utopian purposes, to the extent of having contradictory qualities: they observe incorruptible fidelity toward their
employers; but they think so much of money that they will change
sides for an increase of only a penny a day. Thus the Utopians can
use them confidently, yet betray them unscrupulously. And this
apparently has been going on for hundreds of years, without the
dull Zapoletes ever catching on to the game.) No factions or feuds,
no rankling rivalries or long-drawn-out antipathies complicate the
Utopian record. Like Tolstoy's happy family, it is a family without
a history. A simple verbal device for abolishing time is to narrate
everything about Utopia in the present tense. Hardly anything they
do is the result of present circumstance or past history; it is simply
the way things are and have always been. On the political level, it is
hard to hold in one's mind at the same time the naive little mechanism of More's state and the ferocious intricacy of the milieu
within which Machiavelli had to survive. His Italy, we begin by

noting, was divided into five basic parts—Milan, Venice, Florence, the Papal States, and Naples, with numerous untidy little pockets and leftovers which belonged intermittently to one, the other, or none of the five major powers, depending on circumstances. This was the classic, the almost-ideal arrangement that prevailed till the fatal date of 1492, when Lorenzo de' Medici died. After that date, and throughout Machiavelli's life, Italy as a whole was the football of three major monarchies, Spain, France, and Germany, which perpetually invaded, looted, manipulated, and ravaged the Italian cities in their unending jockeying for advantage. They filled Italy from one end to the other with shiftless, shapeless, leaderless armies of brutal bravos, who spread across the countryside like locusts. Machiavelli himself lived (unhappily) just long enough to hear of the awful looting, sacking, and raping of Rome when a mob of these latter-day barbarians captured the Holy City itself in May 1527. From so simple a caricature of history as this, one sees how much More has simplified his political problems in Utopia, by contrast with those facing a real European prince. The Zapoletes who were imported into Italy by Italian and foreign paymasters did not quietly disappear on request; the historical slate never was and never could be wiped clean. The reason More simplified so radically the politics of Utopia was, of course, that he wanted to concentrate on the essential morality of the state and its citizens; the reason Machiavelli so largely neglected the morality of his prince was that he could not afford to consider that luxury till he had ensured his political survival. That was political survival, not on a nice island in a protecting ocean, but in a jungle swarming with tigers, alligators, and poisonous snakes, who would not go away with a wave of the present tense.

Among other reasons, the moral question is all-important in *Utopia* because it was so important for More personally. He cared hardly at all for one political or social organization as against another—except as it hindered or helped the spiritual and moral development of the citizenry. The Utopians are moral athletes in strict training. They are organized in behalf of morality like a Calvinist phalanx—solidly locked, rigidly disciplined, each man responsible for his neighbors as well as himself—drawn up to war against the beast of appetite within them all. Huey Long, the vintage American politician, had a slogan, "Every Man a King." He meant, or was understood to mean, that every man, at least in Louisiana, should have the privileges and powers of a king. But the slogan could be used in *Utopia* too, though it would mean something very different there. It would mean that every man had the responsibilities of a king—responsibilities that included careful management of the beast within himself and his neighbors. *Management* here implies much more than suppression. When the state is endangered, the beast must be let loose—to betray the ever-gullible Zapoletes, to execute slaves from different districts found conversing together, to assassinate foreign leaders. The beast must even be allowed a certain role in the surveillance of one's neighbors; for no man can sit quietly in a Utopian room and cultivate his reason. He has civic responsibilities, and they extend to supervision of his family, his tribe, his city, his neighbors. Here we must all start to feel slightly uneasy. When I am scandalized—rationally—at my neighbor's insolence or immorality, how can I be sure in my heart of hearts that it isn't because of his pretty wife, who I somehow think would make an even prettier widow? To erase the possibility of such duplicities from the human heart is probably beyond the reach of any social order; but to make every man the watchdog of his neighbor's behavior is probably to invite them. No trick is easier to learn than the best way to prosecute a private vice: it is to profess a public virtue.

Hardly anyone who has looked back and forth at the two societies—wrangling, colorful, dangerous, corrupt, flamboyant Florence; and placid, secure, unvarying, disciplined Utopia—has failed to feel some misgivings about the latter as a place for a full human being to live. And that, of course, is the point; the Utopians aren't full human beings, they have sacrificed certain aspects of their humanity to certain other aspects. Nobody can avoid doing this, but most of us don't have to do it as the Utopians do, everyone along much the same lines, under the guidance of an all-seeing community. An apologist would say they are sacrificing the lower to the higher nature, but they are also sacrificing the complete and various to the incomplete and uniform personality. How much they sacrifice we may remind ourselves by summarizing the little Queens College debate over *Utopia*, which produced, in 1949 and 1952, two important and interesting books on the subject. Russell Ames touched it off with a rebuttal of Chambers's essentially medievalist view of *Utopia*; Jack Hexter responded with a rebuttal of Ames, which went some of the way, but not all, toward reestablishing Chambers. It's always seemed to me that, though Hexter had not only the last word but also the best, it was a radically incomplete word in at least one dimension. The key word of his interpretation is *pride*: and the incomplete dimension is simply the extent of its meaning.

For example, it is pride in Utopia when people are dissatisfied with drab clothing; it is pride when a man becomes attached to a horse he has trained, a garden he has cultivated, an arrangement he has made in the furnishings of his house. It would be pride for a man to declare that his real gift lay in playing the piano, and that he must therefore be exempt from the heavier forms of manual labor, such as farm work. A man who does not like public lectures (sensible fellow), and wants to spend extra time in his shop, is welcome to do so; but it is pride if he decides to make something for himself, his wife, his girlfriend, or any particular individual. If a man learns two trades, hates one and is happy in the other, he may be directed by the state which to follow, in the national interest; and of course it is pride to resist the direction, as it would be insufferable pride to try to free one's brother, son, or husband from slavery. I put these cases in their most extreme and painful form, not because I suppose the Utopians would have been vindictive, but simply to show how much wider and more invidious the word "pride" is in the mouths of the Utopians, Sir Thomas More, and J. H. Hexter, than it would be in the mouths of Aristotle, Cicero, and St. Thomas Aquinas. Here and there it even encroaches on a concept that another society might have called "charity"—not to speak of another completely honorific concept like "magnanimity."

From cradle to grave, then, the Utopians are mustered into a gigantic humility crusade.[3] Their mode of social organization has about it something monastic or reminiscent of monasticism, as has been suggested; it resembles also the reformed church of John Calvin, Augustine's City of God, the church militant, and the Salvation Army. But the special rigidity and ingenuity of Utopia's institutions (thought up once by a clever man and frozen forever against change by other clever men) and its air of social gadgetry mark it as the work of an individual reformer. Utopian society is not only made, it is prefabricated; most emphatically, it has not grown or been allowed to grow. Increase of population is handled mathematically, like a problem in waste disposal. When the nation gets too big, they send the excess off to be colonies; when a city gets too big, they send some people off to start a new city; when a family gets too big, they shift some of its members to another family. Utopia is the product of a moral idea. Like any other ideological society, it tends to convert the safety of the basic idea into a supreme law, and tailor the people to serve it efficiently. Once more, this involves conveniently contradictory qualities. For example, the Utopians are said to be earnest and ardent in the pursuit of abstract learning. But in the areas where learning would be chiefly applied in More's day—theology, philosophy, history, and the law —they are spectacularly and deliberately backward. Their situation

3. We do, indeed, note in Utopia an odd concession or two to the principle of pride; but these exceptions confirm, by their incongruity, the general rule. For example, we are told that the Utopians erect statues to distinguished men as a way of urging citizens to "emulate the glory of their ancestors." But the whole machinery of adoption, which is undertaken so liberally and casually in Utopia, works against passionate feelings about ancestors. And since everyone in Utopia wears the same costume, the statues must be practically indistinguishable and the glory negligible.

in the world, their defensive posture, and their static society prevent them from having a very intricate history; and they frankly avoid most varieties of subtlety or intricate analysis as leading to dispute. These are the people who are avid to liberate and develop their minds, yet they have made it a capital offense to consult together on public affairs outside the senate or the people's assembly. If this set of rules is taken seriously, it is not the thieves but the most ingenious and resolute minds of the nation who will be hanging on gallows, twenty at a batch.

In a word, though he has given his Utopian the safest of all possible islands to inhabit, and complicated their life with an absolute minimum of intractable history, More has been forced to demand inhuman and superhuman qualities of them, in order to give them a decent society. His book, genial and jocose as it is, implies a grim tonality too—as if it were saying: *These are moral athletes, stripped of everything (all impediments, all possessions, all extraneous desires), and conditioned from youth to the austerities of the good life; yet it's only by an absurd concatenation of contradictory qualities that they can solve the problem of good government.* People have said for years that under its jokes, the *Utopia* is a serious book. Under its seriousness, it is also an absurd book.

Pascal in one of his most provoking *Pensées* (No. 139) asks us to think how many of life's problems are due simply to our inability to sit still in a comfortable room. The phrase comes dangerously close to telling us that most of life's problems stem from our unhappy predilection for living. And indeed, a lot of the traditional wisdom on the subject of managing our lives comes down to the recommendation that we live as little as possible. A closed collective society like Utopia does its best to approximate that quiet room; its walls consist simply of our fellow-citizens. But Machiavelli, instead of trying to minimize temptations, concentrates on using to maximum advantage all the human energies of the community. In his most famous book he is writing for and about a prince to whom the option of the retired and contemplative life is by definition not open. In addition, the merit of this prince (his *virtu*) consists in his being able to lead men effectively, to elicit from them the energies of which they are not only capable, but which they are eager to have used. He is a creator, not only of himself and of his office, but of the human materials in which he works; and, like any artist, he is reluctant to disqualify half his palette, for any reason. Machiavelli carefully begins his book by pointing out that no one prince can possibly have, at one time, all the virtues that every prince is supposed to have. When he is being generous, he cannot also be thrifty; to be astute and to be truthful are not easily reconciled; and in the process of being brave, he may well fail to be appropriately gentle. What he can have, and must have if he's to be an effective prince, is the virtue which More considered the ultimate vice, pride. That famous word of Machiavelli's, which takes on a new coloring and a wider meaning every time he uses it, *virtu*, cannot avoid major implications of pride. The prince with *virtu* is an artist of selfhood; he forms an ideal of his self, and then another self capable of living up to the first. Even if he is just a free citizen, the thousandth part of a prince, what sustains him is pride in his own personal dignity, his own manliness. Whatever else the prince may be, he is not an animated idea, but a man swimming boldly across the current of other men's feelings. He can use those feelings fully only if he shares them fully; and that in itself sets him apart from More's pre-programmed automata.

The contrast looks absolute, and on one definition it is. More is medieval in wanting the authoritative, ascetic-spiritual principle to rule over human appetite, Machiavelli much closer to a relativistic, man-oriented modern cosmology in proposing that one set of human appetites can give law—sword-law, if not book-law—to another. On the other hand, there is one ambiguous figure who may bring our contrasted couple closer together, one special person with whom they both had points of intellectual and spiritual contact. This was Girolamo Savonarola, the passionate Dominican friar whose preaching roused Florence, for the brief period of 1494–98, to a political as well as moral revival.

Thomas More, of course, never laid eyes on Savonarola. But it is more than probable that he read his sermons and knew his views, if only because Savonarola wielded overwhelming influence on Pico della Mirandola, whom More admired, and whose life he translated in 1510. And no working society that More could have known came closer in its moral principles to that of Utopia than Savonarolan Florence. It was a republic, governed by a popular assembly and a smaller upper council; it fiercely rejected taxation of the poor for the benefit of the rich; it granted unparalleled authority over the property and behavior of the citizens to men of severe moral principles and unshakable religious conviction. It was as hostile as the Utopians themselves to pride, luxury, and vanity; and though it was not communist, as no European government of the day was,[4] any viewer sympathetic to its moral aims could be excused for thinking that it might have lasted longer had it become so. Its enemies (in addition to Pope Alexander VI) were the rich—("the fat

4. Savonarola's rule as Prior of San Marco was indeed marked by a vigorous onslaught against property. In the interests of spiritual purity, the monastery, which had long been one of the richest and best endowed in Florence, was stripped of its wealth, and the brothers called on to subsist, like mere Utopians, by the labor of their hands. They were even called on to exchange periodically their books, clothing, and cells, (like Utopians exchanging houses by lot) to exterminate from their souls all love of property.

ones," *i grassi*)—within Florence; its vision was of a holy city, a city of God on earth.

It doesn't take much imagination to see that More, with his deep streak of religious dedication, combined with civic patriotism, would naturally have been in sympathy with the idealism of Savonarola. Inevitably, it was distant sympathy; More was only twenty years old when Savonarola was burned in the Piazza della Signoria. Still, as a martyr to conscience and to the purification of the church, as a passionate Christian patriot and the inspiration of his humanist hero Pico, Savonarola could hardly have failed to appeal to More. But how can we suppose that the hard-minded Machiavelli, with his ruthless emphasis on force and fraud, took part in the mass revival-meetings and children's crusades that marked Savonarola's brief ascendancy? Well, one starts by saying bluntly that the ruthless force-and-fraud Machiavelli is to a considerable extent a literary figment. The Machiavelli of *The Prince* is only one, and by no means the most persistent, of several Machiavellis; read in the context of the *Discorsi*, or the familiar letters, or the sparse but important poetry, Machiavelli comes out very far from the crude admirer of bully-boys that formula-writers have supposed him to be. Then, one adds that it wasn't necessary to take part in the excesses of Savonarola's movement to be deeply influenced by it. Machiavelli was a young man during Savonarola's day—not as young as More, but youngish; as a minor functionary in the foreign office, he did not have to commit himself very fully for or against the great Dominican and surely thought it the better part of prudence not to do so. The best friend of his youth, Biagio Buonaccorsi, had been one of the "Piagnoni," the supporters of Savonarola. Doubtless with time and growing disillusion, the active ingredients of Machiavelli's faith, such as they may have been, faded. But throughout his life, he never failed to speak respectfully of Savonarola. He is (*Discorsi*, I.45) the man "whose writings exhibit so much learning, prudence, and courage"; and (in *Discorsi* I.11) he is the great man who, like Numa Pompilius among the Romans, was able to persuade his countrymen of his own divine mission. Like Numa, the parallel implies, Savonarola had it in him to become the founder not simply of a power structure, not simply of a social machine, but of a new human type controlled by a set of religious values. J. H. Whitfield in his seminal study of Savonarola and Machiavelli makes the case, at greater length then is possible here, for a continuing and very positive influence. There's no need to repeat the evidence or spin out the argument at length. To the extent that the point bears on our present thesis, it can be taken as made.

Naturally, More wrote the *Utopia*, as Machiavelli *The Prince*, in full consciousness of Savonarola's disastrous failure. It was a failure that taught both men the same lesson, though Machiavelli is more explicit about it. Armed prophets succeed, he says, and unarmed prophets fail. Savonarola was a type of the prophet unarmed, and the first commandment of the teacher who has learned his lesson is therefore, Get armor. More in *Utopia* seems equally intent on showing the need for total organization, total discipline, total preparedness, if a moral idea is to be made to work. The walls around the Utopian cities, the difficult access to Utopian harbors, the armed guards who stand viligantly by while the camp is being fortified, lest the fortifiers themselves be caught unawares—all these emphases carry a moral weight far beyond their practical functioning: they stand for the armed mind.

Of recent years there has been a tendency, picked up by many people from C. S. Lewis (who didn't like More's communism any better than he liked Milton's Protestantism, and worked hard to burk them both)—a tendency to say that the Utopia is just a joke in the style of Lucian. More couldn't have meant the book "seriously" because—well, because it's too radical, too impractical and one-sided; it's full of mocking puns and verbal tricks of self-deprecation; it's put in the mouth of Hythloday, who is distanced and diminished by the figure of More; and so forth and so on. (A special feature of this argument is the way Harry Berger's zesty rhetoric floats atop the suspicious and diminishing view of the book entertained by R. S. Sylvester and the Yale school of More scholars generally—with the invigorating exception of Hexter.) The effect of the argument is to soften the book's sharp and authentic note of social protest, to make it a mere *jeu d'esprit*, and encourage us to write off its angry and honest critique of contemporary conditions, along with its recommendations for reform, as mere playful fantasies, ridiculous in the eyes of the author himself, like Lucian's imaginary journey to the moon.

The trouble with this argument is simply that it works too well. By labeling them "jokes," it effaces all the sharp points and troubling passages, not only of More's book, but of almost any other book which happens to perturb us with its satiric insights. By this sort of interpretation, Swift and More and Rabelais and Voltaire can all be rounded off into identical, tasteless, digestible bread-pills of thought. Calling an uncomfortable idea a joke is an easy way of cutting down the great disquieting books of the past to the measure of our own parochial preconceptions. I think, however, that there is much more than jest in the *Utopia*. (I don't overlook the possibility that there was more than the author himself would be comfortable with in the long run.) It becomes, indeed, a funnier but at the same time a more painful book, the more closely we associate it with the events of its own tormented time. It means something big, and means it all the way. More was not a sourpuss in his religion, and a certain sober cheerfulness attends his account of human morality, armed and militant, and drawn up for inner and outer battle against the hydra-headed monster, Pride. But our age is perhaps too apt already to take the moral life as a joke; it won't do us any perceptible harm to contemplate for a moment what men like Savonarola and More—yes, and Machiavelli too—meant by it. C. S. Lewis always had some difficulty in seeing that people who weren't high Anglicans might yet have moral standards of a sort; thus he deprecated More the communist as a means of enhancing More the Catholic martyr. By holding the two aspects of the man in a more even balance and actually bending them toward one another, we may be able to see that More meant the *Utopia* (that strange blend of medieval discipline, humanist freedom, and practical bourgeois acquisitiveness) with the same faculties of soul, and almost as seriously, as he meant his resistance to Henry VIII. In both instances, it was the unleashed beast of self-will fueled by appetite and exaggerated by pride, to which he opposed first the flexible fences of philosophy, and then the stiff palisades of religious faith.

HARRY BERGER, JR.

[*Utopia:* Game, Chart, or Prayer?] †

* * *

Criticism of the *Utopia* has in the main recognized certain ambiguities in More's presentation of Hythloday but has tended to overstress the positive side, namely, the fact that More places many of his own ideals in Hythloday's mouth. Yet as Sylvester has pointed out, if they agree about *ends*, the important issue is *means*, and here More differs radically from Hythloday on both esthetic and moral, pleasurable and profitable, grounds. The disagreement is not simply founded on the difference between the uncompromising character of Hythloday's "schole philosophye" and More's pragmatic civil philosophy "whyche knoweth . . . her owne stage . . . and . . . playethe her parte accordinglye with comlynes."[1] More important is the fact that Hythloday is too earnest and intense, that he lacks the sense of play, musing and amused, by which a more

† Harry Berger, Jr., "The Renaissance Imagination: Second World and Green World," *The Centennial Review IX* (Winter 1965), pp. 63–74. Reprinted by permission of *The Centennial Review* and the author. Notes are by R.M.A.; references to *Utopia* have been changed to reflect the paging of this edition.
1. See above, *Utopia*, p. 28.

tentative and self-conscious mind remains negatively capable, alive
to its own limits and to the world's good. Unable to control his distance and detachment within the world, he detaches himself from
the world. (More, like Alberti and other humanists, indicates this
tendency by remarking Hythloday's preference for Greek over
Latin.) Hythloday made his withdrawal easy by getting rid of all
natural and emotional attachments early in life:

> As concernyng my frendes and kynsfolke (quod he) I passe not
> greatly for them. For I thinke I have sufficiently doone my parte
> towardes them already. For these thynges, the other men doo not
> departe from, untyl they be olde and sycke, yea, whiche they be
> then verye lothe to leave, when they canne no longer keepe, those
> very same thynges dyd I beyng not only lustye and in good helth,
> but also in the floure of my youth, divide among my frendes and
> kynsfolkes. Which I thynke with this my liberalitie ought to hold
> them contented, and not require nor to loke that besydes this, I
> shoulde for their sakes geve myselfe in bondage unto kinges.[2]

He is a latter day Odysseus (the analogues are numerous and
pointed) though somewhat in reverse: gladly leaving home he steers
toward fabulous places which, for the Greek hero, were preparations
for homecoming. But if Hythloday would gladly remain in
Phaiakia,[3] at the other end of the world from cyclopean actuality,
More is truer to his model:

> . . . he is in his talke and communication so merye and pleas-
> aunte, yea and that withoute harme, that through his gentyll
> intertaynement, and his sweete and delectable communication, in
> me was greatly abated and diminished the fervent desyre that I
> had to see my native countrey, my wyfe and my chyldren, whom
> then I dyd muche longe and covete to see, because that at that
> time I had been more than iiii. monethes from them.[4]

More is describing Peter Giles, though if Hythloday embodies an
aspect of More's mind, he certainly has this effect in a negative
sense—to diminish "the fervent desyre that I had to see my native
countrey"—but More has resisted the temptation to bear his unsul-
lied ideals far off to Nowhere. As in the case of that truly ideal
idealist, Cardinal Morton, visits from Hythloday—one might say
"attacks" of Hythloday—are reserved for after-dinner conversation,
channeled into recreative occasions.

Morton humors Hythloday as he humors the lawyer, friar and
parasite—a Chaucerian gallery eminently qualified to bring on an
attack. He amuses himself with them, is amused by them, allows

2. See above, *Utopia,* p. 9.
3. More generally, Phaeacia, the land of
Alcinous, Arete, and their daughter
Nausicaa; the last land visited by Odysseus before his return home.
4. See above, *Utopia,* p. 6.

them to vent their vanities and theories at his table, and dismisses them when it is time "to heare his sueters." The Cardinal, controlling his guests as umpire but encouraging them as host, seems in effect to be playing something like Cesare Gonzaga's game as reported by Castiglione:[5]

> . . . we have seen it happen in this house that many who were at first held to be very wise have been known, in the course of time to be full of folly, and this came about through nothing save the attention we gave to it. . . . we, whenever we have detected some hidden trace of folly, have stimulated it so artfully and with such a variety of inducements . . . that finally we have understood what its tendency was; then, having recognized the humor, we agitated it so thoroughly that it was always brought to the perfection of an open folly. . . . wherein . . . we have had some wonderful entertainment. I hold this, then, to be certain: that in each of us there is some seed of folly which, once wakened, can grow almost without limitation. . . . each of us will profit from this game of ours by knowing his faults, the better thereby to guard against them.

But of course the Cardinal, unlike Castiglione's courtiers, is not seated in an ideal circle among trusted and intelligent friends. *The Courtier* describes how persons of spirit and consequence withdraw temporarily and guardedly from the untrustworthy world to the solidarity of that circle, there to seek both pleasurable relief and profitable self-knowledge. Disagreeing with conviction yet seldom with anger, encouraging criticisms and qualifications, they mutually refresh and hone themselves for the return to action. More's Cardinal is a lonelier, more embattled figure who "passed all his tyme in much trouble and busines, beyng continually tumbled and tossed in the waves of dyvers mysfortunes and adversities" by which "he lerned the experience of the worlde." He knows better than to hope by his reason, rather than by his status, to influence or improve the human specimens at his table; yet, though Hythloday is near, he does "not leave and forsake the common wealthe" but continues his direction of the civil stage. Seated among "deaffe hearers", he is for the most part presented as silent and smiling, a giant "of a meane stature, and . . . stricken in age" who fills More's imagination as a model from the *illo tempore* ["distant days"—R. M. A.] of his childhood. What More admires most about him and sees as the secret of his endurance is his ability to *play*, his delight in experimental yet sympathetic engagement of other men:

> He had great delite manye times with roughe speache to his sewters, to prove, but withoute harme, what proper witte and what

5. *The Book of the Courtier*, I.8.

bolde spirite were in every man. In the which, as in a vertue much agreinge with his nature, so that therewith were not joyned impudency, he toke greate delectatyon.[6]

Morton is an anti-Hythloday, and More, if anything, is a lesser Morton, one who has greater need of friends and is more susceptible to attacks of Hythloday. His most severe attack is of course recorded in the second book of *Utopia*, and it is important that this withdrawal to a golden world was written first, to be qualified and contained only later by the return to actuality in Book I. But the second book itself gives witness to its author's essential detachment from the Utopian ideal. The very self-enclosed spatiality of Hythloday's green world is a criticism; it is a womblike retreat protected from the outside world. Since it is a triumph of human art, an ideal system, it is totally unified and homogeneous, purged of that variety —more difficult to control—which springs from accidents of history and differences of individual perspective: "There be in the ilande liiii. large and faire cities, or shiere townes, agreyng all together in one tonge, in lyke maners, institucions and lawes. They all be set and situate alyke, as farforthe as the place or plot sufferethe."[7] Broadest in the middle and narrowest at the ends. Utopia is turned "about a circuit or compasse" so that it bears ironically enough the shape of a new moon between whose points:

> . . . the sea runneth in . . . and there surmountethe into a large and wide sea, which by reason that the land on every side compassethe it about, and shiltreth it from the windes, is not roughe, nor mounteth not with great waves, but almost flowethe quietlye, not muche unlike a greate standinge powle: and maketh welneighe all the space within the bellye of the land in maner of a haven: and to the greate commoditie of the inhabitauntes receaveth in shyppes towardes everye parte of the lande.[8]

But More immediately intersperses a few faint signs of danger which remind us that Utopia may be a risky port to steer for and that Utopians, like Hythloday, jealously guard their purity and exclusiveness, their independence of weaker mortals:

> The forefrontes or frontiers of the ii. corners, what with fords and shelves, and what with rockes be verye jeoperdous and daungerous. In the middle distaunce betwene them bothe standeth up above the water a greate rocke, which therefore is nothing perillous bycause it is in sight. Upon the top of this rocke is a faire and strong tower builded, which they hold with a garrison of men. Other rockes there by lyinge hidde under the water, which therfor be daungerous. The channelles be knowen only to them-

---

6. See above, *Utopia*, p. 11.
7. See above, *Utopia*, p. 35.
8. See above, *Utopia*, p. 34.

selfes. And therefore it seldome chaunceth that anye straunger oneles he be guided by an Utopian can come in to this haven. In so muche that they themselves could skaselye entre withoute jeoperdie, but that their way is directed and ruled by certaine lande markes standing on the shore. By turninge, translatinge, and removinge thies markes into other placse they maye destroye theire enemies navies, be they never so many.[9]

These hints are not developed until later in the second book, for More has given Hythloday's monologue a definite shape: its first half is relatively innocent; the criticisms of actuality are for the most part just, and the defects of Utopia barely touched on. The logic is that of satiric exorcism: "It would be nice if what is wrong with actuality could be screened out. We shall call the corrected image Utopia." The climax of this movement falls almost exactly at the center of the second book. Hythloday has been describing the facility with which the Utopians absorb the small library of humanist culture he has bestowed on them, and he remarks their special interest in the "phisike" of Hippocrates and Galen;[1] even though "there be almost no nation under heaven that hath less nede of phisike then they, . . . phisike is no where in greater honour":

> For whyles they be the helpe of this philosophie searche oute the secrete mysteryes of nature, they thinke themselfes to receave thereby not onlye wonderfull greate pleasure, but also to obteine great thankes and favour of the autour and maker therof. Whome they thinke, according to the fassion of other artificers, to have set furth the marvelous and gorgious frame of the world for man with great affection intentively to beholde. Whom only he hath made of witte and capacitie to considre and understand the excellencie of so great a woork. And therefore he beareth (say they) more goodwil and love to the curious and diligent beholder and vewer of his woork and marvelour of the same, then he doth to him, which . . . hathe no regarde to soo greate and so wonderfull a spectacle.

Two aspects of this passage deserve special attention: 1) The Utopians' gratuitous and somewhat pompous use of "phisike" should be connected with Hythloday's frequent assertions that they are extraordinarily quick learners who "quickelye, almoste at the first meting, made their owne what soever is among us wealthelye devised." Utopia is a Platonic Garden of Adonis[2] a place without pain where everyone learns everything the short smooth way: "amonge the Utopians, where all things be sett in good order," time has no function and history no meaning. The hard-won accomplishments of Western culture are absorbed without sweat or strug-

9. See above, *Utopia*, p. 34.
1. See above, *Utopia*, p. 63.

2. The Garden of Adonis is found in Spenser's *Faerie Queene*, III.vi.

gle; Utopian logic and imagination replace the trial-and-error of human experience. The Utopians are handed the classical inheritance in the Aldine edition, untrammeled by the existential context of past-and-present, loss-and-recovery, which has made that inheritance so precious. That inheritance is to them as Ulysses' tale of painful voyaging was to the Phaiakians.

2) Hythloday's praise of man is so close to Pico's in the *Oratio*[3] as to seem like an echo or allusion: the divine artificer, having finished the creation of the world, and wishing "there were someone to ponder the plan of so great a work, to love its beauty, and to wonder at its vastness," made man, placed him in the middle of the world and addressed him thus:

> Neither a fixed abode nor a form that is thine alone nor any function peculiar to thyself have we given thee, Adam, to the end that according to thy longing and according to thy judgment thou mayest have and possess what abode, what form and what functions thou thyself shalt desire. . . . We have set thee at the world's center that thou mayest from thence more easily observe whatever is in the world. We have made thee neither . . . mortal nor immortal, so that with freedom of choice and with honor, as though the maker and molder of thyself, thou mayest fashion thyself in whatever shape thou shalt prefer. Thou shalt have the power to degenerate into the lower forms of life, which are brutish. Thou shalt have the power . . . to be reborn into the higher forms, which are divine.

Hythloday's echo may of course be a straightforward and conventional piece of *laus hominis* ["praise of man"—R. M. A.], but the context turns it slightly awry. There is something hermetic, something More might indeed have felt in Pico, in the detachment and gratuitous self-delight of curious Utopian observers. The Utopians observe whatever is in the world more easily because they are not located at its center but safely removed to the periphery. Their naiveté about the psychological appeal of such vices as dicing, hunting and love of jewels suggests how little experience they have of the mortal weaknesses from which they are remote. The long discourse on pleasure terminated by the *laus* is vaguely unsatisfying because Hythloday is so concerned to justify the Utopian delight not only in good health *per se* but in good health as a *feeling*, a state of consciousness. Similarly, of mental pleasures, "the chiefe parte of them they think doth come of the exercise of vertue, *and conscience of good life*" (italics mine). To the "delectation that

3. Pico della Mirandola's most famous work was an oration, "On the Dignity of Man," in which he described man as having no fixed character of his own, but being able to take on any other character he chose. A handy English translation is in Ernst Cassirer, Paul Kristeller, and J. H. Randall, *The Renaissance Philosophy of Man* (Chicago: Phoenix Books, 1948).

commeth of the contemplation of treweth . . . is joyned the plea-
saunte remembraunce of the good lyfe paste." That a man should
remind himself of his mere humanity, should love himself and his
neighbor for God's sake, should wear a hairshirt (and still be
happy) is unthinkable:

> . . . for a vaine shaddow of vertue, for the wealth and profite of
> no man, to punishe himselfe, or to the intente he maye be hable
> courragiouslie to suffer adversitie, whiche perchaunce shall never
> come to him; this to do they thinke it a point of extreame
> madnes, and a token of man cruellye minded towardes himselfe,
> and unkind towardes nature, as one so disdaining to be in her
> daunger, that he renounceth and refuseth all her benefites.[4]

As Florentine idealism is in one sense an escape from what man is
to what he would like to be (which Ficino and Pico[5] conflate with
what he should be), so the preferred shape to which the Utopians
have fashioned themselves lead them too often to exclaim, "Happy
to be me!"

In the last half of the second book, the questionable aspects of
Utopia emerge into full view. There are first such isolated instances
as the praise of euthanasia and suicide; here the violation of divine
law is subtly intensified by the previous discussion of pleasure. The
urge to turn a critique whole-hog into a program—that primary
manifestation of the political pleasure-principle—makes itself felt in
the Utopian trick of avoiding corruption in legal procedure by abolishing the procedure—throwing out the form of government
becase the party in power is corrupt. A similar attitude is displayed
toward leagues, though the argument is more roundabout. There is
first the bitter satiric inversion "here in Europa, and especiallye in
these partes where the faith and religion of Christe reigneth, the
majestie of leagues is everye where esteemed holy and inviolable, partlie through the justice and goodness of princes, and partlie at the
reverence and motion of the head bishops." Then follows the
Utopian response: "in that newe founde parte of the world . . . no
trust nor confidence is in leagues" because the neighbors of the
Utopians always violate them. This is not the fault of human
nature, for "men be better and more surely knit together by love
and benevolence, then by covenauntes of leagues." The fault lies in
human institutions, namely leagues, which cause men "to thinke
themselves borne adversaries and enemies one to another." Thus
the Utopian makes his pastoral withdrawal from the painful state of
civilization to the ideal state of nature. More has placed the con-

4. See above, *Utopia*, p. 61.
5. Ficino and Pico were both, after their own fashions, Platonists; that they, or Platonists generally, confused what man is with what he should be is Berger's opinion.

trast to all these Utopian methods, and the criterion by which they are to be judged, in the figure of Cardinal Morton.

In the final two sections, on Utopian welfare and religion, the irony becomes massive, beginning with the Utopian use of cyclopean Zapoletes (the best using the worst, a figure of the end-means split) and ending with the tepid panaceas of the Utopian faith. At the end Hythloday unwittingly supplies an anatomy of the Utopian mind, for he shows how withdrawal is founded on despair of things as they are. Actuality is reduced to the negative ideal: "when I consider and way in my mind all these commen wealthes, which now a dayes any where do florish, so God helpe me, I can perceave nothing but a certain conspiracy of riche men procuringe theire owne commodities under the name and title of the commen wealth."[6] Hythloday's is a solution procured through the verbal magic of personification by which complex issues are simplified, Goldwater-fashion, for quick disposal: do away with those two princesses, Lady Money and Lady Pride. "How great an occasion of wickednes and mischiefe is plucked up by the rotes!" The image recalls one of the more outlandish feats of Utopian husbandry mentioned shortly before Hythloday's praise of man—the Utopians not only matched the farmers of other countries in craft and cunning "to remedie the barrennes of the grounde," they outdid Macduff: "a whole wood by the handes of the people plucked up by the rootes in one place, and set againe in an other place."

Thus More has so shaped Hytholday's account as first to draw us into Utopia, then to push us away from it. This dynamic narrative pattern works against the atemporal and ahistorical life of the island. I find this a simpler and more practical (as well as truer) explanation of the so-called satiric inconsistencies than Arnold Heiserman's elaborate though often perceptive appeal to Chicago genre-theory.[7] What seems most important is the narrative control of the audience. The relations which determine the overall structure of *Utopia* are after all primarily verbal, intelligible and temporal: the three moments which unfold its experience are relatively discrete units, each more condensed and immediate than those which follow it. The letter to Giles frames both parts of the work within the present tense of the writer's experience, while the first book frames Hythloday's monologue in the more realistic and inclusive context of European affairs. The openness and intimacy of More's address to Peter Giles establishes the proper distance for the reader, who is in effect the addressee. Such places of the mind as Hythloday's green world are best dealt with not in lonely voyages but in the friendly play of an afternoon's talk, in the good fellowship of

6. See above, *Utopia*, p. 89.
7. The reference is to A. R. Heiserman's account of *Utopia* as satire, in *PMLA* LXXVIII (1963), pp. 163–74.

men who love and trust each other, in the shared discourse which refreshes weary minds so that they can return to the stage of the actual world next morning. More exorcizes as a purely spatial nowhere the tendency, so obvious in Hythloday, to abolish time and chance.

We may be reminded here of a fact of which Plato was perhaps the first to make systematic use: insofar as landscape is symbolic—even the conversation of the first book of *Utopia* is symbolically placed in a garden, and in the garden of More's *temporary* lodgings —the dimension of space subserves the movement of words and the play of minds which shape and re-shape themselves in time. Plato's unfinished utopian dialogue, the *Critias*, provides an instructive model and analogue of More's method, and I should like briefly to consider it. Critias locates ideal gardens of Adonis at the beginning of history in Atlantis and primeval Attica. He describes them as literal, not metaphoric, places—the state of nature, not the state of myth—and as such they embody Heraclitean ideals.[8] His description emphasizes the great flux and variety of physical things. As their temporal location indicates, these are given rather than earned utopias, and the same fate of decline overtakes the physical luxuriance of Attica and the ethos of the men of Atlantis. The dialogue implies that their loss of self-mastery moved Zeus to put the Atlanteans to the test by sending them out to do battle. It was in the Atlantic invasion of the Mediterranean world that Athens proved her mettle: "when the rest fell off from her, being compelled to stand alone after having undergone the very extremity of danger, she defeated . . . the invaders, and preserved from slavery those who were not yet subjugated, and generously liberated all the rest." The corruption of Atlantis is made the occasion whereby the Athenian ethos is tested and proved heroic: if the Attic gardens decay, their inhabitants—losing the original state of nature—acquire the eros and inner strength through which the soul confronts and masters the experience. The Atlanteans apparently did not meet the test of experience, and when their island was submerged their oceanic power never revived in its human form, while the Athenians, weathering cataclysm after cataclysm, still send roots into their rocky cliff. Their *areté* [virtue] was displaced from body to soul, and this is Plato's historical message: to convert a Heraclitean ideal into a Platonic vision, Athene must confront and defeat Poseidon.[9] The mind must transfer its garden-states from object to image, from perception to thought, from history to myth, from nature to spirit, from the beginning of experience to its end. Critias' narrative is presented as dogmatic rote-work; his mind, resolved and inactive, pas-

8. Heraclitus was an early Greek philosopher, who taught that all things change.   9. Athene, goddess of reason; Poseidon, god of the sea.

sively reproduces the written Egyptian records as accurately as it can; similarly, he describes the laws of Atlantis as tyrannized by convention and the wisdom of the elders. In theme and treatment, Plato's position is diametrically opposed to that of Critias. By sharply outlining the backward-looking attitude which treats the story as literal while he himself presents it as myth or allegory, Plato conveys both the sense of loss and the act of recovery. This act consists in the dialogue itself: here the remembered image is valued not for its pseudo-historical accuracy but for its cognitive significance as an allegory of loss and recovery. The allegory implies that the soul can never simply return to the past or malinger in its green world but must go the long way round until the sense and image of loss have been transformed into the desire and vision of future fulfillment.

The green world seems to possess two essential qualities: first, since it is only metaphorically a place or space, it embodies a condition whose value should not remain fixed, but should rather change according to the temporal process of which it is a part. It appears first as exemplary or appealing and lures us away from the evil or confusion of everyday life. But when it has fulfilled its moral, esthetic, social, cognitive or experimental functions, it becomes inadequate and its creator turns us out. Those who wish to remain, who cannot or will not be discharged, are presented as in some way deficient. Thus the second quality of the green world is that it is ambiguous: its usefulness and dangers arise from the same source. In its positive aspects it provides a temporary haven for recreation or clarification, experiment or relief; in its negative aspects it projects the urge of the paralyzed will to give up, escape, work magic, abolish time and flux and the intrusive reality of other minds.

Insights

FREDERIC SEEBOHM

[A Satire on Crying Abuses]†

The point of the *Utopia* consisted in the contrast presented by
its ideal commonwealth to the condition and habits of the European commonwealths of the period. This contrast is most often left
to be drawn by the reader from his own knowledge of contemporary
politics, and hence the peculiar advantage of the choice by More of
such a vehicle for the bold satire it contained. Upon any other
hypothesis than that the evils against which its satire was directed
were admitted to be real, the romance of *Utopia* must also be admitted to be harmless. To pronounce it to be dangerous was to admit
its truth.

Take, *e.g.*, the following passage relating to the international
policy of the Utopians:—

"While other nations are always entering into leagues, and breaking and renewing them, the Utopians never enter into a league with
any nation. For what is the use of a league? they say. As though
there were no natural tie between man and man! and as though any
one who despised this natural tie would, forsooth, regard mere
words! They hold this opinion all the more strongly, because in that
quarter of the world the leagues and treaties of princes are not observed as faithfully as they should be. For in *Europe*, and especially
in those parts of it where the Christian faith and religion are professed, the sanctity of leagues is held sacred and inviolate; partly
owing to the justice and goodness of princes, and partly from their
fear and reverence of the authority of the Popes, who, as they themselves never enter into obligations which they do not most religiously perform [!], command other princes under all circumstances to
abide by *their* promises, and punish delinquents by pastoral censure
and discipline. For indeed, with good reason, it would be thought a
most scandalous thing for those whose peculiar designation is 'the
faithful,' to be wanting in the faithful observance of treaties. But in

† From Frederic Seebohm, *The Oxford
Reformers* (New York), pp. 146–148.
Reprinted by permission of the publishers, AMS Press, Inc. References to the
text of *Utopia* have been changed to reflect the paging of this edition.

those distant regions . . . no faith is to be placed in leagues, even though confirmed by the most solemn ceremonies. Some flaw is easily found in their wording which is intentionally made ambiguous so as to leave a loop-hole through which the parties may break both their leagues and their faith. Which craft—yes, *fraud* and *deceit*—if it were perpetrated with respect to a contract between private parties, they would indignantly denounce as sacrilege and deserving the gallows, whilst those who suggest these very things to princes, glory in being the authors of them. Whence it comes to pass that justice seems altogether a plebeian and vulgar virtue, quite below the dignity of royalty; or at least there must be two kinds of it, the one for common people and the poor, very narrow and contracted, the other, the virtue of princes, much more dignified and free, so that *that* only is unlawful to *them* which they don't *like*. The morals of princes being such in that region, it is not, I think, without reason that the Utopians enter into no leagues at all. Perhaps they would alter their opinion if they lived amongst us."[1]

Read without reference to the international history of the period, these passages appear perfectly harmless. But read in the light of that political history which, during the past few years, had become so mixed up with the personal history of the Oxford Reformers, recollecting *"how religiously"* treaties had been made and broken by almost every sovereign in Europe—Henry VIII, and the Pope included—the words in which the justice and goodness of European princes is so mildly and modestly extolled become almost as bitter in their tone as the cutting censure of Erasmus in the *Praise of Folly*, or his more recent and open satire upon kings.

Again, bearing in mind the wars of Henry VIII, and how evidently the love of military glory was the motive which induced him to engage in them, the following passage contains almost as direct and pointed a censure of the King's passion for war as the sermon preached by Colet in his presence:—

"The Utopians hate war as plainly brutal, although practised more eagerly by man than by any other animal. And contrary to the sentiment of nearly every other nation, they regard nothing more inglorious than glory derived from war."[2]

Turning from international politics to questions of internal policy, and bearing in mind the hint of Erasmus, that More had in view chiefly the politics of his own country, it is impossible not to recognise in the *Utopia* the expression, again and again, of the *sense* of *wrong* stirred up in More's heart, as he had witnessed how every interest of the commonwealth had been sacrificed to Henry VIII's passion for war; and how, in sharing the burdens it entailed, and

1. See above, *Utopia*, p. 70.   2. See above, *Utopia*, p. 71.

dealing with the social evils it brought to the surface, the interests of the poor had been sacrificed to spare the pockets of the rich; how, whilst the very wages of the labourer had been taxed to support the long-continued war expenditure, a selfish Parliament, under colour of the old "statutes of labourers," had attempted to cut down the amount of his wages, and to rob him of that fair rise in the price of his labour which the drain upon the labour market had produced.

It is impossible not to recognise that the recent statutes of labourers was the target against which More's satire was specially directed in the following paragraph:—

"Let any one dare to compare with the even justice which rules in Utopia, the justice of other nations; amongst whom, let me die, if I find any trace at all of equity and justice. For where is the justice, that noblemen, goldsmiths, and usurers, and those classes who either do nothing at all, or, in what they do, are of no great service to the commonwealth, should live a genteel and splendid life in idleness or unproductive labour; whilst in the meantime the servant, the waggoner, the mechanic, and the peasant, toiling almost longer and harder than the horse, in labour so necessary that no commonwealth could endure a year without it, leading a life so wretched that the condition of the horse seems more to be envied; his labour being less constant, his food more delicious to his palate, and his mind disturbed by no fears for the future? . . .

"Is not that public unjust and ungrateful which confers such benefits upon the gentry (as they are called) and goldsmiths and others of that class, whilst it cares to do nothing at all for the benefit of peasants, colliers, servants, waggoners, and mechanics, without which no republic could exist? Is not that republic unjust which, after these men have spent the springtime of their lives in labour, have become burdened with age and disease, and are in want of every comfort, unmindful of all their toil, and forgetful of all their services, rewards them only by a miserable death?

"Worse than all, the rich constantly endeavour to pare away something further from the daily wages of the poor, by private fraud, *and even by public laws*, so that the already existing injustice (that those from whom the republic derives the most benefit should receive the least reward) is made still more unjust *through the enactments of public law!* Thus, after careful reflection, it seems to me, as I hope for mercy, that our modern republics are nothing but a conspiracy of the rich, pursuing their own selfish interests under the name of a republic. They devise and invent all ways and means whereby they may, in the first place, secure to themselves the possession of what they have amassed by evil means; and, in the second place, secure to their own use and profit the work and labour of the poor at the lowest possible price. And so soon as the rich, in the name of the public (*i.e.* even in the name of the poor), choose to decide that these schemes shall be adopted, then they become law!"[3]

The whole framework of the Utopian commonwealth bears witness to More's conviction that what should be aimed at in his own country and elsewhere was a true *community*—not a rich and educated aristocracy on the one hand, existing side by side with a poor and ignorant peasantry on the other—but *one people, well-to-do and educated throughout.*

Thus, More's opinion was that in England in his time; "far more than four parts of the whole [people], divided into ten, could never read English,"[4] and probably the education of the other six-tenths was anything but satisfactory. He shared Colet's faith in education, and represented that in Utopia *every child was properly educated.*[5]

Again, the great object of the social economy of Utopia was not to increase the abundance of luxuries, or to amass a vast accumulation in few hands, or even in national or royal hands, but to *lessen the hours of labour to the working man.* By spreading the burden of labour more evenly over the whole community—by taking care that there shall be no idle classes, be they beggars or begging friars —More expressed the opinion that hours of labour to the working man might probably be reduced to six.[6]

Again: living himself in Bucklersbury, in the midst of all the dirt and filth of London's narrow streets; surrounded by the unclean, ill-ventilated houses of the poor, whose floors of clay and rushes, never cleansed, were pointed out by Erasmus as breeding pestilence, and inviting the ravages of the sweating sickness; himself a commissioner of sewers, and having thus some practical knowledge of London's sanitary arrangements; More described the towns of Utopia as well and regularly built, with wide streets, waterworks, hospitals, and numerous common halls; all the houses well protected from the weather, as nearly as might be fireproof, three stories high, with plenty of windows, and doors both back and front, the back door always opening into a well-kept garden.[7] All this was Utopian doubtless, and the result in Utopia of the still more Utopian abolition of private property; but the gist and point of it consisted in the contrast it presented with what he saw around him in Europe, and especially in England, and men could hardly fail to draw the lesson he intended to teach.

3. See above, *Utopia*, pp. 88–89.
4. More's English works: *The Apology*, p. 850.
5. See above, *Utopia*, p. 40.
6. See above, *Utopia*, p. 41.
7. See above, *Utopia*, p. 38.

C. S. LEWIS

[A Jolly Invention]†

* * * All seem to be agreed that [*Utopia*] is a great book, but hardly any two agree as to its real significance: we approach it through a cloud of contradictory eulogies. In such a state of affairs a good, though not a certain, clue is the opinion of those who lived nearer the author's time than we. Our starting-point is that Erasmus speaks of it as if it were primarily a comic book; Tyndale despises it as "poetry"; for Harpsfield it is a "iollye inuention," "pleasantly" set forth;[1] More himself in later life classes it and the *Praise of Folly* together as books fitter to be burned than translated in an age prone to misconstruction; Thomas Wilson, fifty years later, mentions it for praise among "feined narrations and wittie invented matters (as though they were true indeed)." This is not the language in which friend or enemy or author (when the author is so honest a man as More) refer to a serious philosophical treatise. It all sounds as if we had to do with a book whose real place is not in the history of political thought so much as in that of fiction and satire. It is, of course, possible that More's sixteenth-century readers, and More himself, were mistaken. But it is at least equally possible that the mistake lies with those modern readers who take the book *au grand sérieux* ["with deadly seriousness"—R.M.A.]. There is a cause specially predisposing them to error in such a matter. They live in a revolutionary age, an age in which modern weapons and the modern revolutionary technique have made it only too easy to produce in the real world states recognizably like those we invent on paper: writing Utopias is now a serious matter. In More's time, or Campanella's, or Bacon's, there was no real hope or fear that the paper states could be "drawn into practice": the man engaged in blowing such bubbles did not need to talk as if he were on his oath. And here we have to do with one who, as the Messenger told him in the *Dialogue*, "used to look so sadly" when he jested that many were deceived.

The *Utopia* has its serious, even its tragic, elements. It is, as its translator Robynson says, "fruitful and profitable." But it is not a consistently serious philosophical treatise, and all attempts to treat it as such break down sooner or later. The interpretation which

† From C. S. Lewis, *English Literature in the Sixteenth Century Excluding Drama*, Vol. III of *The Oxford History of English Literature* (Oxford: The Clarendon Press, 1954), 167–71. Reprinted by permission of The Clarendon Press. Notes are those of R.M.A.

1. Tyndale was the Protestant reformer with whom More disputed. Nicholas Harpsfield wrote a late sixteenth-century life of More; and Thomas Wilson wrote in 1553 a *Rule of Rhetorique*.

breaks down soonest is the "liberal" interpretation. There is nothing in the book on which the later More, the heretic-hunter, need have turned his back. There is no freedom of speech in Utopia. There is nothing liberal in Utopia. From it, as from all other imaginary states, liberty is more successfully banished than the real world, even at its worst, allows. The very charm of these paper citizens is that they cannot in any way resist their author: every man is a dictator in his own book. It is not love of liberty that makes men write Utopias. Nor does the *Utopia* give any color to Tyndale's view that More "knew the truth" of Protestantism and forsook it: the religious orders of the Utopians and their very temples are modelled on the old religion. On the other hand, it is not a defense of that old order against current criticisms; it supports those criticisms by choosing an abbot as its specimen of the bad landlord, and making a friar its most contemptible character. R. W. Chambers, with whom died so much that was sweetest and strongest in English scholarship, advanced a much more plausible view. According to him the Utopians represent the natural virtues working at their ideal best in isolation from the theological; it will be remembered that they hold their Natural Religion only provisionally "onles any godlier be inspired into man from heuen." Yet even this leaves some features unaccounted for. It is doubtful whether More would have regarded euthanasia for incurables and the assassination of hostile princes as things contained in the Law of Nature. And it is very strange that he should make Hedonism the philosophy of the Utopians. Epicurus was not regarded by most Christians as the highest example of the natural light. The truth surely is that as long as we take the *Utopia* for a philosophical treatise it will "give" wherever we lean our weight. It is, to begin with, a dialogue: and we cannot be certain which of the speakers, if any, represents More's considered opinion. When Hythloday explains why his philosophy would be useless in the courts of kings More replies that there is "another philosophy more ciuil" and expounds this less intransigent wisdom so sympathetically that we think we have caught the very More at last; but when I have read Hythloday's retort I am all at sea again. It is even very doubtful what More thought of communism as a practical proposal. We have already had to remind ourselves, when considering Colet, that the traditional admission of communism as the law of uncorrupted Nature need carry with it no consequences in the world of practical sociology. It is certain that in the *Confutation* (1532) More had come to include communism among the "horrible heresies" of the Anabaptists and in the *Dialogue of Comfort* he defends private riches. Those who think of More as a "lost leader" may discount these later utterances. Yet even at the end of the *Utopia* he rejects the Utopian economics as a thing "founded of no good reason." The magnificent rebuke of all existing societies which precedes this may suggest that the rejection is ironical. On the other hand, it may mean that the whole book is only a satiric glass to reveal our own avarice by contrast and is not meant to give us directly practical advice.

These puzzles may give the impression that the *Utopia* is a confused book: and if it were intended as a serious treatise it would be very confused indeed. On my view, however, it appears confused only so long as we are trying to get out of it what it never intended to give. It becomes intelligible and delightful as soon as we take it for what it is—a holiday work, a spontaneous overflow of intellectual high spirits, a revel of debate, paradox, comedy and (above all) of invention, which starts many hares and kills none. It is written by More the translator of Lucian and friend of Erasmus, not More the chancellor or the ascetic. Its place on our shelves is close to *Gulliver* and *Erewhon*, within reasonable distance of Rabelais, a long way from the *Republic* or *New Worlds for Old*.[2] The invention (the "poetry" of which More was accused) is quite as important as the merits of the polity described, and different parts of that polity are on very different levels of seriousness.

Not to recognize this is to do More grave injustice. Thus the suggestion that the acquisitive impulse should be mortified by using gold for purposes of dishonor is infantile if we take it as a practical proposal. If gold in Utopia were plentiful enough to be so used, gold in Utopia would not be a precious metal. But if it is taken simply as satiric invention leading up to the story of the child and the ambassadors, it is delicious. The slow beginning of the tale, luring us on from London to Bruges, from Bruges to Antwerp, and thence by reported speech to fabulous lands beyond the line, has no place in the history of political philosophy: in the history of prose fiction it has a very high place indeed. Hythloday himself, as we first see him, has something of the arresting quality of the Ancient Mariner. The dialogue is admirably managed. Mere conversation holds us contented for the first book and includes that analysis of the contemporary English situation which is the most serious and the most truly political part of the *Utopia*. In the second book More gives his imagination free rein. There is a thread of serious thought running through it, an abundance of daring suggestions, several back-handed blows at European institutions, and, finally, the magnificent peroration. But he does not keep our noses to the grindstone. He says many things for the fun of them, surrendering himself to the sheer pleasure of imagined geography, imagined language, and imagined institutions. That is what readers whose inter-

2. *Erewhon*, a Utopia by Samuel Butler (1872); *New Worlds for Old* by H. G. Wells (1908).

ests are rigidly political do not understand: but everyone who has ever made an imaginary map responds at once.

Tyndale's belief that More "knew the truth and forsook it" is a crude form of the error which finds in the *Utopia* a liberalism inconsistent with More's later career. There is no inconsistency. More was from the first a very orthodox Papist, even an ascetic with a hankering for the monastic life. At the same time it is true that the *Utopia* stands apart from all his other works. Religiously and politically he was consistent: but this is not to say that he did not undergo a gradual and honorable change very like that which overtook Burke and Wordsworth and other friends of liberty as the Revolutionary age began to show its true features. The times altered; and things that would once have seemed to him permissible or even salutary audacities came to seem to him dangerous. That was why he would not then wish to see the *Utopia* translated. In the same way any of us might now make criticisms of democracy which we would not repeat in the hour of its danger. And from the literary point of view there is an even greater gulf between the *Utopia* and the works which followed. It is, to speak simply, beyond comparison better than they.

J. W. ALLEN

[A Sad and Witty Book]†

The 'fruitful, pleasant and witty work, of the best state of a public weal, and of the new isle, called Utopia',[1] written in Latin and published at Louvain in the year 1516,[2] was, for sixteenth-century England, the earliest expression of that same dream. I deal with it last because, logically considered, it lies beyond the point that was reached later. Crowley felt bound to accept the form of society as it stood, for it was to him of divine ordinance. Starkey[3] was at least convinced that the existing form of society must, substantially, be accepted, if one wished to get anything done. But for

† From J. W. Allen, *A History of Political Thought in the Sixteenth Century* (London: Methuen & Co., Ltd.), pp. 153–56. Reprinted by permission of the publisher. Notes are Allen's unless credited to R.M.A. References to *Utopia* have been changed to reflect the paging of the text included in this edition.
1. Title-page of the second edition (1556) of Ralph Robinson's translation, first published in 1551.
2. More's European reputation secured for his book a vogue on the continent it seems to have lacked in England. By 1520 editions had been published at Paris, Basle and Vienna. A German version appeared in 1524, an Italian in 1548, a French version in 1550. No English translation appeared till 1551. In the same year was printed a Dutch version.
3. Robert Crowley and Thomas Starkey wrote respectively *The Way to Wealth* and *A Dialogue between Cardinal Pole and Thomas Lupset*, mid-sixteenth-century tracts on social problems, which Allen contrasts with More's *Utopia* (R. M. A.).

the very practical character of his thought, he too might have sought his remedy in some kind of communism. As it was, he proposed that government should determine rents and organize industry through officials. But More had felt no need of accepting anything as it stood, because in truth he had no hope of getting anything done. It is essentially this lack of faith in the possibility of actually constructing a very and a true commonwealth, that isolates More and separates him from Crowley and Starkey. Crowley declared that the very root of all evil is the notion that a man may do as he wills with his own. Starkey hoped to find remedy and establish the true commonwealth by means of religion and reasonable and thorough regulation. Twenty years before Starkey and Pole, More had come to the conclusion that the mass of men will never become religious, that law can be but a palliative, and that, while private property exists, it is vain to hope that men will think they have no right to do as they will with their own. The inference was obvious: only in a land such as never was and such as is nowhere nor will be, can the perfect commonweal exist. With an irony and in a fantastic form that betray his scepticism, More set forth his dream of that Utopia.

It is a mistake to regard More's *Utopia* as an isolated work of imagination. The thought of its first 'book' is in close accord, up to a certain point, with that of Crowley and of Starkey's *Dialogue*. More is preoccupied with the same evils that are denounced by the later writers: the stupid brutality of criminal law, the excesses of sheep-farming,[4] idleness and frivolity, extravagance and waste, unjust and unnecessary poverty, prevalent selfishness and greed. But so little hope had More that any change for the better could be effected, that he had really no remedial measures to propose . His ' ook became a simple indictment of society. Where Crowley saw eligion as a lever, More saw a vast and stupid, conservative inertia. Every proposal for change is always opposed, simply as suggesting omething new.

'These things, say they, pleased our forefathers and ancestors; would God we could be so wise as they were: and as though they had wittily concluded the matter and with this answer stopped every man's mouth, they sit down again. As who should say it were a very dangerous matter, if a man in any point should be found wiser than his forefathers were.'[5]

While the *Dialogue* saw possibilities of large reconstruction by governmental action, More saw Princes 'employ much more study

---

4. On this particular point there is a difference of opinion. The passage in the *Utopia* in which More speaks of sheep devouring men and houses and cities is very well known. In the *Dialogue*, when Lupset attacks enclosure, Pole expresses the view that more sheep are wanted.

5. See above, *Utopia*, p. 10.

222 · J. W. Allen

how by right or by wrong to enlarge their dominions, than how well
and peaceably to rule and govern that they have already': Princes
who suppose that the property of their subjects is to their own
advantage. If the *Utopia* be a fairy tale, it is the saddest of fairy
tales. More himself says that he had 'taken great pains and labour
in writing the matter'. It was, obviously, so. The book amounts to
an indictment of humanity almost as terrible as *Gulliver's Travels*,
though wholly without Swift's savagery of resentment.

It is excessively difficult to get any change made, and yet everything needs to be changed. Among the nations of Christendom
More's traveller cannot find 'any sign or token of equity and justice'. The rich men who control things

> 'invent and devise all means and crafts, first how to keep safely,
> without fear of losing, that they have unjustly gathered together,
> and next how to hire and abuse the work and labour of the poor
> for as little money as may be. These devices, when the rich men
> have decreed to be kept and observed under colour of the com-
> monalty, that is to say also of the poor people, then they be
> made laws.'[6]

In Starkey's *Dialogue* it was implied that More had disregarded
the actual. But it was the Pole of the *Dialogue* who idealized Parliament, satisfied with the fiction of the common law as to its repre-
sensative character. He had founded on it a great hope of reconstruction. More was possessed by no such illusion and had no such
hope.

'The whole wealth of the body of the realm,' declared an anony-
mous writer, 'cometh out of the labours and works of the common
people.'[7] More's thought was the same. Usurers become rich; but
'labourers, carters, ironsmiths, carpenters and ploughmen', all those
who do the necessary work 'that without it no commonwealth were
able to continue and endure one year', all these labour all their lives
for a pittance, with nothing before them but an 'indigent and beg-
garly old age'.

For this injustice and absurdity there is, it is asserted, but one
conceivable remedy. 'Where possessions be private, where money
beareth all the stroke, it is hard and almost impossible that there
the weal public may justly be governed and prosperously flourish.'
For 'where every man's goods be proper and peculiar to himself'
and where every man 'draweth and plucketh to himself as much as
he can', there will a few 'divide among themselves all the whole
riches' and 'to the residue is left lack and poverty'. So we reach the

6. See above, *Utopia*, p. 89.
7. *How to Reform the Realm in setting
them to work to restore Tillage*, c. 1535.
Attributed uncertainly to Clement Armstrong. Reprinted in *Tudor Economic
Documents* (Tawney and Power), Vol.
III. See p. 115.

conclusion: 'I do fully persuade myself, that no equal and just distribution of things can be made nor that perfect wealth shall ever
be among men unless this propriety be exiled and banished. . . .
Christ instituted among his all things common; and the same community doth yet remain amongst the rightest Christian companies.'
The evils resulting from private ownership may, indeed, be 'somewhat eased' by law and regulation, but 'that they may be perfectly
cured . . . it is not to be hoped for, whiles every man is master of
his own to himself'.

All this is asserted by the mouth of More's imaginary traveller,
not in immediate connection with the account of the isle which is
Nowhere, but in the far more significant discussion that precedes
that account. In his own person More makes the usual objections.
'Men shall never there live wealthily where all things be common.'
Men are driven to work by hope of gain for themselves: under communistic conditions every one will idle. The dilemma is stated, but
it is not resolved. It was hardly worth while attempting to resolve it;
so obvious was it that the remedy proposed by the traveller, Hythloday, was impossible of application. To the doubts expressed by
More, Hythloday can only answer that, if he knew the island of
Nowhere, he would know better. Coming after all that has gone
before, the answer is as sad as it is witty. It was no answer at all;
and it reveals at once the fallacy of what follows. Proof of the assertions made in the first book of the *Utopia* is supplied in the second
by means of a picture of an imaginary commonwealth, in which
communism has actually resulted in all but complete contentment,
prosperity and stability. The picture, obviously, is a mere assumption of what has to be proved. So conscious was More of the fallacy
that, when he came to describe his island of the blessed, he let
fancy loose and became little more than ingenious. He makes, it is
true, in the course of this account certain far-reaching suggestions;
but for the most part it seems to be calculated rather to amuse than
to suggest. It appears, too, after all, that this particular land of
heart's desire is not, on close acquaintance, so very attractive. 'So
must I needs confess and grant,' More concludes, 'that many things
be in the Utopian weal public, which in our cities I may rather wish
for than hope after.' Many things, perhaps; but surely not those
houses all alike, those people so much alike that they are content
hardly to differ in dress, that monotony of grave entertainment and
garnishing of the mind. But it did not matter. More knew that his
Utopia was nowhere and proved nothing. He had declared in effect
that, men being what they are, there is no conceivable remedy for
social evils except, at all events, one that cannot be adopted; and
as to that one, that it is doubtful what, in any case, the result of its
adoption would be. His book is the work of a sceptic in politics,

though of a sceptic whose mind rests in religious faith. The real land of More's heart's desire was not of this world. It was Crowley and Starkey who were the idealists in politics: it was More who had kept to the actual. His Utopia is a *reductio ad absurdum* of their very and true commonweal. He had written the last word first.

ELIZABETH MC CUTCHEON

Denying the Contrary:
More's Use of Litotes in the *Utopia*†

* * *

Still other effects are inherent in litotes,[1] as More uses them. Ambiguity is one, for reasons both logical and psychological. The Renaissance was well aware of the logical complications and ambiguities which result when something is affirmed by negating the contrary. Litotes and ten other figures (an important group in the *Utopia*, including antithesis, irony, paradox and paralipsis) can be specifically related to that topic of invention called opposites, of which there were thought to be four sorts in all: contraries, relatives, privatives, and contradictories. To affirm one contradictory is to deny the other, but litotes based on the first three categories may well be ambiguous. Though immediate contraries (faith/unbelief, for example) have no species between, so that "one or the other must be affirmed",[2] mediate contraries do have a mediate or middle ground between the two extremes. "Not white" is the seemingly inevitable text-book example; as Thomas Wilson says, "if a cloth be not white, it is no reason to call it blacke. For it may bee blewe, greene, redd, russett. . . ."[3] Relatives (Isidore cites "few" and "many") and privatives (sight and blindness, for example, for which a mediate could be an eye inflammation, according to Isidore)[4] can also be ambiguous. On these grounds such common

† Elizabeth McCutcheon, "Litotes: Denying the Contrary," *Moreana*, 31–32 (November 1971), pp. 116–121. Reprinted by permission of Amici Thomae Mori. Notes are McCutcheon's unless credited to R.M.A.

1. Litotes is the rhetorical figure by which one affirms something in the course of denying its contrary. It is a minor though persistent mannerism within More's stylistic and rhetorical gamut; but by concentrating on it, McCutcheon is able to illuminate a really important quality of More's mind (R.M.A.).

2. Sister Miriam Joseph, *Rhetoric in Shakespeare's Time*, p. 322.

3. Thomas Wilson, *The Rule of Reason; Conteining the Art of Logike* [1551] (London, 1567), fol. 52ᵛ, as cited in Sister Miriam Joseph, *Rhetoric in Shakespeare's Time*, p. 322.

4. Isidorus, *Etymologiarum*, in *Patrologiae cursus completus . . . Series latina*, ed. Jacques Paul Migne (Paris, 1844–1864), LXXXII, 153–154 [Book II, ch. 31: "De oppositis"]. [The Latin examples which follow would translate as "not the worst," "no slight," "not a few," "not many," "not often," etc., etc. The numbers are references to page and line of the Yale Latin text.—R.M.A.]

litotes as "non pessime" (48/28, 52/1, 80/16), "non exigui" (46/8, 214/22), "haud pauca" (54/2, 244/14), "haud pauci" (218/9, 224/20–21), "nec pauci" (222/14), "haud multi" (158/5), "haud saepe" (188/25), "non saepe" (184/29), or "haud semel" (212/6) are logically ambiguous. We may, at first, think of their opposites, just as we do with white-black, yet all have one or more species between. "Non pessime", for instance, has to move from *worst* through *rather bad* and *bad* even before it can move towards *good, quite good,* or *the best,* if it does; "haud pauci" may mean *more than a few, some,* or *many,* and "haud semel" [not once] is even more open ended.

A second kind of ambiguity arises from the psychological peculiarity of negating a negation.[5] As Jespersen has observed, ". . . it should be noted that the "double negative always modifies the idea, for the result of the whole expression is somewhat different from the simple idea expressed positively." He calls attention to the same phenomenon which led Puttenham to call litotes the "Moderator", though he interprets it differently, when he adds that "*not uncommon* is weaker than *common,* . . . the psychological reason being that the *detour* through the two mutually destroying negatives weakens the mental energy of the hearer and implies on the part of the speaker a certain hesitation absent from the blunt, outspoken *common* . . ."[6] In fact, since litotes as a rhetorical and literary technique not only moderates but intensifies, so that, as John Smith points out, "*. . . sometimes a word is put down with a sign of negation, when as much is signified as if we had spoken affirmatively, if not more,*"[7] it may be either stronger or weaker. But it is ambiguous. We can and must depend upon the context, of course, but even so we do have to hesitate and decide to what extent a particular litotes is moderating, to what extent emphasizing, or better, attempt to hold two apparently contradictory but equally real effects in our minds at the same time. I do not think, pace Jespersen, that this necessarily "weakens the mental energy of the hearer". More probably it arouses it,[8] requiring us to linger over the construction and its context—hence its particular effectiveness as a figure of emphasis. But we are required to undergo a complex mental action; if something is, for example, *not uncommon,* to pursue

5. Litotic constructions should, logically, be part of Empson's seventh type of ambiguity, but he does not discuss double negations, although he does comment usefully on negatives in general; see William Empson, *Seven Types of Ambiguity,* 3rd ed. (London: Chatto and Windus, 1956), pp. 205–214.

6. Otto Jespersen, *Negation in English and Other Languages,* in *Selected Writings of Otto Jespersen* (1917; rpt. London: George Allen & Unwin Ltd., n.d.), p. 63. Cf. Ch. 24 in his *The Philosophy of Grammar* (1924; rpt. Allen & Unwin, 1948).

7. John Smith, *The Mystery of Rhetorick Unveil'd* (London, 1688), sig. *a4.*

8. See also Lee M. Hollander, "Litotes in Old Norse", p. 1.

Jespersen's example. we move from a *common* which isn't quite stated to the *uncommon* which is, and then, because that is denied, back towards *common* again. But we do not usually know quite where to stop, a process we can visualize this way:

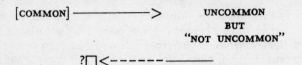

It is just this sort of ambiguous area which a recent cartoon exploits.[9] A husband and wife are standing in front of what should be a welcome mat. But this mat reads, "not unwelcome", to the chagrin of the wife, who says, " *'See what I mean? You're never sure just where you stand with them'* ".

In a larger sense we're never quite sure where we stand in the *Utopia*, either. It is, of course, a commonplace to talk about ambiguity in the *Utopia*. But on the smallest syntactical level ambiguity does exist of a sort which can never be altogether resolved, and probably was not meant to be. For this ambiguity vivifies the text, arouses its readers, and agitates its points, however casually they appear to be made, so that they neither evaporate nor solidify. We are constantly, though obliquely, teased by the many litotes already cited, not least those institutions "non pessime" ["not the worst" —R. M. A.] (52/1) which Raphael found in the new world, or persona More's "haud pauca" (244/14) ["not a few"—R. M. A.] in his concluding speech. Curiously, perhaps consciously, this last "haud pauca" contradicts the implications of another "haud pauca" early in Book I (54/2), which More uses in apparent and ironic antithesis to the positive "multa" (54/1) earlier in the sentence. Here More observes that Raphael did, of course, find many ["multa"] customs which were ill-advised in those new countries, "so he rehearsed not a few points from which our own cities, nations, races, and kingdoms may take example for the correction of their errors" (55/2-4).

We can sense inherent ambiguities and the potential spread of meaning in a given litotes from still another point of view by looking at various translations of the "non exigui momenti negocia" (46/8) of More's first sentence. Ralph Robinson, thinking of litotes as an emphatic and intensifying device, doubles the idea in a positive sense; it becomes "weightye matters, and of great importaunce". Gilbert Burnet, however, preserves the litotic implications, though slightly modifying the meaning, when he renders the litotes

9. *The New Yorker*, February 6, 1971, p. 36. (Cf. Johnson, *Every Man Out of His Humour*, Act. II, Scene 3: "You are not ill-come, neighbor Sordido, though I have not yet said well-come.") R.A.

as "some Differences of no small Consequence". Closer to our period, H. V. S. Ogden, who chiefly hears the moderating possibilities, turns the phrase into "some differences". In an attempt to reconcile the moderating impulse and the emphatic one, Paul Turner writes of "a rather serious difference of opinion".[1] The Yale translation settles for simple emphasis: "certain weighty matters" (47/10). Burnet alone has left some of the ambiguities unresolved; all the other translators have, in a sense, made our minds up for us. But what we gain in clarity we lose elsewhere. The alternatives, and therefore any possible irony, disappear, as does the ambiguity, and with that, the tension and movement of mind, so that nuances of meaning are also dissolved. In short, this litotes becomes far less significant, both in what it says and the way it says it, as an anticipation of the *Utopia* to come. For the phrase More writes certainly calls attention, however obliquely, to the kind of issue being argued about in the known world. He does not, admittedly, spell out the details of what was a massive commercial problem,[2] but he certainly says enough to reinforce our sense of the power and splendor and pride which activates almost all states (except, as we shall discover, Utopia). Indeed, "negocia" itself has commercial overtones which are very unlike the word Raphael will later use for what he thinks of as the public welfare: "salutem publicam" (104/8). By beginning, then, with "non exigui momenti negocia" More is able to raise, for just a moment, a question to which much of the subsequent discussion returns: what sorts of state matters are trifling? And what sorts are not? But, whatever else it does, this first "non" foreshadows the processes of negation and opposites which typify so much of the *Utopia*.

Like all other negatives, only more so, because now the negative is itself negated, litotes speak of a habit of mind, a tendency to see more than one side to a question.[3] Intellectual, judicial, and persuasive, they ask us to weigh and consider alternatives which the writer has himself considered. So each litotes does, then, link writer with reader, who tries to repeat, as best he can, the mental and judi-

1. Ralph Robynson, trans. (1551) in *The Utopia of Sir Thomas More*, ed. J. H. Lupton (Oxford: Clarendon Press, 1895), p. 21; Gilbert Burnet, trans., *Utopia: Written in Latin by Sir Thomas More, Chancellor of England: Translated into English* (London, 1684), p. 1; H. V. S. Ogden, ed. and trans., *Utopia*, by Sir Thomas More (New York: Appleton-Century-Crofts, 1949), p. 1; Paul Turner, trans., *Utopia*, by Thomas More (Harmondsworth, Middlesex, Eng.: Penguin Books Ltd., 1965), p. 37.
2. In this connection see the note to 46/8, 295 in the Yale *Utopia*.
3. More's use of negatives in general,

though beyond the scope of this study, is an important element in his style (and his thought) and needs more investigation. In thinking about negatives, I found some terse comments by Ian Watt on the negative in Henry James illuminating; he talks of what he calls "the right judicial frame of mind". See Ian Watt, "The First Paragraph of *The Ambassadors*: An Explication", *Essays in Criticism*, X (July, 1960), 250–74; rpt. in *Rhetorical Analyses of Literary Works*, ed. Edward P. J. Corbett (New York: Oxford Univ. Press, 1969), pp. 184–203; the words I cite are on p. 190.

cial processes the figure so economically and often ambiguously encloses. As Puttenham says, litotes is a "sensable figure", one which *"alter [s] and affect [s] the minde by alteration of sense"*.[4] The persuasive bias of Renaissance rhetoric is implicit here. Where a modern writer in the ironic mode, like Herman Melville or Henry James, will use this sort of negation to reveal hesitations, qualifications, uncertainties and ambiguous complications in the consciousness of the narrator or a major character in his fiction, More's fiction, though no less ironic, uses litotes, primarily, to affect and alter *our* minds. Yet it is also true that the alternatives were More's to begin with, so that litotes makes us simultaneously much more aware of his mind in action and certain divisions in it; it reinforces our sense of More himself as one who, indeed, saw more than one side of a question.[5]

From this point of view, even such a seemingly conventional litotes as "haud dubie" (62/25, 86/16, 96/32, 236/3) or a more emphatic "Neque dubium est" (216/27–28) or a "non dubito" (242/16) ["Doubtless," "There's no doubt," "I don't doubt"—R. M. A.] implies a process of mental assessment on the part of the speaker. It suggests, as "to be sure" or "certainly" cannot, that someone has weighed the possibilities and reached a decision— hence its usefulness as a persuasive figure. The same effect is multiplied in one of More's favorite litotic constructions, which, unlike most, does spell out (but qualify) its alternatives: some combination of a negative with *minus* or *minus quam*. Like the "nec minus salutaris quam festiuus" of the title page, ["no less beneficial than entertaining"—R. M. A.] or the several *non minus . . . quam* litotes in the passage describing the Utopian way with gold, these constructions seem to ask us to weigh or try to balance different ideas or values, almost as if we were asked to find the balance point on a moving see-saw. The ideas are grammatically "equal",[6] yet, often, the figure is weighted on one side; there is, in other words, a kind of dynamic emphasis which requires that we hold the two elements both together and apart. It can startle, or it can result in ironic or satiric incongruities: things which shouldn't be "equal" are, but things which should be, too often aren't. Raphael's description of the robber, who is in no less danger "if merely condemned for theft" than "if he were convicted of murder as well" (75/8–9) is an instance of the first sort; his description of the Utopian way of

4. Puttenham, *The Arte of English Poesie*, p. 148.
5. An intensive example of a reading on these lines is David Bevington, "The Dialogue in *Utopia*.: Two Sides to the Question", *S.P.*, 58 (1961), 496–509. Compare and contrast with this J. H.

Hexter, *More's Utopia: The Biography of an Idea* (1952; rpt. Torchbook ed., New York: Harper, 1965).
6. Jespersen, *Negation in English and Other Languages*, discusses *non minus quam* briefly, pp. 83–84.

providing for its citizens, an instance of the second: "Then take into account the fact that there is no less provision for those who are now helpless but once worked than for those who are still work-ing" (239/22–25). But most litotes in *Utopia* do not, in fact, spell out the alternative in this way. With litotes like "non pessime" or "haud pauca" ["not the worst," or "not a few"—R. M. A.] it is almost as if we saw one side of a metaphysical see-saw. So the mind is stimulated or teased into the sort of action described earlier, having, often, to construct the opposite which is denied and hold on to contraries which it weighs, each against the other. And once again, though in a more oblique way, we discover a weighting, a persuasive action which often favors Utopian attitudes, however negatively they may appear to be described. As More says, in a fine piece of understatement, which also reveals an awareness of just how complex this sort of question is, Raphael found nations "non pessime institutas" [not the worst established] (52/1). But with this we come back, full circle, to Peacham's point; litotes does, indeed, "praise or dispraise, and that in a modeste forme and manner".[7] In the *Utopia*, more precisely, it praises and dispraises, often almost simultaneously, since to deny something about Utopia is to affirm it, indirectly, of the world as we know it.

More ended his book with a famous wish. My own present hope is a more modest one—that somehow litotes be more systematically retained in translations of *Utopia*, which have, usually, made at best tepid attempts to preserve it, often converting a litotic construction to a simple positive. Obviously, syntactical patterns are difficult to turn from one language to another, and negatives are trickier still. But when, for example, More's final "haud pauca" (244/14) becomes "many" (245/17), or the frequent litotic descriptions of the Polylerites and the Utopians, which comment *via diversa* on the way of this world, are transformed into straightforward descriptions, we lose the emphasis and the understatement, the irony and possi-ble satire, and the ambiguity of the original. The complicated action of More's mind is coarsened, his meaning blurred, the energy and tension of a muscular prose relaxed. On a larger scale, we lose the cumulative effect of a device much repeated, and we have, too often, only one side of what is at least a two-sided vision inherent in every denial of the contrary. In More's hands, litotes was, in fact, a superlative tool for both the exceedingly polite gentleman, the fictional More, and the passionate visionary who had seen Utopia. Avoiding controversy, it constantly calls attention, without seeming to do so, to the purpose and values behind the countless delightful details with which More created both dialogue and discourse; it

7. Peacham, *The Garden of Eloquence*, p. 151.

truly is a figure of and for the mind. Intensive yet understated, emphatic, often drily ironic, sometimes humorous or wry, concealing tremendous energy in its apparent ease and frequent brevity, litotes is not the least of the rhetorical figures in the vision and satire we call *Utopia*.

ARTHUR E. MORGAN

[Is *Utopia* an Account of the Inca Empire?]†

For four hundred years this introduction to *Utopia* has been thought of as purely fanciful. However, if we treat it as simply a factual account we find a story of great interest. In this chapter we will touch but briefly on the evidence that More could have received direct information from Peru.[1] Yet, because it has been generally supposed that he could not have known of the Incas, the evidence is presented at greater length in an appendix. This of itself is an interesting story of pre-Columbian and early post-Columbian voyages to America, and of three expeditions to Peru from the Atlantic coast, before Pizarro.[2]

There are several phases of the evidence which support the theory that More's book in the main is not a fictitious story, but a record of a trip to Peru and of what was observed there. In case the particular trip of Vespucci referred to by More had not been made, there were numerous other possible sources of information which might have been available for writing *Utopia*. There is strong evidence that several Portuguese voyages, both before and after Columbus, reached the east coast of South America in time to have met the conditions required by More's narrative.

† From Arthur E. Morgan, *Nowhere Was Somewhere* (Chapel Hill, N.C.: University of North Carolina Press, 1946), pp. 34–38. Reprinted by permission of The University of North Carolina Press.

1. By contrast with McCutcheon, who has taken a small element of More's style and used it to illuminate the quality of his mind, A. E. Morgan put forward in 1946 a Utopian theory on the grand scale—not much smaller, indeed, than those cosmic romances by Velikovsky and Von Daniken which have enjoyed such a vogue in recent years. More, he proposes, had actually met in Antwerp a real Hythloday, who could describe to him the Inca Empire of Peru, because he had visted it some time before 1515.

The theory faces some practical difficulties. Since they couldn't very well sail through the Panama Canal, these early explorers must either have turned Cape Horn, or plowed 1,600 miles through the Brazilian jungles to Lake Titicaca, and then 1,600 miles back. After which they must have told the story to More in Antwerp, but to nobody else in Europe. This is odd behavior indeed. Still, the curious student should inspect Morgan's evidence critically and decide for himself if the problem to be solved is worth the weight of the explanation involved. Even if the case for influence cannot be made, a detailed comparison is still fascinating: the Inca society was bureaucratic, collectivist, dominated by priests, and ascetic in its practices to a degree that constantly suggests Utopia.

2. Pizarro did not penetrate into the interior of Peru or have firsthand knowledge of the Inca empire till the early 1530s (R.M.A.).

We know now that Peru was first visited, not by Pizarro on his trip down the west coast of South America, but from the Atlantic coast of what is now central or southern Brazil, and the route taken by the first historically recorded expedition is nearly the same, so far as brief descriptions indicate, as that taken by Thomas More's character Raphael Hythloday on his visit to Utopia.

More's description of the life and social system of Utopia corresponds in the main so closely with ancient Peru, both in major features and in small incidental details, that accidental coincidence seems to be out of the question. The statement in *Utopia* that Hythloday was not a common sailor, but an educated traveler, would help to account for the close observation and accurate, detailed descriptions of Peruvian life and economy which are found in More's *Utopia*.

More's brief narrative of the trip across country to Utopia fairly accurately conforms to what so short an account might be of the part of southern Brazil over which his traveler would have passed. The account in *Utopia* tells us that "after many days' journey they came to towns and cities, and to commonwealths, that were both happily governed and well peopled. Under the equator, and as far on both sides as the sun moves, there lay vast deserts that were parched with the perpetual heat of the sun," etc. If "Hythloday" had come along a Guarani Indian trade route to the region of Lake Titicaca, that is about the kind of country he would have found. The description would be accurate for ancient Peru so far as lands under and to the south of the equator are concerned.

On reaching Utopia, "The first vessels they saw were flat-bottomed, their sails were made of reeds and wicker woven close together, only some were made of leather." This is a very good description of the curious and unusual craft used then—and now—on Lake Titicaca. More continues, "but afterward they found ships with round keels and canvas sails, in all respects like our ships." The Peruvian balsa rafts on the Pacific did have cabins and canvas sails. They had keels, but not after the style of European vessels.

* * *

This narrative seems the more probably a factual account in the light of what we now know of the first acquaintance of Europeans with the Inca Empire. Any explorer reaching the east coast of South America and communicating with the natives almost certainly would have heard of that fabulous kingdom. Before Columbus' first voyage there were well traveled trade routes from the Atlantic coast to the land of the Incas. Gold and silver work from Peru had reached the Atlantic coast. Eastern Indians had gone to the land of the Incas, while in one case at least it seems that one of the Inca people visited a fleet which returned to Europe two years before More wrote *Utopia*. Chickens, imported to the eastern coast of South America by Europeans, had been passed across the continent by traders to Peru before the Inca Empire was discovered from the Pacific. A suggestion that Vespucci heard of the Incas on his long voyage in 1502 is supplied in the account of his trip which is accepted as authentic: "The people of the country talk about gold and other metals and drugs and many miracles, but I am from St. Thomas, and time will tell all."

Philip Ainsworth Means, in his book *The Spanish Main*, tells how in 1515 and 1516 Dias de Solis, cruising along the coast of Brazil, probably picked up rumors of the golden kingdom. After the death of de Solis a few survivors of his voyage, on an island off the Brazilian coast, heard stories of the great potentate far away, called the "Great White King." "With amazing courage," Means writes, "this little band of white men, accompanied part of the way by a large number of Indian auxiliaries, made their way westward across immensely difficult country, amid every sort of natural and human peril, until at last they entered what is now south central Bolivia, well within the dominions of the Inca." On the return trip all but two of them were massacred.

In 1525 Sebastian Cabot with two hundred men, supported by merchants of Spain, Italy, and England, stopped on the east coast of Brazil. The ostensible purpose of the expedition was to pass through the Straits of Magellan, but actually, it appears, they wished to search for the fabulous kingdom. Means quotes a Spanish authority as of the opinion that Cabot's expedition, at least, was stimulated by rumors of the Inca country which had reached Europe both from Panama and from the coast of Brazil. A party of fifteen went across country from the coast of Brazil to the land of the Incas, and were entertained by Inca officials. Only seven of the party returned alive. The route from the coast of Brazil to Peru taken by both these historic expeditions is approximately the same, within the limits of meager accounts, as that described by Thomas More in *Utopia*. The expedition of Dias de Solis in 1515 and 1516 was undertaken just at the time Thomas More was writing his famous book.

It is interesting that both More's account of "Raphael Hythloday's" trip across country to Utopia, and the old Spanish accounts of the trip of Dias de Solis, mention the expedition's being accompanied part of the way by a large number of Indian auxiliaries. In the case of de Solis, at least, that is recorded history. It creates a strong presumption that the Indians knew where they were going, along a familiar route.

In 1526 four Portuguese, with two thousand Guarani Indians from the coast, left San Vicente (now Santos) in southern Brazil, went to Peru on a raiding party, and returned to their party in Paraguay with much booty. The commander, Garcia, sent two of his men to Brazil to report. After they left, he and his party, except Garcia's son, were killed by the Indians. During the past century there was discovered in the archives of the Fugger family a record of a voyage to the eastern coast of South America, with the return to Europe in 1514, bringing quite specific information about the wealth of Peru.

In support of the theory that several voyages were made from Portugal to the east coast of South America, on one of which More's informant might have been present, there is considerable historical evidence, which is discussed in the Appendix.

AMERIGO VESPUCCI

The First Voyage†

* * * We sailed with the north-west wind, thus running along the coast with the land ever in sight, continually in our course observing people along the shore: till after having navigated for two days, we found a place sufficiently secure for the ships, and anchored half a league from land, on which we saw a very great number of people: and this same day we put to land with the boats, and sprang on shore full 40 men in good trim: and still the land's people appeared shy of converse with us, and we were unable to encourage them so much as to make them come to speak with us: and this day we laboured so greatly in giving them of our wares, such as rattles and mirrors, beads,[1] *spalline*, and other trifles, that some of them took confidence and came to discourse with us: and after having made good friends with them, the night coming on, we took our leave of them and returned to the ships: and the next day when the dawn appeared we saw that there were infinite numbers of people upon the beach, and they had their women and children with them: we went ashore, and found that they were all laden

† From *The First Four Voyages of Amerigo Vespucci*, translated and annotated by "M. K." (London, 1885), after the first edition written at Lisbon in 1504, printed at Florence in 1505, translated into French, retranslated into Latin, and in that form circulated throughout Europe, starting about 1507. Pp. 7–11, 45–46. Vespucci's letter to Piero Soderini, describing his voyages to America, was the book about American exploration that we know More had

read. It did have certain traceable influences on the *Utopia*; and their quality may usefully be compared with the supposed influence of the Inca explorers. Footnotes are the translator's unless credited to R.M.A.
1. The word is *cente*, supposed to be a misprint for *conte*, an Italianised form of the Spanish *cuentas*. *Spalline* is a word not given in the dictionaries. The Latin translator seems to have read the original as *certe cristalline*.

with their worldly goods[2] which are suchlike as, in its [*proper*][3] place, shall be related: and before we reached the land, many of them jumped into the sea and came swimming to receive us at a bowshot's length [*from the shore*], for they are very great swimmers, with as much confidence as if they had for a long time been acquainted with us: and we were pleased with this their confidence. For so much as we learned of their manner of life and customs, it was that they go entirely naked, as well the men as the women, without covering any shameful part, not otherwise than when they issued from their mother's womb. They are of medium stature, very well proportioned: their flesh is of a colour that verges into red like a lion's mane: and I believe that if they went clothed, they would be as white as we: they have not any hair upon the body, except the hair of the head which is long and black, and especially in the women, whom it renders handsome: in aspect they are not very good-looking, because they have broad faces, so that they would seem Tartar-like: they let no hair grow on their eyebrows nor on their eyelids, nor elsewhere, except the hair of the head: for they hold hairiness to be a filthy thing: they are very light-footed in walking and in running, as well the men as the women: so that a woman recks nothing of running a league or two, as many times we saw them do: and herein they have a very great advantage over us Christians: they swim [*with an expertness*] beyond all belief, and the women better than the men: for we have many times found and seen them swimming two leagues out at sea without any thing to rest upon. Their arms are bows and arrows very well made, save that [*the arrows*] are not [*tipped*] with iron nor any other kind of hard metal: and instead of iron they put animals' or fishes' teeth, or a spike of tough wood, with the point hardened by fire: they are sure marksmen, for they hit whatever they aim at: and in some places the women use these bows: they have other weapons, such as fire-hardened spears, and also clubs with knobs, beautifully carved. Warfare is used amongst them, which they carry on against people not of their own language, very cruelly, without granting life to any one, except [*to reserve him*] for greater suffering. When they go to war, they take their women with them, not that these may fight, but because they carry behind them their worldly goods: for a woman carries on her back for thirty or forty leagues a load which no man could bear: as we have many times seen them do. They are not accustomed to have any Captain, nor do they go in any ordered array, for every one is lord of himself: and the cause of their wars is not for lust of dominion, nor of extending their frontiers, nor for

---

2. *Mantenimenti.* The word "all" (*tucte*) is feminine, and probably refers only to the women.

3. Italicized and bracketed inserts are the work of the translator, to eke out Vespucci's crude Italian (R.M.A.).

inordinate covetousness, but for some ancient enmity which in by-
gone times arose[4] amongst them: and when asked why they made
war, they knew not any other reason to give us than that they did
so to avenge the death of their ancestors, or of their parents: these
people have neither King, nor Lord, nor do they yield obedience to
any one, for they live in their own liberty: and how they be stirred
up to go to war is [*this*] that when the enemies have slain or captured any of them, his oldest kinsman rises up and goes about the
highways haranguing them to go with him and avenge the death of
such his kinsman: and so are they stirred up by fellow-feeling: they
have no judicial system, nor do they punish the ill-doer: nor does
the father, nor the mother chastise the children: and marvellously
[*seldom*] or never did we see any dispute among them: in their
conversation they appear simple, and they are very cunning and
acute in that which concerns them:[5] they speak little and in a low
tone: they use the same articulations as we, since they form their
utterances either with the palate, or with the teeth, or on the lips:[6]
except that they give different names to things. Many are the varieties of tongues: for in every 100 leagues we found a change of language, so that they are not understandable each to the other. The
manner of their living is very barbarous, for they do not eat at certain hours, and as oftentimes as they will: and it is not much of a
boon to them that the will may come more at midnight than by
day, for they eat at all hours:[7] and they eat upon the ground without a table-cloth or any other cover, for they have their meats either
in earthen basins which they make themselves, or in the halves of
pumpkins: they sleep in certain very large nettings made of cotton,[8]
suspended in the air: and although this their [*fashion of*] sleeping
may seem uncomfortable, I say that it is sweet to sleep in those
[*nettings*]: and we slept better in them than in the counterpanes.
They are a people smooth and clean of body, because of so continually washing themselves as they do: when, saving your reverence,
they evacuate the stomach they do their utmost not to be observed:
and as much as in this they are cleanly and bashful, so much the
more are they filthy and shameless in making water: since, while
standing speaking to us, without turning round or shewing any
shame, they let go their nastiness, for in this they have no shame:
there is no custom of marriages amongst them: each man takes as

---

4. The expression in the original is *e
suta*, an error for *è surta*.
5. *Che loro cuple*. The Spanish word
complir, with the sense of being important or suitable.
6. He means that they have no sounds
in their language unknown to European
organs of speech, all being either pala-
tals or dentals or labials.

7. The words from "and it is not much"
down to "at all hours" omitted in the
Latin. I have translated "et non si da
loro molto" as "it is not much of a
boon to them," but it may be "it matters not much to them."
8. *Bambacia*.

many women as he lists: and when he desires to repudiate them, he repudiates them without any imputation of wrong-doing to him, or of disgrace to the woman: for in this the woman has as much liberty as the man: they are not very jealous and are immoderately libidinous, and the women much more so than the men, so that for decency I omit to tell you the artifice they practice to gratify[9] their inordinate lust: they are very prolific women, and do not shirk any work during their pregnancies: and their travails in childbed are so light that, a single day after parturition, they go abroad everywhere, and especially to wash themselves in the rivers, and are [*then*] as sound and healthy as fishes: they are so void of affection and cruel, that if they be angry with their husbands they immediately adopt an artificial method by which the embryo is destroyed in the womb, and procure abortion, and they slay an infinite number of creatures by that means: they are women of elegant persons very well proportioned, so that in their bodies there appears no ill-shaped part or limb: and although they go entirely naked, they are fleshy women, and, of their sexual organ, that portion which he who has never seen it may imagine, is not visible, for they conceal with their thighs everything except that part for which nature did not provide, which is, speaking modestly, the pectignone.[1] In fine, they have no shame of their shameful parts, any more than we have in displaying the nose and the mouth: it is marvellously [*rare*] that you shall see a woman's paps hang low, or her belly fallen in by too much child-bearing, or other wrinkles, for they all appear as though they had never brought forth children: they shewed themselves very desirous of having connexion with us Christians. Amongst those people we did not learn that they had any law, nor can they be called Moors nor Jews, and [*they are*] worse than pagans: because we did not observe that they offered any sacrifice: nor even[2] had they a house of prayer: their manner of living I judge to be Epicurean: their dwellings are in common: and their houses [*are*] made in the style of huts,[3] but strongly made, and constructed with very large trees, and covered over with palm-leaves, secure against storms and winds: and in some places [*they are*] of so great breadth and length, that in one single house we found there were 600 souls: and we saw a village of only thirteen[4] houses where there were four thousand[5] souls: every eight or ten years[6] they change their habitations: and when asked why they did so: [*they said it was*] because of the soil[7]

---

9. In the original, *contar* for *contentar*.
1. Bigger bosom, *mons Veneris*.
2. *Nec etiam non.*
3. Waldseemüller has "bell-towers," having misread *campane* for *capanne*, huts or cabins. [Waldseemüller translated and reprinted Vespucci's letter as a supplement to his *Cosmographiae Introductio* (1507); Varnhagen (below, note 7) is a modern editor.—R.M.A.]
4. Latin has *eight*.
5. Latin, *ten thousand*.
6. Latin has *seven* for *ten*.
7. *Suolo*, the ground or flooring, which Waldseemüller absurdly misread *sole*, the sun. Varnhagen, no less strangely, translates it "the atmosphere."

which, from its filthiness, was already unhealthy and corrupted, and that it bred aches in their bodies, which seemed to us a good reason: their riches consist of birds' plumes of many colours, or of rosaries[8] which they make from fishbones, or of white or green stones which they put in their cheeks and in their lips and ears, and of many other things which we in no wise value: they use no trade, they neither buy nor sell. In fine, they live and are contented with that which nature gives them. The wealth that we enjoy in this our Europe and elsewhere, such as gold, jewels, pearls, and other riches, they hold as nothing: and although they have them in their own lands, they do not labour to obtain them, nor do they value them. * * *

The Fourth Voyage

* * * We had an ordinance of the King which commanded us that whichever of the ships should lose sight of the fleet or of its Captain, should make for the land that we discovered in the previous voyage, at a harbour to which we gave the name of *Badia di tucti e sancti*:[9] and it pleased God to give us such good weather, that in 17 days we reached land therein, which was distant from the island full 300 leagues: where we found neither our Captain nor any other ship of the fleet: in which harbour we waited quite two months and 4 days: and seeing that there came no arrival, we agreed, my partner and I, to run the coast: and we sailed 260 leagues further on, till[1] we arrived in a harbour: where we decided to construct a fort, and we did so: and left therein 24 Christian men whom my partner had for us, whom she had collected from the flagship[2] that had been lost: in which port we stayed full 5 months making the fortress and loading our ships with verzino:[3] as we were unable to proceed further, because we had not men [*enough*] and I was deficient of many pieces of ship-tackle. All this done, we determined to turn our course towards Portugal, which lay in the direction of the wind between north-east and north:[4] and we left the 24 men who remained in the fort with provision for six months, and [*with*] 12 big guns[5] and many other arms, and we pacified all the land's people: of whom no mention has been made in this voyage: not because we did not see and traffic with an infinite number of them: for we went, quite 30 men of us, 40 leagues inland: where I saw so many things that I omit to tell them, reserv-

---

8. *Paternostrini*, necklaces.
9. Mistake for *Bahia de todos os Santos*. This confusion of *d* and *h* in Vespucci's handwriting led to a long-continued error in the maps.

1. *Ttão*, for *tãto*, so far that, until.
2. *Nave capitana.*
3. Brazil-wood, or dye-wood.
4. *Greco* and *tramontano.*
5. *Bombarde.*

ing them for my 4 Giornate.[6] This land lies 18 degrees south of the equinoctial line, and 37 degrees to the west of the longitude of Lisbon, as is demonstrated by our instruments. And all this being done, we took leave of the Christians and the land: and began our navigation to *nornordeste*,[7] which is the wind between north and north-east, with the intention of making our navigation in a direct course to this city of Lisbon: and in 77 days, after so many travails and perils, we entered into this port on the 18 day of June 1504. God [*be*] praised: where we were received very well and beyond all belief: because all the city believed us lost: since the other ships of the fleet had all been lost through the arrogance and folly of our Captain, for so does God reward pride: and at present I find myself here in Lisbon, and I know not what the King will want to do with me, for I desire much to take repose.[8] The present bearer, who is Benvenuto di Domenico Benvenuti, will tell Your Magnificence of my condition, and of some things which, for prolixity, have been left unsaid: for he has seen and felt them, God be . . . . .[9] I have gone on compressing the letter as much as I could, and there have been omitted to be told many natural things,[1] because of avoiding prolixity. May Your Magnificence pardon me: whom I beseech to hold me in the number of your servants: and I recommend to you Ser Antonio Vespucci, my brother, and all my house. I remain, praying of God that he may increase the days of your life, and that the state of this sublime Republic and the honour of Your Magnificence may be exalted, etc. Given in Lisbon on the 4 day of September 1504.

[*Your*] servant AMERIGO VESPUCCI in Lisbon.

6. Vespucci planned to write a longer and fuller account of his journeys, and may actually have done so, but it has been lost. (R.M.A.).
7. It is printed *nornodeste*.
8. The Latin substitutes "this messenger in the meantime commending much to your Majesty. Americus Vesputius. In Lisbon," for all the text which follows the word "repose."
9. *Dio sia ō di*, followed by a blank. This is incomprehensible, and may be "God be . . . ." (Something not understood by the printer), or *di sui occhi . . . .* ("with his own eyes . . . ."), which would imply that Benvenuto had accompanied Vespucci in this voyage.
1. Things relating to natural history.

Bibliography

Adams, Robert P. *The Better Part of Valor: More, Erasmus, Colet and Vives on Humanism, War, and Peace.* Seattle: University of Washington Press, 1962.

Bevington, David M. "The Dialogue in *Utopia,*" *Studies in Philology* 58 (1961): 496–509.

Bridgett, T. E. *Life and Writings of Blessed Thomas More.* London: Burns & Oates, 1891.

Caspari, Fritz. *Humanism and the Social Order in Tudor England.* Chicago: University of Chicago Press, 1954.

Johnson, Robbin S. *More's Utopia: Ideal and Illusion.* New Haven: Yale University Press, 1969.

Marc'hadour, Germain. *L'Univers de Thomas More.* Paris: Vrin, 1969.

Morison, Stanley. *The Likeness of Thomas More.* London: Burns & Oates, 1963. An account of the various portraits and representations of More.

Rogers, E. F., ed. *Correspondence of Sir Thomas More.* Princeton: Princeton University Press, 1947. The Latin letters remain in uncompromising, trotless Latin.

Surtz, Father Edward. *The Praise of Pleasure.* Cambridge, Mass.: Harvard University Press, 1957.

———. *The Praise of Wisdom.* Chicago: Loyola University Press, 1957.

Warren, F. B. *Vasco de Quiroga and his Pueblo-Hospitals of Santa Fe.* Washington, D.C.: Academy of American Franciscan History, 1963. Describes a network of pueblo-hospitals set up in Mexico during the sixteenth century under the direct influence of More's *Utopia.*

Histories of Utopia and collections of Utopian writings are almost beyond number; the reader may choose among smorgasbords prepared by Lewis Mumford (1922), Frances T. Russell (1932), Harry Ross (1938), V. F. Calverton (1941), G. Negley and J. M. Patrick (1952), Richard Gerber (1955), W. H. G. Armytage (1961), J. O. Hertzler (1965). T. Molnar (1967), J. W. Johnson (1968), W. H. G. Armytage again (1968), and A. O. Lewis, Jr. (1971).

Among bibliographies the student may avail himself of R. W. Gibson, *St. Thomas More: A Preliminary Bibliography of his works and of Moreana to the year 1750,* with a bibliography of Utopiana by R. W. Gibson and J. Max Patrick (New Haven: 1961); also Frank and Madjie P. Sullivan, *Moreana: Materials for the Study of St. Thomas More* (four volumes, Los Angeles: Loyola University Press, 1964–66, with an index, 1971). Germain Marc'hadour edits from Angers, France, the quarterly *Moreana*; its atmosphere is a bit close, but fresh air sometimes enters.

NORTON CRITICAL EDITIONS